The Lambert Series—Book Four

LE FIN

(The Ending)

Victoria Taylor Murray

PublishAmerica
Baltimore

First printing

ISBN: 1-59129-874-1
PUBLISHED BY PUBLISHAMERICA, LLLP
www.publishamerica.com
Baltimore

Printed in the United States of America

DEDICATION AND ACKNOWLEDGMENTS

The entire four-book LAMBERT SERIES is dedicated to my amazing son, Michael, and my wonderful daughter, Michelle. Without their never-ending love, encouragement, and much needed assistance with this enormous project, *Thief of Hearts, Forbidden, Friendly Enemies*, and *Le Fin* would still be a life-long dream instead of the reality it has now become. (Thank you, my darlings. ILYTWATC.)

I would also like to dedicate *Le Fin* to my family, the Taylors. (My beautiful sisters) Brenda, Anita, Mary, Millie and Tonya. (My brothers) Brad, John, Joe, Tony, Dan and Tim. My son's beautiful girlfriend, Diane Schewe, and the newest member of the Taylor clan, Jacob Taylor.

Next I would like to acknowledge a few of my wonderful new friends (also writers) who also contributed in the second phase of getting the last two books of my LAMBERT SERIES (*Friendly Enemies* and *Le Fin*) together with me. Thank you, I am forever in your debt…

…Norm Harris, author *Fruit of a Poisonous Tree* and *Arid Sea*

…Christy Tillery French, author *Chasing Horses* and *Wayne's Dead*

…Lynn Barry, author *Puddles* and *Bejoyfl*

…Evelyn Horan, author *Jeannie, A Texas Frontier Girl, Book One* and *Book Two*

…Beverly Scott, author *Righteous Revenge*

…Jeanette Lundgren, California Literary Agent

…John Savoy, Savoy International Motion Pictures

…To PublishAmerica, to which I owe a great deal of gratitude, THANK YOU!

…And last, but far from least, as always I'd like to acknowledge a few of my favorite celebrities (for one personal reason or another)…Harrison Ford, Bill Clinton, Buddy Hodge, Nicholas Cage, Peter Falk, Tom Hanks, Geraldo Rivera, and Pete Rose.

(I love hearing from my readers: vtm_inc@hotmail.com)

Dear Reader,

The four-book LAMBERT SERIES is a ROMANTIC MURDER MYSTERY, written from the viewpoint of the colorful cast of characters. Some of the characters you will love, while others you will love to hate.

Each of the four books in this series has its own storyline connecting the lives of its five keys characters: NOURI ST. CHARLES SOMMERS, ETHAN SOMMERS, CLINT CHAMBERLAIN, CHARLES MASON, and GABE BALDWIN. However, to fully enjoy the overall story, I strongly urge you to read the four-book series in its intended order—starting with book one of THE LAMBERT SERIES, titled *Thief of Hearts*. *Forbidden* is the second book in the series, *Friendly Enemies* the third, and *Le Fin* is the fourth.

My LAMBERT SERIES will provide its readers with hours of entertainment with its many surprising twists and turns: PASSION & ROMANCE; MYSTERY; HUMOR; BETRAYAL; SECRETS; REVENGE; LUST; SKELETONS; SIZZLING CHEMISTRY; ENVY; DISAPPOINTMENT; REGRET; DUTY & HONOR AMONG FRIENDS; AMAZING WILL POWER & INNER STRENGTH; TWO MURDERS TO SOLVE; A KNIGHT IN SHINING ARMOR; RENEWED LOVE; LOST LOVE; REMEMBERED LOVE; AND…A FORBIDDEN LOVE!

But wait! There's still more…A FAIRY TALE MARRIAGE TURNED NIGHTMARE; CHANGES; CHALLENGES; AN UNCERTAIN TOMORROW; AN ATTEMPTED KIDNAPPING; AND…A DEATH THREAT…

THE LAMBERT SERIES will take its readers from Boston to Lambert, from Lambert to Boston, from Boston to Connecticut, from Connecticut to Lambert, from Lambert to France, from France to China, finally returning home to where it all began in Boston. A JOURNEY YOU WON'T WANT TO MISS…

LAMBERT was written for everyone—both ROMANCE LOVERS as well as MYSTERY LOVERS, but its contents were not intended for anyone under eighteen…

So, RELAX, GET A SNACK, KICK BACK, and let the JOURNEY BEGIN…

THE *COLORFUL* CAST OF CHARACTERS

NOURI ST. CHARLES SOMMERS: The main character in the Lambert Series. Nouri is the heart-stoppingly beautiful but bored wife to one of the wealthiest men in the world, Ethan Sommers. Nouri's secret passion is romance. And her favorite pastime is writing in her fantasy journals.

ETHAN SOMMERS: A dashingly handsome and powerful but mysterious and ruthless billionaire businessman who seems to have less and less time for romancing his beautiful, hot-natured wife of only two years. Ethan is a man surrounded by mystery and skeletons from his past. His secret passion is revenge. And his favorite pastime is beautiful super-young women.

CLINT CHAMBERLAIN: Ever so sexy but hot-tempered and sometimes hard to control best friend and high-powered attorney to Ethan Sommers. Also quite the ladies' man. And secret lover from Nouri's past that her husband was never told about. Clint holds the key to Nouri's heart. A man with a few skeletons of his own. His secret passion is Nouri. And his favorite pastime is catering to his one true weakness: beautiful women.

CHARLES MASON: Incredibly manly but obstinate private eye extraordinaire! The best private dick in the country. Quite the ladies' man himself. Charles is also a man from Nouri's past (her first real man) that she will always have deep feelings for. His secret passion is also Nouri. And his favorite pastime is trying to win her back.

GABE BALDWIN: Not only the sexiest but also the best homicide detective on the Boston Police Force—that is, after Charles Mason left the force. His secret passion soon becomes Nouri. And his favorite pastime is nailing the bad guys.

BECKA CHAMBERLAIN: The incredibly beautiful but whacko wife to Clint Chamberlain. Becka is also Nouri's ex-partner in an interior design business—and she happens to hate Nouri with a purple passion. Her secret passion is to become the next Mrs. Ethan Sommers. And her favorite pastime is to destroy Nouri or anyone who tries to get in her way.

RENEA CHANDLIER: A seductive temptress who is hired by Ethan Sommers to help him destroy someone close to him. With Renea's unbelievable beauty, she has zero problems getting close to her intended mark.

GENNA MATTHEWS: Beautiful but wild and zany best friend of seven years to Nouri Sommers. They had met while attending the Fine Arts Academy in Boston. Genna has a dark side that Nouri isn't aware of. Genna's secret passion is Charles Mason. And her favorite pastime is to settle a score!

MAI LI: Originally from China where she worked for The House of Chin—China Royalty. Now she runs the Sommers estate. Mai Li is a beautiful but mature woman who is as mysterious as the well-kept secrets she manages to hide so well.

STEVEN LI: A character with a lot of mystery surrounding him, one of which is his association with the Chinese mob—a.k.a. THE RED DEVIL.

TONYA DAUGHTERY: The District Attorney of Boston. She's also Charles Mason's ex. And even though engaged to someone else now, Charles Mason is still her one true passion in life.

OLIVIA & OTTO LAMBERT: Own and operate the exclusive Lambert paradise. A truly one-of-a-kind couple that takes tremendous pleasure in serving themselves, as well as their guest elite.

KIRSTEN KAMEL: Ethan Sommers' super-young new mistress.

KIKI: Super-young, super-sexy special service employee in Lambert.

THOMAS: Super-sexy special service employee in Lambert. Thomas' special skills make him and his unique service very much in demand on the island elite.

KIRT JARRET: An employee in Lambert with special connections to Otto Lambert, Kirsten Kamel, and Ethan Sommers. His secret passion is Kirsten Kamel.

STACY & STUART GULLAUME: Close friends to the Sommerses, Chamberlains, Matthewses, and Lamberts. Also a couple on the rocks.

GUY MATTHEWS: Billionaire oil tycoon who is married to Nouri's zany best friend, Genna—even though he's thirty years Genna's senior.

CHRISTOPHER GRAHAM: An over-priced attorney who is engaged to the DA of Boston, Tonya Daughtery.

AL BALLARD: Young, inexperienced police detective whom Gabe Baldwin takes under his wing.

LACEY ALEXANDRIA BONNER: Charles Mason's old flame. Also, ex-lover to Gabe Baldwin. Not just another pretty face. Lacey Bonner is also a famous star of stage, screen and television. A lady with a few skeletons and secrets of her own.

KIMBERLY MICHELLE: International supermodel. And Charles Mason's current love interest.
LISA CLAYBORNE: A front page socialite. The baron's daughter, and police detective Gabe Baldwin's on again/off again fiancée.
CELINA SAWYER: Gabe Baldwin's sexy new neighbor in Connecticut—where he owns an A-frame cabin in the woods—the detective's new little hideaway for a little down time between cases.
ISABELLA BEDAUX: Connecticut Police Department's new bombshell detective from France who just happens to have the hots for sexy detective Gabe Baldwin.
JIN TANG: Ethan Sommers' Asian connection to THE RED DEVIL.
ANNA McCALL: Ethan Sommers' private secretary.
VIOLET SMITH: High-priced attorney Clint Chamberlain's beautiful Malaysian private secretary.
TESS: Charles Mason's private secretary.
FREDRICK: The two-generation chauffeur for the Sommerses.
ROBERT BARNET: Stationed in Boston, Robert works undercover for the FBI.
RICK HOBNER: The young police officer in Boston.
PIERRE DuVALL: Famous French clothing designer.
HEIDI: The Sommerses' downtown maid.
JAMES: The Sommerses' downtown chauffeur.
TALULLA: Charles Mason's pet feline.

A WORD ABOUT LAMBERT

Lambert is located in the Eastern Bay area near Cape Cod and neighboring Nantucket. Lambert is isolated from the land mass of New England, where its sands are enclosed by the restless waters that both caress and influence the weather. Lambert is breathtakingly beautiful. The sea has shaped the land itself. Year by year, tide by tide, and storm by storm. Honeysuckle, wild roses, lilacs, mint, and the salty sea scent the air from magnificent sunrise to spectacular sunset!

Lambert is more than a resort on an island, surrounded by sand dunes or salty sea air. It's a hidden hideaway where the super-rich go to find solace from their billionaire empires and super-rich lifestyles. A quaint little village it is not! At this secret haven, guest-elite come and go at will; to unwind, relax, and be pampered in every imagined way; a place where every whim is granted and every demand fulfilled. It is year-round paradise created exclusively for the wealthiest of people, a place where money is never an issue, and, of course, it's scandal free.

That is, scandal free until a double murder is discovered on the island-elite, implicating the wife of one of the wealthiest and most powerful men in the world.

From that moment on, the island paradise will never be the same. Neither will the lives of the many guest-elite who frequent it.

Chapter 1

Heartbreak and disappointment drove Boston homicide detective Gabe Baldwin back into the arms of his ex-fiancée Lisa Clayborne.

Okay, so it wasn't meant to be. Nouri Sommers should've never been allowed to get that close to him. Hell, as far as that goes…to any man!

She was a master at stealing men's hearts and then breaking them. It was a game to her. Gabe had known about her apparent hobby right from the beginning. He should've listened to the voice of reason inside his head instead of the voice of desire. Now look at him, just like all the others before him…in love with a woman that will never be…

At least the Boston homicide detective was determined not to waste seven years of his life mourning what might have been between them—like his friend private investigator Charles Mason had.

Nouri had pulled away from him. Asked him to leave. So be it! It was over; a whirlwind romance that had cost him his heart and even quite possibly his soul. So what! Big deal! He at least still held on to his pride. Who needs a heart anyway?

The telephone rang, interrupting the heartbroken detective's thoughts. He cleared his throat reaching for the phone. "Yeah," he spat gruffly.

"Hi, darling," his fiancée called as she continued to spin around in the new wedding gown that had been hand-delivered from France by no other than the famous clothing designer Pierre Duvall himself.

Gabe released a frustrated sigh. "Yeah, Lisa. What is it? I'm a little busy at the moment." He reached for a cigarette and tossed the six-week-old newspaper that he had been reviewing over to the side of his desk.

"I'm sorry, darling. I know how busy you are, but I just had to phone you. It's my new wedding gown," she squealed excitedly. "It just arrived from…"

The irritated detective cut in. "Lisa, there was nothing wrong with the wedding dress you had Pierre design for you just a few months before," he said, shaking his head with annoyance.

His fiancée made a pouting face and released a sigh. "Darling, that stupid dress was bad luck! You couldn't possibly have expected me to wear the dumb thing after all that's happened now, could you?" she argued, feeling insulted as she placed her hands on her hips and glanced at the famous designer.

Gabe rolled his eyes in disbelief. "I hardly call a fifty-thousand-dollar wedding gown a stupid dress," he snipped sharply.

"Yes, well, this new wedding gown is to-die-for, darling. Here, ask Pierre; he hand-delivered it this morning." Lisa turned to the famous designer again. "Here, Pierre, say hello to Gabe." She handed the telephone to the clothing designer.

"Yes, lovey," the famous designer said. "Hello, Mr. Baldwin. Yes, Ms. Clayborne is right. My newest creation is indeed to-die-for! I just love it. I think I may have really outdone myself this time," he boasted proudly.

"To borrow an old phrase from an old friend of mine—I only have one thing to say about the whole damn thing, Pierre," Gabe returned, shaking his head in amazement.

The designer chuckled. "And what, pray tell, lovey, would that be?"

"Swell!" the detective said, reaching for the six-week-old newspaper again.

"Well, jest if you want, lovey, but I do intend to make this gown so famous it…"

Gabe cut in impatiently. "Listen, Pierre, I really don't have time for this today. I'm very busy. You and Lisa have a wonderful day with all the photographers, the press, and the…"

The designer interrupted the detective in mid-sentence. "But lovey, I must insist you find the time to come join us! We need to have the groom to at least be in a few of the pre-wedding photo shots and…"

"Sorry, old boy. Not today," Gabe cut in. "You'll just have to use one of your male models in the photo shots or something. I can't make it. Not today. Not tomorrow. Not all week, I'm afraid." He sighed.

Pierre tossed his head back with annoyance, waving his right hand in the air with objection. "But lovey, you're getting married in less than two weeks and…"

Gabe jumped in. "Tell Lisa I'll try to phone her later. Bye, Pierre." Gabe shook his head in dismay. "Shit!" he complained under his breath, turning the six-week-old newspaper to page five, the page he was on before the intrusion. He began to read…

Ethan Sommers*, one of the wealthiest men in the world, died this morning at three thirty-two a.m. at an unnamed hospital in China during emergency surgery. A bullet fired at close range was lodged inside his brain. He was flown by helicopter immediately following a bizarre shooting that* *had apparently taken place inside the Shaanxi Museum in China.*

Although we have no official statement from the F.B.I. as of yet, there has been a lot of speculation in the press lately that suggests Mr. Sommers may have been secretly joined at the hip for the past few years to the Asian underworld a.k.a. "The Red Devil."

Also killed inside the Shaanxi Museum were eleven members of the Red Devil, including Jim Tang. Some say Tang was the actual man himself inside the Asian Mob.

Apparently, Ethan Sommers was truly a man with many secrets, and skeletons that may take years to uncover. In the meantime, all we know for certain is that our heartfelt prayers go out to his beautiful young widow Nouri. Although Mrs. Sommers has denied us an interview at this time, we hope she will grant us one in the very near future. Perhaps when the initial shock of her husband's death wears off...

Gabe swallowed hard and pulled out another six-week-old newspaper. Shaking his head with disgust, he glanced at the photograph of the massive turnout of people at the billionaire's funeral. Even the Archbishop. "I don't fucking believe it!" he exclaimed, reaching for another newspaper from the six-week-old pile from the side of his desk. He was curious as to just how many people really knew what a psycho the billionaire businessman had been in reality.

He continued to read…

According to a spokesperson for the F.B.I., and we quote, "We honestly have no idea where the media gets some of their bizarre notions. We have no idea what the press is referring to by 'The Red Devil,' and as far as Mr. Sommers having any connection with the Asian underworld, that notion in itself is bizarre! Mr. Sommers was an innocent bystander inside the Shaanxi Museum apparently in the wrong place at the wrong time when a shootout erupted between the Chinese government and Chinese mob king Jin Tang. Caught in the crossfire..."

"Give me a goddamn break!" Gabe spat, reading the garbage the F.B.I. had fed to the unknowing public about the billionaire tycoon. He shook his head in disbelief as he continued to scan the article about the billionaire.

The United States government in connection with the Chinese government has found no wrongdoing on behalf of Mr. Sommers, involving him, connecting him, or tying him to any illegal activities whatsoever. To our knowledge, Mr. Sommers, as we stated earlier, was simply in the wrong place at the wrong time and sadly got caught in the crossfire. Mr. Sommers will be sorely missed and deeply mourned in the Boston community for years to come. He was a fine and upstanding pillar to our community, just as his father and his grandfather. Thanks to their never-ending generosity and...

Gabe stubbed out his cigarette and nervously reached for another one. "What a crock of shit!" he groaned, lighting up his third cigarette in a row.

He turned the page, suddenly noticing a photograph of Nouri Sommers. The picture of her had immediately gotten his attention. *The Beautiful Grieving Widow* the press had dubbed the photograph. He swallowed hard and continued to sit and stare at the colorful picture in *The Lambert Post & Times Star* of the woman who had so effortlessly stolen his heart.

He lovingly traced his fingertip across the tear-stained face of the beautiful woman staring back at him. "Nouri." He slowly brought his finger to his lips and kissed it and then tenderly placed the kiss across her lips. "Oh, God, I miss you," he whispered, wondering how she was doing. After all, it had been six long, miserable weeks since he had seen her last.

"Go on, Gabe...Get the Hell out of here! Please just leave me alone! Oh God, It's all my fault! I should have forgiven him!" These were the last words she had shouted before he stormed out of the honeymoon suite inside the Carlyle Hotel in France that night six weeks earlier. *Nouri wasn't crying over her husband; she was crying over her lover, high-powered attorney Clint Chamberlain*, Gabe recalled shaking his head sadly. He quickly turned the page of the newspaper; only to suddenly find himself now staring into the face of Nouri's one true love, Clint Chamberlain. *I can't compete with a dead man.* He glanced at the article following the photograph of the attorney.

Clint Chamberlain, high-powered attorney & best friend to billionaire businessman Ethan Sommers, feared dead after his car plummeted off the Ballentines Bridge in Paris, France, early this morning...

Gabe tossed the old newspaper to the side and pulled another one from the pile as he picked up his cold cup of coffee with his other hand.

He glanced at the headlines...

All Hope Lost After Officials Call-Off Exhausting Three-Day Search For American High-Powered Attorney Clint Chamberlain...Heavy rains have forced Paris officials to call off their search efforts for the body of billionaire businessman Ethan Sommers' high-powered attorney after the rented car he was driving plummeted off the Ballentines Bridge early Tuesday morning. Mr. Chamberlain apparently lost control of the car during the early morning fog that had engulfed the entire river area.

His companion still remains unidentified and in serious condition at a local hospital at this time. More details are expected on the mystery lady by the end of the week, according to the spokesperson for the hospital.

Gabe turned the page as the telephone rang, jarring his attention back to the present. Once again he answered the call with distraction. "Yeah," he mumbled, still glancing at the article he had been reading.

"Gabe, this is Charles. Hope I'm not disturbing you," the famous P.I. said nervously.

"Charles, what a surprise!" Gabe returned, surprised to hear from his former partner.

"It's a call that's long overdue, Gabe," he said.

"It's okay, Charles. My fingers weren't broken. I could have—"

The P.I. interrupted, "No, Gabe, I should have been the one."

Gabe reached for a cigarette. "So, what's up?" he asked, lighting up and tossing the newspaper to the side. He glanced at the time.

Charles chuckled. "You mean to tell me that I need a reason to call these days?" he teased.

The homicide detective shook his head and stood to his feet to stretch his legs. "No, of course not, Charles. I guess I'm still a..." He paused, glancing around for his cigarette lighter. "Never mind. Hey, listen, partner. I have a little free time on my hands today. How about lunch? I could use a little company. And we do have a lot to catch up on," he said, walking over to glance out his office window.

"Great, there are a few things I need to talk to you about, too. One o'clock okay?" Charles replied.

Gabe turned from the window, went back to his desk, and sat down. "Le Massionette sound okay?"

"No!" Charles blurted out nervously. "Sorry," he added. "It's just Tonya is having lunch there today with her mother. They're going over the guest list for the wedding. I'd hate to bump into them and have to..."

Gabe interrupted, chuckling. Amused by his friend's apparent nervousness over his upcoming marriage to Tonya Daughtery, the D.A. of Boston. "Okay, I get the message loud and clear, Charles. But you have to admit I was right about the two of you, wasn't I?"

"Swell. Just rub my nose in it, why don't you," the P.I. returned, laughing and glancing at his secretary at the same time. He nodded a thank-you when she handed him a file folder.

"Oh, just listen to yourself, Charles. You've never sounded happier. Admit it!" Gabe chuckled again.

"All right," Charles conceded. "I admit it. I'm a happy man, Gabe. I only wish I could say the same about you, my friend." There was regret in his voice.

"To quote a song by Ol' Blue-Eyes, 'That's Life'!" Gabe returned humorously.

Charles laughed; amused by the detective's attempt at a little dry humor. "At least you didn't quote me the depressing words to 'Send in the Clowns'! So, I know now at least there's still hope, Gabe," he said, shaking his head.

"So, where shall we have lunch if Le Massionette is out?" Gabe asked, checking the time. He suddenly remembered reading in the newspaper about a new restaurant that had recently opened on the north side of town. "I have an idea. Why don't we try the new restaurant that just opened a few weeks ago?" he suggested. "The Fox & Crow. It's where that old country club used to be; what the hell was the name? Bellwood; yeah, that's it."

"Oh, yeah. I've heard the chef there has a different story behind every dish that he prepares." Charles chuckled. "I can hardly wait to hear the story about his Beef Wellington. Or perhaps his filet mignon," he mused. "I've heard des brochettes are the best in the city."

Gabe laughed at his friend's since of humor. "What the hell is with everyone lately and their apparent fascination with speaking French? It drives me nuts! I don't know what's being said to me half the goddamn time." He sighed. "Okay, I give up. What is des brochettes?" he asked.

Charles chuckled. "Gabe, why in hell don't you just give in and learn to speak the goddamn language? You speak almost everything else but French!" he returned.

"For your information, you super-dick—and Charles, I mean that literally," Gabe chuckled. "I know enough French to get by. *Bonjour, merci, l'addition, s'il vous plaît, où sont les toilettes*. See?" he chuckled again.

Charles rolled his eyes in amazement. "Swell," he returned teasingly. "So you can speak the basics. I apologize. Hello, thank you, the bill please, and where are the toilets. Not bad. Now, my friend, you have just learned a new word. *Des brochettes* are kebabs. All joking aside, their kebabs, or at least I'm told, are very good! Shall we find out?"

"Sounds good. One o'clock then?"

"See you there. Bye, Detective."

"Bye, Charles." Smiling, Gabe hung up the phone.

Chapter 2

...Ain't no sunshine when she's gone...and she's always gone too long every time she goes away...

The song was blasting loudly on the radio inside Nouri Sommers' bedroom when the tiny Asian woman that runs the Sommers estate quietly entered and turned down the volume. She smiled lovingly, shaking her head. "Too loud, miss. Can't hear self think," she said, in a teasingly voice.

Nouri sighed sadly. "Sorry, Mai Li. Guess I'm just trying to drown out my thoughts."

The tiny Asian woman walked to the bed and sat down next to her mistress and gently patted Nouri across the shoulder. "You know, miss, you have been in bedroom for past six weeks; that not good. Maybe it be a good idea to get out of bed and come downstairs. Mai Li fix you nice big breakfast, okay?"

Nouri gently removed Mai Li's hand from her shoulder as she scooted up to a sitting position. She smiled. "Thank you, Mai Li. But I don't think so. Not today. I'm just not up to it quite yet," she replied. Sadness clouded her lovely face.

Mail Li took Nouri's hand and held it in her own. "You know, miss, Mai Li very worried about you. Husband and Mr. Chamberlain been gone six weeks now. They died, not you. It's time to let go. Mai Li speak to you like friend, okay?" She smiled with a kind expression in her eyes.

Nouri returned the smile and shot Mai Li an understanding look. She released a deep sigh. "Thank you. I appreciate your caring. But so much has happened in such a short period of time that I don't think I can face it all just yet."

"Miss, hiding in bedroom not answer to problem. Miss need to get out of bed and have breakfast, nice shower, get dressed. And Mai Li will have Fredrick take you to doctor. You don't look well. Too pale, too skinny. Not a good thing," she said, shaking her head as she gazed at her mistress's thin figure.

Nouri couldn't help herself; she chuckled in spite of her mood. "Oh, Mai Li, have I told you lately just how very much you mean to me?" she asked, leaning over to give the tiny woman a heartfelt hug.

Mai Li smiled. "Thank you, miss. You mean a lot to me too. Does that mean you will get out of bed now?" She leveled her gaze at Nouri.

"Oh, all right!" Nouri said, surrendering. "But I'm feeling a little upset to my stomach. I don't know if I will be able to keep anything down." She patted her stomach.

"You feel better after you eat. What would you like Mai Li to fix for breakfast?"

"Oh, I don't know, maybe something sweet. No, wait; make that something tart; no sweet. Oh, hell, I don't know; definitely no coffee! I'll have black rum tea and maybe some raisin toast. No, make that cinnamon; maybe a little fruit. Do we have any melon?" she asked, rising to her feet.

An instant later, Nouri threw her hands up over her mouth and quickly ran to the bathroom, with Mai Li swiftly running behind her. "Oh God, not again!" Nouri cried, leaning over the toilet.

"See, miss, I told you. You need to go see doctor. You sick. Been in bed too long. Not a good thing. Mai Li go call Dr. Douglas now. I'll be right back with your breakfast," she said, taking Nouri by the hand and pulling her out on the balcony. "Here, miss, you sit. Need plenty of fresh air!" she said, in a motherly tone. "Mai Li be back very quick."

Nouri smiled as she watched the tiny woman disappear through the balcony door. "Oh God, what's wrong with me?" she whispered, as she inhaled and exhaled deeply several times. "That's much better," she mumbled, inhaling one more time as she gazed around the south area of the lawn.

It really is a wonderful day. Mai Li is right. I need to go see Dr. Douglas. I probably have a virus or something. She laid her head back on the padded headrest of the chair and closed her eyes. Her mind swiftly drifted back to six weeks earlier.

"Wake up, darling," Gabe lovingly said, gently pushing a fallen strand of hair from her eyes. She squinted a look at the man behind the loving voice.

She smiled, stretched, and then wrapped her arms around his neck, pulling him to her.

"Hi there, Mr. Studly," she murmured, gazing into his beautiful teal-blue eyes. They kissed deeply, passionately.

She smiled at the heated memory as her mind raced on.

"God!" she remembered whispering in his ear after the heart-racing kiss.

"Detective, I've never been happier. I love you so much, Gabe," she whispered softly, tightening her embrace.

A sad expression quickly covered Gabe's handsome face. "Darling, I love you too," he said, releasing himself from her tight embrace.

She looked at him curiously. "What is it, Gabe? You look so sad."

He shook his head hopelessly in silence almost too afraid to speak.

"Gabe," she said nervously, sliding up in bed. "Darling, this isn't the morning after the night before response I was hoping for." She smiled, leveling her eyes to his.

He leaned over and gently ran the palms of his hand down the side of her arm affectionately. "Me neither, Nouri," he said, fighting back his tears.

"Gabe, what is it? You're starting to scare me." She swallowed nervously.

"I...I'm sorry, Nouri. I don't mean to. It's just..." He paused and swallowed hard, trying to get up the nerve to tell her about her husband being shot. "I have something terrible to tell you. And I'm not quite sure how to go about doing it."

She pulled him into her arms. She could feel his body trembling. "Darling, whatever it is, please just tell me," she said, gently rubbing his strong back and shoulders as he continued to lay his head across her chest.

"I'm afraid, Nouri."

"Afraid of what, Gabe?" she asked, lifting his face.

"Afraid of losing you," he replied.

"Gabe, darling, I told you last night, I surrendered myself completely to you. You're the man for me. What's the matter? Don't you believe me? Are you still worried about Clint Chamberlain?"

The loving but sad expression suddenly covering the police detective's face affected her deeply.

"Nouri, until my dying day I'm afraid I'll forever worry over the love you feel for that man, but this has nothing to do with him. This is about..." He stopped talking and swallowed hard.

"Darling, please just tell me what it is!"

"All right, Nouri, but you'll have to promise me something first."

"What's that?"

"Do you promise me?"

"How can I make a promise that I know nothing about?"

Gabe was silent for a few moments before speaking. "All right. It's about your husband. Now will you promise me something?"

"Ethan! You surely aren't afraid that I would ever want to be with him again, are you?"

"So then you won't mind making a promise to me?"

She looked at him curiously. "If you're worried about me going back to that rotten, perverted, miserable husband of mine; all I can tell you is that I can't wait to get away from him and—"

He cut in. "Nouri, Ethan has been shot. He's being flown to a hospital in China. He's not expected to live. I'm...I'm sorry," Gabe said with sadness.

She sat in silence, too stunned to speak.

"Nouri, are you all right?" he asked with concern.

She swallowed hard, trying to pull her thoughts together. After a few moments of uncomfortable silence, she finally responded. "I see. I suppose I should fly to China right away," she said in a whisper. "So what was that promise you wanted from me?"

Gabe pulled her into his arms protectively. "Darling, I need to know that you aren't going to push me away. I couldn't bear it if you tried to shut me out now."

"Oh, Gabe. Just hold me. I love you. I do. Darling, you tell me what it is that you want me to do, and I'll do it," she whispered in his ear, trembling.

"Nouri, I don't know what to tell you to do. I just don't want this to come between us. I couldn't bear it," he said, tightening his arms around her.

Suddenly Mai Li interrupted her thoughts. "Here, miss…breakfast, eat up. Make you feel better," she said with a smile.

Nouri smiled, reaching for her cup of black rum tea. "Thank you, Mai Li. I'll do my best."

"Dr. Douglas said for you to come by his office at two o'clock p.m., okay?"

"All right, Mai Li. Thank you." Nouri watched the tiny woman turn to leave. Then she said, "Mai Li."

Mai Li turned to face her. "Yes, miss."

Nouri smiled warmly. "Will you join me? I'd like to talk to you if you have the time."

Mai Li nodded respectfully. "Yes, miss. Mai Li have plenty of time. Our talk long overdue, yes?" she said, sitting at the table in a chair across from her mistress.

"Yes, it is long overdue," Nouri said, picking up the pot of tea and pouring Mai Li a cup. "Sugar, cream, or lemon?" she offered, pointing to the small silver tray.

"Plain, please."

"Would you care to share my breakfast with me?"

Mai Li shook her head. "Mai Li already had breakfast, miss. Thank you. Just tea is fine."

"Fine. Now, tell me, Mai Li, how have you and Fredrick been holding up?" Nouri studied the tired lines around Mai Li's soft, almond-colored eyes.

Mai Li smiled and nodded. "We okay. Been plenty worried about you though, miss."

"I'll be okay. I just need a little more time, I think. Wow! Everything sure has changed, hasn't it? I still can't believe it." Nouri shook her head in dismay.

"Yes, life can be very strange sometimes, miss."

"Too strange for me at times it seems." Nouri sighed. "I'm really very sorry about your son, Mai Li," she said with sympathy in her voice. "I still find it hard to believe that Steven was your son!" Nouri lifted the teapot and poured herself and Mai Li another cup of tea.

Mai Li struggled hard to fight back her tears. "Steven was a bad seed even as a small boy in China. Angry all the time. Too much hate, too much jealousy, mad at father, mad at me for his being mix blood, hated everything and everybody, including own half-brother." She shrugged defensively.

Nouri nodded. "So it would seem. And even me? It hurts me very much to think that your son actually wanted to see me dead," she said softly as her voice caught on a sob.

"Wrong woman can make man do pretty unthinkable things at times," Mai Li explained sadly as she picked up her cup of tea and took a sip.

"Genna, you mean? How sad. I never would have believed it. Not in a million years. I loved her like a sister. No, actually, I loved Genna Matthews more. She and I were closer than my sister and me. Or so I thought," she said, shaking her head in utter disbelief.

"Mrs. Matthews must've loved Mr. Charles Mason plenty to hold that kind of hate for you for so long, miss."

Nouri nodded. "I've always heard there is a very fine line between love and hate, Mai Li. Apparently that saying must be true to some degree."

"No, Mai Li not agree, miss. Love not supposed to hurt. People make mistakes, sure, but to say I love you to someone should be happy thing; not sad thing, or crazy thing. Wanting to hurt someone over love for someone else is a very bad thing, very sick thing. Ms. Matthews and Steven both very sick, mixed-up people. Too bad. Very sad." She shook her head.

Nouri leaned over and picked up Mai Li's tiny hand, placing it caringly inside her own. "You know, Mai Li, I don't blame you one tiny bit over what Steven tried to do to me. I want you to know that I love you deeply, and I truly appreciate all that you have done for me, as well as continue to do for me. I just want you to know that, okay?"

Mai Li returned Nouri's smile. "Thank you, miss. I love you too, like daughter."

"I know you do, but I need to ask you something. Do you plan to stay here with me now that Ethan's dead, or do you plan on going back to China?" Nouri reached for her cup of tea.

The tiny woman smiled warmly. "Mai Li will stay as long as miss wants me too," she replied.

Nouri gave a deep sigh of relief. "Whew, thank God! I was afraid you might want to leave. Thank you for staying with me, Mai Li. I'll always want you here with me." She smiled.

"This is my home, miss. I love my house Mr. Sommers had built for me here. Don't want to live anywhere else."

"That's good to know." Nouri picked up her fork and began to pick at her food. Mai Li smiled as she watched her mistress finally attempt to get some nourishment.

After a few bites of melon, Nouri continued to speak. "Now that's settled; tell me—is the press still camped out front of the estate?"

May Li nodded. "I'm afraid so, miss."

Nouri sighed as she spread a little jam on her raisin toast. "And the phone calls. Have they stopped yet?"

Mai Li reached inside her apron pocket and pulled out a stack of telephone numbers. She shook her head with dismay. "Calls keep coming in; many every day," she said.

Nouri shook her head again and smiled. "Well, I suppose we'll just have to do something about that, won't we?"

"Like what, miss?" Mai Li asked.

Nouri shrugged. "Oh, I don't know; but I'll think of something." She sat her cup of tea down and then went on. "As long as we're on the subject, are there any phone calls that I should know about?" she asked, silently hoping the homicide detective had called.

"Like?" Mai Li smiled. She knew Nouri was referring to the handsome homicide detective.

"Well, like for instance have I received any calls from—"

Mai Li cut in mischievously. "Like from handsome detective, maybe?"

Nouri's mouth flew open in surprise. "Why, Mai Li, that was the furthest thing from my mind," she lied. "I meant something important like perhaps maybe the authorities may have found Mr. Chamberlain's body. Or perhaps Clint's mystery woman has been located after suddenly vanishing into thin air after she came out of the coma. Something like that." She fought back a smile.

"I see," Mai Li said, with a wee bit of suspicion in her smile. "No, nothing like that, miss."

Nouri took another bite of melon. "Well, since you did bring it up; has the detective phoned lately?" She glanced at her from the corner of her eye, anxiously waiting for her reply.

Mail Li smiled brightly. "Detective calls almost every day to check on you but doesn't actually ask to speak with you. And when handsome detective doesn't call, he has young Ballard to call.

Nouri swallowed nervously. "I see. How about Mr. Mason?"

"Yes, Mr. Mason very worried about you too. He say if miss doesn't return his call soon, he's going to come down here and march into bedroom and…"

Nouri cut in laughing. "Never mind, Mai Li. I have a pretty good idea what Mr. Mason might have said."

"Your father, sister and brother have called many times. Very worried about you too, miss."

"Yes, of course they are. I'll phone them sometime today. Anyone else I need to phone right away?"

Mai Li smiled. "You mean besides handsome detective?"

Nouri glanced at her suspiciously. "Mai Li, what are you trying to tell me?"

Mai Li shook her head innocently "Nothing, miss. None of Mai Li's business. But miss might want to catch up on reading the newspapers," she said, smiling mischievously.

"Excuse me, Mai Li, but I don't understand."

"Mai Li saved newspapers for miss to read when feeling better. And, well, you are feeling better, yes?"

"Well, I suppose a little. But I don't feel much like rehashing old news today."

"Not entire newspaper. Just society page, miss."

"But you know I hate that section, Mai Li."

Mai Li stood to her feet. "I think you might be interested. Detective

Baldwin in it and, well, just take a look and see. You might want to change mind and call handsome detective, okay. I'll go and run your bath now. You have doctor appointment soon." She smiled and turned to leave.

Nouri stopped her. "Not so fast, Mai Li. Just a minute please. Come back here and tell me what it is that you are trying very hard not to tell me."

Mai Li swallowed nervously. "Okay, miss. Handsome detective is getting married in less than two weeks."

Nouri's mouth flew open in surprise. After a few moments, she finally managed to respond. "I see." She paused briefly. "Let me guess. Lisa Clayborne, I would hazard," she added sarcastically.

A surprised expression slowly crept across the tiny woman's face. "You already know, miss?"

"No, not really. But they were engaged before…" Nouri stopped talking and pushed her empty cup of tea off to the side.

"Before what, miss?" Mai Li asked.

"Oh nothing. It wasn't important. Tell me, Mai Li, when was the last time the detective phoned?"

"This morning. Very early. He sounded very depressed. I think he misses you very much, miss."

Nouri chuckled sarcastically. "Yeah right! That's why he went running back into the arms of what's-her-face!" she snapped.

"Maybe you should talk to detective. See what he want," Mai Li suggested.

Nouri shook her head. "I don't think so. Not right now anyway; maybe later. I'd better get my bath and get ready to go to the doctor." She forced a smile still deep in thought over the Boston homicide detective and the woman he was only two weeks away from marrying.

"Yes, miss." Mai Li nodded and turned to leave.

"Oh, by the way, Mai Li, thank you for everything."

Mai Li turned, smiled, and nodded, on her way to fix Nouri's bath.

Nouri poured herself another cup of black rum tea and tried to pull herself together.

Chapter 3

"Okay, lovey, that's a wrap!" the gay clothing designer bellowed to the male stand-in when the photographer snapped the last shot. "You know, lovey, it's amazing just how much you resemble Mr. Baldwin. I still can't believe it! Can you, Lisa?" he asked, removing his right arm from around the tiny waist of the homicide detective's fiancée, as he continued to tap the side of his face with the fingertips of his other hand and stare at the handsome male model.

"It's amazing, Pierre. The model may be a few years younger, but the way you had him posing, no one will know that it isn't Gabe," Lisa agreed.

Pierre chuckled, amused by his own trickery. "That, my dear woman, is one of the many reasons why I am the master of my profession."

"I agree, Pierre! I just can't imagine what I would've done without you! I'm so grateful that you could help me out like this on such a short notice." Lisa gave Pierre a little hug.

"Well, lovey, I'll be here until after the wedding. I'm sure you'll find a suitable hotel for me and my staff, hey, lovey?"

"Oh, of course, Pierre! I'll book your rooms wherever you like. I'll just charge it to Gabe. I'm sure he would insist," she said, shrugging as if the matter was of no consequence.

"I only do the best hotels. You do remember that, don't you, lovey? And of course, I'll need my personal chef flown in," Pierre said, continuing to gaze lustfully at the stand-in model, watching the young man as he removed the clothing he had been wearing for the photo shoot.

"Oh, of course. Whatever you need or want. Gabe would insist." Lisa smiled and turned around. "Here, Pierre, unzip my gown, please," she said, glancing over her shoulder at the famous designer.

"Good," he said, quickly unzipping the wedding gown. "Now my problem is settled. Let's you and I go to the wet bar for a champagne cocktail and catch up on some of our chit-chat, shall we, lovey?"

"Sure, but first we have a few more people from the press to talk to. Remember, Pierre?" Lisa giggled softly.

Pierre cocked an impatient eyebrow. "Oh, lovey, honestly!" he snipped. "I know you're excited, but let them wait. You'll get better press coverage. It's true. I swear! The longer you make them wait, the more they respect you," he chuckled.

"You know, Pierre, I just can't seem to help myself. I'm just so excited about Gabe and me getting back together. For a short time I thought I had lost him to that rich slut! But thank God, he came to his senses and came back to me." She smiled.

"Lovey, Nouri Sommers is hardly a slut! Far from it. Poor dear was just lonely and confused. Or at least that's what I was told. She and Mr. Baldwin just got caught up in a heated moment; that's all. I was told the poor thing hasn't left her bedroom since her husband's death." Pierre shook his head in dismay.

The police detective's fiancée shot the famous clothing designer a questionable glance of annoyance. "Pierre, I thought you were on my side!" she snapped. "And anyway, I hope the bitch stays in that goddamn bedroom of hers, well, at least until after my wedding!" she added, wiggling into her tight-fitting jeans.

Pierre chuckled at her jealousy. "You are shameless, lovey!" he said, enjoying a quick glance at Lisa's well-shaped bare breasts without her noticing. "In a way, Lisa, doesn't this sort of remind you of your first marriage, I mean the wedding part of it, remember? What was his name again, lovey?" he chuckled.

Lisa playfully slapped the designer's arm as she strode past him. "His name was Conrad, and he's still not a topic you want to be discussing with me, Pierre," she said, reaching for her backless summer blouse. She quickly pulled it over her head.

Pierre grinned mischievously. "Temper, temper, lovey. I was only speaking the truth. I bet you about died when you caught him doing the dirty deed with his very own best man only an hour after your wedding vows!"

Lisa shot the nosy designer an angry look. "I'll have you know it wasn't right after our wedding vows, for your information, Pierre! It was the next afternoon. And anyway, it was no big deal to me. It isn't like I was really in love with Conrad or anything. I was young and stupid. I only married him because I wanted to hurt Daddy. I was pissed at him at the time. I knew Conrad was only marrying me to get his hands on some of Daddy's money. I knew, or at least I had my suspicions, about Conrad's honey right from the start. So like I said, it was no big deal," she said, bending over and sliding on her sandals.

Pierre chuckled again. "Tell me something, lovey. Is it true the Baron paid Conrad a million dollars to get him to agree to the annulment?"

Lisa shrugged. "I wouldn't know. I hate being bothered with such petty things," she said, shaking the hairbrush in the designer's face.

Pierre smiled as she brushed her long, beautiful blond hair. "Does Mr. Baldwin know about Conrad, lovey?"

Lisa rolled her eyes, turning to face Pierre. "No, and he doesn't know about Holland either, so just watch it, okay?" She shook the hairbrush in his face again.

"Of course, Lisa. You know me. I keep my mouth shut and my nose out of other people's affairs. Well, usually anyway," he chuckled. "How about that champagne cocktail now, lovey?" He nodded in the direction of the bar.

Lisa grinned. "All right, but I expect you to tell me everything you know about Gabe and Nouri Sommers," she said, sliding her arm inside the designer's.

"What's to tell, lovey? They apparently shared a heated moment. It's over. Case closed!" he returned, patting her hand affectionately.

Lisa sighed. "You know, Pierre, I was a little disappointed that you didn't phone me after you found out they were staying together in the honeymoon suite at the Carlyle while they were in France."

Pierre shrugged defensively. "I just assumed you knew. Who am I to go around spying on people; especially people that spend a fortune buying my line of clothing."

"Huh, well, it's over now. But you must promise me that if something like that ever happens to me again. I mean behind my back—"

Pierre cut in. "Oh, of course. I'd phone you right away. It wouldn't matter to me what Willem would say about it. I'd call anyway. My word, lovey," he said, raising his hand as though he were being sworn inside a courtroom.

"Good. Now tell me what you personally know about Nouri Sommers," Lisa said as she dropped a sugar cube inside Pierre's champagne cocktail.

Pierre sipped his drink. "Mmm, I needed that, lovey. And how thoughtful, Lisa, you remembered the sugar cube."

Lisa smiled and waited patiently for the designer to begin telling her about the beautiful billionairess.

Pierre slid onto a barstool as he began. "Well, lovey, Nouri Sommers is an incredibly beautiful young woman. A real heart-stopper." He shook his head in amazement. "She's probably the only woman in the world that has ever made me turn my head, if you know what I mean. Of course, you must never tell Willem that I even suggested such a thing. He'd...well, he would...well, never mind. Just forget my last remark altogether," he said, using his hand as a substitute fan.

Lisa gave him a heated look. "And this is supposed to make me feel better, Pierre!" she exclaimed.

"Sorry, Lisa. Nouri is simply magnificent, charming, classy, very elegant. I know you want me to tell you something derogatory about her, but lovey, for the life of me, I can't imagine what that might be." He sighed hopelessly.

Lisa shot him a look that was more like a dagger. "Let me see if I can coax you. How does the Holiday Inn sound for your lodging arrangements tonight?" she threatened, slamming her drink down hard on the bar.

Pierre nodded, understanding her threat. "You know, lovey, now that I have had time to think about it for a few moments, it seems as though I do recall a little something scandalous about her after all," he conceded. "It seems Nouri Sommers is not only a little heart-stopper; she is also a huge heartbreaker. A real little thief of hearts.

"It's been rumored that apparently both your hubby-to-be and his ex-partner in crime-fighting were in love with her at the same time. I understand it almost ruined their longtime friendship." Pierre sipped his drink again.

The Baron's daughter stared in open-mouthed disbelief. "You mean to tell me that both private eye extraordinaire Charles Mason and Gabe were having sex with her highness at the same time?" A wicked grin curled the corners of her lips.

Pierre nodded. "Apparently so. Well, at least from what I've been told, it was at least in the same week. The story gets better. It seems that Mr. Mason lost his heart to a Ms. Nouri St. Charles from Boston seven years earlier. And at the time Mr. Baldwin was working undercover on a case and never got around to formally meeting Mr. Mason's main squeeze. So when Mr. Mason asked Mr. Baldwin to babysit Mrs. Sommers right after the Lambert murders, he had no way of knowing Nouri Sommers was in fact the same woman that his friend had been in love with for the past seven years. And..." He paused to take a sip of his champagne cocktail.

"And what? Please don't keep me in suspense," Lisa squealed with interest.

"And the week in question, Mr. Mason had spent the night rekindling his undying passion for her inside her massive bedroom chamber and Mr. Baldwin was unaware. All Mr. Baldwin knew at the time was that his friend needed a favor—the favor being protecting a friend, the friend being Nouri Sommers. Mr. Mason had asked him to personally keep her safe and out of harm's way until his return from France, where he had to go to track down Mr. Sommers and—are you ready for this?" he asked, reaching for his drink.

Lisa squirmed on her barstool excitedly. "Please tell me, Pierre. I can't stand it!"

Pierre chuckled wickedly. "And her lover, high-powered attorney Clint Chamberlain. Which by the way was also not only her husband's attorney, but Mr. Chamberlain was also Mr. Sommers' best friend! Apparently, Mrs. Sommers had had a very romantic week." He shook his head with envy and fanned himself.

Lisa's mouth flew open in stunned belief again. "What? You mean she was doing it with all four men!"

Pierre felt his face flush. "Well, I don't suppose it was like on the same day or anything as tasteless as that, lovey. But yes, it does appear she may had made love to all four men in the same week anyway." He silently drooled at the thought.

"I told you she was a slut, Pierre! No wonder she hasn't left her goddamn bedroom in six weeks. It will probably take her that long to recuperate!" Lisa snipped with an attitude.

"Tsk, tsk, lovey. Nouri Sommers is a very exciting, beautiful young woman. Apparently her husband wasn't getting the job done right, so she let her former fiancé back into the picture. Nouri thought she and Mr. Chamberlain had fallen back in love, but then he disappeared on her too. The poor dear. Lonely and needing a shoulder to cry on, she then turned to her first real man, from what I understand, Mr. Charles Mason. She let him back into the driver's seat, but when she needed Mr. Mason the most, he wasn't there either, but the handsome detective from Boston was, and…"

Lisa interrupted. "Huh! So that gives the bitch the right to steal my man away from me! I don't think so!" Her tone was laced with sarcasm and jealousy.

"Well, in all fairness, lovey, from what I understand, she had been told you and Mr. Baldwin were no longer an item. You were broken up at the time," Pierre said, reaching for the bottle of champagne. He poured himself another glass of bubbling effervescence.

Lisa shrugged. "Well, maybe so, but I still hope the spoiled bitch stays inside her goddamn bedroom, at least until after my marriage to Gabe."

"Well, as I told you earlier, I heard she hasn't left her bedroom for the past six weeks, so there is a good chance you'll get that wish of yours." He glanced at her and smiled.

Lisa set her empty glass on the bar. "Good! Now that we've discussed that, what d'ya say we go and talk to the press. I think we have kept them waiting long enough, don't you think?" She slid off the barstool. "I want to make sure the reporters have enough time to get the info on my wedding in the late edition of the newspaper."

"Fine, lovey. You lead; I'll follow. But I will want to be the one to discuss the gown with them," he said, belting down the last of his drink.

Chapter 4

A very nervous Tori St. Clair a.k.a. Renea Chandlier continued to pace back and forth inside the sleazy motel room on the outskirts of a small town in France.

"Why the hell doesn't he call?" she mumbled, glancing at her watch. "Five o'clock." She sighed, strode to the television set, turned it on, and returned to the ragged overstuffed chair, threw her body down, and waited impatiently for the picture to appear.

"Damn it!" she grumbled as the picture tube struggled to catch up with the sound. "Great!" She stared blankly at the pictureless set.

A few moments later, she glanced nervously at her watch again. "Damn it, come on and call!"

Finally the picture appeared on the television set. "It's about bloody time!" She jumped to her feet and crossed the room to change the channel.

A few seconds later, the telephone rang, giving her an unexpected start. "Oh shit!" she cried, running to answer the phone. "Hello," she whispered nervously into the receiver.

"Sorry I'm late calling. I got tied up at the last minute," the voice on the other end of the line said.

"So?"

"So, I'm going to need a few more days, Tori."

"What!"

"I'm sorry. It's the best I can do. Do you still want me to fix you up?"

"Of course I do, Sean! I have no choice. You have to help me. How much longer do I have to wait here in this roach motel?"

"Maybe a few days; maybe longer. I'm doing my best!"

Tori sighed in frustration. "I'm sorry, Sean. I just hate having to hide in this godforsaken rattrap. It gives me the goddamn creeps." She shivered in disgust.

"I can imagine. You have the gun I got for you, right?"

"Yeah, sure. I wouldn't stay in a place like this without one. I'll tell you that much." She sighed again.

"Sorry, Tori, but you did tell me it had to be someplace where no one would think to look for you, remember?"

"I'm sorry, Sean. I'm just scared. That's all. I don't mean to sound ungrateful. Do you think you might be able to stop by later? I could use the company, and I need a few things. I'm afraid to leave the room."

"Tori, I filled the room with food, clothes, makeup. I even put a few wigs and hats in one of the dresser drawers. Didn't you find them?"

"Yes, but I still need a few things, and besides, I'm lonely."

"Better get used to it, kiddo. Life on the run doesn't get much better. Are you sure that's what you want to do?"

She swallowed hard. "I have no choice. If the Asian Mob finds me, I'm a dead woman. It doesn't matter that Jin Tang is dead. And if the Feds find me, I go to prison. Not much to stay around for, is there?"

"I guess, but…"

"But what?"

"Never mind, Tori. It's your choice, not mine. By the way, how are you feeling?"

"That's hysterical! How the hell do you think I'm feeling, for godsakes?" she snapped angrily.

"Listen, babe, don't take it out on me. I'm not the bad guy here. I'm not the one who got you pregnant or got you into trouble with the Asian Underworld or the Feds, now am I?" the caller returned heatedly.

"Oh God! I miss him so much, Sean," Tori cried, wiping a tear from her eye.

"Yeah, I know. Sorry, kid. Did Chamberlain know you were pregnant?"

"I don't know. Maybe. I think he may have suspected it. I'm not sure; why?" she asked, tugging at the phone cord.

"I have an idea. Maybe I will stop by in a little while, after all."

"What kind of idea?"

"I'll run it by you when I stop by. I'll try and make it by ten tonight. I can take you to get whatever else you might need then too, okay?"

She sighed with relief. "Thanks, Sean. What would I do without you?"

"No problem. I gotta go. I'll see you later." Her friend hung up the payphone he had been using.

Tori sank into the ragged chair and once again stared blankly at the television set. A short time later, her uncontrolled tears began to fall. She covered her face with both hands. "Oh God, Clint! Why did you have to leave me and your baby," she sobbed hopelessly.

She was soon jarred back to reality by the loud knocking on her motel room door. She glanced at her watch. Sean must have decided to drop by earlier than he had told her; she thought as she darted to the door.

"You're early," she said as she jerked the door open. A look of confusion covered her face, and her mouth flew open in stunned disbelief. Too surprised to speak, she slowly backed up against the door to allow her unexpected visitor to enter.

Chapter 5

Homicide detective Gabe Baldwin had glanced at his watch so often that morning he had forgotten how many times. But he checked it again as he pulled another unread six-week-old newspaper out from under a large pile. He nervously thumbed through the pages, deliberately trying to block out everything.

"Man, this place is beginning to drive me crazy!" he grumbled, thinking how much he needed to leave his office for a while. He shoved the newspaper off his desk, jumped to his feet, and reached for his suit jacket just as the telephone rang. He stared at the phone blankly for several moments trying to decide if he wanted to answer it, when his boss walked into his office.

"Well, aren't you going to answer that goddamn thing, Detective?" the police captain asked.

"Fuck it! Let the damn thing ring off the hook for all I care." Gabe reached for his suit jacket again.

The captain shook his head and leveled his gaze to the detective. "Gabe, what the hell is wrong with you today, for chrissakes?"

Gabe sighed and said, "I gotta get out of this damn place for a while. I need a little time to myself." He slipped into his jacket.

His boss gave an understanding shrug. "You want go get a beer and talk about it?"

Gabe covered his face with his hands for a moment and then ran his fingers through his thick hair as he glanced at the police captain. "Thanks, but I don't think so. Maybe some other time, Mark. Right now I just need to be alone. That's all. Care if I leave for the day?" He looked at the time again.

"It's that Sommers broad, isn't it? She's still driving you crazy. It's written all over your face, Gabe," his friend said, shaking his head suspiciously.

"Listen, Mark. I appreciate your concern, but—"

"Now don't go and get a hard-on with me, Gabe," the captain interrupted. "We're friends here. I gotta right to know what's bothering your ass." He shook his head and then went on. "Then if it isn't the Sommers broad, it has to be Lisa?"

Gabe shrugged. "I guess I just have a lot on my mind right now. I should've stayed home. I'm not worth a shit today. I can't even concentrate on forming my next goddamn sentence," he mumbled, throwing himself back in his chair.

The captain walked across the floor, hesitated, and then sat down across from Gabe. "What is it, son? I hate seeing you like this."

Gabe rubbed his chin thoughtfully. He finally leaned over and opened the bottom desk drawer, fumbling around inside it for the bottle of ouzo and two shot glasses that were hidden behind a few fake files.

He set the two shot glasses down on top of his desk and filled them with the clear-colored liquor made in Greece. "Ever tried ouzo before, Captain?" Gabe set the bottle down. "One thing about this Greek liquor," he belted down his shot and cringed at the strong taste of the alcohol burning in his throat, "this stuff will either cure you or kill you, or at least that's what I've been told." He poured himself another shot of the strong but sweet-tasting cure-all.

The police captain hesitantly downed his shot of the Greek white lightning, feeling surprised when the drink took his breath away. "Oh shit! That's some potent stuff, Gabe. What did you say the name of this stuff was?" He used his hand as a fan to cool off his tongue.

The detective chuckled before downing his shot and quickly refilled their shot glass again. "Ouzo, do you like it?"

"Yeah sure." Mark shrugged. "Once you get a shot or two of the stuff in you, it isn't half bad." He chuckled, reaching for his shot glass.

Gabe belted his third shot and poured himself another as his boss downed his third.

The captain watched his troubled friend with concern. "So, tell me, Detective, what's got your dick caught in the wringer today?"

Gabe released another sigh of frustration. "Nothing, and everything." He frowned. "You were right you know, Mark." He swallowed hard. "I can't seem to get Nouri Sommers off my mind. I'm hopelessly in love with her. And can't do anything about it." He reached for the bottle of Greek liquor again, poured himself another shot, and filled the police captain's shot glass again.

"Can't do anything about it, huh?" Mark shook his head. "I'm sorry, but I don't understand your logic, son," he said, shrugging his broad shoulders. "Sounds like you enjoy sleeping with that goddamn stubborn Greek pride of yours. I guess you prefer cold, hard pride to a soft, cuddly body, hey?"

Gabe slammed the liquor bottle on his desk. "Goddamn it, Mark, Nouri told me to get the hell out, and leave her alone! What the hell was I supposed to do?" he snapped, downing another shot.

"Well, running from Nouri Sommers' bedroom to the closest wedding chapel with Lisa Clayborne sure as hell wasn't the goddamn answer! You sit here and tell me how much you're in love with one woman, yet in less than two weeks you're going to swap spit and I-dos with another. Wonderful, simply wonderful, Gabe." Mark shook his head. "I hope you at least like your betrothed! Well, do you?" he added in a fatherly tone.

Gabe downed his sixth shot of ouzo and poured himself another and then slammed the liquor bottle down on top of his desk again without responding to his friend's remark.

"Thank you. Don't mind if I do, Detective," the captain said, reaching for the almost empty bottle of alcohol and helping himself. "So do you at least like the woman you are about to marry?" The two men shared a glance. "Ya know, Gabe, once the I-dos are over, 'forever' can suddenly turn into a lifetime prison term if a man isn't married to someone he really loves. Know what I mean?"

In spite of his surly mood, Gabe chuckled at his friend's fatherly wisdom. "Yeah. I imagine I do understand, Mark, thanks," he said, grinning.

Mark nodded, feeling satisfied that he had given the detective something to think about before he jumped into a marriage he really didn't want, with a woman that he really didn't love, just because of his hurt pride. "Good! Then maybe you should consider postponing your upcoming marriage with Lisa just until you have time to work things out in your mind. Just think about it, Gabe, that's all. I just don't want to see you rush in to something you might live to regret."

Gabe looked thoughtful for a few moments before he opened the desk drawer and pulled out a fresh bottle the Greek white lightning. He glanced at his friend. "If I open this, are you going to help me drink it?" He pointed to the bottle of liquor in his left hand.

Feeling no pain at that point, his boss shrugged and nodded a yes. He slid his empty shot glass across the desk to the detective for a refill. "What the hell! Bev's gone to her mother's for a few days anyway. All I have to go home to when I get there is a dark house and a dog that needs to be fed," he said, picking up his shot of ouzo.

"So where were we, Mark?" Gabe asked before belting another shot.

"I believe I was trying to convince you to postpone your wedding for a while," Mark said, flashing a small grin.

Gabe chuckled. "You know, Mark, I'm only getting married to please my mother. She's dying to be a grandmother." He shrugged defensively. "Don't get me wrong, I enjoy having sex with Lisa, but she can be a real pain in the ass at times. She's spoiled rotten." He glanced at his friend. "You know what she did?" he stated drunkenly shaking his head in dismay.

The captain chuckled at the expression plastered across his friend's face. "No, why don't you tell me? What did she do?"

"She just spent fifty grand of my money on another wedding gown especially designed for her by the famous French clothing designer Pierre Duvall." He rolled his eyes reaching for his shot glass.

The captain cringed. "Ouch! No wonder you want to get drunk today. I'm afraid I'd want to, too. Shit! Fifty grand, that's what I paid for my goddamn house. Unbelievable," he said, picking up the bottle of liquor and pouring them both another shot.

Gabe shook his head again. "Oh, that's not the half of it. Lisa just had Pierre design her a wedding gown just a few months ago. That gown, she says, was bad luck!"

An expression of shock quickly crossed the captain's face. "No shit! So counting both gowns, she spent a hundred large!" He swallowed hard at the thought.

"Yes, that's right. My money! She keeps on spending, and spending, and spending. She's like that goddamn battery-operated bunny that's on TV, the one that keeps going and going and going." He shook his head. "I've had several phone calls already this morning wanting okays on all types of dumb shit she wants me to pay for. Can you fucking believe that?"

The captain chuckled, amused by it all. "Sorry, Gabe. I can't help it. What did she want you to pay for this morning?"

"A two-week stay at the Boston Queen's for Pierre Duvall and his entire staff of male models plus his own private chef that she expects me to fly in from France!" He shook his head in disgust.

The captain shook his head. "I thought the bride's side of the family was supposed to pay for all that happy horse shit?"

Gabe picked up the ouzo bottle and poured them another drink. "She wants to prove to Daddy that I can afford to support her in the manner she's grown accustomed to living. A real pain in the ass, I'm telling you, Mark!" He belted his shot.

"Sounds to me like you need to send her ass back to good ol' Daddy to take care of! After all, he's the one who started the goddamn manner that she has grown so accustomed to living," Mark mused, picking up his shot glass.

Gabe chuckled loudly. "You know, Captain, I see your point there."

"No shit! I'm telling you, son, right to your face, I know you better than most people, and I honestly believe the Baron's daughter isn't the woman for you. Maybe Nouri Sommers isn't either, but at least you owe yourself a little time to think things over; maybe even consider a few other alternatives, right? Who knows, maybe your Ms. Right is still out there somewhere. Maybe you haven't met her yet. Don't rush into anything, son. I..." The captain picked up the empty bottle of alcohol. "Shit! We drank another bottle dry. You got any more stashed somewhere?" Mark's words were beginning to slur.

Gabe nodded drunkenly. "Oh yeah! I think there's still a few bottles around here somewhere." He opened his desk drawer again, fumbled around inside, and pulled out another bottle of the Greek white lightning.

"You know, Gabe, there's something I've been meaning to ask you. That is if you don't mind."

"What's that, Captain?" The detective popped the cork on the liquor with the licorice smell.

"Did you and Mason swap spit and make up yet?"

Gabe glanced at his friend and grinned. "Charles and I are all right. As a matter of fact, we talked this morning. He sounded rather content. Finding out that he had a son seemed to make all the difference in the world; made him real happy. I told you Charles and Tonya were made for each other, didn't I?"

Mark nodded in agreement. "Yeah, I'll give you that one. You know, Gabe, picking up a newspaper with Mason's picture plastered across one of the pages of it somewhere and not seeing him posing with some supermodel anymore isn't going to be the same. I bet he's scared shitless!" He laughed at the thought.

"Maybe a little," Gabe agreed. "But it's high time Charles settled down. Hell, he's knocking forty, the old fart! It's time to let the young guys make their moves on a few of those gorgeous supermodels Charles has been greedily hogging for years. It's only fair, don't you think?" He laughed.

"Oh shit! Speak of the devil," the police captain groaned as the famous P.I. suddenly came bursting into Gabe's office.

Seeing the drunken state of both of his former colleagues, Charles Mason shook his head. "So this is the guy you stood me up for huh, Gabe?" he said playfully. "Hell, what's the captain got that I don't have?"

"A great ass!" Gabe replied. "Stand up, Mark, let Charles have a quick look-see," he said, laughing.

His boss gave a drunken chuckle. "I gotta better idea, Gabe, why don't I drop my boxers, bend over, and let you kiss it!"

The police detective pressed his lips together and made a few loud kissing sounds. "You mean like this, Captain?"

"Something like that, you silly son-of-a-bitch!" Mark shook his head. His face was bright red.

Charles cut in. "Maybe I should leave so you two good ol' boys can be alone," he said.

Gabe laughed. "Fuck you, Mason! Pull up a chair and join us." He opened his desk drawer and pulled out another shot glass and a new bottle of liquor.

Charles' mouth flew open and his eyes widened when he saw the bottle of Greek liquor. "Oh shit, not that stuff, Gabe! You are out to do some serious damage today, huh!"

"Oh yeah!" Gabe drunkenly chuckled, nodding his head. "Here, drink up. You're way the hell behind, Charles," he said, pouring all three of them a shot.

Charles made another cringing face before belting down his shot. "Whew!" he whispered hoarsely, holding out his small shot glass for another shot of the Greek white lightning.

"Bottoms up, Charles!" Gabe said, pouring himself another drink and waiting to pour Charles another.

Charles quickly downed two more shots, attempting to catch up with his two drunken pals, cringing and shaking his head after each shot.

Gabe laughed at his friend. "Well, don't stop now! You have some serious belting to do to catch up with us big boys, Mason!" He poured Charles his fifth shot of liquor.

"Son-of-a-bitch!" Charles spat, loosening his necktie and the top button of his shirt. "So, what are we celebrating, fellas?" he asked before downing his shot of alcohol.

Gabe staggered to his feet and tried to remove his suit jacket. "Oh shit!" he exclaimed.

Charles shook his head. "Here, allow me," he offered, helping the detective take off his jacket. "Better?" he asked, laying the detective's jacket on the back of his chair.

"Much better," Gabe returned, loosening his necktie and also the top button on his shirt.

"Well, what are we celebrating?" the captain remarked, after pondering Charles' question for several moments.

"Ah yes, I remember now. Charles, my dear friend and former partner, the captain and I are celebrating freedom!" Gabe drunkenly slurred, attempting to pour them all another shot of firewater.

Charles intercepted the bottle from Gabe's unsteady hands. "Here, allow me," he said, filling their shot glasses to the brim.

"Charles."

"Yes, Gabe." Charles cringed and swallowed at the same time.

"Pour us another. I feel like making a toast."

"A toast, huh?"

"Yeah, a toast. You gotta problem with that, Charles?"

Charles shook his head. "Problem? No, no, I don't have a problem with that. Please, Gabe, by all means do the honors," he returned, filling the shot glasses again.

"All right, I will. Here's to you, Charles. May Tonya and Chuckie bring you all the good things in life that you deserve," he said.

"Thank you, my friend," Charles said in a solemn voice.

Gabe nodded. "You bet."

"So now what shall we toast to?" Gabe asked, reaching for the bottle of liquor.

"I know," the captain said, raising his empty shot glass in mid-air.

Charles chuckled. "Just a second, Captain, I haven't put anything in your shot glass yet."

"Well, why the hell not?" the captain spat drunkenly.

Charles laughed again. "This is going to be a long afternoon," he mumbled under his breath. He shook his head.

Chapter 6

"What the hell is going on in there, Ballard?" police detective Brad Johnson asked, putting his ear up against the detective's door, attempting to hear what was being said on the other side. He shook his head. All that noise and laughter were echoing out into the adjoining offices.

Newest member to the detectives' squad Al Ballard also put his ear against the door to hear. "How the heck should I know?" he said with a puzzled expression.

"What's going on, guys?" Sergeant Barry asked, noticing both detectives bent over with their ears pressed hard against Detective Baldwin's office door. Curious, she, too, lowered her body and pressed her ear against the door.

Young Ballard glanced at her. "We don't know, Melissa. The captain went in there about three hours ago and has been in with Detective Baldwin ever since."

"And Charles Mason went in to join them about an hour ago and hasn't come out yet," Detective Johnson added.

"Oh shit, this sounds like it could be big! Wonder what's up," Melissa Barry said, watching a female P.B.X. operator heading their way.

The young operator started to knock on the detective's door, but Sergeant Barry quickly stopped her. "I wouldn't bother them if I were you," she said.

"Why? I need to know why Detective Baldwin isn't answering his calls," the young woman replied.

"Apparently, something big must be going down. If I were you, I'd just continue to take the detective's messages and tell whoever is calling that you'll see to it that he gets the message," Melissa suggested, putting her ear back against the door.

"What about the captain?" the young woman asked.

"I don't know. His calls too, I guess," Melissa answered with a shrug of her shoulders.

"But Ms. Daughtery has telephoned for the captain four times now." The young woman swallowed nervously.

"The D.A.? Oh shit!" Detective Johnson cringed.

"Well, I don't know. Maybe if she calls back, you should tell her that he's still in a meeting with…" The female sergeant stopped speaking, straightened, and stared back into the angry eyes of the district attorney, who had just approached.

"With whom, Sergeant Barry? What's going on here?" the female D.A. asked.

"Ah…ah, the captain, Detective Baldwin, and Mr. Mason, ma'am. Something big must be in the works…" Sergeant Barry stammered.

Ms. Daughtery interrupted. "And you, Sergeant Barry and Detectives Johnson and Ballard, make it a point to eavesdrop on your commanding officers' conversations?

Melissa could feel her face turning red. "No, of course not, ma'am. We just…"

Tonya Daughtery cut Sergeant Barry off in mid-sentence. "Why don't you all just go back to whatever it was that you were doing before your curiosity got the better of you," she said, putting her hand on the doorknob.

Tonya slipped inside the office and stood quietly, not believing her eyes. Deciding not to interrupt, she slowly inched her way back out of the door without being noticed. "Oh boy!" she murmured in dismay. What should she do? She sure didn't want to see the captain or the detective in trouble with their boss.

She motioned to young Detective Al Ballard standing nearby. "Detective Ballard," she said quietly. "I need to borrow your pen and notepad please."

The young detective nervously fumbled inside his jacket pocket for a moment and finally pulled out his pen and pad of paper. He handed them to her and swallowed hard.

Tonya Daughtery quickly scribbled a few words on the paper, folded it, and gave the note to the young detective. "I want you to take this note inside Detective Baldwin's office and hand it to Mr. Mason. And, Detective Ballard, when you come back out, I want you to forget about what you saw inside. Do I make myself clear?" She leveled her gaze on the young detective.

Young Ballard swallowed hard, nodded, and then quietly entered the senior detective's office. Slowly crossing the room unnoticed, he handed the famous P.I. the note.

"Thank you, Detective," Charles Mason said, accepting the note being handed him from the nervous young detective. Ballard turned to leave, but Charles Mason stopped him.

Young Ballard swallowed nervously. He could feel his face turning red. "Yes, sir," he said quietly.

"Tell Ms. Daughtery I said thank you. And I will phone her later. And while you're at it, Detective, I want you to phone a limo service and have them pull around to the back of the station. When the driver arrives, come back in here and help me put the captain and the detective inside the limo. Discreetly, okay?" he instructed.

Young Ballard gave an understanding nod and quickly left the office.

In less than thirty minutes, Charles Mason, Detective Baldwin, and the police captain were on their way to the P.I.'s house, after making only one stop; the local liquor store to pick up a case of ouzo.

Yes, it is going to be a very, very, very long night, Charles Mason thought, as he continued to fumble with the lock while his two friends, mumbling and laughing together, sat on the porch steps.

Chapter 7

...Going to the chapel and we're gonna get married. Gee, I really love you and we're gonna get married...

"Rub my face in it, why don't you!" Nouri Sommers snapped at the song as she listened to the radio inside her shiny canary-yellow Viper, zooming past the exit to high-powered attorney Clint Chamberlain's downtown apartment. She was lost in thought, thinking about the young woman Boston homicide detective Gabe Baldwin was going to marry in less than two weeks.

Mrs. Lisa Clayborne Baldwin. Mrs. Lisa Baldwin. "Yuck, gag me with a spoon!" she snipped, rolling her eyes. "Oh excuse me, Ms. Clayborne, I should have said silver spoon! God, I can't believe it, Gabe!" She sighed sadly. "How the hell can you marry a woman like that! She's so transparent, so plastic. Okay, so she is super attractive, and super wealthy, but she's also boring and spoiled!" Nouri continued to mumble under her breath as she zoomed closer to town. "You told me so yourself, Detective!"

Her thoughts shifted back to six weeks earlier. She and Gabe had just returned to France from China. Gabe was to meet with Charles Mason and had told her he would be gone for most of the morning. It was business he couldn't avoid, so he dropped her off at the hotel.

Nouri had no objections. She wanted to secretly say her good-byes to high-powered attorney Clint Chamberlain without Gabe knowing about it. She knew he was extremely jealous of her former lover.

With Nouri's husband now out of the picture and her wanting to move on to a new life with Gabe, she would have to see Clint Chamberlain one final time. A quick good-bye. A kiss on the cheek. And "I wish you well." What could possibly go wrong?

But the police detective had caught her sneaking out of her former lover's hotel suite. It looked bad, and Gabe's heart had managed to get broken yet again. But it hadn't been what he thought. Nouri exited off the freeway. *Why wouldn't he let me explain? Why does he always assume the worst?* She sighed hopelessly and whispered, "Oh well, I guess Gabe and I just weren't meant to be."

Her thoughts raced on...

"Wait, Gabe, please! I know this looks bad, but it's not what you think," she had shouted, running after him inside the hallway of the Bristol Hotel.

He turned to face her. "We'll talk about this later, Nouri. I gotta go!" His tone was one of disbelief.

"Fine, Gabe, think what you like! I really don't care!" Nouri silently mouthed the words as she remembered them. *And moments later, the detective had disappeared out of the front door of the hotel.*

"Oh Gabe, why the hell wouldn't you let me explain?" Nouri murmured. *And now that I've had time to think about it, what the hell were you spying on me for to begin with?* "That son-of-a-bitch, he's as bad as Ethan!" Nouri muttered, suddenly believing the detective must've been following her. How else would he have known she was there? *An educated guess?* "Doubtful!" She dismissed the idea with a negative shake of her head. *Maybe he and Charles were following Clint. Apparently Clint never did tell the F.B.I. where he had hidden the money supposedly belonging to the Asian Mob.* "Umm." She sighed and added the word "Maybe."

...What a difference a day makes...Twenty-four little hours...

"Boy, ain't that the truth!" she mumbled, leaning over to turn down the radio. It was interfering with her thoughts.

"Men!" She shook her head in dismay. "Four men, four lovers, and then, there were none!" she whispered, shifting her thoughts back to France.

Gabe should've been more understanding. More compassionate. After all, Ethan had just died. He should have known I would need to see Clint alone. Even if he didn't understand, he should've trusted me, should've let me explain, but no, what's he do? He pouts at me for two days over catching me sneaking out of Clint's room.

Then just out of the blue, puff, like a cloud of smoke, only two days later, Clint drives his car off that goddamn bridge and suddenly he's dead, too!

And then, after not even speaking to me for two days, Gabe wants to pretend everything is okay between us just because Clint is now out of the picture. I don't think so, mister! Okay, so I was still mad at him for the way he behaved with me a few days earlier; he should have known my anger carried over and that I didn't actually mean for him to get out and leave me alone. I was hurt, confused, and well, I just freaked, that's all. He should have known that. He knew how much I loved him, for chrissakes! I only told him so about a kazillion times that week we were together. He knew it was over between Clint and me. Hell, even Clint and I knew it. Clint was never going to change. Maybe Gabe just used that as an excuse to leave. Maybe he really did want to marry Ms. Lisa Clayborne. Umm...What the hell!

"Speaking of hell! Where in hell am I?" she mumbled, glancing around. Then she recognized the seafood restaurant that she and Gabe had eaten at on their way to Connecticut to his cabin in the woods—where he was taking her to keep her from out of harm's way after she received the death threat following the two Lambert murders.

She glanced at her watch. "Mmm, I'm starving." She pulled her Viper into the restaurant's parking lot, reached for her cell phone, and dialed Mai Li.

"Hi, Mai Li. It's me."

"Miss, thank goodness you call! Mai Li been worried sick."

"I'm sorry, Mai Li. I just needed some time to myself. That's why I had Fredrick drop me off at the condo to get my car after I left Dr. Douglas' office."

"Where are you, miss?"

"You wouldn't believe me if I told you!"

"Where?" Mai Li asked.

"I...I'm fine, Mai Li. I need some time to myself. I've decided to check in to a hotel for a few days. Please don't worry about me. I'll phone every day. I promise, okay?"

"I'm worried about you, miss."

"Please don't worry. No need. I'm fine. Honest."

"What did Dr. Douglas say, miss?"

Nouri swallowed hard. "He said, that I was...was...oh, I'll tell you later. I'm fine. Really I am, Mai Li."

"You sure, miss?"

"Yes, Mai Li. I'm sure."

"Your father called again, miss."

"Well." She sighed. "I'll call him in a few days or so. Next time he phones, tell him that for me, okay?"

"Miss, Mr. Mason phoned again. Said to tell you if you don't phone him by tomorrow, he would track you down like a—"

Nouri cut in. "Yes, Mai Li. I can imagine." She chuckled.

"It's good to hear you laugh again, miss."

"Charles always did have that effect on me," she replied, shaking her head and smiling as she pictured the famous P.I.'s handsome face.

"Miss, did you eat yet?" Mai Li asked in a motherly tone.

"I just pulled into a seafood restaurant a few minutes ago. I'll go in and get a bite after I finish talking to you."

"Okay, miss. You be careful."

"Okay. Bye, Mai Li. I'll talk to you tomorrow." Nouri turned off her cell phone and slid out of her car. Inside the restaurant, she inhaled deeply, enjoying the aroma of the fresh seafood. "Smells wonderful," she whispered.

"A table for…" The host glanced at Nouri standing in front of his podium.

"One please, I'd like a table with a view of the ocean, if possible. I don't mind waiting, if I have to," she said with a smile.

"Certainly, but there is about a thirty-minute wait. Would you care to wait in the lounge, or would you prefer to go out on the patio? You can take a short walk along the beach if you like, ma'am."

Nouri returned the young host's smile. "The lounge will be fine. I've been driving for a while. I could use a drink and freshen up a bit. Thanks." She turned and strolled in the direction of the restroom. A hand reached out and gently grabbed her by the wrist. Nouri's heart leaped in fright. She slowly opened her eyes to see a cute young man.

"I'm sorry, Nouri. I didn't mean to frighten you," he said.

"Do I know you?"

"I'm Rick. I'm a cop from—"

"Rick." She smiled. "Oh, of course. I remember now. Boston Police Department, right?" She smiled and glanced at the two other police officers sitting at a table nearby.

"Yeah, that's right. So, you do remember then?" He smiled.

Nouri chuckled. "How could I forget! That was a night to remember, I'll tell you that!"

"Would you care to join us?" He nodded in the direction of his friends. "My friends and I were just about to order. We'd love for you to eat with us." He smiled hopefully.

"Well." She looked thoughtful for a moment and then smiled. "Ah, if you're sure I wouldn't be imposing."

"Wow, are you kidding?"

Nouri smiled. "All right. You've convinced me," she said, standing near the empty chair.

Rick quickly pulled out the chair for her. "Have you eaten here before?" he asked, helping move her chair in a little closer to the table.

"Only once before. It was great!"

"Yeah, the food is incredible. We love eating here. It's well worth the two-hour drive to get here. Detective Baldwin introduced us to this place a few months ago. We've been coming here every since." He smiled and motioned for the waitress. "What would you like to drink?"

"How about a vodka martini," Nouri said. "No, wait! Better make that a wine spritzer with a lemon twist instead of lime." She smiled. "It's my first drink of the day. I'd hate to get drunk and one of you fellas have to pull me over again," she confessed.

Rick chuckled. "So you have learned your lesson, huh?" he said, playfully.

"Yes, Officer Hobner. I've learned my lesson." She blushed.

"Good," he said with a chuckle. "So, I take it you drove yourself here tonight."

Nouri nodded. "Yes, I needed to get out and about for a little while. I've been cooped up much too long, it seems." She sighed.

"Yeah, I can imagine. Nouri, I'd like you to know that all of us down at the station were awfully sorry to—"

"Yes, thank you, Rick." Nouri stopped him. "Tell everyone I appreciate their concern," she said, squirming uncomfortably in her chair.

Rick noticed her nervousness. He cleared his throat. "Are you okay?"

"As well as can be expected, I guess." She forced a small smile, reaching for her drink.

"That's understandable."

"What's been going on with you, Rick?" Nouri asked, changing the subject.

Rick laughed, picking up his bottle of beer. "Same old, same old."

"Gets pretty boring night after night, huh, Rick?" Nouri said, glancing around the room.

All three guys nodded at the same time and laughed. "Not all the time, but boring enough," Rick responded.

"So if being a cop is that boring, why do you guys continue doing it?" she asked.

"For the adventure," Rick said.

"For the fun of it," his one friend playfully added.

"For the babes; let's be honest, guys!" the third cop teased.

Nouri picked up her wine spritzer, laughing. "Yeah, that's what I thought," she said in playful response as her gaze fell on four people sitting at a table close by. The four people were staring at Nouri and whispering. She shifted uncomfortably in her seat again.

"Nouri, would you like to order now or would you rather have a few more drinks first?" young Hobner asked, and then he downed the remainder of his beer.

"I'm ready to eat if you guys are. Actually, I'm starving." She laughed.

"This restaurant seems to have that effect on me. How about you?"

"Same here. Let's order," Rick said, motioning for the waiter.

"How about I order for everyone? My treat, since you were kind enough to let me join you." Nouri said, glancing nervously over at the table of four again.

"Please order for us, Nouri. But no way are we letting you pick up the tab. We won't hear of it!" Rick returned adamantly.

Chapter 8

"Would you care for another bottle of wine, sir?" the waiter asked the four people sitting several tables away from the three Boston Police officers and Nouri Sommers.

"First, tell me something, waiter, if you can. Do you happen to know if the young woman sitting with the three young gentlemen at the table to our right is billionaire businessman Ethan Sommers' wife?" one of the gentlemen asked, nodding his head in the direction of the other table.

The waiter's gaze followed the direction of his customer's nod. A surprised expression of recognition crossed his face. "Oh, my! Now that you've mentioned it, sir, I believe it very well may be! Umm, yes, yes, it is! I remember she was in here once before about six weeks or so ago. She was with that handsome detective from Boston, the one who's engaged to the Baron's daughter; you know who I mean. What's her name? Oh, I know, it's Lisa Clayborne. I believe the detective's name is Gabe Baldwin. Yes, that's it. And I know for a fact the three gentlemen that are sitting with Mrs. Sommers are Boston Police officers, too. They come here quite often; and on occasion with Detective Baldwin. He has a cabin not too far from here, I recall hearing him mention one time."

"Thank you. You can bring that bottle of wine now, and is there a telephone I can use?"

"I'll bring a cell phone to the table for you if you like, or there's a payphone just down the hall next to the restrooms."

"The cell phone, please." The man smiled smugly at the three people he was with. After the waiter left, he turned his attention back to his newspaper reporter colleagues. "*Cha-Ching!* Get ready for a huge bonus. I can't fucking believe this!" the reporter for *The Boston Enquirer* chuckled softly.

"Gee, how are we going to sneak out to the van to get the camcorder?" the attractive, red-haired, blue-eyed reporter across from him asked, glancing at Nouri Sommers again.

"I'll do it. I'll excuse myself, pretend I am going to the restroom. Instead of going to the john, I'll run out to the van, grab the camcorder, a microphone, a camera, and a tape player. Simple, okay?" another reporter whispered in a low voice.

"What if she leaves before you get back, Ted?"

"I don't think she will. It doesn't look as though they've eaten yet. It won't take me long, Tina."

"Okay, Ted, you do that while I call Steve. Wonder if we still have time to stop the press. The billionaire's grieving widow is going to be our paper's front-page headline tomorrow morning!"

"Yes, but we'd better hurry. Do you think she might answer a few questions for us this time?"

"You mean for her adoring public, don't you, Tina?"

The female reporter rolled her eyes with irritation. "Whatever, Mick, geez!" she snapped.

A few moments later, one of the reporters stood to his feet, excused himself, and quietly snuck out to his van—while one of the other reporters called their boss at *The Boston Enquirer* to tell him to stop the press. And the attractive female reporter, with nothing better to do, fumbled inside her purse for her compact and tube of lipstick.

"How do I look?" she whispered to her colleague after powering her nose and blotting her freshly glossed lips.

"Fabulous," her co-worker mouthed in return as he continued to listen to his boss on the cell phone. A short time later, he handed the phone back to the waiter and thanked him for its use.

After the young police officer noticed Nouri Sommers uncomfortably squirming in her chair several times in a row, he turned to her and said, "Nouri."

"Hmm," she returned in a distracted tone.

"Is something wrong?"

She shrugged with uncertainty. "Rick, you see the people sitting at the table over there?" He nodded. She went on. "They keep staring at me and whispering. It's making me feel very uncomfortable. I think they might be reporters or something." She swallowed hard and picked up her wine spritzer as the reporter from *The Boston Enquirer* walked back toward his table with his video camera turned on and ready to shoot.

The young cop immediately noticed the reporter approaching in their direction from out of the corner of his eye. He instinctively glanced at the other three people. The guy with the camera had been sitting there with them earlier. "I think you might be right. Three of them are standing and making their way over here, and here comes one of them carrying a camcorder. Quick, Nouri, kiss me!" he said, pulling her into his muscular arms as he tried to shield her from the camera and the reporters.

Nouri obeyed without hesitation while the other two young cops jumped to their feet protectively.

The female reporter shouted questions aimed in Nouri's direction as one of her fellow reporters snapped photos of the kissing couple, the third reporter desperately trying to get it all on film.

"Is this the grieving widow's new love interest, Mrs. Sommers? We understand the three gentlemen you're with work for the Boston Police Department. Is this your newest trio of men?"

One of the young cops quickly jumped in. "You guys want to knock this shit off!" he barked heatedly.

"And you are?" The female reporter shoved the microphone into the cop's face. "Are you a police detective like—"

The young cop cut her off in mid-sentence again. "How about you guys just go on about your business!" His tone was sharp.

"Wow! This looks serious. The two lovebirds haven't stopped kissing since we walked over here. We understand, Mrs. Sommers, that your old flame, the handsome detective from Boston, is about to get married to the Baron's beautiful daughter. Do you have a comment you'd like to make about their upcoming—"

The young cop stopped the female reporter again. "Listen, miss, I've asked you for the last time to leave Mrs. Sommers the hell alone or—"

The reporter interrupted him, laughing with triumph. "Thank you, Officer! You just gave me what I needed. So this is indeed Mrs. Ethan Sommers—Boston's very own grieving young widow. Great! Come on, guys, it has been confirmed. We got what we needed, thanks to this cute cop." She and the other reporters made their way through the large crowd of people circling around Nouri's table.

Nouri removed herself from the young cop's tight embrace and warm sweet kisses. She swallowed nervously, reaching for her drink. "Oh God!" She sighed, shaking her head in stunned amazement.

"Are you okay?" Rick asked with concern.

Nouri finished downing her drink before responding. She nodded. "I think so. The damn media! Why can't they just leave people alone?"

The young cop leaned over and gently patted her across the shoulder. "I'm sorry," he said, shaking his head sympathetically.

"Oh, it's not your fault, Rick. It's just the damn press is driving me nuts lately! They stay camped out in front of the estate since my husband died. It's driving me crazy!" Nouri gave a heavy sigh. "Thanks, guys," she added smiling. "I appreciate you trying to protect me."

"Thank you, Mrs. Sommers," they returned in response.

"Oh, please call me Nouri."

"Okay, but only if you stop calling us officers," the young cop closest to her said. "My name is James, and the ugly one over there we call Jerry, among other things." He laughed.

Nouri chuckled. "Fine. Now that that's settled, I think I need a drink." She set her empty glass on the table.

"Waiter," James said, waving him over to the table. "Do you want another wine spritzer or would you prefer something else; maybe something a little stronger?"

Nouri swallowed nervously. "You're right. I think I'd like that martini, now."

Rick nodded. "We understand. After the ordeal you just went through, have as many as you like. I'll see to it that you get home safely tonight." He smiled. "Hey, what are friends for? Right, guys?" he added, reaching for his beer.

Nouri sighed, wishing the waiter would hurry back with her drink. "Thanks, guys. Maybe a good drunk is exactly what I need; especially after the past six weeks I've had."

Rick set his empty bottle down on the table and picked up his fresh one. "Hey, I have an idea, after dinner I know this great bar we can go to and get plastered. How's that sound, you all?"

"Sounds like a plan. I've been needing to let my hair down for a long time," Nouri returned, taking her drink from out of the waiter's hand before he had a chance to even set it down.

After dinner, Rick helped Nouri Sommers dodge the three reporters that were waiting to mob her outside. He quickly ushered her to his car while Jerry and James jumped into her canary-yellow Viper and swiftly pulled off before the reporters from *The Boston Enquirer* knew what had happened.

...Driving along in my automobile...My baby beside me at the wheel...

Young Boston Police officer Rick Hobner glanced at Nouri Sommers. "Great song! I love the oldies channel. Do you mind?" He smiled.

Nouri giggled. "Mind! Are you kidding? The oldies are one of my few true passions in life," she replied, in a playful manner.

Rick glanced at her again with his head bobbing in sync to the song that was being played on the car radio. "See, we do have something in common."

"Yeah, so it would seem." She smiled. "I thought I was the only one who loved that type of music these days. Even though it was popular long before I was born."

Rick shot her a playful wink. "Are you kidding? We're about the same age. I think. I'm twenty-six. How old are you?" he asked.

"Well..." She looked thoughtful for a moment and then teasingly giggled. "I was told a long time ago that there are three things in life a fella shouldn't ask a lady."

"Oh really?" Rick chuckled. "And what might those three things be?" he said, as he continued to tap his fingers on his steering wheel to the tune that was on his car radio.

Nouri giggled. "A woman's age, her weight, and the last deadly sin, or so I've been told...*Is that really yours?*" she mused.

"Okay, I get the age and the weight." He shook his head in playful dismay. "But I just don't get the last thing," he said with a shrug.

Nouri giggled at the expression plastered across her young friend's handsome face. "Oh honestly! You can't mean that, Rick. Haven't you ever hear of; wigs, false eyelashes, collagen-injected lips, breast enhancements, false fingernails? Shall I go on?"

Rick shook his head and smiled. "I get the picture. It's suddenly coming into focus loud and clear." He laughed. "Women!" he added, smiling.

Nouri teasingly leveled her hazel-colored gaze on the cute cop. "I have a newsflash for you, Officer Hobner, it isn't just a women thing, I'll have you know. How about toupees? Public officials, entertainers, and even news anchor men and women alike wear makeup, wigs, etc...in front of the camera." She paused briefly to catch her breath and then went on.

"I once met Engelbert Humperdink in person, and guess what? He had on more makeup than any woman I'd ever met! And while we're on the subject, I heard this guy...he was just a regular down-to-earth type guy...go on a national TV program, and guess what he did? He told the world...I think it was on the Geraldo Rivera show, anyway...this guy announced to the world that for the first time in his life, he felt like a real man. And you want to know why, Rick?" She giggled in spite of her effort not to.

"I'm almost afraid to ask!" he said, glancing in her direction.

Nouri struggled to stop laughing. "Can you imagine how much nerve it must have taken for this poor guy to get in front of a live TV camera and confess to the world that thanks to a new medical miracle, doctors can now take the fat from a person's body—anywhere on this person's body, and inject it into a different part of this person's body." She laughed as she envisioned the TV program she had watched on that day.

Rick shook his head in disbelief. “You don’t mean this guy—”

Nouri cut in. “Exactly! A doctor took the fat out of one part of this guy’s body and injected it into his penis! I swear.” She laughed. “This poor guy said that for the first time in his life he was finally able to urinate in public with the big boys! Can you imagine?” Nouri shook her head in amazement.

Rick chuckled. “So, what line of work was this guy in? A stripper? A gigolo? What?” he asked.

Nouri grinned. “With his newfound inch or two, I seriously doubt it! As I recall, the poor guy went from a pathetic three inches to a manly five!” She laughed.

Rick’s mouth flew open, but he just as quickly closed it. “Oh my God! He actually admitted that on national television?”

“Worse! In front of Geraldo Rivera!” Nouri chuckled.

“Sounds like the poor bastard was almost born a girl!”

“Well, he’s happy, now. That’s all that matters, I guess,” she said.

“Wow! Remind me never to ask another female her age again!” he said, shaking his head. “Maybe we’re better off just singing along to the music being played on the radio for a while. I don’t think I can handle any more of your little anecdotes for a while.”

Nouri giggled. “Just don’t forget you’re the one who started that conversation, Officer Hobner.”

“I what!” Rick returned, not seeing the logic.

“Well, you did!” she said with a smile.

He laughed and shook his head. “And to think I thought that I had just asked you a simple question like how old you were.”

“So, you learned your lesson, huh?” She smiled.

He nodded. “You’d better believe it, ma’am. Next time I get the urge to ask some beautiful lady her age, I’ll do it the easy way,” he said playfully.

“The easy way?”

He laughed, shaking his head. “Yeah, I’ll take their fingerprints and run a make on them down at the station!”

“Very funny!” Nouri said, glancing at the handsome young cop and leaning over to turn the volume on the radio up.

...My boyfriend’s back and you’re gonna be in trouble. Hey nah, hey nah, my boyfriend’s back...

Chapter 9

"Extra! Extra! Read all about it! 'The Grieving Widow' removes black veil after only six weeks of mourning husband's death! Friend or beau? Billionaire businessman Ethan Sommers' beautiful, young widow exchanges public displays of tears for public displays of affection!" a newspaper vendor called across the street from Boston P.I. Charles Mason's office.

"Over here, please! I'll take ten copies," the famous P.I.'s private secretary shouted, running to the stand, waving a five-dollar bill in her hand.

"Extra! Extra! Read all about it! Wealthiest widow in the world takes off her black veil for one of Boston's very own boys in blue! Could it be she has plans to replace the black veil for a white one? You be the judge!" the newspaper hustler shouted near the Boston Police Department.

Boston Police captain Mark Lane stopped in his tracks and paused at the newsstand, not believing his ears. "Oh shit!" he mumbled under his breath, holding his head tightly, as though it was about to explode in his hands. He turned to face the news vendor giving him a wide-eyed stare. "What the hell did you just say?" he snapped.

The excited paper hustler offered the police captain a copy of the newspaper. "Billionaire tycoon Ethan Sommers' beautiful, young widow was spotted inside a seafood restaurant last night sucking some young cop's brains out! The lucky bastard! Best goddamn story we've had all year! I'm selling newspapers faster than the company I work for can drop 'em off to me!" He grinned and chuckled.

"Here, let me see one of those goddamn things!" the captain said, snatching the newspaper from the hustler's hand. In a hangover funk, he tried to focus his bloodshot eyes on the article directly under the photograph showing Nouri Sommers passionately kissing one of Boston's finest. The photo had been dubbed, "The Grieving Widow."

"Hobner, you poor son-of-a-bitch! Wait until Baldwin gets a look at this shit!" he mumbled, shaking his pounding head in total disbelief. "What the hell were you thinking?" he growled, reaching into his trouser pocket for some change to pay the paper hustler.

He turned and rapidly stormed across the street, heading for the police station. With dread in his thoughts, he climbed the cement steps leading to the front entrance of the building, taking them two at a time. He pulled the door open with a powerful jerk. Everyone stared as he entered the room, shouting like a madman, and angrily waving the newspaper high above his head. "I don't want to hear one goddamn word about last night or this morning's newspaper!"

He lowered his arm and strode into his office, then turned to face the police officers. "One more thing, one of you send Hobner to my goddamn office the moment he steps his sorry ass in the front door!" Captain Mark Lane turned and entered his office. Everyone cringed when the captain loudly slammed his office door.

"Goddamn you and your Greek white lightning, Gabe!" Captain Lane complained, trying very hard not to move his head any more than he had to. "This is going to be one hell of a day!" he groaned, opening the top drawer to his desk and fumbling around inside for a bottle of aspirin. The telephone rang, catching him off guard and giving him a surprised start. "Shit!" he spat, closing the desk drawer and reaching for the telephone.

In little more than a whisper, he forced a painstaking greeting. "Yeah, this is Captain Mark Lane."

"It's alive!" the female district attorney said. "Well, Captain?" she added, hiding her laughter.

"I'd hardly call the way I feel this morning *alive*!" He frowned.

She giggled. "I'm surprised you even made it in this morning, Captain."

"That makes two of us, Daughtery. What's up?"

"Would you mind telling me what the hell was going on yesterday, Mark?" she asked sternly.

"What do you mean, Daughtery?" he asked, unaware of her knowledge of yesterday's activities.

"Oh please, Captain! You're just lucky it was me that—"

Mark stopped her in mid-sentence. "All right! So you do know. I don't know how you found out, but you apparently did. So what do you want, a brownie button or something!"

"Don't use that tone with me! A simple thank-you would be nice. Don't you think?" She sighed.

"All right, Tonya. I suppose I owe you that much. So here goes, thank you. Feel better now?" He shook his head and cringed, reminded of his pain from drinking too much Greek liquor the night before.

Understanding what a bear the police captain could be on the outside, she smiled, shaking her head. "Now that wasn't so difficult, was it?" she said. "What's going on? Gabe?"

"If you must know, Daughtery, apparently, Gabe still has it bad for the Sommers broad." He sighed.

"You mean Sommers woman," Tonya corrected lightly.

"Well, pardon me all to hell and back!"

"Mark, honestly! Just because you're hung-over doesn't mean you have to be such an ass! Stop taking it out on me, okay?" she said, reaching for the Styrofoam cup of hot tea.

Mark sighed and settled back in his seat. "You're right, sorry. Have you ever had a hangover from drinking a liquor called ouzo?"

"From drinking what?" she chuckled.

"Ouzo. It's a Greek liquor. Tastes like licorice. Whew! Packs a mighty wallop! Knocked me on my ass, literally! Do yourself a favor and run as fast as your legs will carry you if anyone ever offers you a shot or two of the stuff! The Greeks should have named the stuff white lightning!" He cringed at the thought.

She chuckled. "That bad, huh? I thought Cuervo was. I drank so much of that stuff when Charles and I first split up that I couldn't stand to even look at a bottle of tequila for a long time after that." She shook her head after briefly recalling that fading moment in time.

"Getting that drunk, did it help?" he asked.

"Hardly! If anything, it only made matters worse for me. It prolonged the inevitable." She sighed, remembering.

"That's what's going on with Gabe, now. He wants to punish himself. I think he somehow blames himself for the death of Nouri Sommers' former lover Clint Chamberlain," Mark said.

"That's ridiculous! Why on earth would he think that? The man drove his damn car off a bridge. It had nothing to do with Gabe!"

"I don't think Gabe is even aware that he's blaming himself. It's a long story, Tonya. Do you really want to hear it?" he asked, propping his legs up on top of his desk and laying his head against his chair's padded headrest.

"Yes, Mark. Please," Tonya said, reaching for her cup of tea.

"Gabe was jealous of the man. Plain and simple. Chamberlain was his biggest worry when it came to Nouri Sommers. He was the man who would always hold a piece of her heart, and that scared him. So, when he caught her sneaking out of the man's hotel suite in France, he went ballistic; wouldn't even let her explain what she had been doing there. Gabe clammed up, didn't speak to her for a few days. And so, when her former lover's car went off the bridge and she needed him the most, Gabe wasn't there. He had gone off someplace to cool off and pout for a few days. Nouri had no idea where Gabe had gone, so she had to phone Mason to track him down.

"Charles finally found Gabe in another hotel, getting plastered with some French babe by the name of Veronica. After Mason told Gabe what had happened to Chamberlain, he went rushing to Nouri Sommers' side, but apparently she was both devastated over the high-powered attorney and still pissed off at Gabe for the way he had treated her a few days earlier, so she shoved him away. Told him to get out. Not knowing what to do or how to make things right between them again, Gabe hightailed his stubborn Greek ass back to Boston and back into the waiting arms of his ex-fiancée."

"Wow, that's some story! Has Gabe tried to get in touch with Nouri Sommers since her return to Boston?"

"I don't think so." He sighed, reaching for a cigarette.

"You make it sound like you think it might be a mistake if Gabe goes through with his plans to marry Ms. Clayborne."

"I do, indeed! That would be a huge mistake on the detective's part. He's not in love with the woman. He's in a self-destructive mode right now. Of course, he doesn't see himself that way. His family planned the wedding with the Baron's daughter, and he thinks he's doing what's right now. His mother is dying to be a grandmother. Gabe wants to make his mother happy. And with Lisa, well, I think he feels he would still be in control of what little bit of his heart he has left."

"Oh, that's so sad! I can't believe as handsome as Gabe is, and as wealthy as he is, that he would just settle like that."

"I guess he just doesn't give a shit right now."

"Your choice of words, Mark, honestly!" She smiled, setting her cup down.

"Sorry." He shook his pounding head and frowned.

"Mark, you're his friend; can't you talk him out of rushing into this marriage? Or at the very least can't you try to get him to postpone it?"

"I gave it my best shot yesterday. That's why I got drunk with him. You know, a guy thing."

"And Charles?"

"Mason and Gabe were supposed to have lunch yesterday. Gabe must've forgotten about it. When he was a no-show, Mason came looking for him. After seeing the sorry state the detective and I were in, well, like I said before, it was a guy thing. We spent most of the night at Mason's house doing some serious damage to a case of the shit Gabe seems to love so much. Anyway, when I crawled out of bed this morning, they were still asleep. Hopefully Mason will talk some sense into him."

He sighed and then went on. "I'm hoping Gabe stays away from the station today." Mark paused for the much needed cup of hot black coffee that a file clerk, with an understanding smile, had just brought in for him. He nodded his appreciation.

"Why, for goodness sakes?" Tonya asked. "Working right now might be good for Gabe. It was for me after the Charles thing."

Remembering the headlines splashed across the front pages of *The Boston Enquirer*, he shook his pounding head. "You apparently haven't seen the goddamn headlines in this morning's newspaper yet, have you?" He cringed at the thought of the anger the police detective was going to feel when he saw the morning paper.

Tonya shrugged. "No, I haven't seen the paper, Mark. I haven't had time yet. What's it say?"

"It isn't good. Gabe will go ballistic I'm afraid! Have you ever seen that man angry?" He shook his head at the dreaded thought.

"No. Not real angry, why?"

"Greeks and their tempers! Not a pretty sight. It's a very scary thing to witness. Let's just say I'd hate to be on the receiving end of one of the detective's outbursts!" Mark took a big swallow of his coffee.

"So, what's in the paper this morning that is going to upset him so terribly?"

"It's a front-page doozy! A photograph of Nouri Sommers dubbed 'The Grieving Widow.'"

"Yeah, so? It's not as if it would be the first time anyone has seen an article on her like that since he husband died," she said.

"This one's different, Tonya. It's a photograph of her with one of our boys in blue."

"Like I said, Mark, so?" She shrugged, not seeing the point.

"So," he sighed, "it's a goddamn picture of Officer Rick Hobner sucking her brains out inside some goddamn seafood restaurant last night!" he snapped.

"Oh my lord!" she exclaimed.

"Now, do you see why I said I hope he decides to stay the hell home today?"

"I should say so! Oh my lord! Maybe you should phone Charles and warn him, Mark?"

The captain released a sigh of dread. "Maybe you're right. That is unless you'd like to make the call for me?" he teased.

She chuckled. "Yeah, right. Like that is going to happen, Captain. I'll see you later on this afternoon," she said, shaking her head.

"This afternoon? What's up?"

"I have a few things I need to clear up pertaining to the Genna Matthews and Steven Li cases."

"Oh shit! That reminds me, we need to go over a few things about the Lambert murders, too."

"Like what?"

"We finally got the other kid to confess."

"Thomas?"

"Yeah." The captain nodded. "Poor kid. The product of his environment. A real sick kid," he said, reaching for another cigarette.

"What about the other guy?"

"Kirt Jarret. He's all fucked up, too. You know, in a way I sort of feel sorry for the two poor sons-of-bitches."

"Hmm, well, you can tell me all about it later on this afternoon. I have to go."

"Okay, Tonya. I'll see you later. Bye." Mark hung up the phone, opened his desk drawer, and searched for his bottle of aspirin again.

Chapter 10

Young police officer Rick Hobner watched a sleeping Nouri Sommers, from a safe distance in her bedroom, feeling guilty that he was even staring at her at all.

"God, she's beautiful," he whispered softly, dreading the thought of having to wake her. He couldn't seem to take his eyes off her. His captivated gaze traveled the length of her body, as he enjoyed every sexy curve of her unbelievable beauty.

He tiptoed across the floor to the bed and pulled the sheet up to Nouri's shoulders to cover her semi-nude body, not wanting to risk the embarrassment he knew she would feel if she were not covered when he awakened her.

He reluctantly glanced at the clock sitting on the nightstand, knowing he had to awaken Nouri and take her out of his apartment within the next thirty minutes or he would be late for work.

"Nouri," he spoke her name softly, leaning down from where he was standing, gently tapping her on the shoulder.

She stirred and stretched. And then snuggled back up to the pillow again. He swallowed hard when the sheet slid down once again, exposing the sexy pink-colored nipples of her breast for him to see. He cursed himself for becoming excited and quickly turned to leave.

The wooden floorboard squeaked as he stepped down on one of the loosened boards. The noise made her squirm uncomfortably in bed. She stirred and squinted one bloodshot eye half open. Her focus was too much of a blur to see well. "Gabe, darling, come back to bed. I need you," she whispered hoarsely, gently patting the spot on the bed beside herself.

Rick swallowed hard, cursing under his breath. "She's still in love with the detective; I knew it!" Disappointed, he turned to face her. "Ah no, Nouri. It's not Detective Baldwin. It's me, Rick. Officer Rick Hobner. You spent the night at my apartment, remember?" he said, drawing closer.

Her eyes snapped open. She quickly reached for the sheet and pulled it up to her neck as she forced her body to a sitting position. "Rick!" There was panic in her tone.

He smiled. "Good morning. How are you feeling today?" he asked softly.

She glanced around her unfamiliar surroundings and then cleared her throat. “Ah…ah…Where am I again?”

Rick smiled. “Still in the city. You spent the night here. This is my place.”

“Oh my God!” she exclaimed, assuming the worst.

He chuckled and blushed at the same time. “Wait a minute. Calm down! It’s not what you think. I slept on the couch,” he said with a reassuring smile.

“Whew!” Nouri sighed. “I must have had some night, huh?” She tried to remember something. Anything! She felt her pulse slowly returning to normal.

“I think we all did,” the young cop said.

“I hope I didn’t embarrass myself too badly,” she said, massaging her throbbing temples He smiled. “No, not at all. Would you like a couple of aspirin and some juice? I’m sorry, I don’t have any coffee. I don’t drink the nasty stuff,” he added with a playful cringe.

“Yes, please. Thanks,” she said.

“I’ll be right back. You might want to get out of bed while I’m gone and get dressed. I have to be at work in twenty minutes or so. I’m sorry to have to rush you like this.”

“Oh God, I’m sorry! I’ll be ready in just a minute. Where’s my car?” Nouri asked, jumping out of bed and wrapping the sheet snugly around her body.

Rick grinned at her apparent shyness. “It’s parked outside. I had one of my friends from the club drive it here for you last night. I hope that was okay.” He smiled.

Nouri nodded nervously, hoping Rick would leave the room so she could get dressed. “Oh yeah! Thanks a lot.”

Rick turned to leave after noticing her uneasiness. “I’ll just wait for you in the kitchen,” he said, crossing the room and closing the door after himself.

“Thank God!” Nouri mumbled. She spotted her mini-skirt on the floor beside the large bed, bent down and picked it up, and quickly shimmied into it. “What the hell is wrong with you?” she scolded herself, reaching for her bra and blouse. “What for chrissakes were you thinking, Nouri Sommers?” She fastened her bra and pulled her blouse on over her head. “Oh shit!” she groaned, suddenly remembering the young cop kissing her inside the seafood restaurant the night before in front of the newspaper reporters. She knew the picture would be plastered on every morning newspaper in Boston as well as, in all probability, across the globe. She left the bedroom shaking her throbbing head.

She found the young police officer in the kitchen closing the refrigerator door with his free hand. The other held a glass of juice. He turned to her. "Well, here's your orange juice. I laid the aspirins down on top of the breakfast bar," he said.

Nouri took the juice and eagerly picked up the two aspirins. "Thanks, Rick," she said, swallowing the pills.

He looked at her with concern. "Are you all right?" He checked the time on the wall clock.

She nodded. "I'm fine, thanks. You'll have to tell me what happened last night after we got to your friend's club. Tell me sometime when you aren't in such a rush. I'm afraid most of the evening is a complete blank to me now."

"Not much to tell. We had fun. That's all." His voice was somber. "The four of us."

"What's the matter? Something's wrong; I can tell by the tone of your voice."

Rick flushed, wanting to ask her on a date, but hesitating, since he had earlier discovered she apparently still harbored feelings for Detective Gabe Baldwin. Wondering whether he should risk asking her, he swallowed hard before answering. "I…I was just trying to get the nerve to ask you if ah…ah, you would maybe like to have dinner tonight," he finally managed.

Nouri blushed, realizing the cute young cop had developed a slight crush on her. "A date!" she said, nervously picturing the veteran detective Gabe and his handsome face. It was the face of the man she had allowed herself to fall in love with.

"Yeah, a date! Why not? After all, Detective Baldwin is…" He stopped talking wondering how he must sound. "I'm sorry. If you would rather not, I understand," he said, shrugging his shoulders.

Thinking what harm could it do and deciding she at least owed the young cop a dinner date for looking after her so well the evening before, Nouri said, "Dinner would be nice. Where shall I meet you, and oh yeah, what time?"

Rick gave her a happy smile. "Great! Do you like Greek food? A friend of mine just opened a place a few weeks ago. The Trojan Horse. It's down on Eighth Street. Would that be all right, around seven?"

"The Trojan Horse on Eighth Street at seven it is," she said, reaching for her purse sitting on the breakfast bar beside her key ring.

"Great! I'll see you later, but for now, I have to run. I'm a little late as it is." He smiled, gesturing toward the door.

"I'm ready," she said, walking toward the door. Outside, she turned and watched him lock up. "Rick," she said his name softly.

He turned to face her. "Yeah," he said, only inches away from her inviting full lips. He licked his lips instinctively, remembering how delicious Nouri had tasted the night before when he had kissed her at the seafood restaurant. His gaze dropped to her mouth.

"Thank you for looking after me last night," she said, gently pressing her lips to his briefly.

"My pleasure," he returned, smiling ear-to-ear, grateful for the gesture from the beautiful woman that had just made his day. "There's your car. Think you can manage on your own? I have to split. I'm late as it is," he said, pointing to where her car was parked.

"No, you go right ahead. I understand. I'll be fine," she said.

Rick ran down the short flight of stairs and quickly jumped onto his motorcycle. Nouri waved to him, smiling, as he zoomed out of the driveway. She slowly started to her car, then stopped. Three reporters from the night before were sitting inside a beige-colored minivan. She supposed they were recording her every move on tape. She opened her purse, pulling out a pair of sunglasses and putting them on, swiftly walking to her car while ignoring the questions being whirled at her by the same attractive female reporter from last night, named Tina.

Famous P.I. Charles Mason shook his head in dismay as he continued to take in every word police captain Mark Lane was saying. "Okay, thanks, Mark. I'll take care of it. I'll break it to him gently after he gets out of bed. Thanks for warning me. I'll talk to you later. Bye," he said, glancing at the clock mounted on the wall of his elaborately decorated living room. "Swell!" he groaned, still in his bathrobe, as he walked to the front door and stepped outside to look for the morning newspaper to read the article the police captain had mentioned.

Charles picked up the paper and removed the rubber band around it. "Son-of-a-bitch!" he shouted, storming back in the house with his fury feline Tallulah not far behind. "This is going to be another wonderful day!" He gave a disgusted sigh and shook his head as he put on a pot of coffee in the kitchen.

Charles finished his second cup of strong black coffee, dreading what he must to do next. It wasn't going to be pleasant.

A few moments later, the P.I. entered the spare bedroom where he had carried his former partner in fighting crime, the night before, after he had passed out on the sofa from drinking too much Greek white lightning.

"Good morning, Gabe. Rise and shine," he bellowed in a louder voice than he had intended as he entered, carrying his friend a fresh cup of coffee.

The police detective turned over and groaned in a dry, hoarse voice. “Ugh! You mean I’m still among the living?”

The famous P.I. chuckled “Here. Drink this coffee. It might help.”

Sliding his body up to a sitting position, Gabe gratefully accepted the much needed beverage. “Thanks,” he managed.

Charles shook his head, amused by his friend’s hangover. “You look like shit, Gabe!” he said.

“Not half as bad as I feel, I’m sure, Charles!”

“We going to go at it again, today?” Charles asked.

“What? You mean get plastered again, today?”

Charles nodded understandingly. “Yeah. I’m here for you, my friend. If that’s what you need to do again, well, then I’m…”

“You mean you think I need a babysitter?” Gabe countered, sipping his coffee.

“I was thinking more like you might be needing a friend,” Charles said, flopping down in a chair.

Gabe shook his pounding head. “Sorry. I guess I’m just a little mad at the world lately. I didn’t mean to take it out on you, Charles.”

“No problem. So what’s on your agenda today, Detective?”

“I’m supposed to go to work today,” Gabe said, taking another drink of his coffee.

“Oh, that reminds me, Mark left a message for you. He said to tell you to take a few days off. He suggested you might consider going to that hideaway cabin in the woods of yours. He also said you might want to take this opportunity to start a new romance with that new sexy detective from France they have on the force in Connecticut. He said that you would know the one he was referring to.” He chuckled.

“Oh, I do indeed! Isabella Bedaux. Now that’s not a half bad idea on Mark’s part!” He smiled, picturing the sexy female detective’s beautiful face. “She’s something all right.”

“So I’ve heard.” Charles smiled.

Gabe looked at him curiously. “So you’ve heard of her?”

“I sure have.”

“From who?”

“The district attorney of Connecticut. Chet Hatfield. I was working on a case a short time back that forced me to touch base with him.”

“What did he have to say about her?”

"Said she was amazing in the bedroom and not half bad on top of his desk either!" He chuckled. "Seems he was smitten with Ms. Bedaux for a few weeks."

"A few weeks. That's all? Did he say why he stopped seeing her?" Gabe asked with interest.

Charles laughed, shaking his head. "Seems Hatfield got caught with *the little general* in Ms. Bedaux's beautiful mouth while on the taxpayers' time one afternoon."

"Oh shit! So what happened after that?"

"He was forced to resign."

"No shit!"

Charles nodded. "No shit. It cost him his marriage, too."

"What about Isabella? What happened to her?"

"Last I heard she's got those tight lips of hers snugly wrapped around some guy from Internal Affairs now," he answered, shaking his head in amazement.

"Women!" Gabe muttered sarcastically. "And to think I was under the impression Ms. Bedaux was going to save her sexy self for me!" He laughed taking a drink of his coffee. "What the hell! There's always my sexy neighbor Celina Sawyer. Whew! Talk about sexy!" he added.

"Well, there you go. So does that mean you're going to take a few days off and go to the cabin for a little down time?"

Gabe shook his head and sat the coffee cup down on the nightstand. "I don't think so. I have too much to do."

"What about Lisa?"

Gabe shrugged. "What about her?"

"Duh!" Charles teased.

Gabe smiled. "Oh that! The wedding, huh?"

"Exactly," Charles returned.

Gabe sighed. "I don't know. I'm beginning to have doubts. I wouldn't have money very long married to a woman like Lisa. Hell, she's already spent a quarter of a million of my hard-earned dollars on some of the dumbest shit you can imagine! And now she wants me to look at some mansion this goddamn week that she said used to belong to Cher or somebody like that." He picked up his coffee again and continued, "Oh, it gets better, Charles. She, of course, will have to hire someone to completely renovate it to her liking and—"

"You poor bastard," Charles cut in, shaking his with sympathy. "Gabe, did your bride-to-be ever share the details of her first two marriages with you?"

An expression of shock quickly crossed Gabe's face. "What!" he asked in amazement.

"I take it that you didn't know your beautiful fiancée has been married twice before."

Gabe swallowed hard and shifted his position. "Apparently not! Who was she married to? I mean, do you know their names?"

Charles nodded. "Oh sure. Both times the marriages made the papers, of course. Her first marriage was to a gay gigolo by the name of Conrad Hilton. That marriage only lasted one day as I recall. Lisa apparently caught her new hubby in a compromising position with his very own best man a day after they had exchanged wedding vows." He chuckled, shaking his head at the remembered thought.

"Wonderful!" Gabe said, shaking his head. "I'm half-afraid to ask, but who was the other guy?"

"His name was Holland Madison. A poor little rich boy whose family went belly-up in the stock market. That caused Lisa's marriage to go south."

"Wonderful!"

"So, does knowing any of this help?"

Gabe nodded thoughtfully. "Yes, it does. Thanks, Charles. You are a true friend." He smiled. "I don't care what most people say about you!" he added teasingly.

Charles chuckled. "Does that mean you are going to call your wedding to Lisa off?"

Gabe laughed, shaking his head. "What? And piss off my mother? You know how she can't wait to be a grandmother." He ran a finger around his coffee cup.

"Well?"

"All teasing aside, I don't think I have a choice, now," Gabe said seriously.

"Then it's settled. You'll call off the wedding and go see Nouri, right?"

Gabe shrugged, throwing the sheet off and lowering his feet to the floor. "I'll think about it," he said, after a few moments.

"What's to think, Gabe? You're still in love with her. I can see it in your eyes."

"What the hell are you talking about? She told me to get the hell out, remember? It's over between us. Plain and simple!"

"Forget it, damn it! Just take that goddamn stubborn Greek pride of yours and—"

"What the hell is wrong with you all of a sudden?" Gabe asked.

"You and that stubborn streak of yours!" Charles returned heatedly.

"Listen, Charles, I've already told you. Nouri told me to get the hell out right after Chamberlain drove his goddamn car off that damn bridge. I gave her what she wanted. I can't compete with a dead man!" he said, standing to his feet.

"All right. What about a live one then?" Charles countered.

Gabe shot his friend a confused glance. "A live one? What the hell are you talking about?"

Charles picked up the newspaper he had laid down on the floor and tossed it to the police detective. "Take a look and see for yourself. It seems the beautiful young widow in black has been caught smooching with one of Boston's very own boys in blue at some seafood restaurant last night," Charles said, hoping the news would make Gabe try to contact Nouri again.

Gabe read the article and angrily flung the paper on the floor. "I'm going to choke that slippery little bastard with both of my goddamn bare hands," he promised.

"Calm down, Gabe! I know this looks bad. But I know Nouri. She isn't one for public displays of anything, much less public displays of affection."

"Yeah right! So tell me then just what the hell she's doing sucking Hobner's goddamn brains out in public…"

Charles cut in. "Gabe, you know how the press can be. Look how certain photos in the press made you and me look in the past before. Sometimes things just aren't what they appear to be. Calm down until—"

Gabe interrupted. "I'm not going to calm down until I beat the hell out of that little shit for hitting on my woman!" he shouted.

"Your woman? I thought you said it was over between the two of you?" Charles baited.

"To think she would humiliate me in public like this with a cop! I have half a mind to storm over to her estate and turn her over my goddamn knee and…Who the hell does she think she is!"

Charles smiled, shaking his head. "You mean besides the wealthiest woman in the world?"

Gabe shot his friend a questionable glance. "Wealth! Who gives a shit about money?"

"You mean who besides Lisa Clayborne?" the P.I. inserted. "Gabe, go and take a shower. There are some spare toothbrushes in the guest bathroom and whatever else you might need. Just help yourself. You can also help yourself to some clothes. I'm going downstairs to make a fresh pot of coffee," he said, walking toward the door. He glanced over his shoulder at the detective. "Shall I phone the station and have Mark warn that young cop?"

Gabe shook his head. "Fuck you, Mason, and Pretty Boy Floyd that was kissing Nouri!"

Charles laughed loudly as he made his way down the long spiral staircase.

After putting on a fresh pot of coffee, he made a few telephone calls while he waited for his friend to come downstairs. One call was to Nouri Sommers.

Mai Li quickly told the P.I. that her mistress had informed her the day before that she would be spending a few days away from the estate. She needed a little time to herself. Assuming the worst after talking to Mai Li, Charles phoned police captain Mark Lane to warn him to keep young Hobner away from the station just in case Gabe had decided to go to work that morning.

Charles then telephoned his office, and after talking to his private secretary Tess, he soon learned from her that the mid-morning newspaper had hit the racks earlier than usual. Another feature headline starring none other than the beautiful grieving widow read, "*Grieving Young Widow Trading In Her Black Veil For A Definite Blue One!*"

Nouri Sommers had been photographed leaving her new boyfriend's downtown apartment earlier that morning after apparently spending the entire night with him. The front page also showed another photo of the happy couple sharing another smooch before she waved good-bye to her new love interest young police officer Rick Hobner of the Boston Police Department.

"I don't fucking believe it!" Charles mumbled under his breath as Gabe entered the kitchen.

"What don't you fucking believe?" the police detective asked, reaching across the breakfast bar for the pot of coffee.

Charles shook his head in amazement. "The mid-morning paper is apparently out earlier than usual." He sighed.

"Let me guess. More smooching from The Grieving Widow and Pretty Boy Floyd?"

"Something like that, I'm afraid," Charles returned.

"Wonderful." Gabe shook his head with disgust again. "Do you think she honestly has feelings for that slimy little shit?" he asked jealously.

"Why, hell no! I'm telling you there's something wrong here! There just has to be more to this than meets the eye!"

"Yeah, like what?"

"How the hell would I know? You're just going to have to go talk to her and—"

"Hold on there, back up, Charles! I may be willing to have a few choice words with Hobner—in fact I intend to—but me talk to her—"

"All right. Have it your way, Gabe!" Charles stopped him in mid-sentence. "But if I were you, I wouldn't wait too long to go and talk to her. She's vulnerable right now. The last time she got that way, she rushed into marriage with Ethan Sommers after knowing him for only two short weeks, if you get my drift!"

"And reminding me of this is supposed to do what exactly? Make me feel better?" Gabe shook his head.

"I'm just reminding you that Nouri is the kind of woman who needs to be held at night. Every night! She's been alone for almost six weeks now, and—"

Gabe sat his coffee cup down hard on top of the breakfast bar, stopping Charles from finishing his sentence. "You're sure you are trying to make me feel better right?"

"Of course! What are friends for? I just don't want—"

Gabe cut in. "If you don't mind me saying so, Charles, you need a little work on that bedside manner of yours!"

"Hey, if you don't get that size-eleven foot of yours out of your ass, all joking aside, she just might decide to let someone else comfort her at night. Who knows, maybe even that young, silly-looking cop!"

Gabe picked up his coffee cup, glancing heatedly at his friend. "If it is all the same with you, partner, I'd really rather not hear any more about this right now. I can't deal with it. I already want to go down to the station and literally wring that slimy little shit's neck!"

"So, what are you going to do first?"

Gabe swallowed the remainder of his coffee before responding. "I'm going to go down to the goddamn station and wring that slimy little shit's neck!" he snapped, glancing at his watch, wondering what time the young cop was supposed to be working that day.

"Behave yourself, Gabe! Just go down and talk to the kid. Ask him what happened last night, and—"

"And what, Charles?" Gabe asked curiously.

"And then wring the slimy little shit's neck!" he said with a grin.

Gabe shook his head. "Can I borrow one of your cars?"

Charles nodded. "Sure, if you like. You've borrowed everything else of mine today." He tossed the set of his Mercedes keys to the detective.

Chapter 11

Upon arriving at her downtown condo, Nouri Sommers was immediately swarmed by a massive mob of reporters, from the press as well as television networks from all over the globe. "Fabulous," she complained under her breath as she attempted to exit her canary-yellow Viper.

Without warning, one of the reporters jerked her car door open and leaned inside the car. Practically on top of her, he shoved a microphone into her face covered by her sunglasses.

"Do you mind?" she snapped, shoving the mike back out of her face, and she quickly slid out of the car. She took a deep breath, shaking her head, as she attempted to make her way through the massive mob of reporters, trying to ignore the questions being whirled at her.

Struggling with every step, she was finally forced to stop after a short distance. She swallowed hard, glancing around at all the reporters now encircling her. Gratefully, she finally recognized one of the smiling faces among the group of people staring at her. As their gaze met, she mouthed the word "Help!"

The famous P.I. chuckled and immediately came to her rescue. He began shoving the reporters to the side, swiftly making his way to her.

"Thank you, Charles," she said as he grabbed her arm and led her in the direction of the condo.

"What would you do without me?" he asked, glancing at her frightened pale face.

"Oh God, this is a nightmare!" Nouri cried, jerking free from one of the reporters' tight grips of her upper arm. Charles Mason noticed and was not amused.

"The next son-of-a-bitch who puts their hands on this woman had better have a goddamn good hospital plan!" he shouted heatedly into the massive group of people. "Now, get the hell out of our way!" he added in a threatening tone. Instantly, a path cleared their way.

"You're amazing, big guy!" Nouri whispered in admiration.

"I've been trying to convince you of that for years, sugar!" he returned teasingly.

In a moment, Nouri Sommers and the famous P.I. were inside the building elevator on their way up to her penthouse condo.

Nouri released a deep sigh and glanced at her famous friend. "Oh God! Thank you so much, Charles. I don't know what I would have done without you this morning." She shook her head.

Charles smiled. "Glad I could be of service." His tone took on an edge.

"Service?" she questioned.

"Well, what the hell would you call it?" he returned in a hurt tone.

"Ah, I see. You're still mad at me, huh?" she said, assuming her friend had been referring to her not returning his phone messages after she returned from France.

He leveled his gaze to her. "Hurt would be more like it," he said.

"I'm sorry, Charles. Will you forgive me for not returning your telephone calls? I—"

"It's more than just the telephone calls, Nouri. You not only pushed Gabe away from you in France, but you—"

"I said I was sorry, Charles. Will you forgive me?"

He shook his head. "Well, I'm here, aren't I?" She nodded. He went on. "Nouri, what on earth were you thinking going out by yourself last night? Don't you realize how dangerous that—"

"Please, Charles. I have a hangover this morning and don't feel like being scolded. Do you mind? I just needed to be alone for a while. You understand that, don't you?"

He shook his head. "No, I'm afraid I don't."

A surprised expression covered her face. "No? How can you say that to me after all I've gone through these past few months!"

Charles placed his hand on her arm when the elevator door slid open. "We have a lot of things to talk about this morning, sugar. I haven't eaten yet, and from the look of it, a little food wouldn't hurt you, either." His gaze quickly traveled the length of her body as she stepped out of the elevator.

"And just what the hell is that remark supposed to mean?"

He chuckled. "You've lost too much weight, sugar. You look pale and—"

She stopped him from speaking. "There you go trying to sub for my father yet again!" She giggled.

"Speaking of fathers, have you telephoned yours yet?"

"No," she answered, shaking her head with dread. "No, I haven't. To tell you the truth, Charles, I haven't really felt much like—" She stopped when her maid Heidi jerked the front door to the condo open and looked at them with a worried expression.

"Oh thank goodness, Mrs. Sommers! Are you all right?" she asked.

Nouri smiled. "I'm fine, Heidi. Thanks for asking. Where's James?"

"I'm sorry, ma'am, but he had a few errands to run this morning. You usually telephone if—"

Nouri entered the hallway. "It's okay. I hadn't originally planned on stopping by here today," she said, noticing her maid checking out the famous P.I. She smiled in spite of her mood. "Heidi, this is Charles Mason," she said with a wave of her hand.

Heidi beamed from ear to ear, throwing her hand up and fidgeting with her hair. "Oh, yes. I know who Mr. Mason is. He's...he's very famous." She smiled.

Nouri nodded. "Yes, he is, Heidi. Mr. Mason is an old friend who came to my rescue this morning," she said, smiling at the P.I. "Mr. Mason is going to join me for breakfast; so if you would be kind enough to—"

Heidi excitedly cut in. "Oh, my pleasure, Mrs. Sommers. I'll get right to it!"

"Thank you, Heidi. Mr. Mason will start with some coffee in the living room, and of course, I'll take some tea."

The maid nodded and swiftly left the room.

Charles followed the beautiful billionairess to the living room, speaking to her as they continued to walk. "If I remember correctly, I was asking you about your father."

She glanced over her shoulder, smiling. "So you were, big guy." She sighed. "I haven't talked to anyone since Ethan's funeral. Yesterday was the first time I—"

"I know, sugar. Mai Li told me. She also mentioned that you haven't been feeling well and that you finally went to see your doctor."

Nouri chuckled. "Mai Li said all that to you, did she?"

"She did. A lovely woman."

"With a love for talking, so it would seem!" she said, turning to face him.

Charles smiled. "She cares about you, sugar, that's all."

"Yes, I know. I love Mai Li deeply. I'd be lost without her, to tell you the truth, Charles."

"I know."

"You know what, Charles?" she remarked nervously.

He chuckled at her nervousness. "I know that she cares for you as much as you care for her. That's all. You're a little moody today, aren't you, sugar?" He glanced at her suspiciously.

Nouri shrugged rather matter-of-factly. "Probably. Would you like a

Bloody Mary? I'm going to have one," she said, crossing the room and going to the bar.

"No, I'd better not. I'm nursing one hell of an ouzo hangover this morning!" He cringed at the thought as his mind flashed him a quick reminder of the Greek white lightning he had been drinking the night before.

She chuckled at the expression plastered across her friend's face. "A what hangover?"

He shook his pounding head. "Let's just hope you have the good sense to run like hell if anyone ever offers you a shot or two of the powerful stuff! Whew!"

"That bad, huh?" Nouri laughed.

"You have no idea!" Charles frowned playfully.

"So what were you celebrating; your divorce from Tallulah, perhaps?" She leveled her gaze to him.

"Very funny, sugar! I'm sorry I lied to you about that." He flushed, knowing he had just been busted over the lie he had told her six weeks earlier.

Nouri handed him a Bloody Mary. "Here, drink this. It certainly couldn't hurt. It might even help a little." She handed him the drink and then went on. "So tell me why you lied to me about being married?" she said, taking a sip of her drink.

He took a long drink of the Bloody Mary. "I think you know why; at least by now you should."

She rolled her eyes teasingly. "Let me guess. Didn't have anything to do with that manly pride of yours, did it?" Their gaze met. She smiled knowingly.

He set his drink down on top of the bar and walked over to her. "Speaking of manly pride," he said, tilting her face up with his curled forefinger. "You really hurt Gabe."

Nouri swallowed hard and turned to walk toward the dining room. "Breakfast should almost be ready, Charles," she said, glancing over her shoulder.

"Did you hear what I just said?" he said, stopping her in mid-step and turning her to face him.

"Yes, I heard you. Hurt, you say! Yeah, sure he is, that's why he hightailed his ass back here to Boston. Back into the open arms of Lisa Clayborne!" Her tone was laced with sarcasm. She shook her head, folded her arms, and started walking again.

Charles grabbed her gently by the arm and turned her around again.

"Nouri, you told Gabe to leave you the hell alone and get out. His pride was hurt. What did you expect him to do at the time, for chrissakes?"

"I'm not sure, Charles, but I can tell you one thing for certain," she said, entering the dining room.

"What's that, Nouri?"

She laughed sarcastically, dropping her arms to her sides. "I didn't expect him to go running back into the arms of Lisa Clayborne so quickly! To hear Gabe tell it, she was…" She stopped talking as Heidi appeared with their plates of food.

"Well, here it is. Breakfast is served. I hope you're good and hungry, Mr. Mason. It's been a long time since I've had the opportunity to cook for anyone except for James and myself. Mrs. Sommers is rarely here, and even when she is, she seldom wants anything to eat," she said, smiling brightly, setting their plates down in front of them.

"Ah…smells wonderful, Heidi." Charles smiled. "Biscuits and gravy. I can't tell you how long it has been since I've had a wholesome hungry man's breakfast like this. Thank you." He smiled appreciatively again.

"You're welcome, sir," Heidi responded, then she bowed and left the room.

"I hope you're as hungry as I am, sugar. This looks great!" the P.I. said, quickly diving into his food. "Mmm, the fried potatoes have onions in them," he added, eagerly taking another bite.

Nouri chuckled. "Yes, Heidi is a wonderful down-home cook. She puts gravy and/or onions in just about everything she cooks. She's from the South; one of those little towns along the Kentucky-Tennessee border."

Charles swallowed his bite of food. "I can see that. The grits are a dead giveaway." He chuckled.

"I think Heidi is trying to impress you," Nouri said, reaching for the honey to put on her biscuit.

"Well, she certainly has done that!" Charles helped himself to another biscuit with gravy.

Nouri picked up the silver coffeepot. "More coffee?" she offered.

He nodded. "Yes, thank you. And while you're at it, you can finish telling me what you were saying about Gabe," he said as Heidi entered the room. She checked the coffee in the silver pot and removed a few empty bowls.

"If you don't mind, Charles, I'd rather not talk about Gabe anymore right now," Nouri said. "I'm having enough difficulty dealing with my own little pride thing." She pushed her plate away.

Charles pointed to her plate."What's the matter, sugar; you hardly touched your food."

"Oh, Charles!" Nouri cried, unable to stop herself from jumping to her feet and running to him for comfort.

He pulled her down on his lap and hugged her tightly as she continued to cry on his shoulder. "Shhh, sugar. It's all right. Let it out. You need a good cry. I'm here for you," he whispered in a fatherly tone as he continued to cradle her in his arms.

After a few moments of uncontrollable sobbing, she pulled herself together. "Thank you, big guy. Whatever would I do without you?" she murmured, blotting her tears with the corner of a napkin.

"Well, lucky you'll never have to worry about that now, will you, sugar?" he said, gently caressing her across the back.

"Yeah, right! What about your fiancée?" she countered tearfully.

"Tonya knows how I feel and will always feel about you, sugar. She understands that part between us will never change. You need me; I'll be there. It's that simple. You really are going to like her, Nouri." He smiled.

"Sure I will, big guy. I bet she hates my guts!" She swallowed hard. "Gabe told me all about her and why you stopped seeing her."

"Well, that was before we worked things out between us. You two will become the best of friends. You'll see. Everything is going to be all right; I promise, sugar. And anyway, we'll need you around to keep an eye on Chuckie for us from time to time. 'Auntie Nouri,' now that has a rather nice ring to it, don't you think?" He lifted her chin and gazed into her tear-stained eyes.

Nouri giggled in spite of how she felt. "Little Chuckie. I can hardly wait to meet him. I've been told he looks exactly like you, Charles." She smiled.

The P.I. nodded. "Yeah, he does. It's almost scary. I really love the little fella, Nouri. I can't believe how perfect he is." He shook his head in awe and then continued, "I was pissed at first. I mean when I found out that I had a son...I mean, I wasn't pissed to learn I had a son; I was pissed because I wasn't told I had a son until he was three years old. No woman has the right to keep that kind of secret to herself. The father of the child, no matter who he may be, has the right to know. I was really hot at Tonya at first for keeping her pregnancy from me. I've lost three years of my son's life that I can never get back. It just isn't right! Don't you agree, sugar?" he said, leveling his eyes to hers.

Nouri shifted her position on his lap and began crying hysterically again. "Oh, Charles!" she sobbed.

He gently patted her across the shoulders again. “Nouri, what’s wrong?”

“Everything. Just everything!” she wailed.

“I don’t understand,” he said curiously.

Nouri swallowed hard, trying to pull her emotions back under control again. “I…I can’t tell you. I wish that I could. But I can’t.”

“You can’t tell me what?”

“Nothing.” She shook her head rising to her feet. “I’m sorry. I guess I’m just a little emotional today, that’s all. Let’s go back to the living room. I need a drink,” she said, gesturing in the direction of the hallway.

“Nouri,” Charles said her name softly, causing her to glance back over her shoulder. “Are you all right? I’m worried about you. It’s not normal blocking everything and everyone out of your life for six weeks at a time like you did. Sugar, I understand pain. I understand about losing people that we care about or even love, but to shut the world out like that, well, Nouri, it just isn’t an okay thing to do. I was worried sick about you; so was your father, your sister, and that goofy brother of yours, and so was Gabe, sugar!”

She cleared her throat and started to walk again. “Please, try to understand, Charles, I…I just needed a little time to myself. My whole life has changed practically overnight. Can you imagine what that was like for me? I still can’t believe it. In just one week, Charles, my life as I knew it suddenly didn’t exist anymore. Now, if you ask me, that’s not normal!”

“Yes, I do understand. I was there. Remember? In France, every tear you shed, for chrissakes, I felt! Nouri, you just have to dig deep. Take a deep breath and start from scratch. Locking yourself in your bedroom for weeks on end isn’t the answer. Neither is sucking some young guy’s brains out in public that you barely know!” he snapped.

Nouri chuckled in spite of her efforts not to. “Oh, honestly, Charles! I can explain that. It wasn’t what it appeared to be.”

“Have you seen the headlines in the newspaper yet this morning, by any chance?”

“No, and I don’t care to, either,” she replied.

“The latest headline has you not only kissing your new boy toy in blue good-bye, but you were apparently waving good-bye to him as well after spending the entire night with him, no doubt! Would you care to explain that one?” He shook his head.

Nouri smiled mischievously. “No, not really, Charles,” she said teasingly.

“Very goddamn funny, young lady!” he replied, accepting his drink from her shaking hand.

"Honestly, big guy, you're sounding more and more like my father every day!" She shook her head in playful dismay.

"I'm not your father, Nouri!" he said, leveling his bloodshot gaze to hers, causing her to giggle.

"Okay, I surrender. What is it that you want to know?" She smiled, taking a sip of her drink.

"A lot of things. But for starters you can fill me in on what happened yesterday. Start with the part about your visit with Dr. Douglas."

She swallowed nervously. "The doctor, huh?" She lowered her eyes to her drink.

"Yes, Mai Li told me that's where you had gone to when I phoned for you yesterday afternoon."

"I see. It was nothing. I'm…I'm as healthy as a horse, it seems."

"Yeah, right! And next you will be calling me dumbo, right? That's what you used to say to me when you didn't think I…"

Nouri interrupted. "Yes, I remember, Charles. As a matter of fact, I remember everything about us together." She smiled lovingly.

Charles recognized the needy look in her eyes as he gazed into them. "What's the matter, sugar? Do you need to be held?" he asked.

She smiled. "You know me too well, big guy, but unfortunately you're taken these days." She glanced at him longingly but with sadness.

He nodded. "True, but I'm not married yet, sugar. If you need me, all you have to do is say so." He smiled.

"As tempting as your offer is, Charles, there's something I need to tell you," she said, circling the rim of her glass nervously with the tip of her finger.

"I'm all ears, sugar," he said.

Unable to resist teasing the famous P.I., Nouri traveled her gaze seductively down the length of his manly body and slowly back up again. "Not all ears, Charles." She giggled playfully, trying to lighten the mood.

He chuckled. "Like I just told you, sugar, say the word. Better yet, just walk over here and put your arms around my neck. I'll carry you to the bedroom and…"

She stopped him. "Oh Charles, I do love you. You do know that, don't you, big guy?"

He sighed. "Yeah, I know. You're just not in love with me, right?"

She swallowed hard. "You're taken, remember?"

"So it would seem. But…"

Nouri struggled with her tears, wiping a tear from her eye that fell down her cheek. "I love you, Charles," she whispered softly.

He opened his arms for her to run into. "Come here, sugar," he said.

Nouri didn't walk; she ran into the P.I.'s open arms, throwing hers snugly around his neck.

"Come on, sugar. I'm putting you to bed. You need me right now, and I need to say good-bye to you properly. In a few short weeks I won't be able to hold you in my arms anymore. It's something I really need to do right now, Nouri. What do you say?" He tightened his arms around her.

She gently freed herself from his tight embrace. "Oh Charles," she whispered softly. "I…I can't. I'm sorry."

He swallowed hard to in an effort to calm his need to make love to her.

"What is it, Nouri? Gabe? You're in love with him, aren't you?" he asked.

She sighed deeply. "I told you, Charles, I don't want to talk about Gabe right now," she said, walking to the sofa.

Charles followed. "Nouri, are you blaming Gabe for Chamberlain's death?" he asked curiously.

She wiped another tear from her eye as she sat down in her cozy spot. "No, of course not. But in all honesty, at first I may have. And then I blamed myself. And then I blamed Ethan. And then I blamed you for asking him to stay in France to begin with. But then…" She stopped talking and shook her head with regret.

"Nouri, Gabe is still in love with you. He thinks you blame him for Chamberlain's death."

She shook her head, understanding as much. "I know. And he has every right to think that. Oh Charles, I've treated Gabe so badly. But as it turns out, it was for the best. He's back with Lisa Clayborne and all her millions!" she snipped with a shrug.

Charles chuckled at her jealously over Gabe's beautiful fiancée. "Her what?"

She shot her friend a hurt look. "I'd like to know just what the hell you think is so damn funny! Gabe got what he wanted. A beautiful woman with millions!"

Charles shook his head in playful dismay. "Sugar, that couldn't be further from the truth. You have no idea what the hell you are talking about. Do you? Gabe is worth at least a billion dollars, himself." He chuckled.

A puzzled expression covered Nouri's face as she sat her drink down on the coffee table. "He what?" she exclaimed.

"You heard me the first time. Gabe is a very wealthy man. His family is loaded. Of course, Gabe has his own money, too," he explained.

Nouri sat speechless for several moments, trying to digest what the famous P.I. had just told her. "I would've never believed the detective was into playing games like this! After all his posturing and..." She stopped talking and shook her head angrily. "How dare that son-of-a-bitch! I'll be damned!"

Charles chuckled, amused by it all. "You'll be damned what?"

"That jackass had the nerve to accuse me of taking pleasure in playing games, when all along he...he..."

"Calm down, for chrissakes! Gabe isn't like that, and you should know him well enough to know that by now. He doesn't like flaunting his wealth. He never has. He likes his privacy; likes being his own person. Hell, even his own family disowned him for a while after he joined the Boston Police Force. Whew, was his father pissed!" Charles shook his head at the memory.

"You mean to tell me that he wears those godawful suits of his on purpose!" Nouri exclaimed in utter disbelief, recalling the ugly brown suit he had on the day she had first met him.

"What ugly suit?" Charles asked, remembering what a fancy dresser his former partner could be.

"Never mind," Nouri said, shaking her head.

"So what is it that you wanted to tell me, Nouri?" Charles said, glancing at his watch.

She swallowed hard, patting the spot beside her on the sofa. "Maybe you should sit down first." She smiled nervously, trying to get the courage to tell him about her pregnancy.

"Okay, I'm seated. Now what's this all about?"

"Oh God, Charles! I don't know where to begin. Or as far as that goes, how," she said, shrugging hopelessly.

"Start at the beginning, Nouri. That's always the best place to start," he offered, smiling. He leaned over and patted her on the shoulders.

Just as Nouri started to confide in her friend, the maid entered the room and told her she had a phone call from a police officer—Rick Hobner.

Nouri stood to her feet, swallowing nervously. She glanced at the P.I. with a guilty expression.

"Swell," Charles complained as he watched her leave the room.

Chapter 12

After police detective Gabe Baldwin left P.I. Charles Mason's luxurious mansion, he went to his own, changed clothes, and jumped into one of his own automobiles. "The Maserati will do just fine today," he mumbled, starting the engine.

Gabe's mind was racing as fast as the engine in his car. He released a deep sigh of dread as he drove swiftly to the Baron's mansion. "Not one, but two goddamn ex-husbands! I don't fucking believe that woman!" he angrily spat, remembering what his friend Charles Mason had told him earlier about his fiancée.

After I break her beautiful conniving neck, call off the wedding, and send good ol' Pierre back to France, I'm going to pull Pretty Boy Floyd's goddamn lungs out with my own two goddamn bare hands! And then—

His thoughts were interrupted when his cell phone rang. He answered the call with an angry, "Yeah!"

"Good morning, darling," his soon-to-be ex-fiancée said in a disgustingly pleasant tone of voice, causing the hot-tempered detective to cringe at her phoniness.

"Lisa," he returned with an edge.

"Darling, I tried to reach you by telephone all evening. Where in God's name were you all night long?" she whined childishly.

He rolled his eyes with distaste. "Listen, Lisa, I'm on my way to see you. We have to talk."

"All right, darling. Have you eaten yet this morning?"

He shook his head in dismay. "I don't want any goddamn breakfast," he snapped.

"Hmm, in a cranky mood this morning, I see. Well, not to worry. I know exactly what will put a smile on that handsome face of yours," she whispered seductively. "I'll be in my bedroom when you arrive; just have Martha show you the way." Without waiting for his response, Lisa smacked her lips together, making a kissing sound, and swiftly hung up the telephone.

Gabe shouted her name several times into the receiver, hoping to get her attention, but it was too late. He angrily tossed the cell phone onto the seat next to him and flicked on the radio.

He made a right-hand turn onto the freeway, stepping on the gas pedal, anxious to get rid of at least one of his problems. "Women!" He sighed, thinking first of his conniving fiancée and then of Nouri Sommers sharing a kiss with young police officer Rick Hobner. Tom Jones was singing "Delilah" on the car radio. "Wait until I get my hands on that slimy little prick!" Gabe groaned, switching off the radio. "Women!" he complained under his breath again.

"How could you do this to me with that little shit? Wasn't it bad enough you broke my goddamn heart? Now you want to rub my face into it, too! Fine, have it your way. Let's see if you still find Pretty Boy Floyd as attractive with the fat lip I intend to give him when I get my hands on that slimy little shit!" Gabe continued to rave under his breath as he pulled his car up to the front entrance gate to the Clayborne estate.

He was allowed immediate entrance to the grounds. He peeled rubber all the way to the mansion.

The large, double-width door was answered by a short, round, middle-aged maid. Even with her hefty size she was still rather attractive; her smile was cheery and her eyes sparkled like freshly polished crystal. She was neatly dressed in a crisp black uniform dress covered by a checked black-and-white apron. Her accent was as southern as a mint julep in the month of May. She quickly invited him inside the mansion.

"Good morning, sir." She smiled warmly.

"Good morning, Martha. Lisa is expecting me," he said, returning the smile.

"Yes, Mr. Baldwin. Follow me, please," she said, leading him through another set of double doors onto to a marble-floored hallway. To his left he could see a spiral staircase drifting upward at least four or five levels.

He swallowed nervously when the maid turned to face him.

"Ms. Clayborne's private chambers are on the third level. First door to your left. Can you manage by yourself, or shall I—"

Gabe smiled, sensing the hefty maid dreaded having to go climb the stairs. He cut in, "No, that won't be necessary. I can manage on my own." He inhaled deeply before hurrying up the dreaded long flight of stairs. As the police detective was rounding the corner of the first flight of stairs, ready to take on the second flight, he ran into his fiancée's mother, almost knocking her to the floor. He reached out and grabbed her, pulling her into his protective arms in time to stop the fall. "Oh, God! I'm so sorry, Mrs. Clayborne. Are you all right?" he asked, releasing her from his tight embrace.

Mrs. Clayborne slowly pushed a fallen strand of hair away from her eyes and then moved her hands to smooth her clothing. "I…I think so, Gabe," she said in response, still half-winded from the impact.

Gabe shook his head. "I should've been—"

She interrupted. "Nonsense, I'm fine. Honestly. I'm glad we bumped into one another, actually. You're just the person I've been wanting to see. Come," she said, gesturing with a wave of her hand.

Gabe could feel his face flushing. "Lisa is waiting on—"

She cut in glancing over her shoulder as she continued to walk. "Pooh! Let her wait. I need to talk to you." She smiled mischievously.

"All right." He entered the room, and Mrs. Clayborne shut the door behind him.

"Drink?" she offered, picking up a bottle of dry sherry.

"No thanks." Gabe cringed at the thought.

"Gabe, you look a little under the weather today. Are you feeling all right?" she asked.

He cleared his throat. "I'm fine. Just had a little too much to drink last night, nothing to worry about," he returned, smiling.

"I see," she said, pouring herself a glass of sherry. "You aren't having second thoughts about the wedding again, are you, dear?" she asked bluntly.

He swallowed nervously and lowered his bloodshot eyes. "Maybe I will join you in a drink, after all," he said, walking over and glancing out of the beautiful large bay window.

"Sherry?" she asked again.

He glanced over his shoulder. "Unless you have something a little stronger close by," he said in a hoarse tone.

"Bourbon. Scotch. You name it." She smiled.

"Bourbon will be fine. Better make that a double," he added, walking back across the room away from the scenic view of the pond.

"Sounds serious, Gabe," she said, handing him the drink.

"Thank you." He quickly belted the drink down.

"Another?" she offered, looking at him curiously.

"I can get it myself, thanks. Are you ready for a refill?"

She declined with a shake of her head. "No thanks, I'm still sipping on this one. Come, let's sit on the sofa," she said, leading the way.

"All right."

Mrs. Clayborne leveled her gaze on Gabe. "Now, what's going on between you and Lisa?"

Gabe cleared his throat and said, "Maybe this is a conversation I should be having with your daughter, Mrs. Clayborne."

"Bullshit!" she snapped, staring at him coldly. "This isn't the goddamn dark ages anymore, Gabe. Give me a break, will you?" She shook her head. "You're not going to marry Lisa, are you?" she added angrily.

"Mrs. Clayborne, I…I'm sorry, but I can't," he said, lowering his gaze to his drink.

"It's that Sommers woman, isn't it? You're in love with her, aren't you?" Her tone was sarcastic.

He sighed with regret. "I honestly don't know anymore. What I do know, however, is that I'm not in love with your daughter. I'm sorry."

She smiled faintly. "Maybe in time you could learn to love Lisa. It could happen. You know, not very many know this, but when I married the Baron, I wasn't in love with him either; not at first anyway. But as the years went by, I slowly learned to love him. Maybe in time, if you—"

"I'm sorry," Gabe cut in. "It's just not going to happen. Not today. Not tomorrow. Never," he said coolly.

She looked at him in stunned silence for a brief moment. "If it isn't the Sommers woman as you claim, then what the hell is it?" she demanded.

Gabe sighed heavily. "It isn't just any one thing. It is a lot of things, but mostly because Lisa hasn't been completely honest with me."

"Honest with you, in what way?" she asked, in stunned disbelief.

"Well, for starters, Lisa never told me she had been married before. Twice before, to be exact!" he said.

"She never told you?"

Gabe shook his head. "No. She didn't. I just found out this morning, as a matter of fact."

"Let me guess. The Sommers woman told you, right?" she remarked with sarcasm.

Gabe chuckled. "No, she didn't. I haven't seen or talked to Nouri Sommers in almost six weeks now. Not since I've been back from France. And by the way, Mrs. Clayborne, sarcasm doesn't suit you. It doesn't matter how I found out. The point is I just did. Okay? Lisa should have told me. She chose not to."

"Why don't you take a little time to think about things? I'm sure once you—"

He cut in, "No, the wedding is officially off. I want you to send Pierre back to France. I don't care what you choose to tell your friends, the press, or my mother!" he said sharply.

"I see. Well, I guess there's nothing else to say then, is there, Gabe?"

Gabe sat his glass down the coffee table and stood to his feet. "I'm sorry, Mrs. Clayborne," he said, turning to leave.

"You know, Gabe, the Baron isn't going to like this; he will most surely have plenty to say to you!" Mrs. Clayborne said, escorting him to the door.

He chuckled, glancing over his shoulder at her. "Yeah, I'm sure he will. He knows how to get in touch with me. Good-bye, Mrs. Clayborne." Gabe hurried on to Lisa's private quarters.

After the police detective disengaged himself from his former fiancée, he swiftly departed the Baron's estate. He could hardly wait to get his hands wrapped around young Rick Hobner's slimy little neck as he headed his car into the direction of town.

Chapter 13

When Detective Gabe Baldwin entered the brightly lit corridor of the Boston Police Department, he could hear on the right the loud merriment of his coworkers coming from the men's locker room.

He entered the room, immediately recognizing the loud boasting voice of young police officer Rick Hobner talking with other young friends in blue. Gabe inched his way closer so he could hear better.

"No shit, the body on this woman is to-die-for, I kid you not! When I tried to wake her this morning, and she rolled over and stretched, her beautiful pink nipples suddenly popped into my face. I thought I was going to get off—right then and right there! I'm talking instant hard-on!" he boasted loudly, shaking his head at the heated memory of a few hours earlier. He went on while the homicide detective, standing only a row of lockers away, continued to listen.

"What happened next, Casanova?" young officer Jerry Wright asked excitedly.

Rick laughed wickedly. "Hey, what do you think?" He grinned and shrugged suggestively. "You guys saw this morning's newspaper, and I am late for work, aren't I?

Police officer James Hoskins chuckled, shaking his head. "Yeah, well, Rick, I hope that rich babe was worth dying for. Once Detective Baldwin finds out about your all night love-in with his woman, he's going to kill you!"

Rick laughed nervously. "A price well paid, dickhead!" He grinned again. "I'm telling you, she must've enjoyed herself last night, because we are going at it again tonight!" He smiled wickedly, bending over to lace up his hard shoes. "I'm meeting her at Harvey's new joint tonight. You know, that new Greek restaurant down on Eighth Street," he said, excitedly glancing in the mirror to comb his hair.

"Ah yes! The one with the belly dancers and that Tom Jones wannabe," Officer Brady said.

"Who?" Rick asked.

"You know, that Greek guy who sings like Tom Jones in his native tongue. The Greek language of love; drives the women nuts!" Officer Hauser said, in a playful manner wiggling his eyebrows up and down.

"I hear a few drinks of that Greek white lightning and a few love songs by that Tom Jones wannabe will have most babes ready to spread their legs and go at it in no time at all," Officer Brent Allen remarked, shaking his head. "I swear, you guys! Harvey told me the other night when I stopped in to see him that he gets laid in his office at least five times a night every goddamn night of the week, and are you ready for this?" he asked, glancing around. "And every hard-on is by a different babe every time! Lucky bastard!" He chuckled enviously.

"So what time are you and the Sommers babe going to be there, Rick? We all want to check her out."

Rick glanced back through the mirror. "Eight o'clock. That's when round two of the fireworks begins!" A wicked grin crept across his face.

Officer Hoskins pulled his revolver out to check the clip. Shaking his head in amusement, he said with a chuckle, "That is if you're still among the living, Hobner!"

"Oh shit, Hoskins, give me a goddamn break! I'm not afraid of the detective, if that's what you're implying. He had his chance with her and he blew it! Anyway, a young babe like that needs a younger guy much like myself. Hell, I can go at it all night if that's what it takes," he boasted. "I bet Baldwin had trouble getting it up more than twice a night for her. No wonder she told the poor bastard to get the hell out while they were still in France. Hell, can't say as I blame her." He smiled wickedly.

"Yeah right, Mr. Studly! Just watch your ass. Rumor has it that the detective is still very much in love with Nouri Sommers. There's a pool going on around here today, Hobner, that you might be interested in. A two-to-one shot that the hung-over detective will kick your goddamn ass when he gets here this morning!" young Hoskins said, putting his foot upon the bench and lacing up his shoes, first one, then the other.

Hobner strapped on his revolver. "Ah, fuck that son-of-a-bitch! And anyway, my sex life isn't any of the detective's goddamn business. He's engaged to that other rich bitch now. What the hell is her name?"

"Clayborne. Lisa Clayborne. The Baron's daughter," Officer Brady jumped in the conversation as he buttoned up his shirt.

"Yeah, well, he's still engaged and has no business sticking his nose into mine or Nouri's business," Rick snapped.

"Maybe so, Hobner, but love can make most men do some pretty goddamn bizarre things. Just watch your ass! And if I were you, I'd hightail my ass out of this place and fast; the detective should be here any time now."

Young Rick shook his head arrogantly. "I'll tell you guys like I told the captain this morning—"

One of his friends cut in, "Yeah, yeah, we know, Hobner. You're not afraid of the detective."

Gabe's first reaction to young officer Hobner's remarks was to storm in and break him in two—that is after he finished beating him to a pulp. But after listening to the young cop ramble on, the detective decided that, like it or not, the young cop had made a good argument. The young cop's or Nouri Sommers' love life wasn't any of his business.

Gabe suddenly felt both heartsick and sick to his stomach. He needed a drink, and he needed it badly! He decided to exit the police station as quickly as he had entered it. He quietly left the building without being seen. Then he met the district attorney in the parking lot.

"Gabe…Wait a minute…Please, I want to talk to you!" she shouted, running after him as he continued swiftly making his way to his car. The police detective had heard the D.A. calling out to him, but he was in no mood to respond. He continued on.

"Gabe…please wait!" she shouted, lunging after him, reaching out for his arm. Half-winded, she managed to stop him and turn him to face her. "Didn't you hear me shouting for you, Detective?" she asked, gasping for breath.

His gaze traveled the length of Tonya Daughtery's body. She was a very beautiful woman, he admitted, and she looked exceptionally beautiful that morning. The color of her suit matched her sexy light-blue eye color perfectly. He smiled in spite of himself. "I'm sorry, Tonya. What were you saying to me?" he asked, gazing into her eyes.

She instantly felt guilty after being momentarily mesmerized by the police detective's hypnotic teal-blue gaze. She swallowed hard and instinctively stepped back a few safer inches. She nervously cleared her throat. "I…I was saying that I wanted to talk to you." She paused briefly to jar herself back to her senses. The handsome detective had completely distracted her. "That is, if you have a few free moments," she added smiling shyly.

"Sure, come on. I was just on my way to have a drink. I'll buy you one," he offered, opening his car door and leaning over to press the lock switch to the passenger's side of the car.

She swallowed hard again, briefly hesitating before walking around to the passenger's side of the car. Gabe followed quickly to open her door. "All right. I have a little free time. Where are you taking me, Detective?" she said, smiling.

"I have to run home, first. There's something I need to pick up. We can have a drink there. Is that all right with you?" he said, returning her smile.

She nodded, feeling a twinge of guilt after accepting the invitation to his home so easily. She swallowed, nervously glancing in his direction. "So, how are you feeling today?"

He glanced at her, smiling sheepishly as he gazed into her eyes. "Compared to what?" he returned, shrugging.

She shifted in her seat uncomfortably. *Oh my lord!* she thought awkwardly, noticing her attraction to the handsome detective. She chuckled at his remark. "I mean—"

"You're referring to my getting plastered yesterday?"

"Well, yes," she replied, toying with the top button of her suit jacket unconsciously.

"Do you really want to know? Or are you just being polite?" he asked coolly, lowering his gaze to her impressive large breasts.

"I'm sorry, Gabe. I didn't mean to sound like I was prying or anything like that. I just know you haven't been yourself lately. That's all." She smiled and reached over to pat his hand.

Immediately aroused by her touch, Gabe swallowed hard and quickly pulled his Maserati over to the emergency lane of the freeway. He shut off the engine and pulled her to him and completely took her breath away with one of his impulsive, fiery hot kisses.

Surprisingly, Tonya didn't try to stop him. She didn't want to stop him. His masterful kisses were much too suggestive. Hungry. Needy. Thrilling, actually. *God help me!* she thought to herself as she continued to enjoy his earth-moving kisses.

After removing his lips from hers, he slowly moved his kisses to the side of her neck. "Oh God, Tonya. Please make love to me. I need to be held," he whispered along the side of her throat hoarsely as though he was in pain.

Unable to speak, she gently removed one of his hands, placing it on her right breast, surprising herself as well as him. His need to be held touched her deeply.

She glanced down at his hand where she had placed it on her breast, feeling the heat of reckless desire surge through her body. He slowly unbuttoned her suit jacket with one hand while he continued to nibble on her neck and earlobe.

He instinctively groaned after unfastening the front of her lacy pushup bra and feeling the warm flesh of her firm, round breast in the palm of his large hand. Eagerly he lowered his mouth on her breast and put hungry kisses on each breast, kissing one nipple to tautness, then the other.

She moaned with eager anticipation as he continued to kiss, suck and tease her breast with his fiery hot kisses, tongue and teeth, driving her wild with desire for him.

His need for sexual release was urgent, but he forced himself to hold back. He wanted to take his time and enjoy her body completely, but he also wanted her to feel fulfilled. And he felt relieved that the car's recently tinted windows would block any view of curious passersby.

In complete silence except for an occasional moan, groan or sigh of anticipation, Gabe continued to explore, excite and taste Tonya's incredibly sexy body.

He removed her silk-lace panties, and after hiking her skirt up to her waist, he moved his kisses to the soft, warm spot eagerly open to him between her very shapely thighs. She wrapped one of her legs around his neck as he continued to hungrily taste her. "Oh God, Gabe, that…that feels so wonderful," she breathlessly panted, frantically running her fingers through his beautiful dark-brown hair.

He soon replaced his tongue with two fingers, gently entering her body. She arched, wanting more. "Please," she begged in no more than a whisper, opening her legs wider still. He lowered his mouth to her again and excitedly pleasured her with several oral completions before tearing off his own shirt and tie, and sliding out of his slacks and boxers.

"Make love to me, Tonya," he whispered breathlessly before disarming her completely with another one of his masterful kisses—a kiss so powerful that it touched the very soul of her being. She eagerly obeyed his breathless request. Lowering her head, she anxiously began to shower his very manly body with her deep, hot, wet French kisses. Inch by delicious inch, she drove him mad with desire. Time and again she let him get to the brink of an explosive oral climax, only to suddenly slow down or momentarily stop, causing him to groan in tormented protest. "Oh God, please!" he groaned, with a fierce need for release.

After an eternity of blissful torture, she stopped kissing him and sat on his lap, straddling him. With an urgent need to be filled herself, she slowly lowered her body gently onto his stiff rod of hardened flesh. She could hardly wait to experience his massive erection deep inside her body. She squealed with utter amazement as she slowly began to move her body in sync with his. He sighed lustfully as she continued to whet his desire.

"Deeper, Gabe," she quietly begged in her warm breath as she whispered in his ear. That's all he needed to hear to release the animal he kept locked away deep inside himself. He quickly shifted his position for deeper penetration and set the animal inside himself free. He was ready, more than ready, to give himself so completely to the beautiful, hot-natured woman who currently lusted after his wild embrace.

After their in-sync climax, they collapsed into one another's arms, gasping for air, but both still wanted much more. Still catching his breath, he glanced at the beautiful, flushed-faced woman beside him. "Are you all right?" he said softly. "I'm sorry if I…"

She smiled and quickly silenced the detective with a kiss. After she removed her lips from his, she smiled again. "Gabe, let's go to your house. I want to be with you today," she whispered across his lips with her warm, sweet breath.

Not bothering to put his clothes back on or allowing her to pull her skirt down, he started the engine to the car, pulling her close to him. She smiled understandingly before lowering her head to his lap.

After several emergency stops along the freeway, Gabe finally managed to pull his car into his own driveway, anxious to spend the biggest part of the day enjoying the company of the beautiful woman who seemed to know how to help him chase away the blues associated with a broken heart—a feeling Tonya was apparently an expert at dealing with herself.

Ahhh…Experience! I like that quality in a woman! he thought, unlocking the front door to his house and ushering the beautiful D.A. inside.

Chapter 14

After pacing back and forth to and from the large outdoor balcony and nervously glancing at his Rolex for the tenth straight time in a row, P.I. Charles Mason stormed over to the well-stocked bar in Nouri Sommers' downtown condo and helped himself to his fourth shot of bourbon.

As he slammed the empty shot glass down on top of the bar after belting his drink, Nouri entered the living room with a wide smile.

He glanced at her sharply. "Well, it was nice of you to finally remember that I was still here!"

She chuckled, shaking her head in a playful manner. "Oh honestly, Charles, stop it! I'm sorry it took me so long, but while I was talking to Rick, my call-waiting line beeped. I said good-bye and answered the other line. It was Mai Li checking on me. Knowing this, does it make you feel less angry with me?"

He gave her a sheepish look. "Good! I was beginning to…"

"I know, Charles. I know exactly what was running through that brain of yours, big guy," she said, wagging a finger in his direction.

He playfully grabbed Nouri's finger, pulled it to his lips, and, staring wantonly into her eyes, seductively kissed it. Gasping, she closed her eyes as he began sensually French kissing each finger on her hand. "Oh, Charles," she whispered under her breath.

He pulled her into his heated embrace and kissed her deeply, passionately. "Please, sugar, I need to say good-bye to you properly. Let me make love to you one final time," he whispered in her ear when he was forced to come up for air.

"Oh Charles, I want to! I honestly do, but I can't. I'm sorry," she returned with regret, slowly inching her way back to a slightly safer distance from his manly touches in order to clear her thoughts.

Charles gave her a questioning look as he sank down on a nearby barstool and hung his head sadly. "Is it because you're in love with Gabe?" he asked.

Nouri walked to him and put her arms tightly around his neck. "Oh, big guy, it's more complex than that. I only wish it was as simple as that." She sighed, laying her head on his strong shoulder.

Charles sighed. "Okay, young lady, spit it out! What's going on, and don't tell me it has something to do with that slimy young cop!" he said, in a stern and fatherly voice.

She chuckled. "For the love of Christ, Charles! None of this has anything to do with Rick. He's just someone I feel obligated to have dinner with," she said, giving Charles a fond kiss on the cheek as she went behind the bar. "Want another drink? I'm going to have one. I'm trying to get up enough courage to tell you something." She smiled nervously, reaching for the bottle of vodka.

"All right, in that case, make mine a double shot of bourbon. I got plastered yesterday with Gabe and his boss. I may as well get plastered today with you," he mused as he watched her fix their drinks.

She looked at him curiously. "You got plastered with Gabe? What, a bachelor party or something like that?" she asked handing him his drink.

"Not exactly. Gabe was supposed to meet me for lunch at one of those new restaurants downtown, The Fox and Crow. When he didn't show up, I went to the police station looking for him. I've been a little worried about him lately after hearing a few pretty bizarre…" He stopped for a moment. "Well, he just hasn't been himself since his return from France. Anyway, when I went into his office to chat with him, Gabe and Mark were already half-smashed. To make a long story short, all three of us spent the rest of the day getting plastered in a really big way," he confessed, shaking his head.

Nouri rolled her eyes and then took a sip of her drink. "I see," she said, shaking her head in amusement on her way to the sofa. "So, what were you good old boys celebrating?" she asked.

"Celebrating! Hardly, sugar. Gabe was crying in his beer over you." He leveled his gaze on her. "I told you, Nouri, he's in love with you in a real big way," he added, reaching for his drink. He downed the double shot of bourbon, making a cringing face as he set the shot glass back down on the bar.

"Yeah, right, Charles!" Nouri snipped with an attitude. "That's why he's going to rush into marriage with Ms. Bubblebutt!" She reached for her Bloody Mary on the coffee table.

Charles shook his head. "Ah, no, he isn't. Gabe's breaking the engagement as we speak, as a matter of fact, Ms. Smart Ass," he returned, leveling his eyes to hers.

"Really!" Her tone was one of both surprise and excitement.

He nodded. "Yeah. He finally came to his senses. Well, that is after I shed a little light on the subject." He chuckled, reaching for the bottle of bourbon and pouring himself another short.

"A little light on the subject? What subject, Charles, I don't understand." She smiled nervously.

"I told Gabe about his fiancée's two prior marriages. The very same two marriages she had apparently forgotten to mention to him. Can you believe that shit?"

"Oh, my God! She's been married twice? Wow! I mean…poor Gabe." Nouri picked up her drink again.

Charles crossed the floor, sitting down beside Nouri, placing her hand inside his. "So?" he said, rubbing the warm skin on her hand with the tip of his finger.

"So what, Charles?" Nouri swallowed.

"So, why don't you get that lovely foot of yours out of your shapely ass and give the poor lovesick bastard a call? I know it would make him real happy, sugar."

She pulled her hand away from the P.I.'s warm touches. "I can't do that. It's over between Gabe and me, Charles." She sighed sadly.

Charles could feel himself tensing. "Bullshit! What the hell are you talking about?" he cried, jumping to his feet.

"Charles, just forget it and calm down, for chrissakes!" Nouri leaned over and gently patted the empty spot on the sofa. "Sit back down, big guy."

"Let me go fix us another drink first. I have a feeling it's going to be another long afternoon," he said, shaking his head.

She shot him a questioning glance. "Long afternoon? I don't understand," she said, standing to her feet and following him.

He glanced over his shoulder. "Listen, Nouri, I'm not leaving here today until you do one of two things. The choice is yours, sugar," he said, stubbornly.

She raised her eyebrow. "Choice?"

"Yeah." He nodded, helping her slide onto a barstool. "You can either tell me what's going on with you or…" He turned and walked behind the bar reaching for the vodka bottle.

"I'm listening Charles," she said, watching him make her Bloody Mary.

"Or we can move this conversation into the bedroom and let me have my way with you," he responded, leveling his gaze to hers.

Nouri giggled at her friend's persistence. "All right, I'll tell you, but under one condition. You have to promise me that what I tell will stays between us. You can't tell anyone, or I'll…I'll…"

"Calm down, sugar. You have my word. Whatever it is stays between us. I promise, okay?" He smiled lovingly.

"All right, Charles. But after I finish telling you this, I never want it mentioned again…I mean even between us, okay?"

"For the love of—"

She cut in, "Charles?"

He shook his head in amazement, reluctantly nodding his agreement on the subject. "All right, for chrissakes, agreed!" he surrendered.

Nouri picked up her drink and crossed the room with Charles following closely behind. She sat back down in her cozy spot on the large sofa. "Charles, come sit beside me and hold me for a minute. I need to feel your strength," she said tearfully.

He swallowed hard and stared at her for a moment. "Nouri, you're starting to scare me. Are you sure you're all right? That young cop didn't—"

She stopped him. "No, of course not! Rick was a perfect gentleman. He saved me from three bloodthirsty reporters last night." She patted the spot beside herself again.

He smiled and sat down. "Saved you! God, sugar, haven't you seen the newspapers this morning?" He shook his head.

"No, as I already told you, Charles. And I don't want to. It can't be that bad, for goodness sakes. The kiss in the restaurant was innocent enough, and…"

"Innocent enough! Hey, sugar, the press is having a goddamn field day at your expense. Why the hell do you think I broke my ass getting over here this morning?"

"Fabulous!" She sighed, shaking her head.

"Nouri, seeing those pictures of you sucking that young cop's brains out in the newspaper almost killed Gabe!" He shook his head excitedly. "I pity the poor kid when he gets his hands on him this morning."

"What do you mean?"

"I mean he will probably kill the poor son-of-a-bitch after spending the night with you!"

"Well, that was innocent enough too. He babysat me. I slept in his bed, and he slept on the sofa." She shrugged defensively.

"Maybe it was innocent enough, but even so, the press has you kissing the poor bastard good-bye the following morning after the restaurant thing and…"

"Jesus!" She shook her head in dismay.

"Nouri, I don't think it's a good idea for you to see this young cop again." His tone was one of concern.

"Don't be ridiculous, Charles! I have a dinner date with Rick this evening. And it is a date I intend to keep. I owe him that much, big guy."

"You don't understand, Nouri. Rick isn't the nice guy you seem to think he is. I've heard things about that young cop that aren't very pleasant when it comes to the ladies."

She chuckled. "Will you stop at nothing, Charles? I have a date with Rick tonight. We are having dinner at a new Greek restaurant down on Eighth Street. I've already explained my reasons."

"Listen, Nouri, if you insist on keeping that date tonight, then I insist on being there. Like it or not, that kid's not to be trusted!"

"And what will you tell Tonya? Being away from the woman you plan to marry in a few weeks for two straight nights in a row is not a good thing, big guy! I told you, Rick treats me just fine. I'll be okay. I'll have a drink or two, eat a bite or two of my dinner, then I will have James drive me back to the estate."

"You still don't get it, Nouri. The guy is a press hound; loves seeing photographs of himself in the newspaper. He's a bragger, a jerk, and far from the gentleman that you think he is. And as far as Tonya goes, don't worry about her; she's a full-grown woman who is more than capable of entertaining herself."

"And I'm not?" Nour snapped in a hurt tone.

"That's not what I meant, and you know it!"

"All right, I'll let that one slide," Nouri said. "Charles," she said his name softly.

He pulled her to him and hugged her tightly. "Yes, sugar, what is it? Are you ready to tell me that you're pregnant, now?"

Stunned and speechless, she jerked back and blankly stared at him in dismay. "How on earth did you know?" she finally managed after collecting her scattered thoughts. "I'm…I'm…"

He chuckled at her reaction. "Stunned? Shocked? At a loss for words? Or perhaps you're simply impressed?" he teased.

She smiled, shaking her head. "You are really something, big guy. How did you know?"

He leveled his gaze on her. "I thought you knew me better than that."

"What? Oh, of course," she added. "I'd almost forgotten. You're the best in your field, right?" she teased.

He chuckled. "Ah…that would be correct," he said playfully in return. "But you did forget to mention one small possibility," he added, tilting her chin in the air.

She laughed. "Well, excuse me, Mr. Hotshot! What might that one small thing be?" she said, rolling her eyes in playful dismay.

He shrugged. "Every once in a while, I simply just get lucky! It was a wild guess," he chuckled, pulling her to him again. "Am I the lucky father?" he asked.

"Oh, big guy!" she whispered, wiping a tear from her eye. "I wish." She paused briefly to choose her words carefully, not wanting to hurt him. "I wish in a way you were," she answered softly.

He continued to hold her tightly in his arms for a few silent moments before releasing her arms from around his neck. "Well?" He gently rubbed her arms, making his way down to her hands. He picked them up in his and kissed them—first one, then the other. "Chamberlain?" he asked softly.

She shook her head. "No, and it isn't Ethan either."

"And we're almost certain that it isn't young Hobner, right?" he playfully remarked, causing her to chuckle and slap him across his upper arm.

"Very funny, big guy!" she snipped.

"Umm, well then, that only leaves…"

"The detective," she said, shrugging defensively.

"Swell!" he said. "Come on, young lady. Let's go have another drink. You and I are going to have a serious talk!" He stood to his feet and pulled her to hers. He placed her small hand inside his large one and escorted her to the bar.

Chapter 15

"You tell him!"

"No, you tell him!"

"No, goddamn it! I'm not telling him." Former undercover police detectives Daniel Mosley and Tim Jacobs were arguing with one another as their boss former F.B.I. agent John Harmon suddenly came barreling into the office.

"What the hell are you two arguing about, for chrissakes!" he snapped heatedly, looking at both men in disbelief.

Both men turned to face their boss, shaking their heads at the same time; neither man offering an explanation.

"Well, don't both of you speak at the same time or anything!" he barked with annoyance, crossing the room to join them. "Well?" His tone was demanding.

"You tell him, Tim!" Daniel said nervously.

Tim shook his head as he walked behind his desk and sank down into his chair. "No, not me!" he returned, stubbornly tossing his head back on the headrest of the chair and covering his face with both hands.

"Well, one of you'd better…"

"All right, damn it, I will!" Daniel said. "But you better sit your ass down first, John, because you aren't going to fucking believe it!" Daniel said, sitting down on the corner of Tim's desk. He released another sigh of dread.

John rolled his eyes in aggravation, flopping down in the chair directly behind where he was standing. "Okay, I'm seated, shoot!" he said.

The other two men shared a glance before Daniel turned his attention back to his boss. He inhaled deeply. "Ah…you know Charles Mason wanted us to continue the tail on the D.A. until after the wedding; told us he wanted to make sure Christopher Graham didn't give her any more trouble," he said nervously.

"Yeah, so?" his boss returned.

"So, we followed her to the police station this morning." He stopped talking and cleared his dry throat.

"And, for chrissakes, Daniel?" John snapped impatiently.

"And she flagged down Detective Baldwin in the back parking lot as he was on his way to his car."

"For chrissakes, Daniel, you're causing me stress here!" John nervously fumbled inside his shirt pocket for a cigarette, quickly lighting up. He inhaled deeply.

"Ms. Daughtery got inside the detective's car and left with him." He glanced at his partner.

"Big deal, Mosley!" The former agent shrugged.

"After about a ten-minute drive on the freeway Baldwin pulled over on one of the emergency ramps. Tim and I following not far behind. We passed them trying to get a look inside the car to see what was going on. But between the steam and the tint on the windows we couldn't see a damn thing!"

"So, they were talking." John shrugged again.

"Yeah, that's what we thought, at first," Daniel responded nodding his head in agreement.

"At first?" their boss questioned curiously. "What do you mean?"

Daniel cleared his throat again before replying. "After a forty-five-minute stop on the emergency ramp Baldwin started up his car and took off again. Making two more thirty-minute stops at two more emergency ramps before finally going to his house." Daniel glanced at his friend again.

His boss shook his head in dismay at his two employees. "Maybe I should have Irene bring some tea and cookies in here and we can turn this conversation into a goddamn tea party, for chrissakes, Mosley!" he snapped heatedly.

Daniel shot Tim another look of concern. "Hey, calm down, John; this isn't easy for Tim and me," he said, releasing another sigh.

"Fine, I'm sorry! By all means, please continue; take your goddamn time!" John returned sarcastically.

Tim shook his head with irritation again and glanced at his partner again.

"Tim, just give me the goddamn photos," his said, holding out his hand.

"Here," Tim said, giving the photos to his boss. "Take a look for yourself," he added, turning red in the face.

John snatched the photos from out of Tim's hand and wasted no time looking at them. "You're right. I don't fucking believe it!" he shouted. "Son-of-a-bitch! What the fuck!" he continued to curse, quickly flipping through the stack of photographs. "Oh my God! This is so bad! Un-fucking-believable! Mason will blow both of their goddamn brains out!" he continued to rant and rave excitedly.

"Calm down, John! You're going to have another goddamn heart attack, for chrissakes!" Tim jumped to his feet nervously.

"Baldwin fucked her in the goddamn car, for godsakes!" John shouted, in stunned amazement.

"Hey, with Baldwin it's hard to say just where he might get the urge. Remember the tape we saw of him doing some broad on an elevator in Lambert? That son-of-a-bitch has them waiting in line, doesn't he? The lucky bastard!" Tim said enviously, shaking his head.

The former agent shook his head in amazement. "Yeah, well, if I was hung like that son-of-a-bitch, I'd have them waiting line too, shit! We should be so lucky!" He sighed and then went on. "Whew! Check out the body on the D.A.; can you believe she had a kid? Not a stretch mark on her! Damn, she's hot! I don't care if she is in her thirties; she's got a body like a goddamn teenager!"

Daniel sighed lustfully as he continued to look at the photographs of the sexy female district attorney of Boston. "Yeah, she's something all right. Looking at her like this makes you wonder how she got the nickname dragon lady, doesn't it?"

His boss chuckled. "Oh shit! Don't let that angelic face and dynamite body fool you, guys. Ms. Daughtery can be as tough as nails. She's smoking all right—she's as tough as Mason!" he said, shaking his head.

"Speaking of Mason, what are we going to do about this?" Daniel asked, glancing in the direction of his boss.

The former agent leveled his eyes to Daniel's. "Well, I'll tell you one thing for certain, Mosley, I sure as hell don't want to be the one to break this to him. No way!" He shook his head again.

"So, what are we going to do?"

"You mean besides taking this information to our graves with the three of us?" John returned as an order.

"Yeah," Daniel countered bravely.

"We're going to burn those goddamn pictures and pretend this whole thing never happened. Got it?" John said sharply.

"Sounds like the right thing to do, John," Daniel replied, sharing a glance of uncertainty with his friend.

John held out his hand. "Here, give them to me. I'll burn them myself!" he said, taking the photographs being offered to him, forgetting to ask for the negatives that were lying inside Tim's desk drawer next to several other packs of photographs of another case they had been working on for Charles Mason.

John turned to leave. "Oh, wait a minute, John; you may as well send the photographs of that abandoned warehouse down on Third Street to Mason while you're at it. He told us he wanted to wind that case up today, and he needed the prints A.S.A.P.," he said, pulling his desk drawer open and removing several pack of photographs, unaware that he had also included the incriminating negatives of the P.I.'s fiancée with the naked detective.

John extended his hand to get the warehouse photographs. "Good. I'll drop them off to him myself. I have a meeting with him shortly, anyway," he said, taking the pictures and turning to leave.

"John," Daniel said.

John glanced back over his shoulder. "Yeah," he returned reaching for the doorknob.

"Do you want us to continue the tail on Ms. Daughtery?" he asked nervously.

John nodded. "I guess you'd better, but forget taking any more photographs—especially the incriminating ones with Detective Baldwin!" he said, glancing at both men before leaving the office.

Tim glanced at his friend. "Well, Daniel, that went better than I thought it would. What do you think?" he asked.

"Yeah. A lot better, to tell you the truth," Daniel said, shaking his head. "Man, can you believe it? You just can't trust anyone these days, can you? Poor Mason. Waited all these years to finally settle down and this shit happens! Where's the goddamn justice?"

Tim nodded in agreement. "I never would have believed it, not in a million years! Why do you think it happened?"

"The detective and the D.A.?"

"Duh! That is what we're talking about, isn't it?"

"Oh yeah. Sorry. I guess I'm just still in shock. I always thought Baldwin and Mason were the best of friends," Daniel said. "And Daughtery? I thought Mason was her world, go figure!"

Tim shook his head again, still trying to figure things out in his mind. "I don't know what happened. We've been watching her twenty-four/seven for almost six weeks now, and I personally thought Ms. Daughtery was as close to a saint as anyone could possibly get. I don't get it!" he remarked, still stunned by it all.

"Maybe the detective, the poor bastard, just needed someone to help him get over his broken heart with that Sommers babe. Whew! Talk about a babe; she sure is to-die-for, isn't she?"

"Apparently!" Daniel agreed nodding. "Both Mason and Baldwin got burnt over that broad," he said. "With a body like our foxy D.A.'s, it looks to me like she certainly has the equipment to chase the poor detective's blues away."

"You know, in a way it pisses me off, Daniel." Tim ignored his friend's last remark. "Both Mason and Baldwin have had more goddamn women than most men can only dream of. It just isn't fair. Poor schmucks like us can't even get their goddamn leftovers, for chrissakes!"

Daniel shot his friend a nasty look. "Hey, speak for yourself, jackass! My love life is just fine, thank you very fucking much! It's not my fault your old lady doesn't want to give it up anymore. My 'ex' still gives me plenty! Hell, she probably gives it to me more now than when we were married!" he said with a chuckle.

"Yeah, that's only because she's still trying to get even with your ass for cheating on her with that girlfriend of yours. I know exactly how women are. She's hoping your girlfriend will find out that you're still sleeping with her from time to time. Once Megan finds out that you're doing the mambo with the former Mrs. Mosley, she'll dump your ass! And guess what? After she does, so will the former Mrs. Mosley! Paybacks are hell, Daniel. That's how women get us in the end. All of a sudden we wake up one morning and we're all alone. All we have left is the goddamn shirt on our backs, a jar of instant coffee, and good ol' Rosie and her five sisters in place of a good morning kiss! You know what I mean? Goddamn depressing as hell, isn't it?"

Daniel shook his head at his friend. "No! I'll tell you what is goddamn depressing, Tim—your goddamn male chauvinistic pig remarks! That's what's depressing as hell. Geez!" he said, shaking his head again.

"Fuck you, dickhead!" Tim returned. "No, all teasing aside, Daniel, I'll tell you what's really depressing now that I think about it. Gabe Baldwin and Charles Mason. Those two bastards! They have it all. It's just not fair. Money to burn, for chrissakes! Women all over the goddamn globe. And if those two things aren't bad enough, both of the bastards are hung like goddamn racehorses! Now that's what really frosts my rocks!" Tim said with a heavy sigh of frustration.

Daniel rolled his eyes at his partner. "Well, as depressing as this entire conversation has been, it's going to get a lot more depressing if Mason ever finds out that we didn't tell him about his fiancée making whoopee with his best friend!"

"That is something that will never happen. So, stop worrying about it. John is going to destroy the photographs and the…" Tim stopped talking and jerked his desk drawer open. "Shit! Shit! Shit!" he exclaimed, realizing what he had accidentally done. He kicked the chair to his desk all the way across the room.

Daniel stared at him as though he had just taken leave of his senses. "What the hell is wrong with you, for chrissakes, Tim?"

"Son-of-a-bitch! John is going to wring my goddamn neck but good!"

"What the hell are you talking about?" Daniel asked.

Tim rolled his eyes and then cringed. "The goddamn negatives! That's what the hell I am talking about, Daniel!" Tim swallowed hard.

"What fucking negatives?"

Tim shook his head at his friend. "Hello! Mason's goddamn fiancée with super stud!" He shook his head at the thought.

"Oh my lord! Quick, hand me the telephone. I'll call Tess and try to warn John." Daniel jerked the phone out of Tim's hands.

"Great! Let's just hope we're not too late." Tim swallowed nervously again.

Moments later, Daniel angrily shoved a pile of folders from his partner's desk onto the floor. "Fuck!" he snapped under his breath, nervously pacing back and forth.

"Shit! We were too late, right?" Tim said.

Daniel nodded. "We're dead meat! All we can do now is pray."

After nervously pacing for several moments, trying to figure out what they should do next, Tim reached for the telephone and smiled. "The phone! I'll try John's cell phone. If that doesn't work, then I'll try his pager. Whew!" he sighed in relief.

Daniel glanced around the room, suddenly spotting his boss's pager in the chair he had been sitting in a short time earlier. He went to get the pager. "Ah, partner," he said, glancing at his friend, waving their boss's pager in his hand. "I hate to burst your bubble, at least one of them, but..."

Tim slammed down the receiver. "Fuck! John isn't answering his cell phone either!"

Daniel swallowed nervously, trying to think. "What now?" he asked shaking his head.

"You know, Daniel, I tried to tell John that we were tired. Burned out. We've been overworked for the past goddamn six weeks. We're getting sloppy. You think he would've listened and given us a few weeks off, but no! Mason needs us. He needs us to do this; and he needs us to do that..."

"Oh, stop bellyaching, Tim, will you?" Daniel interrupted. "It's starting to look as though we might get that much needed vacation real soon! Maybe even a permanent one, if Mason gets a look at those goddamn negatives!"

"Well, what next?"

"Grab your jacket. Let's see if we can track John down before he hands Mason the goddamn photos from the warehouse job," Tim said, reaching for his jacket and hurrying out the door.

Chapter 16

After spending the biggest part of the day trying to get his head screwed back on straight and his life back into proper working order thanks to his trusted, very sexy, hot-natured, and compassionately understanding friend, Detective Gabe Baldwin was beginning to feel more like his old self again.

No more crying in his beer over a love affair that was probably never meant to be to begin with. No more feeling sorry for himself over losing his heart to a woman who enjoyed destroying men. And last, but certainly not least, no more tears to be shed over that same woman, Nouri Sommers.

Yes, it's the dawning of a new day. I'm back in the driver's seat. Thanks to the beautiful woman seated beside me, Gabe thought, as he glanced at the sexy female district attorney. He smiled that incredibly sexy smile of his that could melt the heart of the coldest of women.

"Thank you for being there for me today, Tonya. Having you hold me…" He paused, leaning over to slide the warm palm of his hand down inside her suit jacket. He expertly unfastened her lacy-pushup bra eagerly cupping her right breast. "…made all the difference in the world to me," he added, swallowing hard, and then he went on. "I couldn't have snapped out of my silly state of depression if it hadn't been for you. I owe you big time." He pulled her close to him and smiled.

An instant later, he pulled his car off of the freeway onto another emergency ramp. Tonya smiled knowingly, shaking her head in admiration of the detective's large appetite for sex. She spoke to him softly as he unbuttoned her suit jacket. "Glad I could be there for you, Detective," she said, wrapping her arms around his neck. She went on. "I hope you understand that what happened between us today had nothing to do with my love or lack of love for Charles. I want you to know, Gabe, I have no regrets. I made love to you because you needed me." She swallowed hard and then continued, "And of course, I wanted to. You're an amazing lover, and I enjoyed what we shared today very much. It was very special to me."

He smiled appreciatively and then silenced her with another one of his fiery hot kisses. Thirty minutes later, he started the engine to his car on his way back to the police station to drop the D.A. off to her car, which was still parked in the back parking lot of the Boston Police Department.

P.I. extraordinaire Charles Mason was also feeling rather proud of himself after finally convincing Nouri Sommers to stop by the Boston Police Department and have a one-on-one with Detective Gabe Baldwin, the man of her dreams and also the father of the child that was growing inside of her. He had convinced her that Gabe had a right to know about the child.

Charles hoped that when the two star-crossed lovers saw one another again, everything would somehow just magically fall into its proper place for them. "Ah, women." He sighed out loud as he continued to drive to his rescheduled rendezvous point to meet with former federal agent John Harman.

Anxious to pick up the photographs of the abandoned warehouse he had asked the ex-agent to get for him, Charles knew that without them, he couldn't wrap up his current case. *Another productive day.* He picked up his cell phone and attempted to reach his fiancée for the sixth time that day. He released a disappointed sigh when he was told the district attorney had not returned from the Boston Police Department. After thanking Tonya's secretary, he dialed the number to the police station.

After filling the police captain in on "the Nouri and Gabe situation," the private investigator teased with Mark a little about holding his fiancée captive for the biggest part of the day. Hearing that the captain hadn't seen Tonya or Gabe all day was of no major concern to Charles, just a little disappointing.

Of course, on the other hand he did feel a little guilty, knowing he was trying to reach Tonya to cancel yet another dinner date. But he had no choice in the matter—Nouri Sommers needed him, and as usual, she seemed to still be coming in first in his life—a habit he knew he would soon have to break.

Nouri Sommers' downtown chauffeur James dropped her off in the back of the Boston Police Department. She wanted to sneak in the back way hoping to surprise Detective Gabe Baldwin. She asked her driver not to wait, uncertain as to what her plans would be after she saw the detective again.

Nouri was hoping the detective would be so happy to see her that he would rush into her arms, smothering her with hundreds of his much-missed fiery hot kisses and then carry her off into the sunset. Where exactly didn't really matter, as long as they were together again. She released a sigh of eager anticipation, tightly closing her eyes as though she was making a wish.

Opening her eyes again, all feelings of hopefulness quickly vanished as swiftly as they had occurred. She gasped for air and clutched her stomach as she struggled against tears. In stunned dismay she found herself suddenly staring at the man of her dreams, the father of the child she was now carrying, and the man she had swallowed her pride to come and see—standing in front of her eyes, passionately embracing his best friend's fiancée.

"Oh God, this can't be happening!" Nouri cried as she continued to torture herself, watching the two lovers through tear-filled eyes.

She felt her heart skip a beat when the kissing couple disappeared back inside his car. She reached for the wrought iron railing attached to the side of the steps she had been standing on. Holding on with a tight grip, she used the railing as a tool to brace herself as she sat down on the cold, hard step and cried hysterically, unable to control her tears. "Oh God, Gabe! How could you?" she sobbed and sobbed and sobbed.

An eternity passed before the detective and the female district attorney exited the car. Once again Nouri watched as the turned-on couple passionately embraced before the D.A. finally tried to straighten her skirt and matching jacket. Gabe leaned over to kiss Tonya again as she attempted to put her hair back into place. He leaned against the side of his car as Tonya nervously glanced around the parking lot before bringing her attention back to him.

Nouri continued to watch them in heartbroken pain. She had no way of knowing what was actually being said, but if there were any truth to the old saying "a picture paints a thousand words," then the handsome detective and the D.A. were apparently saying plenty!

Suddenly, Charles Mason's fiancée turned to leave, but not before glancing back over her shoulder and blowing a kiss and a wink of her eye to the detective.

Nouri felt heartsick and betrayed as she continued to sit on the cement step, clinging tightly to the rod iron railing.

Several moments later, Tonya sped past where Nouri was seated. She rolled down her car window and waved good-bye to the detective one final time. Nouri quickly turned her face, not wanting Tonya or Gabe to recognize her. Not that they would have; they were both much too preoccupied to notice anything.

As Nouri turned back around to look at the detective, she saw him reach inside his car and pull out his cell phone, straighten his slacks, his shirt, and comb his beautiful thick hair all at the same time. *Obviously a man used to straightening himself up in a hurry!* She forced herself to her feet. Suddenly they felt as heavy as lead. She desperately wanted to run away, but she couldn't move. "Oh God!" she whispered under her breath when the detective looked as though he was going to walk her way. She quickly sat back down on the step and instinctively buried her head in her lap, pulling her arms tightly over her head.

Please don't let him recognize me...Please don't let him recognize me! she was saying over and over in he mind when he suddenly walked up to where she was sitting.

"Are you all right, miss?" he asked in a concerned manner, gently tapping her on the shoulder.

Go away! Go away! she was silently thinking when she heard him repeat himself to her again.

No, I'm not okay, you miserable jackass! I'm carrying your baby while you're out screwing your best friend's fiancée. She wanted to jump to her feet and shout in his face, but instead she nodded her head yes, quietly mumbling the words, "I'm fine."

He shook his head, tapping her on the shoulder again. "Are you sure there isn't anything I can help you with, miss?" he said again.

Yeah, you can go and find a goddamn lake somewhere and jump into it! But she responded to his question with another shake of her head, mumbling, "I'm fine," again.

"Miss, would you please look at me. My name is Detective Gabe Baldwin. Here, you want to see my badge," he said, reaching inside his jacket pocket to pull it out. But he had forgotten to get it when he left his house.

Realizing he had left his badge at home after changing clothes, he shook his head and released a frustrated sigh. "Listen, I'll be right back. I seem to have forgotten my badge. Wait here. I'll be right back. I'll run inside and get another one," he said, patting her gently across the shoulders. An instant later, he ran up the short flight of stairs, taking them two at a time. He glanced at her as he opened the door to the station, thinking to himself there was something oddly familiar about the sobbing woman in distress!

After Gabe completely disappeared out of sight, Nouri quickly jumped to her feet and swiftly began walking as fast as her legs would carry her around the side of the building, hoping she would be far enough out of sight by the time the detective returned. *Whew, that was too close for comfort.* She nervously opened her handbag and pulled out her sunglasses and put them on.

"Where the hell did she disappear to so quickly?" the detective complained, scratching the side of his head and glancing around. He caught a glimpse of her skirt as she rounded the front of the building. He ran after her, but by the time he reached the front of the building, his mystery lady had completely disappeared out of sight.

"Women!" he whispered, under his breath, scratching his head in puzzlement.

Chapter 17

Nouri Sommers had had enough of two-timing men to last her for a lifetime. "Men!" she mumbled angrily as she continued to walk along the busy sidewalks of downtown Boston. She didn't know where she was going exactly, and she didn't care.

"Oh God, I need a drink," she whispered, glancing around her surroundings for a restaurant with a lounge area. "Oh great!" She noticed a neon sign that was brightly flashing the words "B.J.'s Bottoms Up." It showed a decorated toothpick piercing an olive inside the glass.

She hurried inside, taking several moments for her eyes to adjust from the brighter outside light to a more dimly lit one. As her vision adjusted, she glanced around the room, quickly realizing by the massive group of people inside the lounge it must be cocktail hour.

There was no empty table, but she did see an empty barstool at the bar. She slowly pushed her way through the crowd of people and started for the only open seat in the house. But before she could sit down, someone rudely snatched the barstool away. She gave a curse under her breath louder than she had intended.

"Excuse me, miss?" the man who had stolen her seat remarked, overhearing her angry complaint. He smiled brightly, noticing her attractiveness.

She shook her head in annoyance, leveling her angry gaze on the rude man. "Oh, nothing. I was just cursing because you stole that seat right out from under me!"

The middle-aged, well-dressed man smiled at her candor and stood up. "Here, please sit down. I didn't mean to be rude. Let me buy you a drink to make up for my lack of good manners," he said, throwing a hand in mid-air in an attempt to get the attention of one of the busy bartenders. "What would you like?" he added with a grin.

Nouri returned the smile and sat on the barstool. "Oh, I don't know," she said. "Maybe a margarita, oh, and ask them to put extra salt around the rim of the glass, please," she added as a second thought, suddenly craving something both tart and sweet.

As the man glanced back at the attractive young woman for whom he had just ordered a drink, it suddenly dawned on him who was now sitting in his seat. *Oh my God!* He swallowed hard and nervously turned to his friend sitting on the next barstool, poking him in the side with an elbow, silently trying to get his attention without the billionairess noticing. "Ah, my name is Daniel Mosley, and this is my friend Tim Jacobs," he said nervously.

The two former Boston Police detectives quickly exchanged a disbelieving wide-eyed stare. "Holy shit!" Tim whispered under his breath.

Daniel quickly poked his friend in the side again. "Shhh," he whispered quietly, turning his attention back to Nouri Sommers.

"It's nice to meet both of you. My name is Nouri…ah, ah…Nouri St. Charles," she said after much thought, not wanting the two strangers to know her true identity.

Daniel nervously picked up his bottle of beer. "Ah, yeah. It's nice to meet you, too. Do you come here often?" he asked, before downing half his bottle of beer in one long swallow.

She shook her head. "No, actually, this is my first time here. Wow, they sure do get busy, huh? I almost didn't stay." Nouri shifted uncomfortably on her seat. "How about you guys, do you come here often?"

Daniel nodded. "Oh yeah, more than we should, probably." He smiled. "Actually, this place has one of the hottest cocktail hours around. Look over there," he said, pointing in the direction of several long tableclothed tables filled with both hot and cold hors d'oeuvres and appetizers. "Drinks are two-for-one, and you get all you want to eat for free. Best deal around," he went on, causing her to giggle in spite of herself.

He glanced at her curiously when she laughed. "Did I say something funny?"

She chuckled again shaking her head. "No, I'm sorry. It's just that you reminded me of an old friend—your remark, I mean." She smiled.

"An old friend, huh?" he echoed, smiling.

"Yes, a very dear friend. His name is Charles Mas…" She stopped, thinking how much she needed the famous P.I. at that very moment. She swallowed hard. "Oh, never mind. It doesn't matter," she said, lifting her bar napkin and blotting tears from the corners of her eyes, unaware that the running mascara had left small dark smudges beneath her eyes and darkened tear stains on her cheeks.

Daniel was moved by her sadness. "Are you all right? I couldn't help but notice…"

"That I've been crying?" She cleared her throat. "Oh, I'm fine. I…I've just had a tough day. That's all."

"You're sure you're okay?" He smiled, first glancing at her and then at the bartender. "Three more, please," he mouthed the words, nodding to the bartender and pointing to the three of them. The bartender returned the nod and briefly glanced in Nouri's direction.

Realizing how upset the beautiful young billionairess was and having no idea how long she would stay at the bar, Daniel knew he had better inform P.I. Charles Mason of the situation A.S.A.P. There was no way in hell the two former police detectives were going to leave a woman like Nouri Sommers in a bar all by herself, especially in the downtown area with the evening just around the corner. God only knows what could happen to her. Not only had the recent death of her husband suddenly made her the wealthiest woman in the world, but she was also one of the most beautiful women in the world. Charles Mason would have their heads served on a silver platter if anything were to happen to her, and both men knew it. She could be kidnapped, raped, robbed, or worse! Daniel shivered at the chilling thought and decided to excuse himself to go to the restroom, and then he would make that call to the famous Boston P.I.

Turning his attention back to the lovely woman silently sitting beside him nervously toying with the tiny swizzle stick in her drink glass, he set his empty beer bottle down. "Nouri, would you mind watching my beer while I run to the little boys' room?" He glanced at his watch and shrugged. "Guess I'd better make a quick phone call, too," he added playfully.

She giggled at his silliness, agreeing to keep an eye on his empty beer bottle. *Duh!* She rolled her eyes.

Following the silent cue from his partner, Tim moved protectively closer to Nouri. He glanced at her, smiling. "So, do you work around here, Nouri?" he asked, not knowing what else to say on a moment's notice.

She chuckled at his obviousness nervousness to talk to her. "Ah, no, actually, I don't. I'm…ah, unemployed at the present, Tim. That is what your friend said your name is, wasn't it?" she remarked, reaching for her drink.

"Yes, Tim. That's my name," he returned, stealing a glimpse at her unbelievable beauty, silently thinking, *No wonder the famous P.I. and the Boston Police detective are both willing to go to war if necessary over her.* "Whew," he sighed lustfully out loud, shaking his head.

Nouri overheard the sigh and glanced at him suspiciously. "Did you say something?"

He flushed, shifting his gaze from her beautiful, tear-stained face to his beer. "Ah, no actually, I was just thinking out loud," he confessed.

"About what? I mean if you don't mind me asking." She smiled.

"Well, since you asked, I was curious as to why a beautiful woman like yourself, a woman who has very obviously been crying her heart out, would come into a downtown bar like this all alone in all her vulnerability. There are a lot of guys who would love to cash in on an opportunity like that, Nouri."

She chuckled shaking her head. "You were wondering all that, were you, with just one sigh, huh?" she playfully remarked.

He flushed again. "Well, it was a big sigh!" he countered. "And you did ask me what I had been wondering about, didn't you?" he added, waving to the bartender to bring them another round.

"So I did," she said, setting her empty glass down.

"Well?" His tone was curious.

"Well, yes, I have been crying. As you said, that much was obvious. But I'm okay, now. Nothing I can't handle. And as far as being by myself—actually, I'm meeting someone for dinner soon." She picked up her fresh drink and took a sip.

"Well, that's a relief as long as you're not by your…"

Daniel interrupted them when he forced his body between Nouri's barstool and his friend's. He grinned. "Well, did you two miss me?" he teased, making eye contact with his partner.

Nouri giggled.

"So did your date decide to cancel out on you again tonight, Daniel?" his partner remarked—his way of silently asking if his partner had been successful in making contact with the famous P.I.

"Huh?" Daniel said before realizing what his partner was asking. He shook his head and went on, "Oh, Megan. Yeah, well, my life story. Oh well, guess I'll just have to let Nouri here buy me dinner tonight, huh?" He smiled teasingly, flashing her a playful wink.

She laughed out loud, amused by it all. "I don't think my dinner date would like that very much, Daniel, sorry," she said, shrugging her shoulders playfully.

"Your date!" he exclaimed. "Damn, I lose more good women that way!" He flashed her another teasing wink, and she giggled again in spite of her gloom.

Nouri picked up her empty drink glass and began licking the salt around the rim, as Daniel ordered them another round. "So, what do you two funny guys do for a living?" she asked, exciting both men by the way she continued to lick the salt from around the rim of her glass. They swallowed hard. She went on. "I mean, beside trying to pick up on women in bars to buy you dinner," she added, smiling.

Both men laughed without responding. Instead they nervously downed their beers and ordered more.

After she finished her drink Nouri excused herself to go to the ladies' room to freshen her makeup and comb her hair. She had a dinner date soon, and she didn't want her date to know she had been crying.

Having dinner with young Rick Hobner wasn't the only reason she had decided to keep her date that evening. She also knew Charles Mason would be at the restaurant looking for her, and she needed him now more than ever. "Oh, big guy, I need you," she whispered, taking one final glance in the mirror before leaving the ladies' room.

Chapter 18

Private Investigator Charles Mason paused in mid-sentence as he glanced at the telephone number beeping on his pager. He sipped the last of his drink and slid out of the booth he had been sitting in talking to former F.B.I. agent John Harman for the past thirty minutes.

"John, order us another drink. I'll be right back. Tess is paging me. She's beeped in 911. It must be important. Here, give me the photographs of the abandoned warehouse and I'll glance at them while I'm on the payphone," he said, holding out his hand.

John pulled several packs of photos from out of his jacket pocket. "Here you go, Charles," he said, glancing around the lounge for the cocktail waitress.

Charles walked down a small dimly lit hallway looking for a payphone; cursing himself under his breath for leaving his cell phone in the car.

After his private secretary relayed Daniel Mosley's urgent message about Nouri Sommers, Charles shoved the packs of photographs into his jacket pocket and rushed out of the Ye Old Saloon as fast as his long legs would carry him. He was still unaware of the incriminating negatives of his beautiful fiancée and his best friend now safely tucked away inside the inner pocket of his suit jacket.

The former F.B.I. agent shook his head, seeing the famous P.I. flying past him on his way out the door. He hardly heard him mumble the words "I'll phone you later."

The P.I. jumped into his car and was at B.J.'s Bottoms Up in less than five minutes.

Police Detective Gabe Baldwin paused just inside the wide double doors of the Boston Police Department after spotting young police officer Rick Hobner. With a great deal of restraint, he quickly turned to leave, running rapidly down the small set of stairs, only to just as quickly change his mind, run back up the steps and back inside the station; deciding after all to beat the young loudmouth cop's brains out. He raced inside the building without batting an eye, taking the young cop by surprise and grabbing him like a child's rag doll. Gabe shoved him inside the men's locker room before the young cop knew what hit him.

Lucky for the stunned young cop, police captain Mark Lane appeared just in time to stop a punch that surely would have broken the young officer's jawbone.

"Gabe, goddamn it! What the hell is wrong with you, for chrissakes?" the captain shouted, pulling the detective away from the young cop.

"Let me go, Mark! I'm going to kill the slippery, loudmouth, lying, little prick!" Gabe yelled.

Holding the hot-tempered detective up against the wall with his powerful grip, the captain shook his head in amazement. "Gabe, knock it off! And, by God, I mean now!" He leveled his gaze to the detective's.

"Get the fuck off of me, Captain! This is between me and Pretty Boy Floyd over there!" he barked, attempting to remove the captain's strong hold on him.

"Get a grip, for chrissakes, Gabe!"

Gabe could feel his jawbone jerk and the muscles in his face tighten the angrier he became. "Mark, I'm asking you for the last goddamn time to get the fuck off of me! I'm going to kill that little bastard, and no one is going to stop me! Not you, not the goddamn Pope himself! Now move!"

The captain shook his head, tightening his hold on the detective. "Oh really, Detective?" he said, glancing over at the scared young cop. "Get the fuck out of here, Hobner! Take your goddamn ass home and don't leave there until I personally tell you to! Do you understand me? Your eight o'clock dinner date has been canceled!" he shouted.

Without speaking, young Hobner raced out of the locker room as fast his legs would move.

Once the young cop was out of sight, the captain backed away from the police detective. He leveled his gaze on him. "And as for you, Gabriel Anthony Baldwin, let's go! You and I are going down the goddamn street, have a few drinks, and talk this goddamn thing out. Let's go!" he ordered, leading the way.

Once outside, the police captain glanced at his uptight friend, shook his head, and then began laughing.

Gabe glanced at him from the corner of his eye.

"Gabe, you almost blew it back there! You scared that poor goddamn kid half to death. I bet he pissed his pants all the way home!" he said with a chuckle.

"Why did you stop me, Mark?"

"Hey, man, you've got to be kidding!"

Gabe released a frustrated sigh. "Like it or not, I'm going to break that little bastard in half! He's got a good ass-kicking coming, and he knows it," he said, angrily shoving his hands into his trouser pockets.

"For chrissakes, Gabe, I talked to the kid myself this morning, and he explained the photographs. He told me that the first picture of them, the one taken inside that seafood restaurant, wasn't what it appeared to be."

The detective looked at the police captain curiously. "What do you mean?"

"He said that he, James and Jerry ran into Nouri Sommers at the restaurant. She was by herself, so they invited her to join them for dinner. She reluctantly accepted the invitation."

"And the kiss that apparently rocked Pretty Boy Floyd's world?" Gabe asked jealously.

Mark chuckled. "Gabe, shit! The kid was trying to hide her face from the goddamn press. He thought he was protecting her."

"Oh really? Can't wait to hear the reason why she spent the night with the little prick!" His tone was one of disbelief.

Mark frowned, annoyed at his friend's attitude. "Nouri Sommers didn't sleep with Hobner, for chrissakes! She spent the night at his apartment, sure! She had too much to drink. According to Hobner they all did. But he slept on the couch. He gave her his bed to sleep in."

"Yeah, right!"

"It's the truth, Gabe! James and Jerry told me the same story. Said that's exactly how it went down."

"And the photograph of them kissing outside his apartment the next morning?"

"Apparently a kiss of gratitude. You know, 'thanks for looking after me last night.' That kind of kiss, Gabe."

"And that's what Hobner told you?"

"Yes, and Mason says that's what Nouri told him, too."

"Charles?" He sounded surprised.

Mark nodded. "Yeah, Charles told me he went to check on her this morning right after you left his place."

Gabe removed his hands from his pockets and glanced at his friend. "Did Charles say if Nouri had anything else to say?"

"Yeah. She apparently had a great deal to say."

"Like what?" Gabe asked jealously.

"Well, he told me that she had made a date with Hobner for this evening.

A dinner date. She was supposed to meet him at that fancy new Greek joint down on Eighth Street. You know the one I mean?"

Gabe nodded. "Yeah, I do. The Trojan Horse. A date, huh? Why?"

"Mason told me that she felt sorry for the kid. Apparently it took him a long time to get enough courage to ask her to dinner. She didn't want to hurt his feelings, especially after he had taken such good care of her the night before," Mark said, shrugging his broad shoulders rather matter-of-factly, as they continued to walk down the street heading for B.J.'s Bottoms Up, the police captain's favorite watering hole.

"Let me hazard. Another thank-you gesture?" He shook his head.

The captain said with a chuckle, "I guess you could say that."

"Right!" Gabe sighed heavily. "This version is certainly different from the one I heard him boasting about to all the other young cops in the locker room this morning," he added, glancing at the time.

"I'm sure. Hey, we all know how Rick is. Nobody pays the little prick any attention with anything he has to say, especially when it comes to him and the ladies."

"What else did Charles have to say?"

"He said that he made her admit that she was still very much in love with you. He also said she was sorry if she had made you feel responsible for Clint Chamberlain's death in any way. That she never meant to make you feel that way. And he told me that she also said she was sorry for telling you to get out. She never really meant it. She was still angry with you for the way you had been treating her after catching her leaving Chamberlain's hotel. She had only gone to his hotel to say her good-bye to the man. You assumed the worst and that hurt her deeply—you wouldn't let her explain."

"She say anything else to Charles?"

"Yes, he said that she told him that she was going to drop by the station to talk to you. Swallowing her pride and coming to you wasn't an easy thing for her to do, but she sincerely wanted to work things out."

"And when was she supposedly going to do that?"

"Charles said he was at her place having breakfast. He stayed most of the afternoon talking to her, and afterwards he walked her down to the limo. James was supposed to drop her off. That was about an hour or so ago, I think." Mark glanced at his watch.

Suddenly remembering the familiarity of the young woman who had been setting on the stairway at the police station, hiding her face and sobbing her heart out, Gabe swallowed nervously. "Shit!" he spat angrily, stomping his feet on the sidewalk.

"Gabe, what is it? What's wrong?"

As Gabe turned to face his boss, he glanced over his shoulder, quickly recognizing Charles Mason intimately embracing Nouri Sommers as they stood beside his car. He instantly felt the pang of an arrow pierce his heart. "Never mind, Mark," he said.

Mark turned to see what suddenly had Gabe's undivided attention. In stunned amazement, he patted the detective across his shoulders in a fatherly manner. "Come on, son, let's go have that drink, now," he said, pointing across the street to his favorite watering hole.

Too upset to speak, Gabe silently nodded and followed his friend.

Chapter 19

Once inside the police captain's favorite watering hole, Detective Gabe Baldwin instantly spotted two familiar faces. "Come on, Captain, I see someone I want to talk to," he said, nodding in the direction of the bar.

"Who is it?" Mark asked.

"A couple of guys I once worked with. You remember Mosley and Jacobs, don't you? I think they're doing some undercover work for former F.B.I. agent John Harmon, now; mostly jobs for Charles Mason." Gabe pushed his way through the massive crowd of cocktail-hour drinkers, and leaned against the bar, putting his right foot on the top of the brass railing as he faced his two former colleagues. When both men recognized the police detective, they nervously shifted on their barstools and shared a quick glance of surprise.

"Mosley, Jacobs. Remember us?" Gabe asked, in a sarcastic tone, propping his elbow on the padded skirting of the bar.

Daniel swallowed nervously. "Hey Baldwin, Captain, imagine running into you here."

"Small world, ain't it, boys?" the captain said, attempting to flag down one of the busy bartenders.

"So it would seem," Tim remarked, glancing nervously at his friend again and shifting uncomfortably on his barstool. "So what brings you two scoundrels out this time of the day?" he added, picking up his bottle of beer and taking a long swallow.

Gabe noticed and fought back a grin, knowing his presence had disturbed his former co-workers. And he had a pretty good idea why.

The captain chuckled, enjoying himself, watching the two former police detectives squirm around Gabe, remembering there had been no love lost between them in the past. "Just felt like having a few shots. It's been a long day," he returned. "Two shots of bourbon over here, please," he shouted loudly, finally getting the attention of one of the bartenders.

Gabe picked up his shot glass after the bartender sat his drink down. "Bring us a couple more shots of bourbon and whatever those two clowns are drinking," he said, giving a nod in the direction of his two former associates before belting his shot of liquor. He glanced at Daniel and Tim, who seemed to be cringing. "Whew!" Gabe sighed.

"Speaking of clowns," he said with a grin. "What are you two guys up to tonight?"

Daniel set his beer bottle down. "Not much. We just finished doing a little work for Mason involving that abandoned warehouse down on Third Street. Thought we'd relax and have a few." He shrugged.

"Oh yeah, I know the warehouse you're talking about. It's the one that new drug cartel kingpin just abandoned," Gabe said.

"Oh, you know about that, huh?" Daniel sounded surprised.

"Yeah, drug kingpin from Havana." The detective paused thoughtfully for a moment. "Guising as a major corporation these days, I hear," he added, glancing around the bar.

"Yeah that's right, Detective. Feds are going to nail that bastard real soon." Daniel chuckled.

"Mason working with the Feds on that one, Mosley?" Mark asked.

"You know it. He's just about got his end of the investigation wrapped up. John just dropped off the last few sets of photographs on the case this afternoon," Daniel returned, suddenly remembering the incriminating negatives of the district attorney and the naked detective that had been accidentally included in the final set of photographs on the abandoned warehouse. He smiled and flushed at the same time.

Gabe noticed. "That must have been some thought, Daniel. It had you smiling and blushing at the same time," he remarked, reaching for his shot of bourbon.

Daniel cleared his throat nervously. "Oh, it was nothing. You guys ready for another shot?" He quickly glanced at his partner again.

"Sure, why not?" Gabe accepted and then went on, "So tell me, Daniel, I know John mostly does the one-on-ones with Mason, but I was just curious; have you two guys seen him lately? I mean, since his return from France?" he asked, hoping to catch the two men in an out-and-out lie.

Suspecting the detective already knew the answer to that question since he had walked into the bar only moments after the P.I. had left, he found himself suddenly curious as to why Gabe would inquire about something he already knew the answer to. Then it dawned on him. The detective's real question wasn't about the P.I. at all, but more along the lines of who Charles Mason had left the bar with and why.

He grinned and said, "Yeah. As a matter of fact, he just left here with the Sommers broad."

The police captain glanced at the detective, curious as to what he was up to.

"Nouri?" Gabe asked, trying to sound surprised.

Daniel nodded, glancing at his friend mischievously, deciding to rub the police detective's jealous nose in it, for he surmised that Gabe was still very much in love with the beautiful billionairess. Tim nervously shook his head, as a silent warning to his friend to leave it alone.

Shrugging the warning off, Daniel grinned wickedly at his friend and went on. "Yeah, Tim and I spotted her in here." He glanced at his watch. "She was by herself and it was quite obvious she was very upset about something. From the looks of it she had been crying something fierce; had eye makeup running down her cheeks and, well, it was goddamn heartbreaking." He shook his head. "There was no way in hell Tim and I were going to leave her in here by herself…"

Gabe cut in. "Did she say what was wrong?" he asked nervously, already suspecting he was the cause of her unhappiness.

Daniel shot Tim a sneaky grin and then turned his attention back to the detective. "Men in general, I think." He shrugged, throwing his hand in mid-air for the bartender.

"What do you mean?" the police captain jumped into the conversation with interest.

"We overheard her mumbling something about all men were two-timing bastards!" He chuckled. "She may have a point, eh, Detective?" he added, leveling a suspicious gaze at Gabe.

Gabe's expression quickly turned angry. "What the fuck is that supposed to mean, Mosley?" he snapped, slamming his shot glass down on the bar and turning to face him.

Tim slid off his barstool as he remembered the detective's hot temper. "Hey, lighten up, Gabe. Daniel didn't mean anything by it, okay?" he injected on behalf of his friend, silently preparing himself for battle.

Gabe felt his blood begin to boil at an alarming rate. "Okay, Mosley, spit it out! I know your ass too well; what's up?" he demanded.

Tim stopped his friend from speaking with a nudge to the side. "Cool it, Daniel! We could lose our goddamn job if you…"

Daniel cut in angrily. "Fuck it, Tim, I don't give a shit!" he drunkenly spat. "We're going to get our asses fired when Mason sees those goddamn negatives anyway!" he added.

Gabe and Mark glanced curiously at one another. "What fucking negatives?" the police captain asked.

Tim tried to silence his loudmouth friend again. "Please, Daniel, just calm down; it's not worth it!" he cautioned.

"You heard the captain, Mosley—what fucking negatives?" Gabe demanded, reaching for his former colleague's upper arm.

Daniel jerked his arm free, shooting the police detective a dagger. "Okay, Mr. Dynamo! I'll tell the captain. I'm talking about Mr. Stickrod here and the district attorney; that's what I'm talking about!" he shouted drunkenly, glancing at the stunned expression now plastered across Gabe's face.

"You son-of-a-bitch!" Gabe cried with passion, reaching once again for Daniel's upper arm, but the captain quickly stopped him.

"Calm down, Gabe! What the hell is Mosley talking about?"

Gabe ignored his boss's question and reached inside his trouser pocket for his wallet, pulled out a twenty-dollar bill, and tossed it on top of the bar. "Come on, Mark, let's get the fuck out of here before I kill this drunken son-of-a-bitch!" he snapped, jabbing his index finger into Daniel Mosley's chest before turning to leave.

Daniel slid off his barstool. "Hey, Captain," he blurted out loudly, causing Mark to glance back over his shoulder. "Your super-dick detective spent the day fucking her goddamn brains out; that's what I'm talking about!" He laughed wickedly.

Tim shook his head, knowing it was coming, and wasn't surprised when the police detective suddenly punched his friend in the face. The punch was so powerful it instantly broke the poor man's nose. Blood began to spurt everywhere.

Police captain Mark Lane wasted no time trying to make the detective leave. "Come on, Gabe, you son-of-a-bitch!" he said, with a tone of authority as he continued physically shoving the detective out of the bar. "What the fuck is wrong with you, for chrissakes! You want to lose that goddamn badge of yours? Is that what the fuck you're trying to do, for chrissakes?" he continued scolding Gabe until after he finally managed to get him outside.

"You want my goddamn badge, Mark? Then take the son-of-a-bitch!" Gabe shouted, reaching inside his jacket pocket, looking for the badge; momentarily forgetting he had left his badge at home earlier that afternoon. For a few moments he continued to pat himself down, trying to locate his badge, until he remembered where it was. "Shit!" he spat.

"Now what the fuck is wrong, Gabe?" Mark asked with a frown.

"I left my fucking badge at home." Gabe sighed hopelessly.

"Forget the goddamn badge, for chrissakes, I don't want the damn thing!" Mark returned heatedly, shaking his head.

"So what the fuck do you want, Captain? My head on a goddamn platter?" Gabe shot his friend an angry glance.

The police captain released a frustrated sigh and shook his head again. “No, what I want, Gabe, is for you to stop acting this way. Get that goddamn head of yours screwed back on straight and let’s get back to business as usual around here; that’s what the fuck I want! We’ve got unsolved cases out the goddamn wazoo we need to deal with, Detective, in case you have forgotten!”

Mark paused to catch his breath and then continued, “Gabe, get your goddamn act together! And don’t come back to work until you do, got it?” he said sharply, shaking his head and walking away from his friend. A few moments later, he glanced back over his shoulder. “And one more thing while I’m at it, Gabe; maybe you should try keeping it in your goddamn pants more often. Your actions as of late have been hurting a lot of goddamn people, some of whom used to be your goddamn friends!” His tone was one of disappointment. He hung his head, shoved his hands into his pockets, and hurried across the street to the police station.

“Fuck it!” Gabe shouted, angrily kicking an empty beer can that had been lying on the sidewalk. He stood frozen in place as he continued to watch the man who through the years had become closer to him than his real father. He watched as Mark disappeared around the following corner.

Chapter 20

Charles Mason quietly slid out of bed and tiptoed across the room, gently closing the door behind him, trying not to wake the beautiful, heartbroken Nouri Sommers, the woman he had just spent the past several hours making love to.

He quietly cursed under his breath each step he took going down the long, dreaded flight of stairs in his beautiful Victorian mansion. "Gabe, you fucking idiot!" He shook his head angrily at his absent friend, because of what Nouri had witnessed the police detective doing with another woman earlier that evening. Just who the mystery woman was the famous P.I. had no idea; Nouri had not said.

Charles Mason was anxious to fix himself a much needed shot of bourbon and study the photographs former federal agent John Harman had given him on a case he had been working on for the P.I. surrounding an abandoned warehouse down on Third Street. He was also anxious to phone his friend Robert Barnet with the F.B.I. to give him the green light for their long-awaited arrest of drug kingpin Ricardo Montoya of Havana. Charles belted a shot of bourbon to calm the stress of the past twenty-four hours.

Then the private eye crossed the room, heading for his suit jacket lying across an overstuffed chair. He removed the photographs he had tucked away inside one of the pockets. They were the photographs of the case he had been working on since his return from France. As he pulled the stack of photos from the pocket, a stack of negatives fell to the floor. He glanced down and picked up the negatives with one hand as he continued glancing at the first set of prints of the abandoned warehouse in his other hand. He returned to the bar and poured himself another drink, still glancing at the photographs in one hand while clutching the incriminating negatives in the other.

Curious as to what the negatives were, Charles took them inside his study for better examination under the bright light of his desk lamp.

Immediately recognizing his fiancée and the naked police detective, he continued to study the negatives heartbrokenly, for several long moments, while his world seemed to be caving in on him. He opened the desk drawer and placed the graphic negatives inside, shut the drawer and locked it. Visibly shaken, he hurried back to the bar and quickly belted several more shots of liquor before telephoning his fiancée. Sadly, he dialed her number.

"Hi cupcake," he said, forcing himself to sound pleasant.

Hearing her fiancé's voice on the other end of the phone line caused the female D.A. to tense. She swallowed hard, overcome with guilt as she quickly recalled her actions with the heartbroken police detective from earlier in the day. "Hello yourself, darling," she replied nervously.

"I…I tried to reach you several times throughout the day, Tonya. Do you mind telling me where you were all day?" Charles asked with a deep sigh of frustration as he waited for her reply.

After a few moments of uncomfortable silence, she carefully tried to select her words. "I…ah, I was helping a friend who needed me very badly today," she finally managed with a great deal of difficulty, not wanting to confess what she had really been up to or to tell Charles a lie. She swallowed nervously, sensing by his tone and his question that something was wrong—very wrong—and she had a very good idea what that something was. *But how did he find out?*

"I see," he responded, reaching for his drink. "And this friend of yours was a male?" His tone was laced with jealousy.

"Yes, Charles. This friend was male," she replied nervously.

He rubbed his chin thoughtfully before speaking. "I see. And after helping your friend out today." He paused to light a cigarette and then continued. "Did your help make a difference?" he asked, in a hoarse whisper of hurt.

"I'd like to think so, Charles," she answered, setting her brandy snifter down on top of the bar. At that point she no longer had any doubt that the famous P.I. had indeed found out about her afternoon delight with the handsome police detective, his former partner and one-time best friend. She swallowed hard.

"And there would be no more occasion for this friend of yours to seek out your…" He paused swallowing hard trying to stop the tears from building deep inside of him. He calmed his emotions and then went on. "…assistance with his problems in the future?"

"No, Charles. I have no desire to help this friend out again. He needed me. I wanted to help. I…I have no regrets nor apologies to make," she said as she nervously continued to toy with the cord of the telephone line.

Charles cleared the tears from his throat. "I see. And if you should run into this friend of yours again, and he needed your help again, you're telling me that you not only could refuse to help this friend out again, but you wouldn't help this friend out again. Is that what you are telling me, Tonya?" His tone was sharp.

"Yes, Charles, that's what I'm saying."

"And you're quite sure?"

"Yes, darling. I'm quite sure." She struggled to keep from crying at having hurt the man she would forever love.

"And...you still want our marriage to take place?"

"Of course, Charles. What happened between my friend and me today had nothing to do with my love or lack of it for you. I...I love you, darling."

"I see. I'll have to give your afternoon indiscretion a little more thought. In the meantime I have your word that you won't see this friend of yours again in this manner?" He cleared the tears from his throat again.

"Yes, darling. You have my word on it," she said tearfully, hating the thought of having hurt Charles.

"Good. Now I have one final question for you, Tonya, if you don't mind," he went on. "Do you have any more such friends that I should know about before we get married?" he snipped, reaching for the liquor bottle again.

Tonya felt anger surge through her body at Charles' last remark. "That was a cruel and unnecessary thing for you to say to me, Charles. However, you apparently must feel the need. And in a way I suppose I can understand where you are coming from, though I don't agree with your way of dealing with this right now, especially when you go throwing around remarks like that at me. You haven't seen me making a fuss over Nouri Sommers or the time and energy you endlessly continue to..." She stopped talking, hearing the doorbell ring. "Charles," she said, "someone's at my front door. We'll have to continue this later."

Without responding, Charles quietly put the receiver down and walked back behind the bar to open a fresh bottle of bourbon. After he poured himself another shot, he circled the bar and sat on a barstool, glancing over his shoulder at Nouri Sommers, who had been silently standing in the background, listening to his every word.

She smiled, slowly walking up behind him and gently putting her arms snugly around his manly waist. "Big guy, I'm so sorry," she whispered, laying her head across his muscular shoulders.

He returned her smile with tears in his eyes. "Yeah, me too, sugar," he replied in a hoarse whisper as he lovingly patted her hand. After a few moments of silence, Charles gently pulled Nouri around to face him, holding her in his arms. "Why didn't you tell me the woman with Gabe was Tonya?"

She put her arms around his neck and hugged him tightly before bringing her gaze to level his. "Because I didn't want to hurt you, Charles," she said softly.

"I see," he said, putting his arms around her tiny waist. "Come on, Nouri, let's have a drink together and then go back to bed. This time, however, sugar, I'm the one that needs to be held," he said, lowering his head and kissing her softly, gently, sweetly.

Chapter 21

Tonya Daughtery shouted out to her maid as she heard her start down the stairs to answer the front door. "Don't worry about it, Eva. I'll get it," she called out while making her way toward the hallway leading to the front of the house.

She jerked the door open after recognizing the person standing outside. "Captain!" She stepped back, gesturing the police captain inside her home. "What a surprise! Come on in, and I'll fix us a drink," she said, leading the way. "What would you like, Mark?"

"A shot of bourbon will be fine, thanks," he replied, glancing around her home. Tonya gestured toward the large sofa as she made her way to the bar. "Nice place you have here," he added, unfastening the two buttons on his suit jacket as he sat down.

"Yeah, I like it," she replied, from across the room. She poured herself another shot of brandy and the police captain a shot of bourbon. She picked up the two drinks and went to join her friend. "What brings you out this way?" she asked, handing him the drink and then sitting hers on the coffee table, before flopping down into the chair opposite him.

The captain released a deep sigh of frustration before answering her question. "We need to talk, Tonya." His voice was shaky.

"Talk?" She leveled her eyes to him. "All right. What about?"

Mark nervously belted his drink and glanced at her as he set his shot glass on the coffee table. "My biggest concern is Gabe, of course. He's always been like a son to me."

She nodded, understanding how close the two of them had always been. "Yes, I know, Captain. What about Gabe? Has something happened? He is all right, isn't he?"

"Calm down. He hasn't been in an accident or anything like that, if that's what you mean." Mark quickly noticed the relieved expression cross Tonya's face as she lifted her drink.

"Well, then I don't understand. Why did you mention him?"

"Cut the shit, Tonya! We're friends here, aren't we?" he said sharply, shocking the female D.A. into a decisive nod of her head.

"Good. Then I intend to speak frankly." He sighed deeply, stood to his feet, and walked to the bar. He picked up the bottle of bourbon. "May I?" he asked, helping himself to another shot.

"Of course. You were saying, Mark?"

"I don't know where to start, so I'm just going to jump right in if that's okay with you." He swallowed nervously. "Gabe broke some goddamn guy's nose in a bar fight several hours ago," he said, shaking his head in disbelief.

"Oh, my God! Is Gabe all right?"

Mark nodded. "Physically, sure; not too many men can whip his ass!" He chuckled. "But emotionally, I'm not too sure," he added, shaking his head.

"What was the fight over?" Tonya asked, sipping at her drink. "No, wait, let me guess; Nouri Sommers, right?' She rolled her eyes.

"No, actually the fight was over you." He lifted the liquor bottle again.

Tonya could feel herself blushing. "Me!" she exclaimed. "I…I don't understand."

Mark walked back to the sofa with another shot in his hand. "Yeah, over you. Apparently, this guy…"

She cut in with interest. "What guy?"

Mark downed his shot of bourbon. "Maybe I should back up a bit. I think I may be getting a little ahead of myself," he said, nervously shifting his position.

"Maybe you should, Mark," Tonya agreed, reaching for her drink.

"I've got a major problem on my hands this evening surrounding Gabe in more ways than one." He sighed heavily.

"Problem? What problem?"

"The reason I'm here tonight, Tonya, is…that I was hoping to find Gabe. It's important that I find him. His dad is in a hospital in Greece; suffered a heart attack earlier this afternoon. His family has been trying to reach him since it happened. His dad is asking for him. And no one can find him. His family wants him to fly out A.S.A.P. on the company jet. I've got men out all over the goddamn city looking for—"

Tonya interrupted. "Why on earth would you think the detective would be here, for goodness sakes, Mark!"

"There I go getting ahead of myself again. Just let me start at the beginning," he said, jumping to his feet and going to the bar again.

Tonya rolled her eyes in dismay. "For chrissakes, Mark, you're making me a nervous goddamn wreck! Just bring the bottle of bourbon over here, and while you're at it, better bring the bottle of brandy. And for goodness sakes start spitting something out before I have a heart attack!" she snapped.

Trying to find a way to put it all together for the female D.A., the police captain nervously scratched the side of his head as he searched for the right words. "Okay, let me start by asking you a question," he said, picking up the liquor bottle. "Where do you think Charles is right this very moment?" he asked, glancing in her direction.

Tonya rolled her eyes, not understanding why the police detective was acting so strangely. "He's at home of course, Mark. Why?"

The police captain cleared his dry throat. "That's right. And do you know why he's at home, or as far as that goes, do you know who's there with him? Wait, before you say anything. Let me finish, Tonya. Nouri Sommers is there with him," he said, sitting the liquor bottle back down.

"What?" she exclaimed.

"Nouri Sommers is very upset, and apparently Mason is the only one who can comfort her now."

Tonya swallowed hard. "Well, that's just about to change, Captain! Once Charles and I get married, he knows she can't come first anymore," she said.

Ignoring the female D.A.'s remark, Mark continued. "Do you know why Nouri Sommers got so upset—so upset in fact it drove her right back into the strong arms of your fiancé?" He crossed the room carrying the two bottles of liquor.

Tonya shook her head with noticeable irritation. "How on earth would I know something like that?"

Mark noticed Tonya blush as he set the bottles of liquor on the coffee table. "She apparently saw you and Gabe together in the back parking lot of the police station late this afternoon."

Tonya nodded rather matter-of-factly. "I see. And she couldn't wait to go running into Charles' arms ratting me out, right?"

"No, I mean sure, she went running into Mason's arms, and sure, she told him what she had witnessed with her own two eyes, but she had told him that she didn't know who the mystery woman was that had been with Gabe."

"But Charles does know it was me, right?" Tonya asked. Of course he knew, she could tell by the telephone conversation they had had a short time earlier. She released a frustrated sigh shaking her head at the painful memory.

"I think you already know the answer to that question, Tonya!" Mark's tone suddenly took on a fatherly edge, causing her to both blush and shrug at the same time. She nervously picked up her drink.

"So, how did he find out then?" she asked curiously.

"By accident, I believe."

"I'm sorry, Mark, but I'm just not following you."

"Remember, I told you Gabe broke some guy's nose, tonight," he said. Tonya nodded. Mark went on. "Well, the guy's name is Daniel Mosley, he does…"

She cut in. "I know that name. Why?" she asked curiously.

"He used to…"

She cut in again. "I remember now; he used to be on the force. He worked undercover, right?"

"Yes, that's right. Now he and Tim Jacobs work for a former federal agent by the name of John Harman. Most of their work comes from your fiancé these days, I understand."

"Charles!"

The police captain shook his head. "Yeah, that's right. Undercover work on special assignments."

"Special assignments?"

"Yeah, tailing assignments, I spy, surveillance, that type of stuff mostly, I think."

"And you're saying what exactly?"

"Gabe broke Mosley's nose after learning they had been secretly filming every move you have been making for the past…"

Tonya stopped him angrily. "What?"

"Calm down, Tonya. It's not quite as bad as—"

"How dare that son-of-a-bitch have me followed! Who the hell—"

"Tonya, please calm down. It's not quite as bad as it seems. Mason was worried about you. After your episode with Christopher Graham six weeks ago—"

Tonya interrupted again. "I'm stunned, Mark! I can't believe Charles never told me he was having me followed—for my protection or not! He had no right!"

"Maybe you're right, Tonya, but let me finish, okay?" he asked. She nodded. Mark continued. "Anyway, apparently Mosley and Jacobs took some pretty incriminating photographs of you and Gabe…"

"Oh God!" she said, blushing. "Gabe was naked and all I had on was my skirt pulled up to my waist, right?"

"That's right. But after finding out about the photographs the two jerks had taken, their boss had told them never to mention the incident to anyone. Harmon personally burned all the photographs. All's well that ends well, right? Wrong, he forgot about the negatives, and apparently, somehow they got mixed up with the photographs of a case Mosley and Jacobs had been working on for Mason. Not knowing this, Harmon hands Mason the stack of warehouse photos, not realizing the incriminating negatives of you and Gabe…"

She cut in, shaking her head as she spoke, "So, Charles really did find out about my affair with Gabe by accident? Unbelievable! What the hell are the odds on something like that happening, I wonder, Mark?"

"I have no idea!" he said, scratching the side of his head and nervously glancing at his watch.

"All right, the damage is done, but if Mosley and Jacobs were given orders not to mention the photographs, then why did Mosley mention them to Gabe?"

"The two guys got into it. There never has been any love lost between them. Anyway, after one of Gabe's hot-tempered remarks to Mosley, his hurtful comeback was drunkenly spat out about the two of you and—"

"I see." Tonya shook her head in disbelief. "Thank you for telling me about things, Mark. I appreciate it."

"Well, save the thanks, kiddo! If I weren't so damn worried about Gabe right now, I wouldn't be here. He's been acting like a crazy man since last night. And after reading the newspaper about Nouri Sommers and…"

"Yes, I know, Captain."

"Well, shortly before he broke Mosley's nose at the bar, Gabe almost broke that young cop in two down at the station. That's why I took his ass out for a few drinks—to try and cool that goddamn hot-ass temper of his down before he hurts someone over that goddamn broad!"

"I understand, Mark. Gabe's hurting real bad right now. That's why I was with him today. He's miserable. His sadness affected me deeply. He needed to be held. So, I held him. I make no apologies for what I shared with him today. And I will tell you like I told Charles earlier tonight. I have no regrets either! And why should I? From what you have told me, Charles is doing the same goddamn thing to Nouri Sommers right this very minute! You know, Mark, I knew Charles would need to make love to her at least one more time before we got married—his way of saying good-bye for good to her. Charles is in love with her, and a part of him always will be. I've come to terms with that; had to in order to glue our relationship back together.

"But on the same note, I also know that he loves me very much, and of course, he's crazy about our son. And once we get married, a lot of this bullshit with this woman will stop! Charles will become the perfect husband

and devoted father. Charles will forever be in love with Nouri Sommers, something I told him I could live with. I don't expect you to understand our relationship, Mark, but he does love me very much, and I've never loved anyone nor could I ever love anyone more than Charles Mason. Nouri Sommers is no real threat to me or my relationship with Charles or our future together. You know how I know this? Because she isn't in love with Charles. She loves him, sure, but she's in love with Gabe. There's a big difference in loving someone and being in love with them, Mark, take my word for it! Been there and done that a few times in my life—and in my case, Charles is definitely the one! He knows that, and so do I. And in time, Nouri Sommers will know that, too."

The captain shook his head in confusion, reaching for his shot glass. He downed a shot of the strong-tasting liquor. "I talked to Charles before I came over here tonight. I could tell he was hurt over finding out about you and Gabe. It was in his voice. But you're right, he does love you and wants to get through the—"

"Don't even say it, Mark! He can have sex with Nouri Sommers, and I can't…"

"Tonya, please! Let's move on. There's a lot more."

"More? Like what?"

"Like Nouri Sommers is apparently pregnant," he said, reaching for the bottle of bourbon.

"What!" Tonya exclaimed, leveling her eyes angrily on the police captain.

"Relax! Gabe's the father, not Charles," he said.

Tonya sank back in her seat with a relieved expression on her face. "Well, thank God!" she said.

Mark chuckled at her response. "Anyway, Gabe doesn't know yet. And from what I understand, after seeing the two of you together today, she doesn't want him to know. Not now, not ever, according to Charles. He's the one who talked her into going down to the station today and trying to work things out with Gabe. Charles convinced her that Gabe had a right to know about—"

Tonya interrupted. "I agree. Gabe certainly does have a right to know. I made the mistake of not telling Charles about our son Chuckie, and because of that mistake Charles has lost three years of his little boy's life that he can never get back. I was wrong not to tell him. Come on, Captain, we're going to pay Charles and Nouri Sommers a little visit! If anyone knows where Gabe may have gone, it will be Charles." She smiled. "And anyway, I think it's time

Nouri Sommers and I had a little talk. This partner-swapping stuff ends tonight!" she added.

Tonya's outburst caught the police captain off guard. She glanced at him and chuckled. "Snap out of it, Captain! You're going with me," she said, quickly finishing the remainder of her brandy. "I'll be right back. I'm going to run upstairs to kiss little Chuckie good night and let Eva know where I'm going. I'll be back in five minutes," she said, quickly leaving the room.

Mark quickly reached for his cell phone, wanting to warn Charles Mason they were on their way, but the effort was in vain—Charles Mason's phone just rang and rang and rang. "Swell!" he mumbled, clipping the phone back in place on his trousers. "This generation of young adults is going to be the death of me. I just know it!" he was complaining under his breath as Tonya entered the room.

She instantly noticed his flushed face. "What is it, Captain?"

"I don't know about you kids today!" he said, shaking his head.

"What do you mean? And kids, Captain? I'd hardly call Gabe, Charles, or myself kids! Honestly." She chuckled. "Now Nouri Sommers, that's a different story!" she added teasingly.

"Everybody has sex with everybody these goddamn days! How the hell you all can actually sift through all the games and wind up making an actual commitment in marriage is mind-boggling to me!" he said.

Tonya chuckled again. "Captain, sometimes it just takes a few different partners in the sack to—"

Mark stopped her. "Forget it! I don't think I want to hear any more tonight. I'm an old man, and I don't think I can handle any more of this nonsense with you kids. I just want to know one thing, Tonya," he said, scratching the side of his head nervously.

"What's that, Mark?" She chuckled.

"When we walk in and catch Charles Mason and Nouri Sommers doing the wild thing, are you going to do something that we all might live to regret?" he asked.

She shook her head, laughing at the police captain's intended humor. "Of course not! But take my word for it, Captain," she paused, picking up her purse and set of keys, and then went on, "this will be the last time I let that woman make love to Charles!" She looked thoughtful for a moment. "That is to say…and live to tell about it!" she said with a chuckle.

Mark headed in the direction of the front door, shaking his head in total confusion. "Like I said, Tonya, you kids today!" he said, reaching for the doorknob.

"You want to drive, Captain, or would you rather I do?" she asked, playfully dangling the set of keys in her hand.

"No…Hell, No! I'll do the goddamn driving in my own goddamn car! When one of you nutty sons-of-bitches pulls out a gun in a fit of jealous rage, I want to be able to disappear at the drop of a goddamn dime!" he teased, walking out the door.

The female D.A. laughed at the colorful portrait the police captain had so humorously painted for her. "I see your point!" she playfully returned, shaking her head. "Captain, I can just see tomorrow's headlines now…*Police Captain Mark Lane—*"

He interrupted her playful attempt to tease him. "Don't even think about it!" he snapped. "My wife is already upset with me for spending a drunken night out with the boys last night and leaving the goddamn dog home all alone to piss all over the goddamn furniture. I already have hell to pay, don't need any more!"

"So you don't want to make the headlines in tomorrow's newspapers, huh?" she said with a giggle.

"Oh God, don't even tease with me like that! I'm almost half-afraid to be anywhere near Charles Mason or Nouri Sommers right now! They're both two of the hottest media favorites in the world. If the press knew they were together tonight, oh shit!" He sighed as they entered his car. He quickly started the engine of his old, beat-up Ford.

"Yeah, I know what you mean, Mark. Did you get a chance to check out the latest in the afternoon edition of *The Boston Enquirer*? Charles coming to her highness's rescue on his white horse, no doubt!" she chuckled, shaking her head in playful dismay.

"I thought the press had dubbed Gabe her knight in shining armor?" he said, shrugging with uncertainty.

Tonya chuckled. "Oh that! Well, they did, but that's old news—almost six weeks' worth of old news. Apparently, Charles, in a fit of jealous rage, threatened several young reporters this morning when Nouri was mobbed in front of her downtown condo penthouse in the sky. Just out of the blue—*BANG!* He was there standing directly in front of her; there to save the day for the lovely damsel in distress!" Her tone was one of jealously. She went on. "Her new knight in shining armor. Makes you want to puke, doesn't it?" She rolled her eyes.

"The goddamn press made Mason sound like Mighty Mouse, if you ask me!" Mark chuckled. "The whole goddamn thing from the very beginning made me want to puke, if you want to know the goddamn truth about it!" He sighed, reaching inside his shirt pocket for a cigarette.

She grinned as she glanced in his direction. "Can I have one of those, please?" she asked, pointing at the cigarette in his hand.

He shot her a curious glance. "What? A cigarette? But you don't smoke!"

"Yeah, I know. But suddenly I feel like having a cigarette. Do you mind?" She smiled.

"Oh shit! This isn't a bad sign or anything, is it, Daughtery?" he asked.

"I hope not! I mean…I don't think so," she returned in jest.

Mark shook his head, pulling his old car up to the front entrance to the famous P.I.'s house so the female D.A. could press in the secret code into the locked system. "Tonya, all joking aside, I'm not going in there if—"

She cut in laughing. "Mark, please! I promise you I will not get upset if they are in bed together. Everything is fine. I swear, okay? The important thing right now is to track down Gabe. God, I hope his father is going to be all right!" She sighed.

"Yeah, poor Gabe. He's taken a few kicks in the ass these past few months. This just might push him over the edge!"

"God, I hope not!" she replied, pulling out her compact and tube of lipstick as the captain shut off the engine to the car.

"Tonya, are you sure you're okay with all this?" he asked, nodding in the direction of the house.

"Yes. We're technically not married yet. But I will tell you what does bother me though—I mean about this whole thing," she said, powdering her nose and then her chin.

"What's that, Daughtery?" he asked, glancing at her curiously.

"To find out that Charles has been having me followed! Now that pisses me off plenty!" she said, putting her compact back inside her purse.

Mark released a puff of smoke. "I told you Mason only wanted to make sure you and Chuckie were safe. He started the surveillance right after Graham slapped you that night as you were trying to get inside your car. He was worried about you. I guess he just wanted to make sure Graham couldn't get that close to you again. That's all. You can understand that, can't you?"

Tonya looked thoughtful for a brief moment before responding. "I suppose so. But I really hate being spied on!" she added, reaching for the door handle nervously.

"Hey, girly girl, better get used to it! Being married to the most famous P.I. in the country has its fair share of perks as well as disadvantages. And I would imagine once you say 'I do' to Charles, the press will never leave you alone again. So, if I were you, I'd watch that sexy little ass of yours from now on, if you know what I mean!" Mark said, in a fatherly tone of voice.

She glanced at him, shaking her head in complete dismay. "Captain, there aren't a lot of people that can talk to me like that and get away with it," Tonya said, shaking her finger playfully in his direction.

"Yeah, maybe so, Daughtery, but next time, think before you leap! Can you imagine what would have happened if it had been some snoopy reporter from the press that had taken those photographs of you and Gabe, instead of Harman's men? Sweet Jesus! Your career would've been finished here in Boston. And even though Chuckie is only three now, he would have found out about—"

Tonya stopped him from finishing. "Yes, of course, you're right, Mark. I can see that now. I have no desire to ever do... Well, you know what I mean. Come on, let's go inside and get this over with, okay?" She slid out of the car.

After shutting off the alarm system, Tonya let herself and the police captain inside Charles Mason's home.

"The bar is that way," she said, pointing in the direction of the living room as she glanced in the direction of the long spiral staircase leading to the master bedroom. She swallowed hard, turning her attention back to the police captain. "Make yourself comfortable, Mark. This shouldn't take too long."

Once she reached the top of the staircase, Tonya stopped to catch her breath after hurrying up the three flights of stairs. With a great deal of effort she put her hand on the brass doorknob, then swallowed hard one final time, attempting to prepare herself for what she knew would be on the other side of the door. An instant later, she quietly opened it and stepped inside.

Chapter 22

After Tonya Daughtery entered, she crossed the room, heading for the nightstand. As she clicked on the night lamp, she instantly noticed the note Charles was tightly clutching in his right hand. She gave a sigh of both dread and relief upon seeing that Nouri Sommers was not lying in bed beside him. *Thank God!* She gently slid the note out of his hand and straightened the crumbled edges.

The soft sound of the crumbled paper caused the famous P.I. to stir, and through his puffy, tear-stained, half-opened eyes, he squinted a peek at the female D.A. and, swallowing hard, covered his eyes again with his raised left arm to hide the tears still on his face.

"She's gone," he whispered in a deep, raspy voice, fumbling for the pillow Nouri Sommers had been lying on a few hours earlier. He placed it over his head.

Tonya could smell the faint scent of the expensive French perfume his young lover had been wearing still on the satin pillowcase that Charles was holding as she read the note that Nouri Sommers had left behind.

My darling Charles,

I will forever love you. I will forever need you. I will forever think of you, often. But sadly, I have to go. Please don't try to stop me. This is something I need to do. I know you will be hurt. And for this I am so very sorry.

You, my darling, belong with Tonya and Chuckie. This is where your true happiness lies. I know it, and so do you.

As for me, I have tons to think about. Tons of changes in my life to make. And tons of new challenges to face and hopefully conquer.

Surprisingly, big guy, I suddenly find myself looking forward to each of them, starting with the surprise package I'm currently carrying inside. Wow! Who would have thought—me, of all people, a mom! My child is supposed to be a Valentine's Day baby; at least that's what Dr. Douglas told me yesterday.

I haven't decided whether or not I'll ever tell Gabe about our child, but in time I'm sure I'll manage to figure out what's best for the baby as well as myself. I wish I could be as forgiving with Gabe as you have been with Tonya.

But I can't. The love I felt for him was apparently something that just wasn't meant to be. Will I forever keep attracting all the Clint Chamberlains of the world?

Anyway, big guy, thank you for everything. Especially for being the one true love in my life that I could always count on. I will forever miss you, Charles!

Bye, my darling,
Nouri

The note was sealed in a copper-colored lipstick kiss. Nouri's favorite shade.

Visibly moved by Nouri's good-bye note, Tonya wiped a tear from her eye as she tried to remove the pillow from Charles' face. "Please, Charles. Let me…"

He gently shoved her hand away from him. "Don't, Tonya! Please, just leave. I need to be by myself for a while," he said hoarsely through the small opening between the side of the pillow and his muscular arm.

Tonya's first reaction was to leave. Let him just continue to lie there being miserable over the woman that she knew Charles would always be in love with. But after a few moments, she decided to try once again to talk to him.

"Charles," she said his name softly, "I understand your pain. I've been through it myself over you. I know how you must feel. And if this wasn't important I…I…" She paused briefly to clear her throat and then went on, "I have something to talk to you about. It's about Gabe's father," she added with sadness, but Charles continued to just lie there in silence. She went on. "Charles, please, this is important! Gabe's father has suffered a heart attack. He's in a hospital in Greece asking for his son. Gabe has disappeared. No one can find him anywhere. Mark stopped by my house as you and I were talking on the phone earlier and…" She stopped talking and shook her head with annoyance.

"Charles, are you listening to me? Mark is downstairs waiting for you. We have to find Gabe," she said, trying to remove the exotic-smelling pillow from his face again.

Once again he gently pushed her hand away. "Tonya, please, I want both you and Mark to leave. I'll pull myself together in a little while and then I'll try and hunt Gabe down myself. I'm sorry, but I don't want to talk to you right now."

His sharp words hit her just like a slap to the face; just as painful. She angrily shot back, “Fine! If you really want me to leave, then I’m out of here! If it’s Nouri Sommers you want, then it’s Nouri Sommers you can have, but before I go, I just want you to know that I think you are a hypocrite, Charles Mason! How dare you lie there making me out to be the bad guy in this relationship, when in fact you’re just as guilty as I am!” she shouted heatedly, jumping to her feet and storming out of the bedroom, slamming the door very hard behind her.

She ran down the long spiral staircase, crying, into the protective arms of Captain Mark Lane.

Moments later, both the D.A. and the police captain were on their way back to her house, with Tonya giving him the play-by-play on what had transpired inside the famous P.I.’s bedroom.

“Well, Mark, that’s when I got mad and ran out of the bedroom,” she said with a sigh of frustration.

“Wonderful!” Mark said in response, shaking his head in disbelief.

Chapter 23

Searching for evidence that the past several years of her life hadn't all been a complete lie, Nouri Sommers suddenly found herself unlocking the front door to the five-bedroom apartment downtown where it all began. She swallowed hard before taking a deep breath, then slowly released it before reaching for the light switch to the right of the wall as she entered. She closed her eyes, swallowing hard again as she shut the door behind her.

As she turned around and opened her eyes, she stopped breathing; her mind began to race as though she had no control over it. She shivered, forcing herself to breathe. Her heart had been ripped from her chest right here in this very room. "Oh God, Clint!" she cried out his name at the hurtful memory of yesteryear, then walked to the bar and poured herself a shot of brandy.

With the drink in her trembling hand, she walked across the room to the patio and gazed out of the large sliding glass door at the city silhouetted along the busy streets of downtown Boston. The moon was full, bright, and more golden than usual for a mid-summer moon. Her mind drifted as she continued to stare blankly around the downtown area below.

"Mmm, it smells wonderful. What is it?" she asked, smiling at the handsome attorney sitting across the table from her.

"Western-style omelets. I put everything but the kitchen sink in it," high-powered attorney Clint Chamberlain had replied, returning her smile.

The beautiful, young billionairess smiled as she continued to listen to the voices from her past being played out inside her mind.

Her mind raced on.

"Oh my goodness! Where are all the workers?" she asked while glancing nervously at the sexy attorney.

"I gave them all the day off. You don't want them to start calling you a slave driver, do you?"

"How dare you!"

Clint silenced her with a kiss.

Nouri jarred herself back to the present and walked back to the bar, setting her brandy snifter down on top of it.

Longing desperately to find some sort of peace within herself, she began to do a mental room-by-room inventory of her past memories with the man who at one time held the key to her heart. Her gaze scanned inside each and every room, as the memories one by one continued to flow in and out of her mind.

Down to the final two rooms in the massive apartment, she slowly opened the door to the bedroom; the very room that had given her both pleasure and pain. She walked over to the bed and sat down on Clint Chamberlain's side, staring blankly at his pillow as her mind wandered.

"I want you, sweetness," he whispered with urgency, brushing the outline of her ear with his tongue.

"Mmm," she responded, still half-asleep, instinctively moving her hand behind her back in an effort to find the man behind the words and pull him closer to her. Even in her sleep she wanted to respond to him...to his touch...to his kisses...

"I'm sorry, sweetness," he whispered in her ear with his warm breath.

"I know you are, darling," she mouthed the words as she continued to remember the last time they had made love in the room.

"Oh Clint," she whispered his name sadly as her mind continued to torture her with the memory of their last night together in their downtown apartment. The very night that had changed her life forever.

While Clint was in the shower, not hearing the telephone ring, she had answered it. Unaware at the time it would be a phone call she would later regret having answered.

"Hello, Clint honey, I know you can't talk. That's okay. You don't have to say anything. I hope I didn't wake her. I just wanted to tell you something. If you ever decide to leave that snooty bitch you're living with, I would love to give us another chance. Making love with you tonight after all this time away from you has only made me miss you all over again, baby. Please telephone me tomorrow. You still have my number. I...I still love you, Clint. Goodnight," the sexy female on the other end of the phone line had said.

After recalling the painful memory, Nouri reached for her stomach, feeling as though she were going to vomit again. She curled her body up in a knot and let herself fall in the middle of the bed. Unable to stop herself, she began to cry.

"Damn you, Clinton Jerome Chamberlain!" she sobbed angrily. "You and your damn women! I've always known what a skirt-chasing jackass you were from day one!" She tried to stop crying and swallowed hard, gazing around the room. Her gaze stopped at the beautiful antique dresser on the far side of the room. She cleared her throat, forcing herself to her feet, and walked to the dresser. She slowly opened the top drawer. "I don't believe it!" she exclaimed, reaching for one of her earlier fantasy journals lying on top of a pair of the high-powered attorney's silk boxer shorts.

She hesitantly opened it, sighing as she wiped tears from her eyes, seeing the diamond and gold wedding band Clint had taped across the first page of her journal. She gently peeled back the tape, removing it with her trembling fingers. She slid the ring on behind the wedding ring her husband had placed on her finger two years earlier during their wedding vows.

She glanced through the timeless journal, remembering each entry as though she had just written it the night before. She smiled, closed the journal tightly, and clutched it to her breast. She looked for the silver, jeweled box she usually kept her journal in. She placed the journal inside and carried it with her into the study.

She clicked on the light switch and glanced around the room. Everything was exactly as she had furnished it four years earlier. She smiled as she walked behind the large, expensive, handmade desk she had specially made for Clint on his thirty-fifth birthday and sank into the soft, leather cushion of his comfortable chair.

The photograph on the desk to her right caught her gaze. She picked it up and lovingly smiled at both faces smiling back at her. "Clint, Ethan," she whispered their names, tracing an outline with the tip of her fingernail of both handsome faces sporting wide, mischievous smiles.

Nouri wondered why Clint had never displayed the photograph while they were together. Perhaps if she would've known the two men were friends, she would've never married Ethan Sommers to begin with. "More secrets!" she angrily whispered, setting the photograph back down in its proper place. She tossed her head back and propped her feet up on the desk, folding both hands behind her head. "Why doesn't anything make any sense to me anymore?" she asked, racking her brain for answers.

As her mind drifted back, the past four years began to haunt her. Crystal clear images, voices, ghosts from her past.

...Clint, Ethan, Becka, and Genna. Friends or enemies? Lovers or fools? A wife without a husband...lies...secrets..."Oh God!" The images all far too clear! Too painful! Glowing reminders of a young woman's fairytale dream turned nightmare!

"Oh God! Lies...lies...the past four years of my life have all been lies!" She sobbed hysterically, jumped to her feet, and ran out of the study with the silver, jeweled box tightly clutched to her breast.

She wept for the friendships she had trusted, for a love that she had given the key to her heart, for a husband who never existed, and for the past four years of her life that had absolutely no meaning or purpose—not one thing to show for her love or her sorrow.

As Nouri Sommers locked the door to Clint Chamberlain's downtown apartment, she sighed sadly, knowing that once she pulled away from the building, she would be closing the door on a chapter in her life that sadly she had no business being involved in; completely pointless, with zero value. Nothing real or tangible remained; that is, except for the silver, jeweled box that housed her most intimate thoughts of passion and two slightly used diamond and gold wedding bands. She slid the wedding bands off her finger and gently placed them inside the silver, jeweled box with her fantasy journal of yesterday.

With a sigh of hopelessness, she glanced at the shiny jeweled box one final time before turning on the radio, as she started the engine to the shiny canary-yellow Viper. Quickly closing the chapter of a young woman's shattered dream, she found herself feeling like a young child who had just discovered there was no real Santa Claus.

*...Yesterday, all my troubles seemed so far away. Now it looks as though they're here to stay...*echoed the song on the car radio as Nouri glanced for one last time through the rear-view mirror at the building that had started it all. Moments later, she swiftly made a right turn, heading for the nearest on-ramp to the freeway.

"Ah, one final good-bye to deal with," she whispered under her breath, putting the pedal to the metal and cranking up the volume on the radio another notch or two.

Chapter 24

*...Shotgun! Shoot 'im 'fore he runs now. Do the jerk, baby...*was the song blasting loudly on the jukebox inside a downtown girly joint called "Honey for the Bears."

"Yo, bartender!" Gabe Baldwin drunkenly called, trying to get the attention of the scantily clad female making drinks behind the bar. She glanced in the police detective's direction. He grinned mischievously and then continued, "When Twinkletits up on stage gets finished shaking that shapely fanny of hers, I'd like to buy her a bottle of the hundred-dollar grape juice that she drinks," he shouted, reaching for his drink.

"Twinkletits," he quietly pronounced the name again, instantly recalling Nouri Sommers branding the sexy female detective in Connecticut that silly nickname out of jealousy. He chuckled as he continued to watch the semi-nude dancer on stage shake her tail-feather to the oldies but goodies song titled *Shotgun*. He shook his head, amused by it all; wondering how many years it had been since he had frequented an establishment such as this.

He shook his head, not quite believing that places of this kind still actually existed. "Men and their toys," he mumbled under his breath, content with his reasoning on why girlie joints were still as much in demand today as they were back in the seventies.

An instant later, Ms. Twinkletits stepped off the stage and headed in his direction. He chuckled as he watched the red-haired temptress gracefully make her way to the bar area. The way she seemed to glide toward him reminded him of an exotic cat of sorts. He smiled lustfully when she joined him.

"Hi there, my name is Bambi." Her tone of voice was soft and seductive.

He smiled. "You can call me whatever you like, Bambi. How about Harry? That sounds like a manly name, don't you think?" he remarked in a playful manner, motioning for the barmaid.

The red-haired dancer giggled at the police detective's playfulness. "Harry, huh?" she said, making eye contact with the barmaid.

Gabe noticed and shook his head chuckling. "Ah, yeah. Harry's a nice name. What's the matter, don't you think I look like a Harry?" He reached for his drink with one hand as he playfully traced the index finger from his other hand seductively across the warm flesh of Bambi's shapely thigh.

The dancer gasped and shivered at the same time from the unexpected sensation. Their gazes met. She swallowed hard. "Ah, Harry." She let the name roll off her tongue. "No, that's not it," she said, turning herself on the barstool to completely face the handsome detective. With the tip of her finger she suggestively traced the outline of his beautiful full lips as she continued to speak. "I know who you are. I've seen your handsome face in the newspaper before. As a matter of fact, I saw it in the paper just a few days ago." She paused and licked her lips erotically, gazing back into his eyes with interest. "You're engaged to the Baron's daughter. You're that handsome police detective everyone is talking about." She smiled knowingly.

He raised his hand and removed her finger from his lips, teasingly biting it before kissing it and then releasing it. "Oh, I am. Am I?" He chuckled, picking up his drink.

"Mmm." She nodded, reaching for her glass of grape juice.

"Well, tonight, Bambi, I'm Harry," he said in response, glancing around the room. "Been a dancer long?" he asked, returning his attention to the dancer.

She squirmed uncomfortably on the barstool, causing Gabe to glance at her. He studied the small makeup-hidden lines around the dancer's eyes. *About my age, give or take*, he thought to himself as he continued to half-listen to her reply.

"Most of my life. At one time I thought I could make it big. You know, in New York, or maybe Las Vegas, someplace like that." She shrugged her shoulders with disappointment.

"Oh yeah," he responded, looking into her eyes. "So what happened?" He set his drink glass on top of the bar and motioned for the bartender to bring them another round.

"Oh, I don't know. A few wrong choices can be hell on a young gal's dreams, know what I mean, Harry?" She forced a smile.

"Only too well, Bambi," he said in a sad tone as the beautiful face of Nouri Sommers suddenly jumped inside his mind. He quickly blinked the vision away, but the guilt he had been dealing with for the past several hours still remained.

"What about you, Detective?" she asked, remembering too late he had asked her to call him Harry. "Oops, I mean Harry." She smiled and shrugged.

"What do you mean?" he asked, still trying to get Nouri off his mind.

"I read that you're supposed to be getting married in a few weeks. I just assumed a man like you would want to be spending as much time with his fiancée—especially with a fiancée like Ms. Clayborne and all. Wow! She's really something, ain't she?" The exotic dancer shook her head with envy and reached for her champagne glass filled with grape juice.

Gabe chuckled. "Well, Bambi, I guess you could say it's the boys' night out," he mused, picking up his drink and downing it in one long swallow.

The dancer laughed. "So where's all the boys?" she asked teasingly.

"Would you believe I started without them?" He smiled, glancing around the room again.

"What's the matter, Harry? You seem a little uneasy. Is something wrong?" she asked, gazing into his eyes.

He shook his head. "Nope, everything is just hunky-dory. Truth is that I just don't like having my back facing the door, that's all. A habit I picked up in bars a long time ago."

"Would you like to move over to a table?" she asked.

Gabe released a deep sigh and shook his head before speaking. "No, actually, Bambi, I won't be staying that long. To tell you the truth I don't even know why I stopped in here to begin with. No offense intended. I think I'll have one more drink, buy you another bottle of that hundred-dollar grape juice, and then bolt," he said, motioning for the barmaid again.

"Too bad. I get off in a few hours, Harry. I thought maybe—"

Gabe leaned over and kissed the dancer on the cheek, interrupting her. "Thanks, but I can't. I have something I need to do tonight and a long drive ahead of me. Maybe some other time," he said, flashing her a wink.

She smiled, knowing she would never see the handsome detective again. "Sure, anytime, Harry. I'm always here." She shrugged her shoulders in disappointment as she watched him down his drink, stand to his feet, and disappear out the door as quickly as he had entered.

What the hell is wrong with you, Gabe? You're losing it! Are you trying to lose that goddamn badge of yours? You need to get your goddamn head screwed back on straight and don't come back to the station until you do! Got it!

Just like a broken record, police captain Mark Lane's words kept playing over and over inside his mind as Gabe continued to walk along the busy streets of downtown Boston.

When the detective passed a coffee shop, the aroma of the coffee from inside instantly caught his attention. "Mmm, that smells good," he whispered under his breath, changing his direction and rushing inside the restaurant. He sat at the counter and drank several cups of the fresh-brewed coffee. Then he took an extra large cup to go with him.

Spotting a cab parked on the street, he jumped inside, asking the cab driver to drop him off in the back parking lot of the Boston Police Department.

Once there, Gabe wasted no time getting into his car. He swiftly and quietly turned on the key to the ignition and sped out of the parking lot before anyone had a chance to see him. He wanted to run home, take a shower, and pack a suitcase, realizing he needed a few days away from everything and everybody to get his head screwed back on straight. And the most secluded place in the world to him was his A-frame cabin in the woods. *Where better to be alone?* he thought, entering the ramp on the freeway, heading home with his radio blasting a song by the Righteous Brothers on Nouri Sommers' favorite radio station.

...Baby, baby, I'd get down on my knees for you...if you would only love me like you used to do...

Chapter 25

Charles Mason was angry with himself for not even trying to stop his fiancée from leaving earlier in the evening. "God, I acted like such a jerk!" he groaned angrily, as he picked up his fury feline Tallulah. "Oh, Tallulah, I'm such an idiot!" he said to the cat, scratching her behind the ears. "Are you hungry, baby?" he asked his pet, forcing himself out of bed and onto his feet. He crossed the room with Tallulah under his arm.

"Come on, girl, Daddy will feed you now," he continued to talk to his cat as he reached for his bathrobe with one hand and slid it on, leaving it untied. He made his way downstairs, wanting to feed his soft, white, fluffy friend.

After he fed Tallulah, he made a quick telephone call. The person he was phoning answered immediately.

"Hi, John, sorry to disturb you," he said, sitting at the breakfast bar as he waited for the coffee. "Yeah, she's fine, or at least I guess she is…. What? When…? Shit! Is Daniel all right?" he asked. "Ouch! Poor bastard. Let me guess, over my fiancée, right…? Hey, it's okay, John, I would have found out about it sooner or later," he said, glancing around for a cigarette lighter.

"No please! It's not necessary. I insist they were only doing their job…. Like I said, it's not a problem…. Don't worry about it. I'm a big boy, remember?" he said, clearing his dry throat with a small cough.

"Hey, John," he went on. "The reason I'm phoning so late is that I need for you to locate Gabe Baldwin," he said, glancing at the coffeepot. "What? No, of course not…! No, it's not about Tonya, either." He shook his head and reached for the coffeepot. He poured himself a cup of coffee and then turned his attention back to his phone conversation with former federal agent John Harmon.

"It's important that we find Gabe right away. His father has apparently suffered a heart attack…. No, he's in a hospital in Greece…. Hey, I wish I knew, but I have no idea…. I couldn't begin to tell you where to start looking. When Gabe's in one of his moods, it's hard to say," he said as he continued to playfully wiggle his toes at his fury feline.

"I thought I'd try a few places on my own in the morning. I need to go and talk to Tonya first…. What? No nothing like that. It's me. I was a real jerk…! Oh, John, it's a long story; how about I tell you about it later…? What? Yeah, some, I would imagine.... Hey, she had every right to be upset with me tonight.... I guess Nouri being here with me tonight had something to do with it, sure....

"Not entirely. She left while I was asleep. I'm worried sick about her. She left me a good-bye note. Tore me up pretty good.... What? No, she asked me not to. But I thought I'd give her a few days by herself and then maybe I'll try and track her down." He picked up his cup of coffee and took a drink.

"What? No, I don't think so, John.... Hey listen, I'd better go on over to Tonya's before it's too late for the 'I'm sorrys.' If you find Gabe, let me know right away. Beep me. I'll take my pager with me.... I don't care what time of the night or day it is, just find him. His family is holding the company jet for him, ready to leave at a moment's notice.... Yeah, make sure he knows that.... No, not much. Mark just said he thinks Gabe might be out and about tying on a good one. Captain also had to chew his ass out pretty good.... Yeah, I know how hard that must have been for him. He loves Gabe like a son.... Yeah, sure.... Listen, I have to go. Call me just as soon as you hear anything.... Okay, bye," he said, hanging up the phone, picking up his cup of coffee, and going to his study after turning on the stereo system. Charles left it on the oldies but goodies channel Nouri had put it on earlier in the evening. He made his way to the study as he listened to the current song.

...Do you know where you're going to? Do you like the things that life is showing you?

Charles sat in the chair behind his large, antique desk, put his head back, and continued to listen to the song that strangely seemed to be asking him questions that he had already begun asking himself a short time earlier.

He continued sitting behind his desk, listening to the song being played, reflecting on many things in his mind. Questions, so many questions, that he needed answered before he could go forward with his life; a life with a woman who truly loved him. The very same woman that he shared a beautiful little boy with. A woman he in turn loved very much, even if it was a different kind of love than he felt for another woman. Make that *the* woman. The very woman who had stolen his heart and his soul seven years earlier—Nouri.

Would he ever be able to give her up completely? Doubtful! Especially now that she was so alone. And on top of that she was pregnant. Pregnant by a man she would have never known had it not been for him. "God, I've ruined her life!" he whispered sadly.

"Oh God, sugar! I'm so sorry," he cried as the tears flowed again.

The famous P.I. began blaming himself for everything that had happened to Nouri Sommers for the past several months. After all, the fact of the matter clearly remains: had it not been for him, both her husband and her former lover would still be alive today.

It was he who had insisted the high-powered attorney stay in France and help track down the mysterious billionaire businessman. Had he not interfered, perhaps Ethan Sommers would be sitting inside some jail cell by now instead of being killed by his friends in the F.B.I. And perhaps Clint Chamberlain would have come back to Boston as well and back into the arms of the only woman he had ever truly loved; according to the high-powered attorney anyway.

And what about Gabe? Had he been honest with the police detective right up front about his love for Nouri, maybe she wouldn't be in the mess she was in today. The telephone rang, jarring him back to the present.

"Yeah," he said hoarsely, forcing back his tears.

The deep, baritone voice on the other end of the phone line was noticeably nervous. Charles cleared his throat before responding. "Yes, this is Charles Mason, what can I do for you?"

"This is Dr. Edward Holloway. I'm chief of staff here at St. Mary's Hospital in Connecticut."

Thinking something might have happened to Gabe, remembering he had a cabin in the woods in Connecticut, Charles nervously jumped to his feet. "Yes, Dr. Holloway, what is it?"

"I'm not sure, Mr. Mason, if you're the person I should be speaking to about this or not, but we just performed emergency surgery on a young woman. She had no I.D. on her. The only thing we found with even a clue as to who she might be was a business card with your telephone number on it." He paused to give Charles an opportunity to say something, but the P.I. was too stunned for words, so the doctor went on.

"As I was saying, Mr. Mason, we have no idea who this young woman might be, so we were hoping you might be able to help us. Apparently her car slid off the road during the rainstorm we had here in Connecticut earlier this evening. She had no I.D., just a purse full of cash, a silver, jeweled box with a fantasy journal in it dated three years ago, and two different diamond and gold wedding bands...one expensive; the other one very, very expensive. Do you have any idea who this young woman is?"

Charles could feel the blood slowly drain from his body. He closed his eyes tightly, falling back into his chair, fighting hard to keep from crying out loud. With a great deal of effort, he finally managed to respond, "Oh my God!

It sounds like Nouri, but it can't be. Oh dear God, please don't let it be her!" he said, shaking his head in disbelief.

"So you do know her?" Dr. Holloway said, in a relieved tone of voice.

Charles cleared the tears from his throat again before speaking, "Is this young woman very beautiful? Dark-brown, curly hair with red highlights? Some people might call it auburn," he offered, excitedly wiping the sweat from his forehead with the arm of his terrycloth bathrobe.

"Yes, and our mystery lady has hazel-colored eyes."

Charles flew to his feet again. "Oh my God, it sounds like Nouri Sommers!" His tone was one of total disbelief.

"You mean the widow of—"

Charles cut in, breathing heavily, "Yes."

"Are you the person I should be discussing this matter with?" the doctor asked, realizing who his mystery lady was.

"Yes, I'll be there as quickly as possible," Charles said, starting to hang up the phone when the doctor spoke again.

"Don't you want to know—"

Charles cut in sharply, "Yes, of course I do. I'm sorry, Dr. Holloway. How is she?" he asked, glancing at the clock on his desk.

Chapter 26

...Listen to the rhythm of the falling rain telling me just what a fool I've been...

"Ah, no you don't!" police detective Gabe Baldwin mumbled under his breath, lowering his hand to turn off the radio inside his Maserati. "I'm not going to think about Nouri Sommers another time tonight!" he continued to mumble to himself, quickly remembering how much she had loved the oldies but goodies channel. She had been the reason he had begun listening to the bubble-gum channel to begin with.

Not being able to get over her as easily as he had hoped after his return from France, he found himself doing anything he could to keep her memory clear in his mind, including changing all of the radio channels he had in his possession; at home, the office, his automobiles, and even inside his secret downtown apartment that no one knew about. Well, that is to say, except for a few sexy mid-afternoon snacks with no last names.

After realizing Captain Mark Lane had been right—he did indeed need some time to himself if nothing else but to reflect, Gabe decided his cabin in the woods was exactly the place for him to get the rest he so desperately needed as well as a great place to get his head screwed back on straight. Mark had hit the nail on the head. It was time to get back to the business at hand. His captain needed him, even if Nouri Sommers did not.

His mind drifted...

Who needs a woman like her anyway? After seeing the way she ran back into Charles' arms, how could I ever trust her again? That is to say if she wanted me back, and it was painfully clear by the way they were so tightly embracing she apparently did not! Of course, after seeing me with Tonya the way she had, can't say as I blame her much...

He sighed as his mind raced on, trying to analyze the past six weeks of his life, starting with the morning he first met the beautiful young woman who seemed to continue to hold a sort of magic over him.

He gasped when Nouri Sommers' beautiful face flashed before him. He felt his heart begin to race madly and his hand tremble as he continued to study the beautiful face of the young woman in his thoughts.

God, she's beautiful! Those eyes. That smile. He shivered at the memory of their first meeting. He smiled, recalling how he felt. *She was something else all right!* It was like a bolt of lightning shooting through his body.

"Good morning, Officers. How may I help you?" She had smiled gracefully, brushing past him on her way to the sofa. Her unbelievable beauty had completely taken him off guard and caused him to lose his train of thought. He smiled at the memory, recalling how easily she had distracted him and how clumsy young homicide detective Al Ballard had been over her graceful and hypnotic greeting.

"I'm...ah, ah...Detective Al—" He interrupted the young detective, taking charge of the interview.

"I'm Detective Gabe Baldwin, and this is Detective Al Ballard," he said, gazing in her eyes with deep rapture.

He swallowed hard, attempting to stop his heart from beating so wildly. *Calm down, old boy, this is only a memory. Something I need to deal with now so I can put it away forever*, he thought, releasing a deep sigh.

He continued to reflect…

He remembered how their eyes had never left one another, causing young Ballard to blush and become impatient at the same time. Gabe chuckled at the thought.

"What happened back there, Detective?" Ballard asked, not believing how the senior detective (his idol among detectives) had behaved with the beautiful suspect in a double homicide investigation.

Gabe laughed, remembering how amused he had been at the time.

His thoughts drifted forward to the afternoon he had met his former partner in fighting crime Charles Mason for lunch to discuss a favor.

"How does Mrs. Sommers feel about me babysitting her?" he asked, his chest pounding as he waited for Charles Mason to answer the question.

"She hates the idea," he said in response.

Gabe felt his heart drop again just like it had six weeks earlier during this conversation over lunch.

He recalled how relieved and childish he had felt after his friend had explained that Nouri, of course, hadn't meant her remark towards the detective personally. He chuckled at the memory.

"God, I had it bad. Right from the beginning," he mumbled with a sigh, remembering more of their conversation about the beautiful young woman who so effortlessly had stolen his heart as well as the hearts of many other men.

His thoughts continued to race on…

"Where are you taking me, Detective?" Nouri had asked in a frightened tone of voice after the death threat she had received.

"Connecticut. I have a small cabin in the woods there. You'll be perfectly safe. I promise, ma'am." He smiled, desperately longing to pull her into his arms.

She gazed at him helplessly. "Who will be staying there with me?" She continued to gaze into his eyes.

He remembered melting at her penetrating gaze. Gabe fumbled for a cigarette as he again mumbled his reply to her, "I will. The fewer people that know where you are, the safer you will be."

Gabe swallowed again, reaching for his cigarette lighter as he continued his journey down memory lane. Some of the more humorous memories caused him to chuckle, like the time they were driving to his cabin in Connecticut and she had fallen asleep. Her head had dropped down to his lap, causing an instant reaction in the lower region of his trousers. He smiled, fondly recalling how easily she could get him turned on, whether she had meant to or not. And the time she had jealously acted out his telephone message from his former fiancée Lisa Clayborne at the cabin.

Suddenly he remembered The Kiss. Their very first kiss. He was hopelessly in love from that moment on. "More like doomed!" he sighed. "I fell for her like a ton of bricks!" he said, shaking his head and glancing instinctively at the rear-view mirror after passing a tow truck coming up out of a sunken ditch underneath an overpass. "Oh my God!" he mumbled, when the shiny canary-yellow Viper suddenly caught his eye. He slammed on the brakes, turned his car around, and wasted no time going after the tow truck.

The driver of the truck pulled over immediately after the police detective almost ran him off the road. He jumped out of the truck with a baseball bat tightly clutched in his right fist. "You son-of-a-bitch!" he shouted angrily, walking towards Gabe.

Gabe quickly brought his badge out of his jacket pocket and flashed it, feeling suddenly grateful he had remembered to grab it before leaving his home. "Calm down. Sorry I scared you. I didn't mean to. My name is Gabe Baldwin. I'm a homicide detective with the Boston Police Department," he said.

"I don't give a shit who you are, buddy! You almost ran me off the goddamn road back there!"

"I said I was sorry, man. Calm down! This is important. Who owns the automobile you're towing?" he asked, walking past the driver to get a better look at the car and its tags.

The driver shrugged his broad shoulders. "Hell, I don't know. Some young broad from Boston; she didn't have an I.D. on her. Cops said only thing inside the car was a small overnight bag with a few clothes. You know, one of them weekend jobbies. That and some kind of fancy jewelry box with a fantasy journal and a couple of diamond wedding bands inside it."

"I see," Gabe replied, glancing inside the car. "Anything else?" he asked, with growing interest.

"I think one of the cops said she had a business card with some big shot P.I.'s number from Boston in her purse too."

"Was she all right?" Gabe asked, staring into the huge man's icy-blue eyes.

The driver removed his ball cap, scratched the side of his head, and then put the hat back on before speaking. "I don't rightly know, Detective. The one ambulance driver said it didn't look good. Said he thought it looked as though she may have suffered a miscarriage."

"What!" the detective exclaimed in stunned disbelief.

"She was apparently pregnant, and one of the…"

Gabe stopped him in mid-sentence. "Never mind! Where did they take her?" he asked, turning to go back to his car.

"St. Mary's. It's the hospital out by the airport."

After thanking the driver, Gabe jumped in his car, quickly changed directions, and put the pedal to the metal en route to St. Mary's Hospital on the other side of town.

"God, please let Nouri be all right!" he prayed, clutching his chest as if he were trying to start his breathing again. "I'm so sorry, darling," he murmured, racing in the direction of the hospital.

His brain rapidly bounced from one thought to another as he desperately searched for answers as to why Nouri Sommers would have attempted something so foolish. Driving in a town she obviously knew nothing about, and on top of that driving during a thunderstorm. *What was she thinking?*

Could she have actually been trying to find my cabin after only being there once? If so, why? Had she and Charles Mason gotten into an argument? Maybe Tonya and Nouri had gotten into an argument? Over Charles? Over me? Why the hell didn't she just go back to the mansion, her apartment, or her condo for the night? His mind continued to run rampant.

"Oh God, baby!" he whispered, in torment after remembering his entire conversation with the tow truck driver. He wiped a tear from his eye, knowing if Nouri was indeed pregnant, then he was without a doubt the father. He suddenly recalled the plan-B method he had used, wanting to steal her away entirely from high-powered attorney Clint Chamberlain while they were in France. He wiped a stream of tears away from his cheek with his thumb and his forefinger.

"Oh my God, pregnant! Why didn't she tell me?" *Please dear God, let Nouri and my baby be all right!* he silently prayed again, pulling his car into the emergency entrance of St. Mary's Hospital. Without thinking, he jumped out of the car, leaving the door open and the engine running.

He went charging into the hospital as fast as his long legs would carry him. "Where is the doctor on duty?" he demanded loudly even before the self-closing doors had a chance to close completely.

A large intern swiftly came from behind the front desk, demanding the detective to lower his voice. The police detective flashed his badge excitedly. "Like I said, pal, I need to speak to the—"

Dr. Holloway came up rushing up from behind him. He extended his hand. "You must be Charles Mason. I'm Dr. Holloway," he said, swallowing nervously.

Gabe felt his face flush and his jawbone tighten. "No, my name is Gabe Baldwin. I'm a homicide detective with the Boston Police Department," he said, reluctantly extending his hand to the good doctor.

The doctor nodded. "Oh yes, I remember seeing your picture in the newspap—"

"Never mind about that, Doctor. I want to see Nouri Sommers right away; how is she? And of course the baby?" he asked, tightly closing his eyes briefly in an attempt to stop himself from crying.

Dr. Holloway glanced at the police detective, nervously nodding with his head. "She's this way, Detective." He ignored Gabe's question about Nouri Sommers' condition. "Would you mind telling me what the Boston Police Department's interest is in this young woman, Detective Baldwin?" he asked with curious interest.

Gabe stopped walking and shoved his hands into his trouser pockets, leveling his eyes on the doctor as he answered. “None, actually, Doctor. It’s personal,” he said, pulling his hands back out of his pockets.

A looked of confusion covered the doctor’s face. “I don’t know, Detective. Maybe we should wait for Mr. Mason to arrive before—”

Gabe angrily interrupted him. “Listen, Doctor, I have more right to be with Mrs. Sommers than Mr. Mason does,” he stated coolly.

“I’m sorry, Detective, I don’t understand. Mr. Mason said—”

Gabe heatedly cut in again. “Listen, Dr. Holloway, I don’t know what Mr. Mason has told you, and quite frankly, I don’t care. Mrs. Sommers is carrying my child; I’d say that takes top billing over—”

The doctor stopped the detective from finishing his sentence. “I see. Yes, of course. This way, please,” he said, gesturing.

“Well?” Gabe remarked impatiently as they continued walking down the long hallway. “Are you going to make me wait forever before you tell me how she’s doing?” He could feel a knot forming in the pit of his stomach. He released a deep sigh and swallowed hard.

Dr. Holloway cleared his throat nervously. “Yes, of course. I’m sorry, Detective. I’m…I’m sorry, but it doesn’t look good. I had to perform emergency surgery to stop her from bleeding to death. The steering wheel of the car was jammed up against her stomach during the impact from what we were told by the police officer on the scene. She had to be flying across the overpass to have had an impact like that,” he said, shaking his head.

“Is that all the officer had to say about the accident?”

“No, he also said Mrs. Sommers had been drinking, but at this point…”

The doctor stopped talking and reached for the detective’s arm in an attempt to keep Gabe from falling as he staggered and leaned against the wall. “Are you all right, Detective?” The doctor gestured for him to sit down on the bench beside him.

Gabe swallowed hard. “No, I mean yes, I’m fine. I need to see her. What were you saying?” he asked, lowering his hands to his sides, silently praying he wouldn’t pass out.

They began walking again. “I stopped the massive flow of bleeding, but it’s hard to say if the babies will survive. Something only time will tell, I’m afraid. It will be a few days before we know for certain, but—”

A stunned expression quickly covered Gabe’s face. He stopped walking again and leaned against the wall. “Excuse me!” he remarked, in stunned disbelief.

The doctor stopped walking and turned to face the detective again. "Yes…? Listen, Detective, are you sure—"

Gabe silenced him with a wave of his head in mid-air. "Babies. You said babies, Doctor?" he said, in a low whisper.

"Oh, I see. Apparently you didn't know? Yes, Mrs. Sommers is carrying three babies."

It was all Gabe could do to continue standing. He swallowed hard and nervously ran his fingers through his hair. "Three?" He looked at Dr. Holloway in dismay. "Maybe I'd better sit down after all for a few moments."

"Here, Detective. I'll sit with you for a moment," the doctor said, gesturing to a nearby bench. He went on. "As I was saying, Detective. "It's too early to predict if the babies will survive or not. We should know more in a few days. As far as Mrs. Sommers is concerned, I am sorry. She slipped in a coma right after surgery. Her head injury was extremely severe, and with the swelling," he paused, shaking his head sadly before he continued, "well, we just have to wait it out, I'm afraid," he said, extending his arm and patting the detective across the shoulders. "I'm sorry."

Gabe struggled with tears. "Thank you, Doctor. Of course, you understand money is not an issue here. I want the best. I mean the very best for her that is available. I don't give a damn how many specialists you have to fly in here. Understand?" he said, jumping to his feet.

"Yes of course, Detective, but we have some of the finest doctors in the world right here in Connecticut already. We'll take care of her just fine. Regarding her being in a coma," he paused just outside the I.C.U. before he continued, "that is something she will have to pull through on her own. The mind is like a complex machine. Mrs. Sommers will have to will herself to come back from the dark recesses of her subconscious mind."

"I see. And there's nothing else that can be done for her right now?" Gabe asked, wiping a tear from his eye.

The doctor shook his head, sadly opening the door to the I.C.U. for him. "No, Detective. However, a prayer or two certainly couldn't hurt."

Chapter 27

Private investigator Charles Mason could hardly hear the telephone conversation that he was having with former federal agent John Harmon. The loud noise from the engine of his private helicopter was overwhelming.

"I can barely hear what you're saying, John; can you shout a little louder?" Charles yelled into the cell phone.

"Sure," John responded loudly. "I was telling you about a conversation that I had had with a dancer who works at some girly joint downtown, Honey for the Bears. It's down by—"

Charles cut in, "Bottom line, John. I'm in a hurry. On my way to Connecticut. Nouri Sommers was in an automobile accident. She's been admitted to a hospital there. St. Mary's. I need you to get me a full report on the hospital as well as the hospital staff."

"Okay, consider it done. Maybe that's where Baldwin was heading. I was telling you about a conversation I had with some dancer downtown. Her name is Bambi. Anyway, she told me that he had stopped in the club. Had a few drinks. And then told her he had a long drive ahead of him."

"Sounds like Gabe might be on his way to Connecticut. Maybe Nouri was going there to meet him," he shouted loudly, shaking his head at the thought of her driving alone.

"Wonder how Baldwin got in touch with her so fast?"

"I don't know. Maybe he didn't. Could be just a coincidence. She's apparently making her rounds saying her good-byes to her past, it seems."

"What! You mean you think she tried to kill herself deliberately tonight?"

"God, I hope not, John! I just meant first she left me a good-bye note and then I found out after talking to the maid at her downtown condo that Nouri had been there earlier. She had been dropped off by a cab. She packed a small weekend bag and then had her chauffeur bring the Viper around for her. She told the maid that she was going to do a quick run by Clint Chamberlain's downtown apartment. And then she asked Heidi to phone Mai Li to let her know that she needed to be alone for a few days." Charles released a sigh, gesturing to the helicopter pilot that he would be there in a moment.

"You want me to run by Chamberlain's apartment and snoop around a little? Maybe she left a note or something," John offered.

Charles swallowed, hoping Nouri hadn't deliberately tried to harm herself. "Yeah, thanks. Check it out. See if there was anything there that might have upset her or—"

John cut in, "I'll take care of it, Charles. What about Baldwin? Should we keep looking for him?"

"Yeah, just in case he's not at the cabin. He has a secret pad no one is supposed to know about down on Maple, check it out. In the meantime, I'll make a quick stop at his cabin in Connecticut while I'm there; after I check in on Nouri at St. Mary's."

"Anything else you want me to do?"

"Call the captain down at the station. Fill him in on what we have so far. Ask him to get in touch with someone at the Connecticut Police Department and find out all he can about the car accident. Tell him I'm on my way there. He can reach me at St. Mary's Hospital. Tell him I'll be waiting for his call. You can give him my cell phone number." He paused briefly to think, holding up a finger to the helicopter pilot again to let him know he needed a few more moments to finish his call. "Oh, and ask Mark to phone Tonya for me," he added. "Tell him I said to tell her that I would telephone her later to let her know what has happened, and while he's at it tell him to also tell her that I'll check to see if Gabe is at his cabin. I know she's worried sick about him."

"Will do. Is that it?"

"I guess, for now anyway. Call me if you get anything else, thanks," Charles said, clicking the cell phone off and putting it away as he made his way to the waiting helicopter.

His heart was racing, and his mind seemed to be bouncing off the four corners of the helicopter.

God! Has Nouri actually tried to kill herself? If so, over what? Or who? Me? The baby she is carrying? Clint Chamberlain? No, he concluded.

It could only be over one thing. Better make that one person. It had to be over her forbidden lover. The stranger who had somehow managed to steal her away from both himself as well as away from the high-powered attorney who secretly held the key to her heart. Yes, it was over Gabe Baldwin. His former partner on the police force as well as his one-time best friend.

Oh God, Nouri! I'm so sorry! Charles cried out in his thoughts.

I should have never agreed to meet with you at Pompillio's that day. I should have never accepted your telephone call. I should have left the door from our past closed. Now look at what's happened. He shook his head in utter disbelief as his thoughts continued to run rampant.

Oh, sugar, you were right to leave me seven years ago. All I've ever exposed you to has been heartbreak, tears and danger. Even from the beginning, starting with Genna. God, I'm so sorry. If it had been you coming home that night instead of me, you would have been killed, stabbed by Genna. And even seven years later, look what her insane love for me has cost you. Oh please forgive me, sugar. He released another sigh as he continued to mentally torture himself.

You would have been better off if you had never known me. Please don't die, sugar! I swear I'll find a way to make things up to you. Please just live so I can say all these things to you in person...

A few moments later, the pilot tapped him on the shoulder to get his attention, nodding his head to the rooftop of the building coming into view; the top of St. Mary's Hospital. Charles quickly put his thoughts of regret and guilt away for a later time.

"Here we are, Charles, St. Mary's Hospital. Shall I wait for you?" the pilot asked, raising his voice over the loud engines of the helicopter.

Charles shook his head, clearing his throat from tears so he could speak to the pilot. "No, no need to wait. I'll be here a while. But you can do me a favor and do a quick run by Gabe's cabin for me to see if he's there. If he is, tell him I'm here at St. Mary's waiting for him. Here's a map I've drawn up for you to his place. It isn't far from here," he said, handing the map to the pilot.

The pilot accepted the map and glanced at it as he spoke. "Sure. Should I fly back to Boston after I do the run-by?"

Charles nodded as he opened the door to the helicopter. "Yes, be sure to call me on my cell phone before you leave, though. I'll be waiting for your call," he said, jumping out of the helicopter and slamming the door shut.

Chapter 28

"Just what the hell do you think you're doing, man?" a dark shadowy figure of a man shouted as he stepped into the light glaring from P.I. Charles Mason's helicopter.

Charles motioned for the pilot to take off before responding to the man behind the loud voice. He glanced at the man now standing beside him. He nodded and then began walking in the direction of the elevator door on the far side of the rooftop as he spoke to the man. "My name is Charles Mason. Dr Holloway is expecting me," he said coolly, pressing the button to the elevator. What floor is his office on?"

The man removed his ball cap to wipe the sweat beads from his forehead as he answered the P.I. "Mr. Holloway is the chief of staff here at St. Mary's. You'll probably find him on the main floor."

Charles stepped inside the elevator, pressing the "M" button. He nodded to the curious man as the doors slid shut. He swallowed nervously as the conflicting emotions continued to surge through his body. "Damn, sugar!" he whispered under his breath with dread as the elevator door suddenly slid open. He stepped out of the elevator and into the main lobby of the hospital and stopped the first person walking past him to get directions to Dr. Holloway's office.

The person he had stopped was the doctor, who smiled, extending his hand to the P.I. "You must be Charles Mason," he said.

Charles nodded. "Yes, Doctor. It's nice to meet you. I appreciate your phoning me. How is Nouri?"

"There's been no change since our last conversation."

"May I see her?"

The doctor glanced at him nervously before speaking. "Certainly, Mr. Mason, but only for a few moments. I should probably tell you there's already someone in—"

Charles cut in, "Hmm. A Boston Police detective right? Gabe Baldwin," he remarked, suspecting as much.

"Yes, that's right. Detective Baldwin said he's the father of the bab—"

Charles interrupted again, "Yes, that's right. He is. I'm just surprised that he's here, that's all. He didn't come here with her, did he?" he asked curiously.

"No, he arrived about an hour ago."

"I'm ready to see her now if you don't mind, Dr. Holloway."

"Certainly, this way, Mr. Mason," he said, leading the way. "That was some telephone conversation we had earlier. Would you mind telling me what exactly is your relationship to Mrs. Sommers?"

Charles leveled his gaze on the doctor when he put his hand on the door of the I.C.U. before entering it. "Well, Dr. Holloway, our conversation was no joke, and you can take it to the bank I will become your worst nightmare if Nouri doesn't pull through this," he replied, brushing past him. He spotted Gabe, who had his head lying down beside the hand he was tightly clutching.

Charles was suddenly filled with compassion for his former partner. He swallowed hard before moving closer. "Gabe," he said his name softly.

Gabe turned to face the P.I. "Charles, look what's happened to Nouri and my babi…" He stopped talking and began to cry. He laid his head back down beside Nouri's hand and continued to sob in despair.

Charles fought back his own tears at the heart-wrenching sight and gently patted his friend across the shoulders before leaning over to kiss his beautiful sugar on the cheek. "Oh God, sugar!" he whispered under his breath, close to her right ear.

He raised up and glanced down at Gabe. "Come on, Gabe. I'll buy us a cup of coffee. We need to talk," he said, reaching over to help the distraught detective to his feet.

Gabe shook his head no. "No, I want to stay here with Nouri and my babi—"

"Please, Gabe," Charles insisted, reaching for his arm, refusing to take no for an answer. "It's important. It's about your father," he said.

Gabe swallowed hard, using the sleeve of his expensive dress shirt as a handkerchief to wipe away his tears. He glanced curiously at the P.I. through his bloodshot eyes. "My father?" he asked.

"Come on, let's go have that cup of coffee," Charles said, helping his friend to his feet.

Charles asked the shift nurse where they could find a cup of coffee at such a late hour, suspecting the hospital cafeteria was closed. In silence the two men went to the waiting room to the right of the I.C.U.

"Black, right?" the P.I. said, handing a cup of coffee to the heartbroken detective. "Gabe, your father suffered a heart attack earlier this evening. Half of the goddamn town has been trying to track you down all night," he said, shaking his head.

Gabe could feel what little blood he had left in his body slowly begin to drain out of it. He swallowed hard. "Is he…Is my father all right?" he asked.

"I don't know. I was told the family jet is waiting to rush you to Greece. Maybe you should call Franklin for an update."

Gabe shook his head in amazement. "Shit! Can you fucking believe this night? Why don't I just go ahead and blow my goddamn brains out tonight and get it over with?" he moaned, glancing at his friend.

Charles shook his head impatiently. "Talk like that, Gabe, isn't doing anyone any good! Especially yourself. Pull yourself together, for chrissakes! Too many people are counting on you right now," he said sharply, reaching for his cell phone. "Here," he said, handing his friend the phone. "Call your family."

Gabe shook his head with dread, taking the last drink of his coffee before accepting the phone. He dialed his family's mansion in Boston.

Before the Baldwins' longtime butler could even get out a hello, Gabe began speaking into the receiver of the phone. "*Signomi*, Franklin. (Sorry, Franklin.) It's me. I just found out about *Patera* (Father). How is he?"

"Apparently he seems to be okay and resting. His doctors managed to get to him in time. Thank God, sir!"

"Indeed, Franklin. Thank God! What happened? Is he still in Greece?"

"He was on the golf course, sir, seventh hole, when he suddenly kneeled over and started gasping for air and clutching his chest. Yes, he's still in Greece."

"Where's *Mitera* (Mother)?" he asked nervously.

"She and Todd flew out right away to be with him, of course, sir. Mrs. Baldwin said for you to get there as soon as you could."

"I see. Would you do me a favor please, Franklin?"

"No, sir! Not if it means calling your *mitera*! She told me to tell you that if you tried to…" He stopped talking and swallowed nervously. "Shall I use her exact words, sir?" Franklin asked nervously.

"No, that won't be necessary," Gabe said, shaking his head and smiling knowing what a hot temper his full-blooded Greek mother had. "I have a pretty good idea what she had to say, Franklin.

"Franklin, all joking aside, I need for you to telephone her for me. Tell her I will phone her later to check on Father. This is important, Franklin, or I wouldn't ask. Is she staying at the Zákinthos villa or the Mykonos flat?"

"She's staying in Zákinthos, sir. She said she wanted to do a little redecorating on the villa while she's there. Says she's depressed since you broke your engagement to Ms. Clayborne, sir. She's back on her I'll-never-be-a-grandmother kick, I'm afraid." Franklin rolled his eyes.

Gabe chuckled, knowing how humorous his mother could be over the least little thing. "Listen, Franklin, something terrible has happened. The woman I am in love with was in a terrible car accident last night. I'm in Connecticut now with her at the hospital here. St. Mary's. Tell Mother I would be there for Father if I could, but someone that I have every intention of marrying as soon as she can mumble the 'I do' words needs me here with her right now. Will you do that for me, Franklin? Also, tell Mother that I have a wonderful surprise that I can hardly wait to share with her. I'll explain in detail when I phone her later, all right?"

"All right, sir. I'll say a small prayer for your friend, sir."

Gabe handed Charles back his phone. "Thanks," Gabe said, glancing nervously at the time. "Apparently Father is doing better and resting now. Thank God!"

"That's good news, Gabe. Tell me something if you don't mind. How did you find out about Nouri's accident so quickly?"

"By luck actually. I had decided earlier to go to my cabin for a few days and get my head screwed back on straight, so I was on my way there when I noticed a tow truck pulling Nouri's Viper up out of a ditch. Needless to say, I was in shock. He told me where they had brought her. So here I am."

"Did Dr. Holloway tell you about her—"

"Yes, of course. After all, I am the father!"

Charles smiled and patted his pocket. "Let's go outside for a smoke."

Gabe nodded and followed his friend outside. "Dr. Holloway explained why he had phoned you. Wonder why she didn't have her driver's license on her."

"I don't know."

"We have a lot to talk about, Charles, but to tell you the truth, I'm just not up to it. Can we deal with our problems later, please?"

"Sure. Nouri takes priority over everything and everyone right now. I'm so thankful Dr. Holloway called. I think I scared the shit out of the poor bastard." Charles chuckled, shaking his head.

Gabe glanced at his friend. "What do you mean?" he asked.

"Well, the good doctor didn't sound too optimistic about Nouri's condition. He painted a pretty gruesome picture to tell you the truth…one I couldn't handle too well…one I wasn't ready to accept. So I told him that she would be well again and she would pull through no matter what!"

"And?" Gabe stated curiously.

"And he kept rattling off all this medical mumbo jumbo, so I sort of got mad."

"Mad?"

"Yeah, real mad. I told the good doctor that, contrary to what he thought, he must do whatever was necessary to pull her back from the jaws of death. I told him I was dead serious. I told him to do what was necessary to pull her through this. If that didn't work, to do the unimaginable. And if that didn't work, to do the unthinkable. But I assured him whatever the cost she would pull through this ordeal!" He flicked his cigarette to the ground.

"Good God, Charles!" Gabe sighed.

Charles shot Gabe a questioning look. "What?"

Gabe swallowed hard before speaking. "Damn it, Charles! Will you forever be in lover with her?"

A question the P.I. had been asking himself most of the evening. Charles glanced at the detective with a look of uncertainty and released a heavy sigh. "Gabe, considering the tragedy that we both are forced to deal with right now, I'm going to ignore the tone you just used with me. That's number one." He paused, reaching into his shirt pocket for another cigarette, and then continued. "Number two. Let's not do this right now. It's neither the time nor the place." He blew out a puff of smoke and then leveled his eyes on Gabe again. "And number three." He sighed. "I think you already know the answer to that question." He propped his foot on the side of the brass railing and glanced down at the hospital's emergency entrance.

Knowing it would probably take at least half a special unit task force to separate him and his former partner if they were to come to blows, Gabe lowered his hands to his sides with a great deal of willpower. Gabe also knew that Charles was right about one thing. This was not the time or the place for a street fight, especially between friends. And certainly not over a woman, even if that woman was a woman they were both in love with. And God help them, both probably always would be.

Gabe stood in silence for a few moments to cool off and released a sigh of built-up frustration. He closed his eyes tightly and swallowed hard in an attempt to make himself behave.

After another few seconds of uncomfortable silence, he spoke in a hoarse, hurt, but nonetheless determined tone of voice. "Charles, in love with Nouri or not, you should understand this. From this moment on she is my wife and I am her husband. There are no other men for her nor women for me. She is going to pull through this ordeal, and we will be married. And she will bless me by giving birth to many, many children in our lifetime together, if God be willing.

"From the first moment our eyes gazed into each other, I knew she and I were meant to be. And God Himself knows I tried to fight it and deny it, off and on, for the past six weeks. All the past bullshit between her and me ends here now, on this very night.

"Whether Nouri dies tonight or one hundred years from tonight, I have no intention of leaving her again," he said slowly, turning to leave. He glanced back over his shoulder. "I just wanted you to know that, Charles," he added, then swallowed hard. "I'm going to go back to Nouri now. You're of course welcome to come along if you like."

Having said what he felt needed to be said to the famous P.I., Gabe slowly went back inside the hospital, leaving Charles Mason staring blankly after him until he was completely out of sight.

Chapter 29

As the painfully slow hours of late night dragged on into the early hours of a new day, the first flicker of hope in police detective Gabe Baldwin's heart finally jarred his attention from the depths of despair when he heard Nouri Sommers mumble in her sleep.

"Gabe, darling, please come back to bed. I need you," she groggily moaned from the depths of her subconscious mind.

"Oh God, darling, I'm here! I'm here!" he hoarsely shouted, smothering her face with hundreds of tiny little kisses. "Hmm," she moaned in response, with her eyes still tightly closed.

"Darling, please open your eyes!" he said as he continued to tightly clutch her hand inside of his.

And then there was the eerie sound of silence staring him in the face again. He felt the muscles in her hands go limp. In panic he pressed the buzzer for the nurse.

Both the nurse and Dr. Holloway immediately entered the intensive care unit. "Yes, Detective, what is it?" the doctor asked.

Gabe turned to face the doctor with a look of fright. "It's…it's Nouri," he said, swallowing hard and moving his position to the side to make room for the doctor to examine her.

"Yes, what about Mrs. Sommers, Detective?" the doctor replied, lowering his head to listen to her heart. He then checked her pulse. He glanced at Gabe as he turned his small flashlight on. With his free hand he held her eyelid open to examine her pupils.

"She spoke. Called out to me. And then I felt her hand relax. It scared me. Is she—"

"No, she's still with us. Relax, Detective," Dr. Holloway stopped him from finishing. He turned his attention back to his patient. "There doesn't seem to be any change in her condition. I don't see how it would be possible for her…" He suddenly stopped talking, not wanting to hurt the detective's feelings, and glanced back at him. He continued, "But of course, if you think she may have said something…" He paused, shrugging his shoulders in disbelief. "I…I, ah…mean if she did speak, of course, this would be a good sign." He bent over to say a few words to his patient in order to appease the police detective. "Mrs. Sommers, my name is Dr. Hollaway. You were in a car accident. Now you are in the I.C.U. of St. Mary's Hospital. If you can hear what I am saying to you, please open your eyes and blink," he said, gently patting her hand. When she didn't respond, he released her hand and straightened his position, glancing back at the detective. "I'm sorry, Detective, but in her current condition there is no way Mrs. Sommers could have said anything. As much as you would like to believe she spoke—"

Charles Mason came rushing into the room, interrupting the doctor in mid-sentence. "Gabe, what's going on?" he asked.

The police detective swallowed hard, shaking his head in hopeless despair. "I…I thought I heard Nouri call out to me," he said in confusion.

Dr. Holloway said, "I'm afraid the detective thought—"

Charles interrupted the doctor. "Doctor," he said, nodding in the direction of the door. "I'd like a word with you in private." As the two men were turning to leave the room, Nouri softly called out again.

"Gabe, darling, come back to bed. I need you."

The doctor blinked his eyes in stunned disbelief.

Gabe lovingly placed her hand in his. "See, I told you, Doctor!" he said.

The doctor pulled out his small flashlight and opened her eyelids and checked her pupils again. "This is amazing!" he remarked, shaking his head.

Gabe and Charles exchanged an excited glance. "Thank you, dear God!" the detective whispered under his breath.

Charles walked over and slapped his friend across the broad shoulders. "Yes indeed! Thank you, Lord!" he said, smiling brightly.

"Well, Doctor?" both men asked at the same time.

"I'll bring in a specialist right away. We should know something in several hours," he said.

As soon as the doctor left the room, Gabe held Nouri's hand again. And Charles circled the bed and picked up her left hand. Both of them bent over to kiss her. Gabe kissed her right cheek and Charles kissed her left. Gabe whispered softly, in her right ear, "I love you, darling." And Charles in turn did the same in her left ear. Teasingly, but even so, his tone was laced with an ample supply of jealousy. Gabe smiled in spite of himself at his former partner and shook his head in surrender.

The P.I. glanced at his friend mischievously. "Hey, old habits die hard," he said, shrugging defensively.

"So I see," the police detective returned, feeling happy for the first time in a very long time. He lowered his head back down to Nouri, whispering more words of love softly in her ear.

A few moments later, the nurse asked both men to leave. The specialists were on their way, and they needed to get her ready for a series of tests.

Both the detective and the P.I. left, but not without a great deal of objection first.

Once outside the I.C.U., Charles turned to his friend, patting him on the back. "Come on, my friend, let's hail a cab, go to your cabin for a few drinks to celebrate, take a shower, get a bite to eat, and have a heart-to-heart! What do you say? After all, we suddenly have nothing but time on our hands. Dr. Holloway has given strict orders to the hospital staff not to let us back in there until late this afternoon," he said, pressing the button to the elevator.

The police detective stepped inside the elevator with his former partner. "All right." He nodded.

Chapter 30

The late evening air rustled the drapes inside the bedroom of Tonya Daughtery, the district attorney of Boston and the fiancée to Boston's most in-demand private investigator Charles Mason.

The stirring of the drapes made the room seem as on edge as she was. "Damn," she mumbled angrily under her breath as she tossed and turned, then turned and tossed. "This is ridiculous!" she complained, forcing her eyes to close shut.

She shifted her position several times in bed trying to get comfortable enough to sleep. It was useless. "Damn it!" she cursed, opening her baby-blues, only to suddenly find herself blankly staring at the ceiling. "Damn you, Charles!" She sighed hopelessly, sitting up in bed.

She glanced at the brightly lit clock sitting on the nightstand, wondering why her fiancé hadn't phoned yet. She lowered her feet, sliding them into her fluffy-pink sandal house shoes as she reached for the matching silk robe to her teddy. She stood to her feet, putting the robe on.

"Oh God, I need you, Charles!" She sighed in frustration, needing to be held. She crossed the room and flipped on the light switch, aimlessly glancing around her bedroom. The large, full-length, antique mirror caught her roving eye. She walked over to the mirror and began to study the image staring back at her.

"Not bad," she said in a quiet voice, gazing the length of her body. *Thirty-five and I still look as though I'm in my mid-twenties. Well, in the face, anyway.* She continued to think while untying the silk robe and letting it fall in a circle around her feet. "Humm." She continued to look closely at herself. After a few thoughtful moments, she removed her teddy and matching silk undies and then stood nude in front of the mirror.

Not one stretch mark! she thought proudly, suddenly remembering the great pains of self-sacrifice and willpower she had forced herself to endure during her pregnancy.

She had eaten enough fruit and cottage cheese and lettuce with no dressing on it to last her a lifetime. No meat. No sugar. No bread…her one true weakness in food. And of course, no coffee, only allowing herself herbal teas. And from the looks of it, the sacrifice had been well worth it! She looked amazing. And rightfully so. She had worked hard at keeping her body looking slim, trim, and in great shape.

Charles Mason loved her body. And God knows she loved his manly body just as much. *What a man!* she lustfully thought, suddenly getting the urge to screw her manly fiancé's brains out.

Oh God, Charles, I need you! She sighed with desire, gently cupping her large breasts in her hands. She gently began to tease the nipples of her breasts with her fingers. "Oh God!" she moaned, lowering her warm hands to roam over her smooth, flat stomach. "Mmm," she groaned softly, letting her right hand roam lower still. She slowly inserted several fingers inside herself. "Ahh…ahh…ahh," she whimpered excitedly, when her mind suddenly flashed her a crystal-clear image of Gabe Baldwin's handsome face. "Oh Gabe! Gabe! God, you were incredible!" she lustfully panted, mentally reliving the heated memory in her brain, quickly bringing herself to an explosive climax. "Oh God!" She swallowed hard, not believing what she had just done to herself after thinking about the handsome detective and what they had shared together earlier that day.

She swallowed hard again, trying to rid her mind of the feelings of guilt she was now experiencing. *Stop it!* she was silently scolding herself for such shameless behavior, when the telephone rang. Shaking her head to clear her mind, she quickly picked up the telephone after glancing at the caller I.D. It was the familiar telephone number of the Boston Police Department.

She answered the call with a half-winded, "Hello."

"Sorry to disturb you, Tonya," the police captain said in a nervous tone.

"Mark! What is it? Did you find Gabe? Oh my God, it isn't Charles, is it?" she returned in panic.

"For chrissakes, get a grip, Tonya! They're both fine. I just called to see if you wanted to go to Connecticut with me. I could use the company, and we need to talk."

"Connecticut! I don't understand, Captain," she replied with confusion.

"Listen, I don't have time to get into this now. I'll explain everything on the airplane. It's…It's Nouri Sommers. She was in an automobile accident there. Both Gabe and Charles are already there apparently, or else en route. Charles had asked John Harman to contact me. So you want to go with me?"

"Oh my God! Is Mrs. Sommers all right?"

"I don't know. Are you going?"

"How did Charles find out about—"

"Listen, Tonya, I don't have time for twenty goddamn questions, are you going with me or not?"

She released a sigh of frustration. "Gee, I don't know. Charles and I haven't officially made up yet. He's got some serious apolog—"

"I don't have time for this bullshit, Daughtery! Are you going or not?" He rolled his eyes with irritation.

"I want to go, but what if he gets mad—"

"Shit, Tonya! You won't know that until you get there, now will you?"

"I suppose you're right. He and I definitely need to talk. Okay, I'll meet you at the airport. Have you made your reservations yet?"

"Yeah, I got a ticket for you too, just in case. Plane leaves in about an hour."

"Then I'd better stop talking to you and get in gear. What airline?"

"Delta is ready when you are!" he said.

"Cute, Mark! Okay, I'll meet you there," she said, quickly hanging up the phone.

The female district attorney was showered, dressed, packed, and on her way to the airport within forty-five minutes of Mark's telephone call.

She could hardly wait to run into the open waiting embrace of Charles Mason, the man of her dreams. She could just picture it now; they would run into one another's arms, passionately kiss, and then find the nearest hotel so they could make up properly. Right?

Wrong! It wasn't the lustful reception Tonya had hoped it would be or expected.

"What the hell are you doing here, Tonya?" the P.I. snapped angrily after turning to see who had just entered the waiting room where he had been nervously pacing back and forth for quite some time.

Tonya stared at him, hurt, fighting back her tears. "Oh, silly me. Where is my head! I was hoping you might want me to be with you at a time like this," she countered heatedly.

Without responding, the hot-tempered P.I. angrily brushed past her, storming out the door of the waiting room.

Mark crossed the room to join her. "I'm sorry, Tonya. It's all my fault. I shouldn't have interfered," he said, patting her across the shoulders.

She wiped away a tear that was rolling down her cheek. "That's all right, Mark. Charles is still apparently in a mood. It's hard for him to let anyone in, especially when it comes to Nouri Sommers. I should've known better."

"Apparently!" the police captain returned, shaking his head. "But she isn't in love with Charles. It's Gabe she is in love with. She's told Charles that time and again, I understand," he said, shrugging his shoulders.

"Don't worry about it, Mark; it will work itself out. Go and find him. Find out how Nouri Sommers is doing and of course Gabe, too. I think I'll go and find a hotel to check in to. I'm pretty bushed," she said, glancing around the waiting room, hoping Charles Mason would come strolling back in.

Mark glanced at her sympathetically. "No, just stay put. I'll pop in the I.C.U. to check on Nouri and say hello to Gabe. I'll get the keys to his cabin in the woods. I'm sure he would want us to crash there," he said, smiling.

She shook her head in objection. "No, Captain. Thanks. I would rather find a hotel out this way, something close to the airport. I intend to catch the first flight back to Boston in the morning. If it's meant for Charles Mason and me to be together, then he will have to come after me this time. I've had it with him!" She sighed hopelessly.

Mark nodded his head understandingly. "All right. Which hotel do you think you might be staying at? I'll phone you later to check on you."

"I'm not sure. And anyway, I'm a big girl. I can take care of myself. Just phone me on my cell phone after you find out more about Mrs. Sommers' condition." She stood on her tiptoes and kissed the huge, burly police captain on the cheek. "Thanks, Mark, I'll talk to you later," she said, turning and walking out the door.

Mark watched the upset D.A. fade out of sight before going to the I.C.U. to check on Nouri Sommers and of course the police detective who had become like a son to him through the years.

After gently closing the door behind him as he entered the I.C.U. of St. Mary's Hospital, the police captain quietly walked up behind Gabe and tapped him across the shoulder. "Gabe, how are you, son?" His tone was one of a caring father.

The crushed homicide detective lifted his head, wiping a tear from his eye with one hand while still holding Nouri's hand with his other hand. "Mark." His tone was one of surprise.

"Hi, son. Can we step in the waiting room for a few minutes? I'd like to talk to you."

As softly as a butterfly's kiss the police detective lowered his head and brushed his lips loving across his sleeping damsel's lips. "I'll be back, darling," he whispered in her ear with his warm breath. The feel of his warm breath kissing her skin made her slightly stir in her sleep. She moaned so softly it was hardly noticeable to anyone but himself. He swallowed hard and glanced at his captain in hopeless despair.

"Well, maybe for a moment. I want to be beside her if…I mean when she wakes up," he said tearfully.

"I understand, son," the captain responded, leading the way out of the room. He crossed the hallway, heading in the direction of the waiting room.

Gabe was walking beside him. He glanced at his friend. "Mark, I'm surprised to see you," he remarked nervously, quickly remembering what an ass he had been the evening before.

"I know. But I had to come. We care about you down at the department. You know that, don't you? Gabe, I'm worried about you, son."

Gabe stopped walking and turned to face his friend. He threw his arms around him as though he were embracing his own father. "I know, Mark. And I appreciate your concern for me."

Mark patted his friend across the back before Gabe pulled away. He cleared his throat. "I said a lot of things last night that I didn't mean, Gabe, and—"

"It's okay, Captain," Gabe cut in. "I had it coming. Don't give it another thought. I had no right behaving the way I did. I am the one who owes you an apology." He released a sigh of regret. "How's Mosley doing?" he added mischievously, not able to resist.

"You broke the poor bastard's nose! How the hell do you think he feels?" Mark responded with a chuckle.

Gabe shook his head angrily. "He's damn lucky I didn't break his legs in two!" he snapped, but he quickly caught himself and calmed down. "It's just he had no right taking those goddamn pictures of Tonya and me to begin with!" He swallowed hard again. "How is Tonya, by the way?" he asked, quickly glancing around the room to make sure Charles Mason wasn't close by.

"Not good. Mason is treating her like a piece of shit!" he said, shaking his head in disbelief.

Gabe shot him an apologetic look. "Maybe I should talk to him about it? Tonya doesn't deserve to be treated like that. It wasn't her fault; it was mine."

"I don't know, Gabe. I don't think Mason is angry at her so much over sleeping with you. No, it is something else that's bugging him and I think whatever it is, he is taking it out on Tonya," he said reaching for a cigarette. "Oops, can't smoke this damn thing in here. Come on, let's go outside and have one."

Gabe nodded while the captain continued to talk. "I don't know, Gabe. I thought if Tonya came to Connecticut with me, Mason might be happy to see her. They would kiss and make up and…well, you know what I mean, right?" He sighed.

"Did you just say Tonya came here with you?"

"Yeah, but Mason was not happy to see her. He got pissed and stormed off. I think he got mad at me for inviting her to come along." He shrugged defensively.

"Where is she?"

"I don't know. Said she was going to find a hotel close by the airport. She's going to catch the first flight back to Boston in the morning." He shook his head. "She's really hurting inside. I feel for her. I shouldn't have asked her to come along."

Gabe sighed. "I can't believe Charles is acting this way with her! Damn, that pisses me off! I'll talk to him about it. If he wants to take his mood out on somebody, he can take it out on me. He and I are destined to go at it sooner or later. May as well go at it now and get it over with," he said heatedly.

The captain flicked his cigarette to the ground. "Don't talk like that, Gabe. You have more important things to worry about now. Your father for instance. And of course Nouri. By the way, how are they both doing?" he asked with concern.

"Well, my father is apparently resting comfortably now. Looks like the worst is over. Thank God!" He sighed. "And as for Nouri, all we can do at the moment is hope and pray. The doctors are waiting for the results of a few tests they had to do on her. She's still in a coma. And the doctors still aren't sure if my babies will make it or not," he said tearfully. "They said it might be a few days before they know for certain. But I'm hopeful."

The captain's mouth flew open in surprise. "What! Babies? Did I hear you correctly, son?" he asked excitedly.

Gabe smiled proudly. "Yeah, three of them; can you believe it? Can you imagine that, Mark? If they pull through, I'll be the—"

The captain interrupted, "Gabe, Nouri and your babies are going to pull through this just fine. Everything is going to work out. You have to believe that, son."

Gabe smiled. "Yeah, Captain, I have to think that way or I'll go nuts!" he said, struggling with his tears again.

The captain looked at his friend. "I talked to the chief of police here in Connecticut earlier today over the telephone. He told me that Nouri had been drinking heavily. Said she was going at a high rate of speed, and with the heavy downpour of rain, she didn't stand a chance." He shook his head sadly.

"He went on to tell me that she didn't have any I.D. on her or in the car. His conclusion was that she might have tried to kill herself. Sorry, son, there was no easy way for me to say this to you."

Gabe swallowed hard as he felt the blood slowly begin to drain the life from his body. He shook his head in objection. "No, hell no! Nouri would never have tried to hurt herself! I don't believe that for a minute!" he countered anxiously.

"Gabe, I'm sorry. I'm just the messenger here. There's something else if you want to hear it."

"What?" the distraught detective replied in a low whisper, not really sure how much more his aching heart could stand at this point.

"One of Mason's men was spotted going into Clint Chamberlain's downtown apartment. Apparently snooping around. We went in after he left but couldn't find anything. Rumor and speculation suggest he might have been looking for a suicide note left by Nouri."

Gabe shook his head firmly. "No, Mark! Everyone is barking up the wrong goddamn tree here. Nouri would never take her own life. No way!" he said stubbornly.

The police captain reached inside his jacket pocket and pulled out a crumbled piece of paper taken from a set of stationary with the famous P.I.'s name and logo on it. "Here, read this. It's in Nouri Sommers' handwriting. She had left it for Charles before she left his house last night. Apparently she left after he had fallen asleep.

"Tonya told me about a note she had removed from Charles' hand last night. She and I had stopped by his place looking for you. Or at least hoping he might have a good idea where you might have gone to sulk. Anyway, I remember what Tonya had said about the note, so I sent a couple of young cops over to break into Mason's place to get the note after I talked to the police chief here in Connecticut. I wanted to read the note for myself. Gabe, it's a good-bye note. Could it mean more? I don't know, that's why I'm asking you to look at it. I…I mean if you're up to it." He handed the detective the piece of paper.

Gabe accepted the note with trembling fingers.

My darling Charles,

I will forever love you. I will forever need you. I will forever think of you, often. But sadly, I have to go. Please don't try to stop me. This is something I need to do. I know you will be hurt. And for this I am so very sorry.

You, my darling, belong with Tonya and Chuckie. This is where your true happiness lies. I know it, and so do you.

As for me, I have tons to think about. Tons of changes in my life to make. And tons of new challenges to face and hopefully conquer.

Surprisingly, big guy, I suddenly find myself looking forward to each of them, starting with the surprise package I'm currently carrying inside. Wow! Who would have thought—me, of all people, a mom! My child is supposed to be a Valentine's Day baby; at least that's what Dr. Douglas told me yesterday.

I haven't decided whether or not I'll ever tell Gabe about our child, but in time I'm sure I'll manage to figure out what's best for the baby as well as myself. I wish I could be as forgiving with Gabe as you have been with Tonya. But I can't. The love I felt for him was apparently something that just wasn't meant to be. Will I forever keep attracting all the Clint Chamberlains of the world?

Anyway, big guy, thank you for everything. Especially for being the one true love in my life that I could always count on. I will forever miss you, Charles!

Bye, my darling,
Nouri

After reading Nouri's heart-wrenching note to Charles Mason, the police detective stood silently staring blankly at it for several long moments, too moved to speak.

The captain glanced at him with concern. "Son, are you all right?"

Gabe was too busy to hear what his friend had just said. Inwardly he was fighting a battle within himself, struggling hard to hold back his tears. An instant later, the battle was over. He had lost the war. The floodgate sprang open, and the tears began to freely flow down his face. "Oh God!" he cried in agony, covering his face with both of his muscular hands. "Mark, it's my fault! Nouri and my babies are inside the hospital struggling for their lives, and it's all because of me and that goddamn Greek pride of mine. Oh God! What have I done?" he sobbed loudly, falling to his knees.

The police captain was so moved by his friend's pain that he began to weep as he continued to pat him comfortingly across the shoulders. "It's okay, son, let it out! Let it all out. Everything is going to be all right," he said, helping his friend to his feet. "Nouri will pull through this ordeal, and your babies will be fine, Gabe. It isn't your fault! Well, not entirely, son. There's enough blame to pass around," he said, embracing the detective as a son again.

Gabe nodded without speaking as his friend gestured toward the glass revolving doors leading into the hospital. "Come on, Gabe. Let's go inside and check on Nouri, and then you and I are going to get something to eat. I won't take no for an answer. Nouri needs her rest, and from the looks of it, you could use a few z's yourself!"

Chapter 31

The Boston D.A. followed the Boston Police detective out on the balcony of her Connecticut high-rise hotel suite, intensely aware of the distance he was continuing to keep between them. His expression had been strained throughout their entire conversation.

Reflecting in her mind how easily she had made him smile just the afternoon before suddenly caused her to feel a pang of regret. God, how she longed for him to pull her into his arms.

She was hurt at Charles Mason and desperately needed to be held. *Please make love to me*, was what she longed to whisper in his ear, but instead she forced herself to ask, "Have the doctors said any more about Nouri's condition?"

Gabe swallowed hard as he gazed at her beautiful face, sexy eyes, and full, pouting lips. He licked his lips, bringing his gaze back to her eyes.

"No, Tonya. Actually, it might be several days before they're able to tell us something—something substantial, anyway," he said, fighting back his need for a warm body to comfort him.

She glanced at his handsome face, understanding his pain. "That's too bad. I'm sorry. I know how much in love with her you are." She forced a smile.

He sighed. "Yeah, well, all I can do at this point is to be hopeful. And of course, pray." He shrugged.

She cleared her throat, gesturing for them to go back inside. "Can I fix you a drink?"

He nodded appreciatively. "Sure, why not? We need to talk, anyway. I didn't sneak away from the captain tonight just to track you down for idle chit-chat." He released another sigh and then went on, "Tonya, I'm sorry. I never meant to cause you any grief with Charles. Is there anything I can do to make it up to you?" He paused to accept the drink from her trembling hand. "Do you want me to speak with him about the way he has been treating you?"

Tonya shook her head, wiping a tear from her eye. "No, thank you, Gabe; this is something he and I will just have to work out, I'm afraid. And to tell you the truth, I don't believe my making love to you has all that much to do with it anyway; it's something else..." She stopped talking and downed her shot of brandy in one long swallow. She glanced needfully at him, biting her lower lip.

Gabe knew what she wanted. And after all, he did owe her. And on top of that, he hated to admit it, but suddenly he needed to be held, too. *But this has to be the last time*, he thought as they both continued to gaze knowingly at one another for several uncomfortable moments, trying to fight their strong attraction for one another as well as their urgent need to be held.

He finally shook himself free from his raging hormones. He swallowed hard. "How about another drink?" he said, loosening his necktie and sliding off his jacket. He smiled nervously, knowing where things between them were heading. It was inevitable.

Tonya knew as well and found it difficult to control the chemistry escalating between them.

She realized he was going to stay. *Hopefully for the whole night.* She took the glass from out of his hand and gasped when his warm hand touched hers. *God, please let him make love to me, now.*

"Where's Charles, do you know?" Gabe asked. "I haven't seen him all afternoon. Earlier at the hospital he went outside for a smoke, but he never did come back inside," he said, glancing at the time. It was ten o'clock.

Tonya set the bottle of brandy on top of the bar and picked up their glasses, handing him his. She smiled faintly. "I have no idea, and at this point I could care less!" Her tone was filled with both hurt and stubborn pride.

Gabe belted his drink down as he sat down on the sofa. He patted the spot beside himself. "Come here. Sit beside me while we talk," he said softly.

She swallowed nervously and quickly obeyed. "All right," she whispered.

He smiled as she sat down, leveling his disturbing teal-blue gaze to her nervous light-crystal blue eyes as he spoke. "You need me to hold you, don't you?" he whispered.

Unable to speak, she simply swallowed hard and nodded.

Gabe smiled understandingly and tilted her face to meet his open mouth. She moaned with urgency, eagerly unbuttoning his shirt. "Oh please, Gabe, I can't wait!" she whispered, jerking her head back and reaching for the zipper to his trousers.

"Oh God, help me," he cried in hopeless despair as his hormones continued to rage out of control.

Tonya unfastened his trousers, anxious to feel his steel-rod of hardened flesh deep inside her mouth again. He eagerly gave in to her animal want for his body. Moments later he shouted his explosive release. "Oh God, Tonya," he cried, running his fingers through her long, shiny black hair.

"Please, Gabe," Tonya breathlessly panted, struggling to help him remove the remainder of his clothing. She just as urgently removed hers and then excitedly positioned herself straddling across his lap, hungrily kissing, sucking and nibbling the side of his throat, mouth and manly chest. "Please," she continued to softly beg, attempting to get him hard again.

Moments later, he was ready to give in to her urgent plea for sexual release. She eagerly inserted the tip of his hardness inside herself, urgently slammed her body down hard on top of his lap, taking the entire shaft of his hardness deep inside, crying with both whimpers of pain and pleasure as she continued to savagely move her body up and down to match his own wild movements.

Soon they both shouted blissful release. Too drained to move, they sat holding one another tightly as they continued to gasp for breath.

"Damn it!" Gabe cursed himself angrily under his breath for his weakness of the flesh in times like this when he needed to be held. He swallowed hard and shook his head.

Understanding his guilt, Tonya tilted his face to hers. "Please, Gabe, don't blame yourself. We needed one another. We haven't done anything wrong," she whispered softly. "Please, let's go to the bedroom and hold each other for a while," she added, whispering in his ear with her warm breath.

Her soft, comforting words and warm breath touching the flesh of his skin caused him instantly to become aroused again. He swallowed hard and gently lifted her in his arms.

After hours of comforting one another and both of them promising this time had to be their last time together, the female district attorney finally fell asleep with a contented smile on her beautiful face.

Gabe slid out of bed, took a quick shower, and left her hotel suite, but not before placing a beautiful long-stemmed pink rose on top of the pillow where he had been lying a short time earlier.

Someone had sent three dozen roses to the beautiful D.A. earlier that afternoon. The police detective figured it had to have been Charles Mason who had sent them. *After all, who else could it have been?* He glanced at his watch, hoping police captain Mark Lane would still be asleep when he got back to the cabin. It was two o'clock a.m.

Chapter 32

"She's an incredible fuck isn't she, Gabe!" Charles Mason snapped as his former partner in fighting crime, the homicide detective from Boston, walked past the chair where he had been sitting in the lobby.

An expression of guilt quickly masked the police detective's face when he stopped and turned to face the man who had just spoken to him. He nervously cleared his throat. "Let's take this outside, Charles," he said, gesturing toward the glass and brass revolving doors directly in front of them.

"Sure thing, Detective!" the P.I. returned, jumping to his feet.

Once outside, they walked to the park across the street from the hotel.

Gabe glanced at his friend from the corner of his eye as he unbuttoned his jacket and started to remove it. Charles quickly stopped him. He swallowed hard, shaking his head. "That won't be necessary, Gabe. I don't want to fight with you. It would be too much like punching my own brother in the face, for godsakes! And anyway, what right do we have waking up the whole goddamn town?"

Gabe looked at him curiously for a moment. "So, what the hell do you want, Charles?"

The P.I. leveled his hurt gaze on the detective. "I want you to promise me that you will stay the hell away from Tonya from now on. She is after all my fiancée and the mother of my son. Or have you forgotten that, my friend?" His tone was sharp and demanding.

Gabe stood in silence several moments, praying that his heart would stop beating so rapidly. The shock of the famous P.I. popping from out of nowhere on him like he had had sent the detective's heart racing. He finally managed a sigh of relief. The last thing he wanted between them was a fight. He nodded. "All right. I can do that, Charles. But only if you're willing to stay away from Nouri as well," he countered just as smugly.

Charles shook his head. "That's a hard one, my friend. I don't think I will ever be able to give her up completely to you or any other man, Gabe. I bet you didn't know she was a virgin the first time I made love to her," he said, closing his eyes as though he were still savoring the thought.

Gabe swallowed hard again, not wanting to hear what Charles had to say. He remained silent, trying to stop the jealous rage now surging through his body.

Charles knew he had upset Gabe, but he continued to talk anyway. "Yeah, she really was. Of course, she never knew that I was aware of the fact. She wanted me to think she was experienced, so hot, so horny. But the moment I entered her body…" He paused, as he reached inside his pocket for a cigarette. He lit up and then offered the police detective one. "Well…" he started and suddenly changed his mind. He released a puff of cigarette smoke. "Bottom line, Gabe, Nouri was the only woman that I had made love to who hadn't been with anyone else. How the hell can any man really ever let a woman like that go? I'm not sure I can." He shook his head.

Gabe stared at the P.I. sharply. "I'm sorry, Charles, but your days with Nouri have come to an end. She and I are hopelessly in love. And just as soon as she is up to it, we'll be married. You have no choice in the matter. All Nouri has ever felt for you is—"

Charles interrupted him with a chuckle. "Allow me. She loves me, but she's just not in love with me. Right?" He flicked his cigarette to the ground.

Gabe flicked his cigarette to the ground as well. "Listen, Charles, the woman you should be worrying about right now is across the street upstairs in bed sleeping inside a hotel suite. She needs you, and like it or not, Nouri needs me. It's me she is in love with, and it's my three babies that she is carrying inside her. Deal with it!" he said sharply.

"I'll tell you what, Gabe, after Nouri is up to it, she can tell me that herself! If she can't, then I've got news for you, Detective; I'm here for the duration. Got it?" Charles huffed arrogantly.

Gabe shook his head in amazement. "You poor bastard! Why don't you just let it go? Do you honestly want to destroy our friendship beyond repair, Charles?"

"Nouri needs me. She always has, and like it or not, Gabe, she always will. Who the hell do you think she comes running to every goddamn time she gets upset!" he shouted.

"That was yesterday's news, Charles! I'm all the man Nouri will ever need from now on. I'm not trying to hurt you. I'm just trying to be honest with you." He swallowed. "I…I'm also trying to save our friendship here. Let it go! Do you hear what I'm saying to you?" he snapped heatedly.

Charles chuckled arrogantly. "Yeah! All man, huh?" he returned angrily. "Is that why you were in the hotel across the street fucking Tonya's brains out, while poor sugar is in the hospital fighting for her life and the life of your babies!" he countered excitedly.

Too angry to speak, Gabe doubled up his fist and punched his one-time best friend in the face, instantly breaking his nose. The next moments that followed were bloody and gruesome. All bloody hell broke loose. It took ten uniformed police officers to finally separate the two men from one another.

After being patched up and receiving several matching sets of bandages, slings and casts, the two men were read their rights and tossed into opposite jail cells, anxiously waiting for the district attorney of Boston and the captain of the Boston Police Department to come and bail them out.

"Boy, they sure fucked up this time, Tonya," the police captain said into the phone. He shook his head in disbelief.

"You can say that again, Mark!" the female D.A. said, wondering if the fight between the P.I. and the police detective had anything to do with her having had sex with the detective again.

"I have half a mind to let Gabe sit in his goddamn cell for a while and think about it!"

"Yeah, Charles could use a little time to think about things, too," she replied.

"Wonder what they fought over," Mark said curiously.

Tonya swallowed nervously. "I'd like to know that myself," she said, feeling guilty.

"Boy, the goddamn newspapers are going to have a field day over this one!" Mark said.

"Oh God, I can hardly wait! We'll all probably lose our jobs over this mess!" Tonya added.

"You might be right. Well, guess we'd better get our tails down to the station and bail those two out. I'll meet you down there in an hour or so. The police chief is sending a car for me. I'll see you there," Mark said, hanging up the telephone on his end.

Chapter 33

As the Boston district attorney waited patiently for the Boston Police captain to meet her inside the Connecticut Police Department so they could make arrangements to have the Boston Police detective and the Boston private investigator released into their custody, she continued to mentally study the seductive moves of the sexy new female detective from France.

Tonya rolled her eyes in amazement as she continued to quietly watch a few of the male detectives openly flirt with the sexy young woman in the super tight-fitting short skirt as they took turns one by one stopping by her desk. She chuckled in spite of herself when one of the men came up behind the young woman and rubbed his noticeable erection across her shapely bottom as she bent halfway across the desk to reach for a file.

Isabella Bedaux turned to face the horny detective, suggestively biting her lower lip before releasing it slowly, sliding her gaze with interest to the young man's thick, full lips.

The detective glanced around the busy room as he discreetly slid her hand inside his, slowly sliding their hands downward, stopping when he reached the front of his trousers. He gently pressed her hand against his zipper. His hardened condition was still obvious. He grinned at the seductive little minx, wickedly nodding in the direction of the empty room directly across from them.

The female district attorney quickly found herself thinking it was a damn good thing the empty room had a door on it. She smiled, shaking her head at the turned-on couple. An instant later, she remembered a recent conversation between herself and Charles Mason; one in which he had shared a story with her about the former district attorney of Connecticut and a sexy bombshell detective from France. "Jesus! That must be her," Tonya whispered under her breath, standing to her feet as the Boston Police captain rushed in her direction.

Before the police captain reached the female district attorney, Isabella Bedaux grabbed him by the arm. "Excuse me. Are you the police captain from Boston?" she asked, gesturing with a wave of her hand for the young male detective to take a hike.

"Yes, I am. Mark Lane," he returned, glancing at the young woman questioningly.

"Hi, my name is Isabella Bedaux. Our captain said I should keep a lookout for you and let him know when you got here." She smiled brightly.

"Yeah, well, I'm here, Ms. Bedaux. Will you go and get—"

The Connecticut Police captain walked up behind Mark, startling him. "Hello, Captain. Sorry to have to drag your ass down here over something this ridiculous!"

"Tonya," Mark said, motioning her into the conversation. "Captain, yes it is, a goddamn pity. I have half a mind to—"

Tonya interrupted, "Hello, Captain. I'm the district attorney of Boston, Tonya Daughtery," she said, extending her hand.

"Wow, you're quite beautiful, Ms. Daughtery, if you don't mind me saying so."

"Thank you, Captain. Please call me Tonya." She smiled.

"I see you have met Ms. Bedaux. She'll take you two down to the holding cell after we finish a little paperwork. Sure you want to get those two hellions out of jail tonight? Still a lot of passion brewing between them the last time I checked on them. Maybe you should let them sleep it off. I don't know if our city can handle them getting it on again tonight." The Connecticut Police captain's tone was one of uncertainty.

Mark stifled a chuckle and glanced at the female D.A. "I don't know, Tonya, what d'ya think? Think we should give them a little time to cool off with one another?"

Tonya shrugged, glancing at the female detective who was standing beside her, hanging on to every word being exchanged. "I don't know, Mark, maybe we should. I'd feel terrible if they went at it again tonight. On the other hand, maybe we should at least talk to them first."

The Connecticut Police captain nodded. "Okay, I'll take you two down in a minute. Isabella, go down to the holding cell and let Mr. Mason and Captain Baldwin know that the captain and Ms. Daughtery are here and I'll bring them down in a few moments. Captain, I need to discuss a few things with you and Ms. Daughtery first if you don't mind," he said, gesturing toward his office.

As Tonya and Mark followed the Connecticut Police captain to his office, she glanced back over her shoulder at the female detective who was hurriedly applying a fresh coat of lipstick. Their gaze met briefly, and Tonya could've sworn she saw a wicked grin tug at the corners of the young woman's mouth.

After filling out the proper release forms and catching up on the situation surrounding Nouri Sommers' accident, the captain escorted them to the elevator leading to the holding cell.

"Remember, Tonya, talking to these two was your idea, not mine!" Mark said, shaking his head, dreading the thought of seeing either one of his hot-tempered friends. "Oh, and if Mason starts any more of his bullshit with you, I want you to leave his ass in here until hell freezes over, okay?" he added, smiling and patting her across the back in a fatherly manner.

Tonya smiled and stepped off the elevator as it came to a stop.

"Well, it's the door on the right. If you need anything, just have one of the guards let me know. It was nice meeting both of you," the police captain said, shaking first Tonya's hand and then the Boston Police captain's.

Moments later, they walked into a room surrounding them in wall-to-wall jail cells.

Tonya and Mark shared a glance, shaking their heads as they witnessed the sexy female detective busy at work trying to seduce the handsome police detective from Boston.

The captain interrupted them when he laughed loudly. "I can't take that poor son-of-a-bitch anywhere, can I, Baldwin?" he remarked, deliberately trying to spoil the mood.

Gabe chuckled in spite of his physical pain. "Guess not, Captain," he said, blushing profoundly.

"Can you excuse us, Ms. Bedaux?" Mark remarked coolly.

Isabella leaned back over to face Gabe and suggestively kissed the police detective on the cheek, causing Tonya to jealously want to rip the young woman's heart out with her two bare hands. If looks could kill, Ms. Bedaux would be dead.

"I'll be upstairs if you need me to drive you back to your cabin, Gabe," she said seductively, quickly shooting a dagger in the direction of the female D.A.

Mark noticed the tension between the two women mounting over Gabe. He leaned over to whisper in her ear. "Down, girl, your master is watching," he said, causing Tonya to both blush and glance at the famous P.I. at the same time.

After Isabella left the holding cell, the police captain looked first at the detective and then at the famous P.I. "Boy oh boy!" he started. "Just look at both of you crazy sons-of-bitches! Your goddamn left leg is broken, Charles. And your right one, Gabe! Wonderful!" He shook his head and then went on. "Your left arm is in a sling." He rolled his eyes at the P.I. as he continued. And Gabe, so is your right one! Wonderful! Mason, your goddamn nose is broken, and so is yours, Gabe. Once again, men, all I can say is 'wonderful'!" He shook his head again in utter dismay. "What the hell is going on between you two lunatics?" He scratched the side of his head in confusion.

Both men remained silent, refusing to comment.

Mark glanced at Tonya and released a frustrated sigh. "Well, gentlemen?" he stated sharply. But still both men refused to comment. "Wonderful!" he sighed.

"Okay, fine! You two don't want to talk. Good!" he shouted. "Then both of you can sleep on it! Maybe you'll feel like talking about it in the morning."

He nodded in the direction of the door. "Come on, Tonya. Let's go," he said, turning to leave.

Tonya glanced at Charles helplessly, and he shot her an icy dagger in return. She swallowed hard. "Fine, Captain. I'm ready if you are," she returned, shaking her head with disappointment at her fiancé.

Before she reached the door, the P.I. shouted in her direction. "Goddamn it, Tonya! Get back here and get me the hell out of here!" His tone was sharp and demanding.

She glanced at him angrily and then turned her attention back to the police captain. "Shall we, Mark?" she remarked, nodding in the direction of the door.

"Swell!" Tonya heard the hot-tempered P.I. complaining under his breath before the door closed shut behind her and Mark.

Chapter 34

Tonya Daughtery stepped out of her morning shower and reached for the hotel bathrobe with one hand and a towel with the other. She walked into the bedroom, toweling dry her hair. She glanced at the clock on the nightstand, wondering what time the Boston Police captain was going to phone her.

She was anxious to meet with him that morning so they could get her fiancé out of jail. She really hated the thought of having to leave him sitting it out in a jail cell all night, and quite frankly she missed him.

She sat on the side of the bed and picked of the telephone and dialed room service.

"Good morning. Would you please send me up a pot of herb tea, two slices of dry whole-wheat toast, a small glass of prune juice, and a copy of this morning's newspaper? Oh, and if you can find me one, I'd like a copy of this morning's newspaper from Boston as well. Thanks," she said, placing the receiver back on its hook.

A short time later, while applying her makeup, she was startled by the sudden appearance of a man standing inside her bedroom doorway. He was holding a copy of a newspaper in his hand. She turned to face the intruder and the chilling gaze of lust on his face. She instinctively checked the belt fastened around her bathrobe to make sure it was securely fastened in place.

"You should have knocked first!" she snapped, crossing the room and briskly snatching the newspaper from the young man's hand, recognizing the young guy who worked for the hotel. She shot him a heated dagger as she glanced over her shoulder and strode past him.

"Ahh…I did, miss, but apparently you didn't hear me," he replied in a seductive tone, gazing lustfully at her again.

"Well," she remarked, with a snip, not believing him. "That will be all. Where's the tab?"

"Are you sure there's nothing else I can do for you while I'm here, miss?" he replied suggestively, slowly traveling his gaze down her body.

She cleared her throat and snatched the tab from the cocky young man's hand as he teasingly waved it in mid-air.

"Yes, I'm sure," she said sharply, quickly adding, "and by the way, young man, don't address me as miss." She paused to sign the tab for her breakfast and then continued. "It's District Attorney to you! Have a nice day," she said, handing him the room service check and nodding toward the door silently, suggesting he do himself a favor and leave. She gave a sigh of relief after he had left the room.

The young guy had given her the creeps. He reminded her of a case she had tried a month earlier in Boston, a case in which a young bellhop working in one of Boston's finest hotels had raped and robbed a wealthy middle-aged woman who had come to their city on vacation. Tonya swiftly shook the unpleasant thought from her mind and reached for the belt to her bathrobe again, making sure it was still snugly in place.

After putting the chain lock on the door to her hotel suite, she sat down to have her breakfast. She removed the rubber band from around Connecticut's local newspaper and then poured herself a cup of tea. She straightened out the newspaper and picked up her cup and took a sip as her gaze scanned the headlines. "Oh shit!" she squealed, spitting out a mouthful of hot tea after seeing the headlines.

Boston's Dynamic Duo Together Again...But Wait...Stop The Press...

Instead of waltzing in to stop a crime they seem to be doing a new dance step together! Shall we call this new dance of theirs the fisticuff shuffle?

Boston's very own cop of the year, homicide detective Gabe Baldwin, and one-time partner, best friend, and also cop of the year, now International P.I. of the Year, Charles Mason, were photographed fist-fighting at a local park close to the airport in the wee hours of the morning.

According to an eyewitness there on the scene it took an entire special unit task force to separate the two men.

What started it all? Perhaps another rumor, who knows? Lips are tightly sealed on this one, folks! But according to one of the photographs posted below, it shows both men leaving The Embassy Towers, Connecticut's newest and most exciting hotel.

Our reporters discovered that even though neither man was registered at the hotel, the beautiful fiancée to Charles Mason, who is also the district attorney of Boston, was registered there.

Big deal, you say? Well, it most certainly could be! The person that sold The Connecticut Herald *this photograph, along with several others, spoke of the Boston Police detective entering Ms. Daughtery's hotel suite at nine thirty p.m. last night and leaving her suite at two thirty a.m. this morning (you can plainly note the time of his arrival and departure from the photograph provided by the camera that took the actual shots), and as you can see by the next photograph, both men had a short discussion in the downstairs lobby of the hotel shortly before the fight. And once again, as you can see by the time on the photograph, it was less than twenty minutes after they had left the hotel.*

The remaining photographs on the following few pages were taken every ten minutes following that photo, ending with both men being read their rights and arrested following their release from the emergency visit at St. Mary's Hospital, where another rumor quickly surfaced after our reporters arrived on the scene.

The rumor involves the beautiful young widow to billionaire tycoon Ethan Sommers. Apparently Ms. Sommers had been admitted to the emergency room following a late-night car accident the night before.

Our reporters are working around the clock on both stories and will give our readers a full report as soon as the pieces to both puzzling stories are put together.

Tonya Daughtery sat staring blankly at the newspaper she was still tightly clutching. "Oh my God!" she mumbled, sliding her chair back and standing to answer the telephone.

She put the receiver to her ear and heard the police captain shouting excitedly even before she had had an opportunity to say hello. "Have you seen the goddamn newspaper yet this morning?" he bellowed loudly through the phone lines.

"I have," she said.

"The one from Boston?" he asked sharply.

"No, the local paper."

"Get your hands on one from Boston A.S.A.P. I'm on my way to your hotel. I'll be there in about thirty minutes!" he snapped. Before she could respond, she heard the loud click of the police captain slamming the phone down on his end.

"Swell," she mumbled, sticking her index finger in her ear to try and stop the echoing.

Eager to read the headlines in her hometown newspaper she hurried across the room and sat back down at the dining cart and quickly removed the rubber band from around the paper. She took a sip of her tea and opened the newspaper with trembling fingers. Her eyes widened. She swallowed hard, attempting to read the article below the incriminating photograph of herself with the naked detective.

Our Tax Dollars Busy At Work...Not!

Boston's very own district attorney caught with her lace panties down. But wait, who's that she's with? Oh no! It's...It's...Boston's very own Cop of the Year, homicide detective Gabe Baldwin, isn't it?

The female district attorney swallowed hard, too shocked to move, too stunned to cry, and too upset to think clearly. *Oh my lord! This can't be happening to me! How could the newspaper reporters have gotten their hands on this!* she wondered as she continued to glance at the photograph in the newspaper. "How can I ever show my face in Boston again?" she whispered under her breath, sliding her chair back to answer the door.

"Who is it?" she asked, struggling with tears.

"It's me, Tonya. Mark."

Tonya unlocked the door and jerked it open, throwing herself into the police captain's muscular arms. "Oh thank God!" she cried, hugging him tightly. "What am I going to do, Mark?"

Mark gently patted her across the shoulders as he spoke. "I don't know, Tonya, but I promise you I'll think of something," he returned protectively.

"I don't understand any of this! How could the newspaper get their hands on that photograph? Who could do this to me? Why, for chrissakes!" She continued to cry.

"Mosley gets my vote, but then again..." He paused, released her from his embrace, and stepped inside the hotel suite. "The walls apparently around this goddamn place have ears!" he added, closing the door.

He noticed the silver coffeepot sitting on the dining cart and headed across the room in that direction. He poured himself a cup of tea, thinking it was coffee. "Whew! Just what I need," he said, taking a drink, only to just as quickly spit it back out of his mouth. "What the hell was that shit!" he asked.

The female D.A. chuckled in spite of everything falling apart around her ears. "It's herb tea, Captain. I don't drink coffee," she added, shaking her head in playful dismay.

"Well, it tastes like shit! Let's get a pot of goddamn coffee up here while we try to—"

Their conversation was put on hold by a knock on the door. They exchanged a curious glance before the captain started toward it. "I'll get it while you call room service," he said, reaching for the doorknob. He glanced back over his shoulder. "While you're at it, order me an egg sandwich on toast or something, will you? I'm starving to death," he said, jerking the door open and staring Gabe Baldwin in the face.

"Hi, Captain, can I come in?" the homicide detective asked.

"What the hell? Sure, come on in. How the hell did you get out of jail?" he asked, curiously scratching the side of his head as he backed away from the door to allow the police detective to hobble in.

"You mean after you and Tonya left us stranded there?" Gabe asked angrily.

Tonya returned to the living room after ordering room service, noticeably stunned to see Gabe standing there talking to the police captain. Their gazes met. "Tonya," he said in a hurt tone. She nodded.

The captain went on. "Where's Mason?" he asked curiously, closing the door.

"I don't know." Gabe shook his head.

"Who got you out?"

"Isabella Bedaux offered after she found out you guys left me stranded," he returned with an icy edge, shooting an angry dagger at the female D.A., and then he turned his attention back to the police captain. "After Isabella bailed me out, we left. As you might imagine, Charles and I were still not speaking, so I left him there. We got halfway to her place when I suddenly had a change of heart, so we went back to bail his ass out. By the time we got there, he was gone. I don't know who bailed his ass out, and they wouldn't tell me!" He sighed.

The captain shook his head. "Gabe, go sit down on the sofa. Just looking at your sorry ass is causing me pain here!" he barked, following behind him. "Have you seen the headlines in *The Boston Enquirer* yet?" he asked.

Gabe nodded. "Yeah, that's why I'm here this morning," he said, cringing as he sat down. He laid the crutches off to the side of the sofa and then shifted his position. He released a sigh of regret.

"What the hell are we going to do? I'm not just going to stand by and let Tonya be humiliated over this!" Mark said, in a protective tone of voice.

Gabe shook his pounding head. "Me neither! Got any ideas, Mark?"

"No, not a one. Do you?" He shook his head again. "Who do you think was the miserable bastard that did this?" he asked angrily.

Gabe released another painful sigh. "I don't know. We all have made our fair share of enemies. The business we're in. It could have been any one of at least a hundred people give or take. Charles has so many enemies I've lost count." He shook his head thoughtfully. "Could've been someone wanting to humiliate him by using his fiancée. And of course, I have just as many enemies who would love to see me humiliated."

"True! And of course Tonya herself has put a lot of scum away. Could be someone wanted to get even with her one way or another. But even so, Mosley gets my vote, the prick!" the police captain said with heated passion.

Gabe chuckled in spite of his pain. "Yeah, well, that was my first thought, Mark, but after I thought about it for a few moments, I suddenly remembered what a chicken-shit bastard he was when he was still on the force. Frankly, he doesn't have the stones for anything that clever. He's not that bright. And anyway, he knows I would break his scrawny little ass in two over something like this. Take my word for it, he's plenty afraid of me! No, it isn't Mosley. But you can bet your sweet ass it's someone close to home!"

Their conversation was interrupted when room service buzzed. "I'll get it, Tonya," the captain said, walking toward the door.

Tonya swallowed nervously as she joined the police detective on the sofa after he motioned her over by patting the empty spot next to him. She glanced at him as she sat down, mixed emotions running rampant. Regret, hurt, anger, sympathy, and need.

Gabe swallowed hard, gazing at her. "God, I'm so sorry, Tonya," he whispered hoarsely, reaching for her hand. She quickly pulled away from his touch, folding her arms angrily. "Isabella Bedaux, Gabe?" she whispered, momentarily forgetting the real issue at hand.

He rolled his eyes in disbelief. "Tonya, please don't pull that jealousy shit on me. Not now, I can't handle it! I thought during our conversation last night that we both agreed—"

The police captain entered the room feeling as though he was in the way. "Excuse me, I forgot something," he said, quickly exiting the room, allowing them a few moments to be alone.

She turned her attention back to the detective. He lifted her hand to his lips, gently kissing it as he continued to speak. "Don't be like that with me. I can't bear for you to be angry with me." He swallowed hard.

She gazed into his bloodshot eyes. "Did you?" she asked suggestively, suddenly feeling the need to know if he had slept with the sexy bombshell detective from France.

He gently ran his soft fingertips across the knuckles of her right as he continued to look into her eyes. "Tonya, what choice did I have? You and the captain left me stranded in that goddamn jail cell all night."

A tear of disappointment slowly trickled down her cheek as she slowly removed her hand from his. "I'm sorry, Gabe, I just needed to know." She swallowed hard.

He released a sigh of regret. "Listen, Tonya, you're not in love with me.

It's Charles you're in love with. Like you said. We didn't do anything wrong. We needed one another. We comforted each other, period! It ends there, right?" he whispered, reaching for her hand again.

She bit her lower lip nervously. "Of course. It's just now, I mean, since we've made love, I…I'm confused. I do love Charles, and I do understand your being in love with Nouri Sommers, but—"

He cut in, silencing her, "Tonya, there is no us. We needed one another. You needed to be held. I needed to be held. We both needed a warm body. It happened. Now it's over. You go to Charles. And I return to Nouri."

"And what about Isabella Beadux? I know I have no right feeling the way I do, but—"

"Tonya, for what it's worth, I didn't make love to Isabella. I had sex with her. I made love to you. There's a difference. I'll always care about you, and if you ever really need me, I'll be there, Charles or no Charles. Do you understand what I'm trying to say?"

She gazed at him longingly. "Will you at least kiss me one final time?" she asked tearfully.

He smiled, pulling her into his heated embrace. The next instant he took her breath away with one of his masterful, fiery hot kisses.

"Oh God, Gabe," she breathlessly whispered as the police captain entered the room. He cleared his throat loudly, separating the star-crossed lovers.

"Shall we get back to the issue at hand here, please!" he barked, as an order.

Chapter 35

Still carrying around the cell phone her boss had given to her the day he left for France six weeks earlier, the private secretary to high-powered attorney Clint Chamberlain entered his law office for the final time.

Violet Smith crossed the room that held so many memories of their past together, then slowly circled the six-foot-long solid oak desk, traveling her index finger along its top from corner to corner.

She continued to be lost in thought, recalling a few of the last conversations she had had with her friend, who also happened to be her boss. She laid the cell phone down and sat in his overstuffed padded chair, tossing her head back on the headrest and propping her legs up on top of the desk. She closed her eyes as her mind raced on.

"Wake up, sleeping beauty," he said in a nervous tone of voice.

"Clint! Clint Chamberlain, is that you?" Violet smiled remembering.

"I'm fine, Violet, calm down!" he said as she forced herself to sit up in bed wiping the sleep from her eyes.

"Violet, Ethan Sommers has gone crazy. I think he may have killed a young woman tonight."

"Oh my God! What happened, Clint?"

"I don't have time to explain right now. I'll tell you everything I know when you meet me at the airport. I'll be arriving in about an hour. I need a favor. I need for you to run by my apartment and pack me a suitcase. Don't forget my passport. I'll meet you inside a restaurant called Michael's."

"But—"

He cut in, "I'm sorry, love, I don't have time for explanations. I'll explain everything when I see you. Now be a good girl and hop to it. You don't have much time."

Her mind raced forward.

"Violet, I need you to transfer one billion dollars of Ethan Sommers' money into a new account in Switzerland. Make up a name or number. I don't care which. Just don't give that information to anyone, including Ethan

Sommers. I'll call you later for the new account number. Oh, and Violet, I want you to gather up every file, video tape, record, computer disk, or whatever we have on The Medallion Corporation and put it into a safety deposit box under your name. I want it to appear as though we have never even heard of the name Ethan Sommers. Got it?"

"Yes, anything else?"

"Yes, keep my cell phone with you at all times while I'm gone. It will be my way of keeping in touch with you. When I phone, don't use my name or call me 'boss.' I have my reasons. Call me Traz, okay?"

Violet opened her eyes to glance at her watch as her memories continued to haunt her. Suddenly the high-powered attorney's cell phone rang. "Oh shit!" she squealed, almost falling out her boss's overstuffed chair. She nervously picked up the cell phone.

"Hello," she said in a shaky voice.

After a brief moment of silence on his end, the high-powered attorney spoke. "Hi, Violet, this is Traz. I need to see you right away. Can you meet me?" he said nervously.

"Oh my Lord! Is it really you?" she exclaimed, not believing her ears.

"Yes. Can you meet me?" His voice was so low she could hardly hear him.

"Of course, where?" she asked nervously.

"Is anyone in the office with you?" he asked cautiously.

"No. Everyone's gone. I'm here by myself," she said, quickly glancing around the room to make sure.

He sighed. "Good. Go and unlock the back door. And then put on a pot of coffee. I'll be there in ten minutes."

Too stunned to move a muscle, Violet sat staring blankly at the cell phone she was tightly clutching in her right hand. An instant later, she forced herself to her feet, not remembering later how she had managed to unlock the back door to the office or put on a pot of coffee as she eagerly waited for the high-powered attorney to arrive.

After a tearful reunion she freed herself from his embrace, stepping back a few steps, tearfully gazed at him, before slapping him across his up upper arm.

"Damn you, Clint Chamberlain! I ought to kill you for letting me grieve over you so. Why the hell didn't you telephone me, for chrissakes! Surely you knew how upset I would be thinking you were dead!" She shook her head angrily as she continued to yell at her friend. "And all this time—"

He cut in, flashing her his to-die-for grin, instantly silencing her. "I missed you too, Violet," he said, pulling her back into his arms.

"God, I still can't believe it!" she said embracing him snugly for a few moments before pulling free from his arms. She stepped back and smiled. "What's going on? Everyone thinks you're dead, and you apparently want them to, why?" she asked, wiping the tears of joy from her cheek.

He smiled again. "Why don't you get us a cup of coffee and we'll have a long talk, okay?" He walked to his desk and glanced around his office, shaking his head as he sat down. "God, the walls look so bare. The file cabinets are all gone. Where is everything, Violet?" he asked, slouching back in his seat.

She handed him a cup of coffee with her trembling hand. "You're dead, remember? Your brother stopped by a few days ago and—"

He interrupted. "Never mind. I can only imagine, knowing Clark as well as I do." He shook his head. "You didn't turn over anything I asked you to put in a safety deposit box did you?" he asked.

She smiled, sitting down on the corner of the desk. "I'm surprised you even asked me that question, Clint Chamberlain!" She rolled her eyes in hurt dismay.

He flashed an apologetic grin. "I'm sorry, love. Of course you didn't. You're right, I do know better, Violet." He sighed, reaching for the coffee cup.

"Have you been in town long? I mean are you aware of what happened—"

"You mean Nouri's car accident?" he cut in. "Yes, I know; that's why I'm here. I saw the newspaper this morning."

"I don't understand."

"What's to understand? I need to see her."

"But what about Charles Mason and that homicide detective?"

"What about the two bastards?" he snapped.

"I just meant with the cloak and dagger thingy you apparently—"

"Yes, you're right. I don't want anyone to know I'm alive. With Ethan Sommers dead and gone, I knew the federal government would come after me with a vengeance over all his illegal activities. They would be out for blood. And the one billion dollars I have that belongs to the Asian Mob!

"So, after my car went off the bridge in London, it gave me an idea. I knew death would be my only way out of this mess. The opportunity presented itself. I had to take it. My one-time shot for freedom. No way in hell was I going to rot in some jail cell over Ethan's mistakes."

"But I don't understand. The newspaper reported the Feds ran a complete investigation on Mr. Sommers and could find no wrongdoing whatsoever on his part."

He shook his head and sat his cup down. "Yeah, sure they did! That was just a ploy on their part to flush me out! I'm telling you, Violet, they want to get their greedy little hands on the Mob's money and—"

"But even if Mr. Sommers was mixed up in some illegal activity with the Mob, I know you well enough to know you would never be a part of any of it, right?"

He released a sigh. "Violet, my pet, I'm not exactly the angel you would like to believe I am, I'm afraid," he said, shrugging defensively.

"Clint Chamberlain, I know you. And if you were doing anything illegal, it was to protect Ethan Sommers."

"Yeah, well, just the same, if the Feds or Mason had their way about it, I'd be hung by the neck at high noon!"

"Oh, that's ridiculous! I think you're overreacting. I know you can work things out here, for chrissakes. No need to live the rest of your life hiding in the shadows!"

"Listen, Violet, maybe you're right, but to work something out with them, I would have to hand over the billion dollars that belongs to the Asian Mob. No way in hell am I going to do that! And of course, there is also the little problem concerning the Mob. Even though Jin Tang is dead, the man stepping into his shoes will hunt me down like a dog because of that money, so as you can see, I really don't have much of a choice here."

"So what are you going to do?

"I have a plan. A wonderful plan, Violet, my pet!" He smiled mischievously.

"Mmhmm. Which is?" she questioned suspiciously.

"Well, actually, I've already set the plan into motion. You see, Violet, I've bought an island."

"A what?"

"Well, actually, it's a big island. An island paradise. I figure I could start a new life there with you, my loyal and devoted secretary and best friend. And of course Nouri. And—"

"So that's why you came back to Boston? To kidnap Nouri Sommers!"

"Yes, I can't live without her, Violet."

"But?"

"Yes, I know she supposedly fell in love with the horny detective from

Boston. But I also read where he was engaged to the Baron's daughter Lisa Clayborne. And as far as Mr. Super Dick goes—"

She cut in giggling. "Who?" she remarked with a laugh.

"Mason, P.I. extraordinaire," he said. "As far as Mason is concerned, I read in *The Boston Enquirer* he too was engaged. He's supposed to be getting married to the D.A. of Boston. So you see, Violet, there's no one left to take care of Nouri. She needs me."

"Well, maybe so, but according to this morning's newspaper, both men are still hopelessly in love with her and were actually put in jail last night because of a fight they had over her."

"Yes, and the paper also reported that Super Dick caught Super Cop sneaking out of his fiancée's hotel room in the early pre-dawn hours of the a.m. So that proves that Mason is still in love with his fiancée. What's he need Nouri for now?"

"Yes, that's true. But there's also one thing you're overlooking, Clint."

"What's that?"

"The paper reported Nouri slipped into a coma right out of surgery. It doesn't look good for her, I'm afraid."

"Yes, I know. But I plan on getting her the best doctors money can buy to make her well again."

"I see."

"Yes, I have everything all planned out. We'll be one happy family on our island paradise."

"Clint, what about the woman that—"

"Oh, well, I got that worked out too. Her name is Tori St. Clair." He paused, reaching nervously for his cup of coffee. He continued, "Hold on to your bonnet, Violet, for what I'm about to share with you." He swallowed nervously. "She is…ah, ah…she will be…ah, ah…"

"Clint Chamberlain, spit it out, what will she be—"

He cut in with a mischievous chuckle, "All right. Tori will be joining us on the island. I have no choice. I have to bring her with us. You see, Violet, Tori is carrying my baby. A little girl actually. Due around Valentine's Day."

"Oh my God!" she said in stunned disbelief.

"Close your mouth, Violet," he said with a laugh.

"I don't understand. I thought you said you came back for Nouri." Her tone was one of confusion.

"I did. I can't live without her."

"I think we need to have a second opinion on the CAT scan the hospital in

France apparently forgot to take on that sick brain of yours, Clinton Jerome Chamberlain! There isn't a woman in the world who would let you—"

He stopped her with a laugh. "What, Violet? Have my cake and eat it, too!" he mused, shaking his head. "I told you, I have everything worked out. My two women will never see one another. Tori will be on one side of the island, and Nouri will be on the other. No one will be the wiser."

"Oh my God!"

He laughed again. "Calm down, Violet, I have everything under control," he said, standing to his feet and walking around the desk, pulling his secretary up into his arms and playfully swinging her around the room in a circle. "Now, all we have to do is go to Connecticut and sneak Nouri out of the hospital," he said, whirling her around in a circle again.

Chapter 36

P.I. Charles Mason continued to curse under his breath after reading the morning headlines of *The Boston Enquirer* newspaper for the fifth straight time in a row. "Son-of-a-bitch!" he shouted angrily.

"Why do you keep torturing yourself, Charles, let it go! There's nothing we can do about it, is there? The damage has been done!" his friend Robert Barnet from the F.B.I. said, shaking his head in utter disbelief over the situation.

"Damn it! There's got to be something we can do. I can't just stand by and let Tonya be humiliated like this, man!" Charles said.

Robert nodded, understanding his friend's frustration over the incident. "Yeah, you're right, of course. Maybe if we knew who sold the negatives of Tonya and Gabe together to the goddamn newspaper, we could think of something, but unfortunately…" He paused briefly to stub out his cigarette.

Then Charles smiled for the first time in days. "That's it! Thanks, Robert. You gave me an idea."

Robert raised a questioning eyebrow. "Oh shit! Who do you expect me to kill?" he asked, reaching for another cigarette.

Charles chuckled at his friend's dramatic query. "No one—if it comes to that, I'll do that part myself!"

Robert shook his head. "I didn't hear that, Charles! As a matter of fact, we're not having this conversation!" He chuckled. "Okay, playtime is over, what's this brilliant idea of yours?"

"Can't tell you. That is unless you're—"

"Shit!" Robert cut in. "I knew it! You want me to be a part of this idea, right?"

"Well, of course you don't have to be. I can always have—"

"Enough, all ready! Stop doing that shit! I hate it when you do that!"

Charles chuckled. "You hate it when I do what exactly, Robert?" he teased.

"Forget it! I'm probably going to live to regret this, Charles." He paused. "All right, count me in."

Charles smiled. "Good! Now all we have to do is break into the main office of *The Boston Enquirer*. They surely must keep some sort of records of their secret payoffs to the sons-of-bitches that sell them shit like the fucking negatives of Tonya and Gabe, right? Well, all we have to do is hunt down the bastard who sold them the negatives and force him to admit to using some sort of trickery, making it appear the—"

"Oh, I get it. You want me to make the bastard change his tune. Say it was someone other than Tonya or Gabe in the photographs, right?"

Charles nodded, releasing a puff of cigarette smoke from one corner of his mouth that wasn't still swollen. "Yeah, that pretty much sums it up, Robert. What do you think?"

Robert considered his friend's idea thoughtfully for a moment. "Yeah, it might work. But what if the son-of-a-bitch is someone we can't bully that easily?" he asked with concern.

"Well, one thing's for damn sure; we won't know that until after we find out who the bastard is, right? So I suggest before we come up with a plan B, we—"

"Right. I'll take care of the break-in myself. Your sorry ass is obviously out of commission for a while. Jesus! What the hell is going on between you and Gabe, for chrissakes?"

Charles felt his face suddenly flush and the muscle in his jaw instinctively jerk when the image of Gabe and Tonya intimately embracing jumped back inside his brain. He swallowed hard, glancing sharply at the federal agent. "You mean besides him fucking my fiancée every goddamn time he gets the urge!" he barked jealously.

Knowing his friend as well as he did, the P.I.'s response made Robert chuckle. "Give me a goddamn break! I know both you and Gabe a hell of a lot better than that! There's more to it between you good ol' boys than that! You guys have shared women before; plenty of them in the past. Nope, not buying it! It's that Sommers broad, isn't it?"

Charles nervously picked up his cup of coffee with one hand, slowly running his fingers through his hair with the other. He released a sigh. "Truthfully, I don't know what the hell is wrong with me. I suppose I'm confused. Tried to take my shit out on Gabe. Sure Nouri has something to do with it, I guess. Don't get me wrong, Gabe having sex with Tonya really pissed me off, but nothing I can't handle. But when he told me to back away from Nouri, I don't know if it was the way he said it to me, or his tone, but in any case, something inside of me went nuts! And of course before I exploded, there were other things building up inside me, too."

"Like what?"

"Well, someone has to take the blame. I mean what has happened to Nouri. Jesus!"

"Charles, I understand your pain, and I even understand your confusion. But I honestly can't understand why you feel the need to place any blame."

Charles swallowed his last drink of coffee and then set the cup down. "The blame, all of it, everything, lies on my shoulders. And I'll tell you why. Since Nouri has asked for my help, she has lost her husband, her lover Clint Chamberlain, and on top of that, the man I personally entrusted her care and safety to has gotten her pregnant. Yes, that's right, Robert; Nouri is carrying not one but three tiny little babies inside her who belong to Gabe Baldwin! And on top of all that, I'm beginning to think maybe her accident wasn't an accident after all!" He shook his head sadly.

"What! You mean you think someone tried to kill her?" Robert said.

"No, I mean I think she tried to—"

"Suicide!" the federal agent exclaimed. "Why on earth would you think she wanted to take her own life, for godsakes, Charles?"

"Because she saw Tonya and Gabe being intimate with one another. It broke her goddamn heart!"

"And Nouri seeing them together that way makes you jump to this conclusion?"

"Well, what else can I think?"

"I don't understand."

Charles wiped a tear from his eye. His friend crossed the room and patted him across the back. "I'm sorry, Charles. Let me get you another cup of coffee, and you can explain things to me," he said, reaching for the P.I.'s coffee cup.

Charles nodded and cleared his throat. "I think everything that has transpired in the past few months was probably more than she could deal with. First of all there was the mystery surrounding her husband before his death—the Lambert murders, implicating her. Then Clint Chamberlain suddenly disappears into thin air right after her husband vanished off the face of the earth. The death threat. The attempted kidnapping. Catching first her husband cheating on her. And then her lover doing the same. She finds out that her best friend of seven years is the one who had wanted to see her dead for the past seven years. Poor thing has fallen in love, out of love, and in love again, only to have her heart ripped from her chest after catching her new lover cheating on her as well. Then she goes through the trauma of discovering she has somehow managed to get pregnant along the way. Jesus,

Robert, no one in their right mind should have to face something like that alone!" He shook his head sadly again.

"Yeah, poor kid has had it rough, no denying that," the federal agent responded, reaching for the coffeepot again.

"I think she might have been saying good-bye to her past that night. Starting with her note to me."

"What note?"

"She left a note on the pillow she'd been sleeping on earlier that night before she tiptoed out of my place. Later I found out that she had stopped by Chamberlain's downtown apartment. And then, the next thing I know, I get a goddamn phone call from the chief of staff at St. Mary's Hospital in Connecticut."

"I'm sorry, Charles, but I still don't see what makes you think she may have tried to commit suicide. Everything you have told me so far has been speculation and circumstantial."

Charles nodded to his friend and held up his empty cup for a refill. "Robert, Nouri didn't have any I.D. on her, and she had been drinking heavily before the accident." His voice was filled with pain.

"I see. So you're willing to ruin a friendship over speculation, misplaced guilt, and jealousy?"

Charles shot his friend a curious glance. "Is that how you honestly see it, Robert?"

"I'm sorry, my friend. I know that's not what you want to hear, but that's how I honestly see it. I think you should have at least waited until Nouri has an opportunity to tell her side of the story. You could be way the hell off base here, Charles," he said, returning to the comfort of his chair.

"Ah, I don't know. Maybe you're right. Maybe I did take my guilt out on Gabe. And maybe I am jumping to conclusions with Nouri. Hopefully it was just an accident. But with Gabe, I'm afraid it's a little too late for the 'I'm sorrys.' The damage between us has already been done!"

"Ah shit, Charles! I hate it when…" Robert suddenly stopped talking and shook his head, knowing how stubborn his friend could be when he already had his mind made up about something.

"When what, Robert?"

"Never mind. I'm sure you'll figure it all out when you're ready, Charles. In the meantime, what are you two guys going to do when you run into one another at the hospital?"

"I'll make arrangements to fly down and see her after visiting hours are over. They make most visitors leave at eight o'clock every night."

"I see. And what about Tonya, have you talked to her yet?"

Charles slid a cigarette from out of the pack and lit up. "No, my friend. That is something I'm not up to yet." He sighed and then continued. "Now, how about we get back to clearing her name. What d'ya say?" He forced a small smile, even though it felt very painful.

Chapter 37

With every intention of carrying Nouri Sommers out of St. Mary's Hospital in Connecticut and disappearing with her forever, high-powered attorney Clint Chamberlain and his private secretary Violet Smith managed to slip past the nurses' station off to the right of the I.C.U. where Nouri was safely being cared for while she was still in a coma.

"Shhh," Violet whispered to Clint after his left foot kicked the corner of a food cart parked in the middle of the floor.

"Sorry," he whispered, tiptoeing behind his secretary into the room where Nouri was sleeping restfully.

Several machines were hooked up, monitoring her sleep and breathing patterns as well as her heart rate. Clint released a deep sigh of sadness. "Oh my God, Violet! Look at my beautiful sweetness," he whispered tearfully.

"Poor thing," she replied, shaking her head.

Clint walked to the bed and lowered his head, brushing his lips softly across hers in a kiss. "Oh God, sweetness," he whispered against the side of her throat. He swallowed nervously. "Nouri, can you hear me? It's me, sweetness, Clint. I've come for you." He sighed with sadness. "But now I'm afraid to try and take you out of here. I'm afraid if I take you off the machines, you might die on me or something, baby. Can you hear what I'm telling you? Sweetness, I love you so much! I'm going crazy without you. I miss you so much.

"Baby, I know how upset you must have been thinking I had died when my car went off that bridge in Paris, and I'm sorry for not getting in touch with you sooner. But you have to believe me when I tell you that I wanted to, but I just couldn't. I had my reasons. We can discuss all that after you're better. Listen, sweetness, I have to go now. If the police catch me here, they'll toss my ass in jail. But don't worry, baby, I'll be back for you in a few days. Hopefully, you'll be off this machine by then," he whispered, then swallowed, nervously glancing at his secretary, who was now motioning for him to leave.

"Hurry up, Clint, someone is coming!" she said in a nervous whisper before poking her head out the door again.

"Shit!" he spat in a hushed tone, lowering his head to Nouri's ear. "Baby,

I have to go now, but I'll be back. Please get better, sweetness. I...I love you," he whispered in her ear with his warm breath, causing her to slightly stir. He kissed his sleeping beauty gently across the mouth and then quickly exited the room, closely following behind his secretary.

"Oh shit!" he whispered, seeing homicide detective Gabe Baldwin heading in their direction from the other end of the hallway.

Violet grabbed her boss by the arm and pulled him around the corner to their right.

"Jesus, that was close!" Clint said, swallowing nervously.

An instant later, they quietly disappeared.

Curious as to who the clumsy couple was leaving the I.C.U., Gabe hobbled as fast as his crutches would allow him to the nurses' station.

"Who were the two people that just came out of the I.C.U.?" he asked the head nurse behind the counter.

"What two people, Detective? I never saw anyone, but then again, I wasn't watching that closely," she said, shrugging.

Gabe's face flushed with anger. "Don't you realize just who the hell you have in there, miss?" he snapped sharply, and with his next sentence he was demanding to see Dr. Holloway.

Within the following hour the homicide detective had made all of the arrangements to have Nouri Sommers transferred to the Sommers mansion in Boston along with a round-the-clock staff of both doctors and nurses, of course, with a great deal of protest from Dr. Holloway. But Gabe did it anyway.

The specialist the detective had asked his mother to arrange for and have flown in earlier that morning from Greece to care for his beloved Nouri agreed the staff at St. Mary's Hospital in Connecticut had done all they could for her. At this point there was nothing left for them to do for her. The hard part, Nouri Sommers would have to do on her own. She would have to want to wake up.

Mai Li, the tiny Asian woman who ran the massive Sommers estate, came running out of the mansion to greet the helicopter carrying both Nouri Sommers and homicide detective Gabe Baldwin. "Oh, Detective, thank you for bringing the miss home for Mai Li to take care of. I've been so worried about her," she shouted tearfully over the loud engine of the helicopter.

"You're welcome, Mai Li. I'm hoping familiar surroundings will be good for her. Of course you understand…" He stopped shouting and shook his head with annoyance at the loud engine noise. "Let's talk inside; it's too noisy out here, and anyway, I want to make sure Nouri is safely put in bed and is resting comfortably before we talk, okay?"

The tiny woman nodded. "Yes, of course. Mai Li understand. I'll go put on some coffee. You look like you could use a cup," she said smiling.

"Yes, thank you. And before I forget to tell you, we will need to use all the spare bedrooms inside the mansion for the staff of doctors and nurses. Would you please help everyone get a room and get settled in? You can double them up if you have to."

"Mai Li see to it right away, sir," she said, stepping to the side so the police detective could hobble in the house with his crutches.

Soon Nouri Sommers was safely and comfortably sleeping inside her own bedroom. As Gabe gently closed the door to Nouri's bedroom behind her departing attendants, he turned to face his sleeping beauty, releasing a deep sigh of hopefulness as he stared at her. Then alone he heard her softly repeat the words she had mumbled in her sleep at the hospital.

"Gabe, darling, come back to bed, I need you."

He smiled and crossed the room to join her. "Darling," he said softly, sitting down beside her on the bed. "I'm here," he whispered against the side of her warm neck. He laid his head on her chest for several moments and wept. "Oh darling, please come back to me. I need you so much. Our babies need you so much. Do you understand?" he sobbed.

She stirred, attempting to roll on her side, causing Gabe to jump to his feet excitedly. He ran out of the room in search of the specialist his mother had flown in from Greece.

"Dr. Kavala, come quick, please!" he shouted excitedly down the hall.

The doctor jerked the bedroom door open after hearing the summons. "Yes, Detective, what is it?" he asked, rushing to the detective.

Gabe motioned him inside Nouri's bedroom. "*Peraste*. (Come in.) She moved, Doctor. Almost rolled to her side; please hurry."

"*Fysika* (Of course)," the doctor responded excitedly, entering the room and rushing to Nouri's side.

Mai Li had heard the detective shout for the doctor and came running. She stood quietly inside the doorway, nervously wringing her hands. Gabe noticed and went to her, gently taking her by the hand. "You're part of this family, Mai Li. I haven't had time to tell you until now, but Nouri is going to pull through this tragedy and bless me with three babies. She's pregnant." He smiled proudly as he watched the specialist check Nouri's vital signs.

Mai Li swallowed hard. "Miss is going to be a—"

Gabe cut in with a chuckle, "Yeah, isn't it great? She'll be a wonderful mother to my children. We will be married the moment she's well enough to mumble the words 'I do'!" He smiled again.

"Oh, Detective, I'm so happy! I suspected she was with child; that's why I made her go and see Dr. Douglas. Miss been throwing up every day since she came back from France. She would first want something sweet to eat and then something sour. And then couldn't make up mind what she want. Mai Li knew. I'm so happy for you and miss, Detective." She smiled warmly. "Mai Li be good nanny to young detectives!" she said with pride.

"Yes, of course you will, Mai Li. An excellent nanny indeed!" He smiled, patted her hand, and then crossed the room to join the doctor. "Well, Dr. Kavala?" he asked anxiously.

The doctor glanced at the detective. "Detective Baldwin, would it be possible for you to excuse us. I need to work with Ms. Sommers for a while. I should have some answers for you soon."

"But she is all right, isn't she?" he asked with concern.

"Well, at the moment there doesn't seem to be much of a change. But I still need to work with her for a bit. I'll run a few minor tests, check the babies, and tell you something as soon as I can," Dr. Kavala said in response, patting Nouri gently on the hand, causing her to stir again. The two men exchanged a hopeful glance and smiled.

"All right. I have a few things I need to take care of," Gabe said, glancing over his shoulder at Mail Li. "Come on, Mai Li, I could use some coffee, and I need to make a few telephone calls."

After the police detective phoned his father to check on him, he phoned his mother to thank her for sending Dr. Kavala to take care of his bride-to-be, the same beautiful woman who was going to pull through this terrible ordeal and make his mother a grandmother by Valentine's Day. Becoming a grandparent was something his mother had been dwelling on for a very long time.

After a good scolding from his mother for his shameful behavior as of late and a tearful good-bye, Gabe made several telephone calls in an attempt to track down Charles Mason, but with no luck. He gave up on the effort and phoned the Boston Police Department instead, hoping his young partner Al

Ballard hadn't gone home for the day. He had an assignment posed as a favor to ask of him, one that could get young Ballard into a lot of trouble if he got caught completing it.

The assignment was to break into a locker belonging to the young loudmouth cop that Gabe believed might have been the person responsible for making the incriminating photographs public of himself and D.A. Tonya Daughtery. With any luck, there would be some evidence linking police officer Rick Hobner to the dirty deed.

Within an hour, the young detective phoned his senior partner at the Sommers estate and asked to meet him at one of their favorite downtown coffee shops. He had good news.

The police detective swiftly left the Sommers mansion, borrowing Nouri's shiny candy-apple-red Corvette. Anxious to meet with his young partner, he sped swiftly downtown.

His young partner noticed him the moment he hobbled into the coffee shop. Al jumped to his feet and waved to him.

Before Gabe could slide into the booth, his excited young friend handed him an envelope containing a set of the incriminating photographs of the detective and the sexy female D.A. of Boston along with a bank deposit slip for a very large sum of money made out to young police officer Rick Hobner.

"Fabulous!" Gabe said with a sigh.

"Looks like you were right about Rick, Detective," young Ballard remarked, shaking his head with disgust.

Gabe nodded his head with a decisive yes. "Is he working tonight?"

"No, the captain hasn't called him back to work yet. But he did stop in yesterday to see the captain. But the captain had already left for Connecticut with Ms. Daughtery."

Gabe drummed his fingers thoughtfully on the table for a brief moment. "Do you know where the little prick lives, Ballard?"

The young detective shook his head again. "No, Rick and I have never really been friends. He's not one of my favorite people, if you know what I mean. But I understand he has been hanging around down on Eighth Street a lot since his friend opened a restaurant. A Greek joint. The Trojan Horse I think is the name of it."

Gabe released a frustrated sigh. "You want to do a quick run by the place with me? You might be able to keep me from killing the slimy little prick, but

I doubt it," he said, shaking his head angrily.

The young detective swallowed hard. "From the looks of it, sir, you don't look much like kicking anyone's rear right at the moment," he said, smiling and shaking his head.

Gabe chuckled at his young friend. "Don't worry about me, kid. Don't let this cast fool you, I can handle myself just fine," he returned in a playful tone.

Young Ballard blushed. "No doubt, sir," he said. "Oh, by the way, I understand the captain and Ms. Daughtery are on their way back to Boston, sir. He's pretty mad at you for not telling him you were coming back to Boston tonight."

Gabe shrugged defensively. "Yeah, well, I didn't know myself until after it happened. It was a spur of the moment thing. I got spooked after I thought I saw two people coming out of the I.C.U. at St. Mary's. Thought it best to bring her back to Boston after that. I think I made the right choice for her," he said, glancing at the time. He waved for the waitress, who was busy flirting with a guy at the counter. He wanted her to bring them a refill on their coffee.

Later on, the search at the Greek restaurant down on Eighth Street turned out to be fruitless. Gabe released a disappointed sigh. Police officer Rick Hobner was not there.

"Well, sir, do you want to hang around here for a while? See if Hobner shows up?" young Ballard asked.

"No, I don't think so, Ballard. Hop in, I'll drop you back to your car. I can't waste any more time on this tonight. I need to get back to the Sommers estate. I don't want to be away from Nouri too long. Go back to the station and see if the captain is back yet. Tell him I broke into Hobner's locker and tell him what I found. I don't want you taking any heat for me, kid. Tell him to phone me at Nouri's house. See what he wants to do about Hobner. Ask him if he wants to handle it or should I. There's no way in hell I intend to let Tonya lose her job over my stupidity."

"Sir."

"Yes, Ballard."

"Do you want me to get Hobner's address? I'm pretty sure I can get it without the captain or anyone else knowing." He smiled nervously.

Gabe pulled the car door shut and started the engine and quickly pulled out into traffic. He glanced at his young friend. "You know, Ballard, at first all I could think about was killing that slimy little bastard. He's been nothing but a thorn in my ass for the last six weeks. Since the night he brought Nouri down to the station after stopping her for a D.U.I." He paused to light a cigarette and then went on. "But now, suddenly killing him isn't all that important to me now. All I care about is Nouri and the three babies that she is carrying. My babies, Ballard. Three of them," he stated proudly.

Young Ballard's mouth flew open in stunned surprise. "What? You're going to be a father, sir?" he finally managed after the shock of it sank in.

Gabe smiled. "Yeah, can you believe it? I'm so happy about it I could bust!"

"I knew the first time you two laid eyes on one another there was something magical going on between you two."

"Yeah, me too," Gabe agreed, smiling. "Remember I told you after we left the mansion that I felt like I had been struck by a—"

Young Ballard cut in, "A bolt of lightning, yeah, I remember, Detective." He smiled.

"Well, kid, I'm hopelessly in love with her. And I can't wait until she gets well enough to marry me. My bachelor days are over; she is the one!"

"You're going to leave behind a lot of broken hearts, sir," Al responded teasingly.

"My wife-to-be is also going to be leaving a broken heart or two behind, Ballard." He smiled.

"Mr. Mason?"

"Yes, I'm afraid he will be the most heartbroken of all, kid. But he belongs with Tonya and Chuckie. He knows it, and in time he'll realize that."

"If you don't mind me asking, sir. Is Mrs. Sommers the reason you two got in that fight yesterday?"

Gabe looked thoughtful briefly, flicking his cigarette out of the car window. "Mostly, I think. You see, Ballard, Mr. Mason has been in love with Nouri for a very long time. He sees himself as her personal protector. She was a kid when they first met. Anyway, he fell hopelessly in love with her. She was in 'like.' After a while, she left him. She needed room to grow. Charles never stopped loving her. In his heart, he felt as though someday she would come back to him. Through the years, he kept her alive in his heart and in his head. One day she needed him again. Not necessarily what he had in mind, but a start, or so he thought. Nouri does love Charles, but she just isn't 'in love' with him.

"There are many different types of love, Ballard, and even though you don't understand what I'm trying to share with you right now, someday you will. You see, kid, you can have sex with anyone. That doesn't necessarily mean you are in love with that person. Although a lot of people sometimes misconstrue sex for love. Not until Nouri Sommers did I even understand the real meaning of love. To honestly be in love with someone is the most amazing feeling in the world, Ballard. It goes far beyond the physical aspect of a relationship. Right now, Ballard, I would sell my soul to the Devil if he would let her and my three babies be all right. Before Nouri, I could've never imagined myself saying something like that, much less admitting something like that so openly," he said, smiling, as he pulled the Corvette alongside of the young detective's car.

"Wow, the Devil, sir?" Young Ballard cringed at the thought, causing Gabe to chuckle.

"It's just an expression, Ballard! I just mean there is no price that I wouldn't pay if I could guarantee Nouri's and my children's health and safety."

"I understand, sir." He nodded. "Topic change, sir. So what do you want me to do about Hobner, sir? Forget about him?"

"For the time being anyway. Have the captain phone me. I'll talk it over with him and see what he wants to do first. Tell him that I said I'll be waiting for his call. Now, my young friend, thanks for all your help tonight, but I guess I'd better bolt. I need to get back to Nouri," he said as the young detective hopped out of the car.

Young Ballard glanced over his shoulder and watched the senior detective in the shiny candy-apple-red Corvette disappear out of sight.

Chapter 38

With little effort on his part, F.B.I. agent Robert Barnet, along with two other federal agents, secretly entered the main office of the Boston Enquirer Building, swiftly locating the hidden files listing the names of people who would prefer to remain anonymous after they had accepted large amounts of money for inside information on political, high-society, or celebrity-status individuals.

The latest entry in the journal was to police officer Rick Hobner of Boston. The amount paid was staggering.

"Whew, we're in the wrong profession, gentlemen," the federal agent told the two secret agents with him.

Both men nodded their agreement as they continued to photograph the evidence inside the file.

Robert Barnet handed over his findings to private investigator Charles Mason thirty minutes later in his home on the south side of the city.

"Well, well, well, one of Boston's finest. Maybe we should do a quick background check on our young friend before I rip his goddamn head off! What do you think, Robert?" Charles said.

Robert nodded. "I told you, Charles, that I'd handle it, and I will. Give me a couple of days and I guarantee you young Hobner will be making all types of press-related apologies to both the detective and Ms. Daughtery, and of course to all the fine tax-paying people of Boston for—"

Charles cut in, "And after this apology, Ms. Daughtery will of course show what a kind and forgiving heart she has by deciding not to sue the young cop for malicious slander and character defamation, right?"

"Exactly. Young Hobner will be reduced to traffic duty for the rest of his life; that is, unless he decides to quit the force first."

"Now, there's only one thing we need to do."

"What's that, Charles?"

"Where are we going to find a couple of actors to say they were paid to dress up and pretend to be the detective and the district attorney?" Charles asked curiously.

Robert shrugged. "Well, with all your millions, Charles, that should be easy enough for you to arrange. I'm sure there are a lot of starving actors out there that would love to strike it rich overnight, right?" He smiled.

"All right, but what about Gabe's car? Were his tags caught on any of the photographs?"

"I don't think so. But even if they were, we'll make Hobner admit publicly that he borrowed the detective's car the day in question."

Charles looked thoughtful for a moment. "Have we covered our asses in every possible angle of this? I'd hate to have something unexpected pop up and—"

"Except for one small thing."

Charles cringed knowingly. "The fight we had in the park back in Connecticut, right?"

"Yes, and Gabe entering Tonya's hotel room that night at nine thirty and not leaving until two in the morning."

"Shit!" Charles sighed in.

"Well, Charles, what do you want to do about that?"

"You've already had the charges on us dropped. How about Gabe and I kiss and make up in public. We'll call it a misunderstanding. I'll get the captain to tell the press that he had business with Tonya earlier in her room, and when Gabe arrived he was there, and he was still there long after Gabe left. Mark can lie about some case they were working on secretly or something or another." Charles stood to his feet and hobbled over to the bar to pour himself another shot of bourbon.

The federal agent nodded his approval of the P.I.'s plan to clear the police detective and the D.A. in the scandal surrounding them. "Sounds believable. Are you going to get in touch with Gabe and Tonya tonight? We don't have a lot of time, Charles."

Charles released a deep sigh. "Yeah. I'll take care of Gabe and Tonya. And you take care of persuading young Hobner to go along with the new program. I'll get in touch with the captain, too. You'd better get going. You have a lot to do. I'll meet you back here in about twelve hours, okay?"

Robert nodded, glancing at his watch. "I'm out of here then."

Charles smiled appreciatively, sliding off the barstool and standing to his feet. "Thanks, Robert. I owe you one," he said as his gazed followed his friend to the front door.

Robert glanced over his shoulder as he opened the door to leave. "Better get off that leg for a while." He smiled and walked out the door.

Chapter 39

As Gabe Baldwin continued to struggle with the silk black bow tie he was trying to fasten around his muscular neck, his mind was racing as rapidly as his heart was beating. Giving up on his efforts to properly fasten the tie, he crossed the room to the large walk-on balcony inside his bedroom at his family's Greek villa.

Walking outside for some fresh air, he inhaled deeply as he nervously glanced at all the activity going on around the beautiful estate. He chuckled as he overheard his mother giving the staff of servants some last-minute duties to attend to. She appeared to be as nervous as he was. Hey, who could blame her? After all, he had made her wait an eternity for her only son to get married. *That is to say, her only blood son*, he thought after seeing his spoiled and pampered adopted brother making his usual grand appearance.

There had never been a real bond between them as children. Thinking they would never have children of their own, his mother had driven his father crazy until he finally gave in and let her adopt their first child. The family's wealth had created a real spoiled brat in his older brother. He remembered Todd's ever-growing jealousy of him while they were growing up.

Too bad! I would've really loved for us to have become good friends, especially on a day like today. I could use a good friend. Gabe sighed, watching Todd immediately demand his fair share of attention.

"Hey, over here, Dimitris! *Tha ithela enna ouiskee.* (I would like a whiskey.)"

"*Tipota allo* (Will that be all)?" Dimitris, the newest member of the Baldwin family staff, asked politely.

"Did I ask for anything else, Dimitris?" Todd spat rudely. Gabe shook his head, irritated with his spoiled older brother, and turned his gaze in the direction of his favorite aunt on his father's side of the family, Aunt Marsha.

"*Kalimera, thia Marsha* (Good morning, Aunt Marsha)," Franklin, the family's head butler, said warmly.

"*Yassas, Franklin.* (Hello, Franklin.) It's nice to see you again," she replied, smiling.

"*Boro na sas prosfero enna poto, madam* (May I offer you a drink, ma'am)?"

"*Stin anglika, sas parakalo* (In English please)," she said with a chuckle.

"May I offer you something to drink, ma'am?" he asked, suddenly remembering her limited Greek vocabulary.

"No thanks, Franklin. I'm certainly capable of waiting on myself. But I appreciate the offer. Say, tell me, Franklin, how's that handsome nephew of mine doing?" she asked with a giggle. "I can hardly wait to meet the lucky lady who has stolen him away from his good old Aunt Marsha," she added teasingly.

Gabe smiled lovingly as he shifted his attention over to where his father was standing with his golfing buddies. He could hear them talking.

"Gabriel, I've heard your son's fiancée is even more beautiful in person than in her photographs. I can hardly wait to meet her."

"Yes, Nouri is lovely. And being pregnant by my son only adds to her beauty."

Gabe smiled lovingly at his father for the kind words he had just spoken.

"I understand, Gabriel, that it was touch and go for her and the babies for quite some time."

His father nodded in agreement to what his friend had just said. "Yes. Nouri had us all plenty worried for a while. But thank God she and my future grandchildren pulled through it all like little champs. I did tell you all three of the babies are little boys, didn't I, gentlemen?" his father remarked proudly.

"Only several hundred times now, Gabriel," his one friend reminded.

"Well, it's the first time I've heard it, Yannis," his father's other friend cut in teasingly.

"You know, Gabriel, we've heard it rumored your son's fiancée hasn't gotten her memory back yet. Is that true?"

His father nodded in agreement again. "Yes, that is true. But nonetheless I've never seen a couple more in love. *Thelo na kano mya proposil* (I'd like to make a toast)!" he said, holding his glass in mid-air. "*Kali creksil* (Cheers)!"

"*Sinharitiria* (Congratulations)!"

"*Efcharisto para poli. Aspro pato* (Thank you very much. Bottoms up)!" his father said with pride, holding his glass high in the air for everyone to see.

Gabe smiled warmly and walked back inside his bedroom, quickly making his way to the wet bar to pour himself a shot of brandy.

Sitting in a chair, he reached for the telephone, desperately hoping this time he would finally be able to make contact with Charles Mason, his one-time best friend and former partner in fighting crime.

Gabe was still devastated over what had transpired between them a few months earlier. He missed Charles' friendship, and the thought of not having the famous P.I. in attendance at his wedding was very upsetting to him.

Unable to reach him, Gabe released another disappointed sigh before belting down his shot of brandy. He put the empty brandy snifter down on the brass and gold coffee table and laid his head back, closing his eyes. Even with all the loud outdoor activities going on around him, his mind soon drifted backwards in time, to three months earlier.

"Nouri, darling please wake up. I need you desperately," he said, whispering in her ear. Suddenly she opened her eyes, yawned, and seductively stretched.

He could hardly believe his eyes. He began to sob tears of unbelievable joy. "Nouri! Oh God, darling!" he whispered in amazement.

She looked at him strangely, smiled nervously, and then glanced around her surroundings. "Where am I?" she whispered softly, sliding herself up in a sitting position.

"Darling, you're home. I had you brought here three days ago," he explained as he lovingly continued to stroke the side of her cheek with his curled index finger.

She cleared her throat nervously. "Three days ago?" she remarked, trying to remember something...anything.

"Yes, that's right, darling. Three days ago."

"Darling? Why do you keep calling me darling?" she asked, reaching for the satin sheet and pulling it up to her chin shyly.

He continued to gently travel his finger down the side of her arm as he spoke. "You...you don't know who I am?" he said in a hurt tone.

She shook her head no without speaking.

As he gazed into her eyes with deep rapture, he felt himself become instantly excited. He noticed the effect his instant condition had on her and smiled when he noticed her shiver and nervously bite her lower lip. He smiled knowingly. "Ahhh...so you do remember me," he playfully returned, knowing that even if she hadn't remembered him, her body certainly had.

She smiled shyly. "Remember what?" she asked, sliding her gaze down to his full, sexy lips. She swallowed hard.

"Me, darling." He smiled seductively.

She blushed and swallowed hard, bringing her gaze back to his incredibly sexy teal-blue eyes. She smiled and instinctively gasped for breath.

He chuckled. "What's the matter, darling? Would you like for me to open the patio doors and let in a little fresh air?" he said, gesturing in the direction of the patio with a wave of his hand.

She nodded nervously. "Air? Ahhh...ah yes. Thank you, that would be nice," she replied softly, raising her hand up to touch the hot flesh of her flushed cheek and neck.

He slowly stood to his feet, happy to silently announce how much he wanted her. He chuckled as her gaze followed him and the huge bulge in the front of his trousers to the patio and back. She licked her lips wantonly. "Do you know who I am now, darling?" he asked, walking back across the floor and sitting beside her again. Her gaze traveled slowly upward on his well-built body until she reached his gaze. He smiled and leaned over to kiss her.

Not knowing why she hadn't tried to stop him, he kissed her softly, sweetly, gently at first and then, no longer able to control himself, he kissed her urgently, wantonly, passionately with one of his fiery hot kisses, completely taking her breath away. "Oh God!" she breathlessly panted after he reluctantly pulled his lips from hers.

He chuckled, knowing how she had always loved his masterful kisses.

"Do you know who I am now, darling?" he asked, slowly lifting himself up to a sitting position only several inches away from her quivering lips.

She slowly opened her eyes. "Whew!" was her one-word response.

"Darling," he said her name with a chuckle. "Your name is Nouri Sommers. I'm police detective Gabe Baldwin. I'm with the Boston Police Department. We're recklessly in love and we plan to be married just as soon as you're up to it. Oh, and maybe I should mention one more small detail so you don't kick me out of bed tonight," he said teasingly as he continued to trace the warm flesh of her arm with the tip of his finger.

"Small detail?" she echoed with curious confusion. Her eyes widened curiously.

"Yes, darling. Actually three small details," he said teasingly. "You're carrying my three babies." He smiled lovingly. "We should know in a day or two what sex they're going to be. Isn't that wonderful, darling?" he stated proudly.

A shocked expression quickly covered her face. "I'm...I'm pregnant? Three babies? I...I can't believe it!" she exclaimed excitedly, reaching first for her head and then instinctively for her stomach.

"What is it, darling? Do you have a headache?" he asked with concern.

"Yes, I mean no! Wow! This is all so...I'm sorry." She paused and shook

her head in disbelief. "I'm sorry, mister, but I don't remember you! I don't seem to be able to remember anything, I'm afraid." She frowned.

He leaned over, gently embracing her. "Darling, I have a staff of round-the-clock doctors and nurses here at the estate to take care of you until you have completely recovered from your accident. I also had a specialist flown in. He's your primary doctor. His name is Dr. Kavala. Dr. T.C. Kavala. I'll go and get him for you. I'll be right back. Oh, and darling, I love you," he whispered, lovingly kissing her on the cheek before standing to his feet.

He glanced over his shoulder as he reached for the doorknob. "I'll be right back, darling," he said, leaving the room.

Suddenly the telephone rang, jarring Gabe back to the present.

It was the family's head butler informing him that the Boston Police captain had arrived.

"And he would like to speak to you if you're not too busy, sir."

"Put Mark on, Franklin. I'm never to busy for a friend," he replied.

The police captain continued to gaze around the corridor of the beautiful Greek mansion as Franklin handed him the telephone. "Hey, Detective. I just wanted to let you know that I couldn't be more happy for you than if you were my own son," he said tearfully.

Gabe smiled at the sound of the captain's voice. "Thank you. Your friendship means a lot to me, too. I don't think I could have pulled through these past few months of my life if it hadn't been for you, Mark. You, my dear friend, mean a lot to me," he said.

Mark cleared his throat. "Hey, listen, I know how busy a man can be on the morning of his wedding, so I won't keep you. I just wanted to wish you the best, Gabe. Are you and Nouri taking off right after the 'I dos'?"

Gabe chuckled. "Well, sometime during the reception that follows anyway. You know me—I can't wait to get her off to myself."

"Where are you taking her for the honeymoon?"

Gabe chuckled again. "That, my dear friend, is a secret! Even my own mother and father haven't been given that information. I intend not to be interrupted for the next two weeks, no matter what!" he said teasingly.

"I can certainly understand that, son! Listen, I'll let you get back to whatever you were in the middle of doing. I'll see you later, Detective."

"Mark, hold on just a second, I wanted to asked you if all my friends in blue were able to make it?"

"Sure did. They are having the time of their lives!"

Gabe laughed, shaking his head, knowing what a rowdy bunch his coworkers could be while partying. "Well, I hope everyone will enjoy their rooms as well as their three-day visit here on the island."

"What? Are you nuts! The accommodations are like staying in a goddamn palace! What's not to enjoy? I bet I'll have one hell of a time getting everyone to leave come Monday morning!" Mark said, laughing.

"Well, everyone is welcome to stay as long as they like. You know that, Mark. Say listen, I was curious, have you heard from Charles lately? I've been trying for the past two months to reach him. I miss our friendship, Mark. He won't return my calls; it's very upsetting to me. I mean what happened between us," Gabe said sadly.

Mark cleared his throat again. "Listen, Detective, Franklin is in a hurry to show me to my room. I'll see you after the wedding. Congratulations, son!" he said, deliberately not answering his friend's question about the famous P.I. He swiftly put the receiver down.

Gabe shook his head with amusement. "I'll take that as a no!" he mumbled under his breath, replacing the phone and then heading back to the bar.

Upset that he couldn't get through to his one-time best friend and former partner, he downed a shot of brandy and then slouched back down in his cozy chair. Soon his thoughts drifted again.

"Captain, just how in hell did Charles pull this off? It's amazing! If I didn't know better, I'd swear that guy was really me. And that young woman, God, she's a dead ringer for Tonya!" Gabe said, pointing to a newspaper of two actors that Charles Mason had hired to pose as the homicide detective and the district attorney of Boston.

"I heard it cost him plenty getting them to publicly admit to a frame-up that really wasn't a frame-up." Mark chuckled, amused by it all. *"Yeah, Mason's a piece of work, all right!" He shook his head at the thought of what the famous P.I. was capable of.*

Gabe glanced at the newspaper of the two actors and the young cop who had sold the incriminating negatives to The Boston Enquirer. *"Look at that slimy little bastard. He got off easy as far as I'm concerned," he said, pointing to police officer Rick Hobner of the Boston Police Department.*

The captain nodded, stifling a grin. "Yeah, I can't believe how easily he confessed to trying to frame you and Tonya," he said in playful dismay.

Gabe chuckled. "We're a shameless bunch, aren't we?" He shook his head also in playful dismay.

"Yeah, but only when it comes to protecting our own," the captain returned, sinking down in his chair behind his large, ugly, wooden desk.

"I'm glad Hobner saw the light and decided to go back home. He's not the right shade of blue for around these parts!" Gabe said, tossing the newspaper down on top of the captain's desk.

"Yeah, he's gone back home to one of those down-home states where yellow is their state's most popular color," the captain said, laughing.

"Have you spoken with Charles since all this bullshit has calmed down, Mark?"

Mark shook his head. "No, and I understand he hasn't gotten in touch with Tonya either. Seems to have disappeared off the face of the earth," he said, leaning over and pulling open the bottom desk drawer, grinning like the cat who just ate the canary. "Shall we, for old times' sake, Detective?" he asked, teasingly pulling out a bottle of the detective's favorite liquor.

Gabe chuckled. "A man after my own heart. Let's do it, Captain, but this time I can only have a few! I want to be sober when Dr. Kavala tells me the sex of my babies."

Gabe smiled, remembering just how happy he had been that day as his thoughts continued to race on.

"Well, Mr. Baldwin, I've just finished examining Mrs. Sommers, and other than the loss of her memory, she seems to be doing much better than we could have hoped possible in such a short period of time." Dr. Kavala smiled excitedly.

"And my babies, Doctor?" Gabe asked excitedly.

"They're doing wonderful! They're completely out of danger now and..."

Gabe cut in excitedly, "Yes, what? I can't stand it!" He remembered how excited he had been, waiting for the doctor to tell him.

The doctor smiled knowingly. "It appears you are going to be the proud father of three happy, healthy baby boys!"

Gabe smiled at the memory of how excited he had been after the doctor had told him about his children. *He picked up the small doctor and joyfully whirled him around the room a few times before asking him if he had told Nouri the exciting news yet.*

"No, I knew that was something you might want to tell her yourself, sir."

"Thank you, Dr. Kavala," Gabe said as he left the doctor to share the glorious news with the beloved woman of his dreams.

He popped his head inside the bedroom door playfully, but Nouri was sleeping. He entered, quietly walking over to kiss her on the cheek. She gently stirred and seductively stretched, driving him instantly insane with want for her. But he knew it was too soon. He leaned down and brushed his lips ever so softly across hers. She moaned.

"Gabe, darling. Come back to bed. I need you." He smiled lovingly at her subconscious memory of him and leaned down to kiss her again. But this time she opened her eyes and pulled him to her. "Please, come to bed and hold me for a while, Detective. Will you?" she asked softly, needingly.

"My pleasure, ma'am," he playfully responded in his professional tone of voice, causing her to giggle. He shed his clothing and anxiously joined her in bed, glad to finally be lying beside her in bed again. "God, I love you, darling," he whispered, holding her warm body close to him.

"What are we going to do, Gabe, if I don't ever get my memory back?" she asked, clinging desperately to him.

He kissed her gently on top of the head as he lovingly began to caress her satin soft body. "We'll take our time and fall in love all over again. Make new memories together, darling. Our love is something that is meant to be, Nouri. We'll be married as planned. After all, my babies need their father's name, don't they? And by the way, darling, our babies are all boys. I'm so overwhelmed with joy, Nouri—"

She silenced him with a kiss. "Shhh. Enough talk, Detective. I may not remember who you are just yet, but strangely I certainly remember your heart-racing, fiery hot kisses," she whispered, eagerly pulling his head down for another masterful kiss.

He smiled at the memory and stood to his feet, stretched, and walked back to the bar for another drink.

"I was doomed the first moment I laid eyes on her," he whispered under his breath, mentally picturing her beautiful face. "God, I love you, darling," he said with a sigh. He went back to his cozy spot and sat down. He took a sip of his brandy as he continued his trip down memory lane.

"Thank you, Dr. Kavala. I appreciate everything you have done for Nouri and me. I'm sorry to see you leave."

"Mrs. Sommers is doing remarkable. To be honest with you, I'm still amazed at her recovery, physically speaking of course. As for her memory, sadly, she may never get it back again. With the head injury she suffered, it's

hard to say, Detective. That is something only time will tell, I'm afraid. You know how to reach me if you should need me before my next monthly visit. I have taken the liberty of dismissing all the other doctors and nurses, except one. Ms. Helman will stay for as long as needed."

"Thank you again, Doctor."

Gabe made his way to the kitchen in search of Mai Li to ask her to give everyone the evening off.

He smiled, remembering how he had asked her to make all the arrangements for a romantic candle-lit dinner for himself and Nouri that evening.

"Oh yes, Detective, just the medicine the miss needs, sir," Mai Li responded excitedly.

He returned her smile and then showed her the diamond engagement ring he had planned to surprise Nouri with at dinner that evening. The tiny Asian woman was as excited as he had been.

He chuckled after recalling how Mai Li had almost fainted when he had asked her to order an entire room full of red roses for the special occasion.

"Oh, Detective! Too expensive on policeman's salary," she said, unaware of his family's vast fortune. He smiled at the memory.

"It will be all right, Mai Li. Nothing I can't handle. Then you'll arrange everything for me?"

"Happy to, Detective. Anything else you need Mai Li to do?"

He smiled mischievously. "As a matter of fact—yes, there is, Mai Li. You can tell my beautiful fiancée that I said to wear something incredibly erotic for dinner. I'm feeling very romantic tonight!" he said, playfully wiggling his eyebrows up and down, causing Mai Li to giggle.

"May I have this dance, darling?" he whispered seductively across Nouri's neck.

"Why, Detective," she responded, blushing.

He molded his body suggestively to hers, letting her feel his excitement for her. "God, you are so beautiful, darling," he whispered in her ear, sending goose bumps up her spine.

"What are we doing, Detective?" she whispered softly as they continued

to sway back and forth to the soft music being played by the hired violinist.

"I think they call it falling in love, darling," he whispered along the side of her throat.

"Oh God, Gabe! Let's go make love," she breathlessly surrendered.

"Not before I put this on your finger, darling. It's long overdue," he said, pulling the diamond engagement ring out of his jacket pocket. He gazed into her eyes lovingly as he lifted her hand. "May I, darling?" he asked hopefully as he continued to gaze with deep rapture into her eyes.

She smiled lovingly, eagerly accepting, not really knowing why, except for the fact it just felt so right. "Oh God, Detective! Can I have one of your masterful kisses now?" she asked softly, throwing her arms around his neck and pulling his head down to meet her eagerly open mouth in a knee-buckling kiss.

Gabe's present thoughts were put on hold again. There was a loud knock on the door, demanding immediate attention. He shook his head to clear his mind, released a deep sigh, and swiftly crossed the floor to answer the door.

Chapter 40

"Oh my, miss! You look so very beautiful. Makes me want to cry," Mai Li said as she fought back tears of joy.

Nouri Sommers glanced at the tiny Asian woman as she continued to gaze approvingly into the large antique mirror inside her bedroom of the Baldwin family villa in Greece.

"Thank you, Mai Li. Oh God, I'm so nervous I can hardly stand it!"

"How you feeling today, miss?" Mai Li asked, taking Nouri by the hand and leading her to a chair for a rest.

Nouri smiled fondly. "Fine, I think. I mean other than being so nervous. Gosh, it was so weird finally meeting a family that I know is mine but have no memory of. Not my father, my brother, or even my sister. I know that hurts them, but I can't help it. And knowing this makes me feel even more out of place around them. Even so, I'm glad Gabe flew them here for the wedding." She released a sigh of frustration, angry with herself for not being able to remember one shred of her past.

Mai Li nodded. "It's understandable how you feel about your family. They are like strangers to you. Be patient. I'm sure everything will come back to you in time. You'll see. You shouldn't worry so much. I think your family understands what you are going through." She patted Nouri's hand affectionately.

Nouri sighed. "I hope you're right. You just imagine how awful it is not knowing who you are or what it is you're supposed to be doing, Mai Li. It's sort of like living in a dreamworld where nothing is as it seems," she said, shaking her head with sadness.

Mai Li glanced at her mistress curiously. "Don't you remember anything at all, miss?"

Nouri swallowed hard. "No, not really, that is to say, except sometimes certain things seem somewhat familiar to me. And Gabe…" She said his name with a lustful sigh. "Wow! Being with him feels so right; so familiar. Perfect, actually. God, I'm such a lucky woman." She sighed. "Can you believe how sexy he is, Mai Li? I wonder how I got so lucky."

The tiny woman giggled. "It is the detective that is the lucky one, miss. Many men crazy for you before handsome detective." She shook her head.

Nouri glanced at Mai Li in surprise. “Oh my, really? What about my husband?” she asked with interest.

Mai Li chuckled. “Before husband. There was famous P.I. His name was Charles Mason. And then there was high-powered attorney Clint Chamberlain,” she offered, smiling fondly as the handsome attorney’s face popped inside her mind.

“Umm, Charles Mason. Clint Chamberlain.” Nouri rolled the names off her tongue. “You know, those names do seem distantly familiar to me. Were they just admirers or did I actually date them, I mean before my marriage to Ethan Sommers?”

The small woman nodded her head, hoping Nouri had finally remembered a small piece of her past. “Yes, you did, miss. Mr. Mason was your first real love. He crazy for you. Very crazy for you. His nickname for you was…”

Nouri instinctively whispered the pet name the P.I. had given her seven years earlier. “Sugar. He used to call me that silly pet name all the time, didn’t he?” she asked, excitedly standing to her feet. “Oh my God! I remembered that, didn’t I? I can’t put a face with his name, but oddly I can remember that damn silly pet name!” She smiled, excitedly glancing at the tiny woman standing beside her.

“See, miss. In time you will remember again. What about Mr. Chamberlain? Do you remember his pet name for you?” Mai Li asked with excitement.

“Clint Chamberlain. Clint…Clint Chamberlain,” she said the name several times thoughtfully in an attempt to jog her memory. She finally shook her head sadly and sighed. “No, nothing familiar there, I’m afraid. Did I date this man as well?”

“Yes, Mr. Chamberlain crazy for you too, miss. He died right after Mr. Sommers got killed. Drove his car off bridge in the fog,” she said, shaking her with sadness at the memory.

“Pity.” Nouri swallowed hard, shaking her head, and then continued. “How long ago did I date Mr. Chamberlain?”

“You were engaged to him before you marry Mr. Som—”

Nouri interrupted in stunned disbelief, “What? I was engaged to him too! Oh my goodness. I can’t believe it. Wow, I was a fickle woman, wasn’t I? Not to mention apparently a naughty one as well.” She swallowed nervously. “How could Gabe fall for such a shameless little tart?” She shook her head.

Mai replied with a giggle, “No, miss. You nothing like that. Nice girl. You very nice girl. You had three lovers in seven years’ time; that’s not a bad thing in today's world," she offered in an attempt to calm her mistress.

"Well, if you say so. I would honestly hate to think of myself as having once been a shameless harlot or something like that! Whew! Were there any more men in my life I should know about before my marriage to Gabe?" Her tone was one of concern.

Mai Li smiled, shaking her head and blushing. "No, miss. Not that I am aware of."

Nouri sighed and glanced at Mai Li. "Mai Li, would you please get us both a glass of juice or something and come sit beside me. I want you to tell me how you and I met. How Gabe and I met. And how Ethan Sommers and I met. We still have some time before the wedding, and you know how protective Gabe has been with me not letting anyone say more than a sentence or two to me since the accident. I really need to hear a few things from my past. You have no idea how desperately I long to remember who I am," she said, swallowing nervously.

Mai Li started towards the bar. "Okay, miss, I just hope handsome detective don't get mad at me when he finds out," she replied, crossing the room. She glanced over her shoulder. "Are you sure you wouldn't care for a sip or two of champagne before the wedding?"

Nouri smiled declining the suggestion. "No thank you."

"Maybe juice would be better. Detective don't want you drinking while you're pregnant anyway," Mai Li responded, pouring two glasses of orange juice for them.

"Well, I wouldn't say that exactly. It's not just Gabe. I don't like alcohol. I hate the taste of the nasty stuff. It makes me sick!" she said, cringing. "He offers me a sip of whatever he's drinking from time to time, and after the tiny sample of his drink I find myself questioning how on earth anyone could possibly find any enjoyment out of the nasty-tasting stuff. Yuck!" she said, cringing again.

Mai Li chuckled out loud. "Well maybe you feel that way now, miss, but before the car accident you drank plenty," she said with a giggle and shake of her head.

"Really?" Nouri remarked in surprise.

May Li nodded. "Yes, sometimes like a fish," she said, waving a scolding finger playfully at her mistress.

Nouri released another deep sigh of disbelief. "Oh my! And you're reasonably certain that I was a nice girl, huh?" she said, teasing and making a frown.

Mai Li smiled fondly again. "Very nice girl, miss. The best!"

"Okay, if you say so, I'll take your word for it, but now I want you to be serious. I need for you to tell me about Charles Mason, Clint Chamberlain, Ethan Sommers, and, of course, everything about the handsome detective and myself."

After Mai Li filled in many of the missing pieces of Nouri Sommers' life, at least those of the past seven years, the beautiful bride-to-be released a sigh of amazement. "No wonder my subconscious has suddenly decided to block everything out! Wow!"

Mai Li gently patted her hand affectionately. "That is why handsome detective is so protective of you, miss," she said.

"So it would seem. But I still can't understand why he never told me about Ms. Bubblebutt!" she said in a jealous tone of voice.

"Ms. Bubblebutt?" the tiny woman questioned with a giggle.

Nouri chuckled in spite of herself. "You know, it's the damnedest thing, suddenly the pet name of Gabe's former fiancée Lisa Clayborne just popped inside my brain! Wonder why he never mentioned being engaged to her?"

"Don't know, miss. Maybe because he feel it wasn't important."

Nouri released a sigh. "And you're sure Gabe really loves me and isn't just pitying me because of the babies or my accident?" she asked, nervously wringing her hands together.

Mai Li gently patted her mistress's hand again as she spoke. "Yes, miss. You and handsome detective belong together. I've never seen a couple more in love!"

Nouri wiped a tear from her eye and leaned over to hug the tiny woman tightly. "Thank you, Mai Li, you're right. I know Gabe loves me and our babies. And I also know in time my memories will return. But from the sound of my life, at least the past several years of it, it might not be such a terrible thing if it didn't!" she said, standing to her feet. She went on, "Maybe I should touch up my makeup before my father knocks on the door to escort me down the aisle." She smiled and then quickly lowered her hand to her stomach, frowning.

An expression of concern quickly crossed Mai Li's face. "Miss, you all right? Should I go and get—"

Nouri stopped her in mid-sentence. She smiled. "No, I'm fine. The babies just suddenly decided to kick the living daylights out of their poor mother," she said, chuckling and gently patting the area on her stomach that hurt.

"There, there, my little darlings. I know…I know you miss your father. I do, too. He'll be here soon to sing your lullaby, I promise. Shh…" she whispered comfortingly to the three tiny baby inside of her.

Mai Li smiled approvingly at Nouri's gentleness and genuine love for the tiny babies still growing inside her. "You're going to be a wonderful mother, miss!" she remarked, walking back to the mirror with the mother-to-be.

Chapter 41

"Charles!" Gabe said his name excitedly after opening the door and seeing him standing on the other side of it. "My God, I can't believe it!" he added in stunned dismay.

"Gabe, may I come in?" Charles asked, walking past the police detective without waiting for him to respond.

Gabe chuckled. "Sure. Please enter. Don't wait for me to invite you. Just walk right in."

"I usually do," Charles teased, walking crossing the room and heading to the bar. "May I?" he asked, gesturing in the direction of the bourbon bottle.

The detective chuckled as he closed the door and then started across the room to join his former partner in fighting crime. "Certainly. Might as well pour me one, too, while you're at it."

Charles picked up the bottle of alcohol and poured them each a shot. "So, you're surprised to see me, huh?" His tone was playful.

Gabe smiled from ear to ear, shaking his head and reaching for his drink. "Boy, you can say that again!"

Charles chuckled. "You honestly didn't think I'd let you get married to Nouri…" He paused briefly and downed his shot of bourbon. After he made a cringing face, he went on, "…without me being here, did you?" he added mischievously.

Gabe chuckled, nervously shaking his head in relief. "Shit! You scared me for a moment," he returned, flushing.

Charles smiled. "Here, let's have a toast," he said, reaching for the bottle of bourbon again and filling their glasses. "If I remember correctly after all, it is customary for the groom's best man to offer a toast to the blushing groom in waiting, right?" He leveled his mischievous gaze to the red-faced detective.

"My best man?" A curious expression quickly masked the detective's handsome face.

Charles nodded. "Yeah, you're damn straight! You didn't honestly think I'd let that goddamn old shit downstairs that you call 'Captain' take my job away from me this afternoon did you, Detective?" he stated in a teasing manner.

Gabe shook his head in disbelief. "You mean that old fart knew you would be here and never told me? Hell, Charles, I've been terribly upset over what happened between us. I…I'm so glad you're here," he said, throwing his arms around his longtime friend in a friendship embrace.

Charles returned the manly embrace and then slapped his friend across his broad shoulders. He stepped back a few feet and reached for the bottle of bourbon again. "So, you missed me, huh?" he said with a chuckle.

Gabe nodded. "Something like that, my friend." He held his glass over to Charles for a refill.

After Charles filled the two glasses, he said, "Here's to you, my friend; much happiness to you and Nouri. I truly wish you all the wonderful things that life has to offer." He gently tapped his glass to the detective's.

"Hear, hear," Gabe said, holding his glass in mid-air before belting the drink down.

"So, how is she doing?" the P.I. asked with concern.

Gabe smiled. "She's doing much better than I could have hoped. And my three sons are doing just fine, too," he said, blushing nervously.

"And her memory?"

"The doctors say she may never get her memory back again. That's something only time will tell, it seems."

"So how did you get her to agree to marry you then?"

"We fell in love all over again, Charles," Gabe responded in an arrogant tone, causing his friend to chuckle.

"Oh, I remember now. The only man she will ever need from now on, right, Detective?" he playfully remarked, picking up the bottle of bourbon again.

Gabe shook his head, blushing. "Yeah, Charles, exactly!" he returned, leveling his gaze on the P.I. jealously.

Charles laughed loudly. "Hey, down, boy! I've learned my lesson and my place, so it seems. Tonya set me straight."

Gabe cleared his throat as he pictured the female district attorney's beautiful face.

"Now, just how in the hell do you think my wife is doing being married to a stubborn old jackass like myself!" he said, laughing.

A look of surprise crossed the detective's face. "What! You and Tonya got married? But when, for chrissakes!"

Charles laughed excitedly. "We got hitched a week ago. Right after I got my head screwed back on straight. I realized what a jerk I had been. So I went calling on her when I got back in town with a preacher in tow. I wasn't going to take no for an answer!" He chuckled and blushed at the same time. "Spending a little time away from her made me see the error of my ways; not to mention the void in my life without her and my son. So I came to my senses, decided to let go of the past and move to the future!"

"You say you've been back in Boston for a week now? Why didn't you return any of my calls, for chrissakes?"

"I don't know. Guess I just wasn't of a mind to do so, Detective," he responded teasingly. "All joking aside, my friend, I guess it took me a little time to clear my head and my heart. I just needed a little time alone, I guess. The important thing right now is that I'm back. And I'm bigger and better than I've ever been, with a new outlook on life, and an even bigger attitude to go along with it!" he said, grinning from ear to ear.

Gabe laughed. "Oh please, Charles! You sound like you're as high as a kite. How much have you had to drink, anyway?" he asked, playfully taking the bottle of alcohol out of his friend's hand.

Charles laughed, taking the bottle back from his friend and pouring them another round. "High? I'm high all right; high on life, my friend. High on life! I've never been happier, Gabe. I mean that sincerely. Thanks to Tonya and little Chuckie, my life is finally complete. I've come full circle, it seems!"

"And what about your feelings for Nouri?" the detective asked nervously.

Charles set his drink glass down and embraced his friend tightly. "Nouri, my beautiful sugar." He paused, stepping back a few feet and wiping a fallen tear from off his cheek before the police detective had a chance to notice. He cleared his throat and continued, "I'll forever love her. You know that, and so do I. But her heart belongs to you completely now. I, my dear friend, stand aside. I surrender. Toss in the towel. I'm not the man she needs anymore to fight battles for her. That has become your job now. Just please do me one favor, Detective," he said in a hoarse tone.

"What's that, Charles?" Gabe asked with interest.

Charles cleared the tears from his throat, not wanting Gabe to know just how shaken up over Nouri he really was. A brief moment later, Charles forced himself to chuckle. "Just stay the hell away from my wife, and I'll do the same, deal?" he said in jest, slapping his friend across the shoulder before extending his hand in a friendship shake.

Gabe knew how his friend felt and in all probability how he would forever feel about Nouri Sommers. He swallowed hard as he released his hand from his friend's. "Charles, if Nouri should ever get her memory back, I'll let you have a few private moments alone with her. I know she would want that," he said, reaching for his drink. "And as for that beautiful wife of yours, I'd like to kiss her." He paused mischievously as he watched the expression suddenly change on his friend's face. "That is a kiss of congratulations on her lovely cheek with your permission of course, my friend," he said, gesturing toward the bottle of bourbon before glancing at the time. "I think we have time for a short one. It's almost time for the moment I've been breathlessly waiting for my entire life. God, I love her, Charles," he said, wiping a tear from his eye.

Epilogue

Detective Gabe Baldwin and his incredibly beautiful wife Nouri had just finished putting their three-month-old triplet sons to bed for the evening, Gabriel Anthony Baldwin II, Charles Xavier Baldwin, and the smallest of the three, Clinton Jerome Baldwin. Gabe lovingly pulled his wife into his arms.

"Oh God, darling, I'm the happiest, most contented man in the world. I can't imagine anything giving me more pride than my beautiful wife and adorable little sons," he said lovingly, tilting her face and gazing into her eyes with deep rapture.

She smiled. "Oh, I don't know, darling," she whispered mischievously, slowly stepping back a step or two. She lowered her hand gently patting her stomach. She felt herself blush. "How about saving some of that manly pride of yours for our little daughter," she said softly.

A stunned expression quickly covered the detective's handsome face. He swallowed hard to keep himself from fainting. Nouri quickly reached out for his arm, shaking her head and giggling.

He silenced her with one of his fiery hot kisses. She moaned wantonly, causing him to stop and chuckle at her never-ending need to be fulfilled. "I adore you, darling," he said, picking her up into his arms. "Let's go and see if we can turn our daughter into triplets too," he whispered against the side of her sexy neck.

"Really, darling! Can we do that?" she asked as he continued walking out of the nursery, still carrying her in his arms.

He chuckled. "I'm not sure, darling, but it might be fun trying," he whispered as he continued to nibble on her ear and shoulders suggestively.

As he put his beautiful wife on the bed, she eagerly pulled him to her. "I love you, darling," she whispered in his ear, her warm breath sending goose bumps instantly up his spine.

"As I do you, darling," he panted excitedly, rubbing his huge mass of hardened excitement across the sexy curve of her inner thigh.

"Mmm, Detective Baldwin, is that a pistol in your pocket, or are ya just glad to see me?" she playfully teased.

He chuckled at her playfulness. "Now, what do you think, Mrs. Baldwin?" His response was breathless as he continued to nibble his way to her shoulders again.

The telephone rang, causing Nouri to groan in complaint. "Don't you dare stop doing what you're doing, Detective. I'll get it," she said, reaching over her head, fumbling for the receiver while Gabe continued to hungrily kiss his beautiful wife's shoulder while his fingers were busy unfastening the buttons on her satin blouse.

After struggling to free the phone cord from around her neck, she finally managed to speak into the receiver. "Hello," she responded in a distracted tone of voice. "Who? I'm sorry, you must have the wrong number," she added, rolling her eyes and hanging up the phone, anxious to return to her husband's heated embrace.

"Who was it, darling?" he asked, shifting his position so he could remove her blouse.

She shrugged unknowingly. "A wrong number, I suppose. Some guy thought he was phoning some woman he called 'sweetness,'" she replied, glancing at her husband's strange expression.

Gabe sat up straight and quickly unplugged the telephone. Nouri watched him curiously, shaking her head. An instant later, he lay back down in bed, pulling her to him. He cleared his throat. "You know, darling, now that I've had a few months to think about it, maybe we should reconsider accepting the wedding gift my family offered us on our wedding day. I think our children might enjoy growing up on a Greek island paradise after all." He released a nervous sigh. And then went on. "What do you think?" He smiled mischievously, lowering his head and smothering her with another one of his masterful kisses.

"Mmm," she sighed contentedly, tightening her arms around her husband's neck.

Printed in the United Kingdom
by Lightning Source UK Ltd.
131849UK00002B/176/A

9 781591 298748